# GOING ALL IN

STEPHANIE C. LYONS-KEELEY
WAYNE J. KEELEY

Copyright © 2017 by Stephanie C. Lyons-Keeley & Wayne J. Keeley

ISBN: 978-1-68046-480-1

Melange Books, LLC
White Bear Lake, MN 55110
www.melange-books.com

Names, characters, and incidents depicted in this book are products of the author's imagination or are used fictitiously. Any resemblance to actual events, locales, organizations, or persons, living or dead, is entirely coincidental and beyond the intent of the author or the publisher. No part of this book may be reproduced or transmitted in any form or by any means, electronic or mechanical, including photocopying, recording, or by any information storage and retrieval system, without permission in writing from the publisher except for the use of brief quotations in a book review or scholarly journal.

Published in the United States of America.

Cover Design by Ashley Redbird Designs

# PROLOGUE

*It is nothing to die. It is frightful not to live.*

—Victor Hugo, *Les Misérables*

Somebody was dead.

There was no doubt about it.

To the crowd of onlookers, the four state police cruisers parked haphazardly in the middle of the block might have been their tip-off. The synchronous, revolving red and blue lights imbued a strobe-like, Christmassy glow despite the humidity of the late September evening. With Indian summer still going strong, it felt more like July than what had already turned to autumn. The citizens of the tony, sleepy town of New Fairfield, Connecticut—a 'burb tightly tucked between the larger cities of Danbury and its neighboring Brewster, New York—were unused to this kind of activity. Ordinarily there never would be more than a single town police cruiser driving lazily through the streets, rarely citing anyone for an offense greater than blowing off a stop sign or using a hand-held mobile device.

It also might have been the presence of the volunteer fire truck which was only dispatched for emergencies, fire-related or otherwise. Then again, it might have been the handful of paramedics busying themselves in and around the city of Danbury's ambulances. New Fairfield did not have any of their own. Or, it might have been the hum of the throng of onlookers themselves who filled the sidewalk-less street, spilling over onto neighbors' lawns while they craned their necks to get a better look at the unfolding scene.

The atmosphere was downright electric.

It might have been all of those things that hissed of death in the air; visceral yet at the same time palpable, like the sight of the Grim Reaper's scythe. But it became a certainty when two paramedics appeared in the doorway, deftly rolling a gurney from the house. On it was a body draped in a white sheet, belted tightly, as if they were trying to keep it safe from harm.

The low hum quickly turned to a buzz, pulsating through the crowd from front to back; at first questioning then demanding. The prattle of the onlookers became more intense by the minute. The confirmation of a death became supplanted by a headier, more potent possibility. Could it have been —murder?

Homicide was almost unheard of in New Fairfield. The exception, perhaps, was an incident a few years before when a beloved, retired elementary school teacher had shot his mail carrier. He had developed dementia and mistook him for an intruder. But that certainly was an anomaly; a definite aberration in the order of things. Indeed, New Fairfield did not have a homicide division or a coroner, instead relying upon Danbury to come in and clean up such messes.

---

CLARENCE LEE PERKINS, who only just had celebrated his fifteenth birthday, had never seen a dead body. Although his grandmother had passed away of cancer the year prior, his parents protectively kept him from her deathbed while she was in the hospital, and it was a closed casket at her wake. Clarence—or Doogie, the moniker coined by his parents because of his resemblance to the television character Doogie Howser, and then later adopted by his friends—made his way to the front of the crowd to get a better view of the deceased. Seeing his first dead body was exciting, a rite of passage of sorts, and he wanted to make sure he had a front row seat. As with the rest of the masses, he could not tell if it was a man or woman under the formless sheet, but there was no mistaking the growing blood stain about the head.

"Did you get any pictures, Doog?"

Doogie nearly jumped out of his skin. He turned to find his best friend, Vinny the Mole, standing directly behind him. Vinny acquired his nickname, not because of his penchant for spying—although he definitely was a good spy—but rather, because of an unusually large mole dotting his right eyebrow, creating the impression that he was always questioning something.

"You scared the crap out of me!" Doogie shrieked.

"Dude, you need to get some photo action. Insta, Snapchat, the works. We need to go viral with this."

"Don't you have any respect for the dead?"

Vinny's eyebrow shot up, sending his mole straight into his hairline. "Um, no, I don't, asshole. Why the hell should I? This is awesome shit!"

The boys now were fronting the crowd—which seemed to be doubling by the second—and they watched intently as the paramedics prepared to load the body into the back of the ambulance. Suddenly the air fell eerily silent.

"Do you think it's *her*?" the Mole whispered.

"Dunno," Doogie responded in the same hushed tone. "Can't tell. They covered the damn body before they brought it out."

"Well, I hope it's not her. I'd have to find a new fantasy babe. There's something really wrong about jacking off to a dead person."

"Yeah, man. Whatevs'. I just hope it's the dude. What a fuckin' weirdo."

The boys were mesmerized as the paramedics carefully folded the legs and lifted the gurney into the ambulance. It was all playing out like in the movies. But just as the gurney was almost completely inside, the bottom edge of the sheet caught under one of the wheels tugging off the corner which had been covering the victim's head.

The identity of the body was exposed.

"Fuck me!" the Mole screeched.

# 1

## THE GAME

"I think I'm going to go all in," Scarlett said as she leaned over the table to study the flop, her impossibly tight red tank top scarcely covering a black lacy bra.

C. Thomas, her significant other for lack of a better term, sighed and hit his forehead with the heel of his hand. "How many times," he began in a lecturing tone, "have I told you that you can*not* tell the other players what you're thinking?

"I like to think out loud!" she fired back. For a dumb shit, he sure likes to come off as quite the know-it-all in front of the gang, she thought. He might have been right, but what Scarlett really wanted to do was to tell him just to shut the hell up.

C. Thomas shook his head in frustration. "The whole point of the game is to *not* reveal what you are thinking and to avoid 'tells.' Not only are you *not* avoiding tells," C. Thomas continued, "but you are actually explicitly *telling* us your tell."

"Maybe that's her strategy," Marty offered almost curtly to C. Thomas. He then turned to Scarlett and said in a softened tone, "Take whatever time you need, Scarlett, and feel free to speak your mind."

She continued studying the flop, and either advertently or inadvertently displayed most of her breasts down to the barely there tan lines. Marty had just taken a sip from his drink and began gagging.

"You okay, Marty?" Steve looked up from his cards at Marty, noticing that his eyes had widened to such an extent that it reminded him of one of those eye-popping tropes in cartoons.

"Yeah," Marty choked out a response. He looked around the table to see if anyone else had noticed Scarlett's cleavage, but they were oblivious, consumed with their own hands and whether to bet or not and how much.

Scarlett leaned further over the table providing Marty with an even greater view of what was inside of her tank top. Steve was sure that any moment he was going to see Marty's optic nerves exposed and dangling when his eyeballs flew out of their sockets.

"I'm going all in," Scarlett declared.

"You sure?" C. Thomas asked.

"Yes, I'm *sure*." Scarlett leaned back in her chair and pushed her entire pile of chips into the middle of the table.

C. Thomas smacked his lips. "Well, that lets me out." He took a long drink of his beer as he leaned back in his chair.

"Me, too," Katie chimed.

"I fold," Erin said.

"Fold," Marty said, disappointed that his peep show was over.

"Up to you, Steve-O," C. Thomas said.

Scarlett flashed a dazzling smile at Steve. "Careful, Baby, I'm holding something *good*."

"No fair," Marty said. "She's using her feminine wiles to manipulate the game."

It was Steve's turn to smile. "That's why she's a damn good player."

Katie glared at her husband, although he was too caught up in Scarlett's coquetry to notice.

Scarlett puckered her lips and blew a kiss to Steve. Marty clucked his disapproval. "Can we just move the game along?"

"All-in," Steve announced. Careful not to spill his drink, he slid his stacks of chips into the middle of the table where they cascaded into one huge pile.

"I hope you have what it takes," Scarlett said, continuing the coy banter.

Marty rolled his eyes.

"We'll see," Steve said, attempting but failing to maintain a neutral tone.

She overturned her two down cards. She had a queen and a ten. With the board cards, she had three queens.

"Three ladies," Scarlett said.

She reached for the pile of chips, but Steve stopped her, placing a warm hand firmly over hers. "Not so fast." He turned over his hole cards. A pair of kings. The board gave him an extra king with the pair of queens. "Full boat. Three cowboys and two ladies."

"Damn!" Scarlett muttered. "That finishes me." She rose, picked up her glass of wine, and dejectedly walked to the loveseat in the corner of the room where she kicked off her shoes and stretched out on it. She was a competitive woman and didn't like losing. To Steve she looked like a spoiled child on the tail end of a tantrum; he smiled to himself. It's a cute look for her, he thought.

Marty leaned back in his chair, but his eyes were still fixed on Scarlett. She was the real eye candy of the group with the kind of beauty that turned heads, both men's and women's. He never paused to care whether his wife, Erin, took notice of his voyeuristic exploits.

"Looks like we'll all be done in a few minutes," Erin said. "Except for Steve, of course."

"Steve has a real talent for the game," Scarlett offered, much to Marty's chagrin. She already was coming out of her funk.

"It's all luck," Marty grumbled. "He had a pair of kings in the hole and one on the board. It was a gift." Now it was Marty's turn to act like the sore loser.

"Yeah, I was just lucky," Steve said as he raked in the pile of chips and started to stack them in tall, neat piles. Steve never gloated, despite the fact he usually beat the pants off of the others in nearly every game.

"It's luck *and* skill," Katie said, defending her husband and then walking over to place a proprietary hand on his shoulder. "I'm parched. Does anyone else want a refill?"

"Sure," Erin responded. Katie retrieved Erin's glass and picked up a near-empty tray of snacks to refill from the kitchen.

It had been Steve and Katie's turn to host the twice-monthly card game. That meant that they were responsible for the refreshments, a variety of assorted edibles and more importantly, plenty of alcohol. Katie always went above and beyond the others' offerings, often looking up new and extravagant recipes on the internet. She'd get lost on Pinterest. In addition to the extra expense, it meant Katie had to do double time to ensure the house passed the white glove test. Not that their guests cared or even noticed the presence or absence of a layer of dust or a few fingerprints on the mirror, but Katie always felt compelled. Since the games began, she probably had spent a small fortune on those cute, little decorative soaps, replacing them every time someone had the audacity to actually use them.

"Hey, Steve, maybe you should invest in a seat in Vegas next year for the WSOP," C. Thomas said.

"What the heck is the WSOP?" Erin asked.

"It's the World Series of Poker," C. Thomas responded. "I could see Steve sittin' there all casual with a stogie, a pair of Ray-Bans, and his ear buds waitin' on that multi-million-dollar cash prize."

"I don't think I'd last ten minutes at the WSOP," Steve responded deprecatingly.

"Oh, I bet you would last *way* more than that," Scarlett's voice was suddenly throaty.

Steve couldn't help but do a double-take. Scarlett always had been somewhat of a tease with everyone, but was tonight different? Was it his imagination?

Katie raised an eyebrow. "Steve can last and I can vouch for him," she said, throwing yet another stake of ownership into the mix.

Marty again clucked his disapproval.

The card game resumed without Scarlett.

The triptych of card-playing couples had been friends and neighbors for years. Despite their varying ages and mixed social and political views—Steve and Katie, the forty-something republicans; Marty and Erin, the mid-thirties democrats; and Scarlett and C. Thomas, the late-twenties independents —they all seemed to enjoy each other's company. The origin of the friendship was now shrouded by misty yesteryear. A school outing, a friend of a friend's party, a few random meetings in public, and suddenly there were six friends. It was easy. They all lived within walking distance of one another's homes. Then one evening when they all were snowed in during an infamous Connecticut Nor'easter, they converged at Steve and Katie's, lit a roaring fire, pulled out more than a few bottles of Merlot and a deck of cards, and played a game of poker. On the game nights that followed, Steve and Katie's teen daughters usually babysat for Marty and Erin's very boisterous twin sons.

Steve dealt the river card face-up on the table. It was a queen, the third royal in a row. The other four cards of mixed suits were another queen, a king, a four, and a six. A flush or a straight seemed unlikely. Everyone was still in the hand at this point.

"You know, Las Vegas may be a good place to plan our next joint vacation," Erin said, deliberately changing the subject. She was very adept at playing peacemaker. With a challenge like Marty under the same roof, she had a lot of experience. "What do you guys think?"

C. Thomas nodded. "Sounds good to me. I can probably combine it with a bit of business. Maybe get a few more DVD kiosks set up." From across the room Scarlett let out a muted groan. She'd been trying to tell him for years that DVDs were going the way of the dinosaurs, overtaken by online streaming and whatnot.

"What about you, Scarlett?" Marty asked.

"I am quite sure I won't have any trouble taking off of work. I'm hardly there anyway," Scarlett said, rolling her eyes. "The manager at Lola's already called me off twice this week, not that I love telling rude, pretentious, flabby old women how great they look in gaudy, overpriced clothing."

"Great!" Katie said and, ever the organizer, offered, "I'll start looking into hotels and airlines if everyone agrees."

"I'll have to check the school schedule to see when the twins are off. Maybe I can talk my parents into babysitting for a week."

"Fat chance," Marty said. "She thinks our monsters are the spawn of Satan."

"She only considers that they are half-blooded relatives of Satan, *Dear*," Erin said.

Everyone chuckled at that one with the exception of Marty, of course. He had gone all-in on a pair of twos and was the next refugee from the game.

"How can you go all in on a pair of deuces?" C. Thomas asked.

"It was a bluff that didn't work," Marty retorted. He stood and stretched then casually sauntered his way over to Scarlett on the love seat. He was hoping she'd make room although there were both an unoccupied couch and an invitingly comfy, overstuffed side chair.

"How about squeezing in another loser?" he asked Scarlett.

Erin glanced over and was about to say something, but shook her head. It wasn't as if it mattered.

Scarlett picked up her feet so that Marty could sit and then lowered them into his lap. "Hope you don't mind, it's a bit squishy with two."

"Not at all," he replied. He immediately noticed a rather large, dark purple bruise on her shin. "Rough sex?"

"Hardly. Can't walk and chew gum at the same time, you know? I should look where I'm going. I'm such a klutz."

C. Thomas shot her a sly look, but she ignored it.

Marty's plan had worked out better than he had expected. His all-in play on the pair of twos had not been a bluff at all, but just a desperate attempt to lose so he could spend time cozying up to Scarlett on the loveseat while the rest of the group continued the game. He felt her heels pressing on his jewels. He was sure it had to be on purpose. He was getting a boner. Would she realize it? Would she care?

Scarlett did realize and did care in a half-assed sort of way. She felt his hardness almost immediately and was smugly satisfied. What would Mother think? she wondered. She slowly but not subtly rocked her heels over his hardening organ. Maybe she could make him come in his pants. Wouldn't that be a hoot? How could he possibly explain that to Erin later?

Scarlett decided to up the ante. "Hey, Marty, can you do me a big favor?" she hissed, her heel digging more aggressively into his hardness as she spoke. "Can you massage my feet? They're *killing* me."

"Absolutely!" Marty replied a little too quickly and a little too eagerly.

Erin cast a sidelong glare at him. Now he was going a bit too far.

"Make sure you do a good job, Marty," C. Thomas said. "I need her feet in good working condition." He gave Scarlett a furtive wink.

If Scarlett could read minds, she would have been pleased to know that Marty was now in real crisis. Deeply concerned, he knew that at any moment he *was* going to come in his pants. What on God's green earth would he do then? She has to be aware of what she's doing, he thought.

Beads of sweat broke out on his forehead. The last time he came in his pants was at his sixteenth birthday party when he slow danced with Jessica Honeywell. He remembered that his body felt like it had been struck by a thunderbolt. He had frozen at first, then gyrated backward, almost knocking down several other classmates as he scrambled to the bathroom, leaving poor Jessica stupefied and scarred for life. Marty's high school experience—which never had been good—became a nightmare after that. He would forever be known as the kid who either had epilepsy or a bad case of the runs. He often wondered if he would have fared better had the real truth come out—pun intended.

Massaging her slender, perfect feet only made things worse. He glanced down at the perfectly painted red toenails. Hot. So hot. His balls felt as if they were going to explode any second. He tried to distract himself. *Who won the last Super Bowl?* Not a good diversion since he wasn't the least bit interested in sports. *No man is an island, entire of itself.* No, reciting archaic poetry wasn't the answer, either. He thought about excusing himself and finishing the job on his own in the bathroom. He wondered what Katie would say about that.

The sweat was rolling down his face. He was almost there—almost at the brink—he had to something—*Now!*

Marty abruptly stood up nearly knocking Scarlett to the floor and walked to the window. "Is it me or is it hot in here?" He was tugging at the neck of his wrinkled, holey T-shirt.

"I can crank the A/C," Katie offered.

"I think it's already cool enough," Erin said.

Marty turned to face the window, desperate to hide his hard-on. Suddenly he was sixteen again and on the dance floor. When he first stood up, Scarlett spotted the bulge protruding from his unflattering plaid shorts, and she chuckled to herself. She was rather stunned at how big it actually appeared to be. She never figured Marty to be hung.

"Maybe we should change the damn game," Marty said over his shoulder, prancing in place and again trying to distract himself. "I'm tired of losing to Steve all the time."

"Hmm. I think the problem could be motivation," C. Thomas offered. "Maybe we need something more important to play for besides pocket change."

"Don't try to make us play strip poker again," Erin said, a hint of annoyance in her tone. "I am *not* taking off my clothes in front of all of you." One night several months earlier when they were all drunk and playing five-and seven-card poker at Scarlett and C. Thomas's house, her lecherous husband had the bright idea that they should try strip poker in an effort to spice up the game. Needless to say, things came to an abrupt halt when Erin refused to take off anything except her shoes and a pair of earrings.

"And no more truth or dare," quipped Marty. "Finding out that Steve wears tighty whities was too much over-sharing for me."

"I think briefs are sexy," Erin told Katie. "I wish Marty would wear them."

"Erin!" Marty yelled. He spun around, his shorts finally almost back to their normal fit. "Do you have to say shit like that?"

Erin was laughing. "I was just telling the truth."

"I love it when a man doesn't wear any underwear—you know —*commando*," Scarlett said.

All heads turned in unison toward C. Thomas who only shrugged. "Don't look at me. I ain't telling you guys a fuckin' thing."

"Good," Steve said, shuffling the cards for the next round. "We really don't want to know. Now, can we please finish this game?"

"Not so fast," Marty said. "I think C. Thomas is right."

"I am?" C. Thomas asked.

"Yes," Marty continued. "Maybe we need to be more invested in the game."

"What could we possibly play for besides money?" Katie asked.

Katie later would think back upon this pivotal moment. To a large extent, everything that happened next was as a result of this simple question. *When a butterfly flaps its wings…*

"Why don't we play for a—person?" C. Thomas suggested.

Inquisitive looks and muttered "Huhs?" and "Whats?" went around the room. Only Scarlett was quiet and raised a pensive eyebrow. She had a fairly good idea of what C. Thomas was going to propose. What really surprised her was she actually felt a twinge of excitement at the prospect.

"How long have we known each other?" C. Thomas asked.

"Too long," Steve said. "Jeez, can we just get on with the game?"

"I'm serious," C. Thomas said. "How long have you and Katie been friends with Marty and Erin? Ten years?"

"Eleven," Erin corrected.

"Scarlett and I have known all of you for at least three years. Right?"

"Is this going somewhere?" Marty asked.

Scarlett smiled to herself. For once she agreed with C. Thomas. She now knew *exactly* where this was going.

"I have an idea," C. Thomas began, "about how to spice up the game and —ahhhh—maybe our dreary *lives*." He was dragging it all out to significant effect.

"Dreary lives? Speak for yourself," Steve said

"C'mon, Steve-O. We all could use some novelty once in a while."

"If I want novelty, I'll try a new restaurant, or I'll vacation somewhere I've never been," Steve retorted.

"Well, what about your wife? Will she think that's *novel* enough?" Marty interjected.

"Yeah, man. This means something for *everyone*," C. Thomas went on.

"O-M-G," Steve said, throwing up his hands. "Can you get to the damn *bottom line*?"

"Suppose the winner of the game gets to choose somebody else's partner to spend the night with?"

There was a momentary dead silence while the others stared blankly at C. Thomas as they waited for what he said to register. Then they all erupted in gales of laughter, with the exception of Scarlett. Katie and Erin nearly fell over on top of one another. Now sitting up in the loveseat, Scarlett's complete attention was focused on C. Thomas, probably for the first time since they'd began dating.

"Familiarity breeds contempt!" Steve said jokingly. "I knew it would happen sooner or later."

"I thought wife-swapping went out in the seventies," Erin was snarky.

"This has nothing to do with wife-swapping," C. Thomas responded. He was completely deadpan. "This is a *reward* for winning the game. Only the winner gets to choose."

"And whomever the winner chooses has to go along with it?" Katie ventured.

"Yes, but there would be some ground rules."

"Can we just finish the current game?" Steve asked shooting Katie a look, unamused by the entire conversation.

"I'm *serious*," C. Thomas said. "I think it could really work."

Marty looked at Scarlett. "What do you think about your man's bold plan?"

All eyes turned to her. She didn't immediately answer. She looked contemplative and after something of a pregnant pause, finally said, "I think it could be—um, interesting."

It was Steve's turn to raise a pensive eyebrow.

"So what would the ground rules be?" Katie asked, now showing genuine interest in the prospect.

"Don't egg him on, Katie," Steve said with more than a hint of annoyance in his tone. He couldn't believe she even was entertaining C. Thomas's ludicrous proposal.

"It's simple and elegant," C. Thomas began. "The winner chooses somebody else's partner to spend the evening with. What they do—*or don't do*—is totally up to the winner. Both parties are forbidden from ever telling anyone what transpired."

"Did you really use the word *transpired*? How long have you been practicing this speech?" Steve needled, still unamused.

"It can be anyone's partner," C. Thomas said, ignoring Steve.

"So it's not about sleeping with each other?" Erin asked.

Marty shook his head. "It is if you choose to do it. Let's face it. What the hell else are you going to do all night together? Make popcorn and watch Netflix?"

"Sure, Netflix and *chill*," Scarlett chuckled.

"Where would you go?" Katie asked. "New Fairfield's only no-tell motel? I'm sure that would raise some hairy eyeballs all over town."

"Oh, yeah," Erin agreed. "In this hokey place? The gossip would spread like wildfire."

"Not a problem," C. Thomas explained, becoming more animated by the prospect that everyone might really be on board. "I inherited my dad's cabin right on Candlewood Lake. Ten minutes from here. She's just sitting there waiting to be used."

Steve lowered his head and started banging his forehead on the table in obvious frustration. "I can't believe we are even discussing this as if it were a real possibility."

"It *is* a real possibility, Steve-O," C. Thomas chastised. "We've all known each other for a long time. There's a trust we've built among us. Are you telling me that all during this time no one has ever fantasized about being with somebody else?"

Dead silence pervaded the room again. The tension was so thick you could cut it with a knife.

Finally, Marty spoke. "Are you telling me you've had sexual fantasies about our wives?"

"Are you telling *me*, Marty, that as a healthy, heterosexual male you've never once—even for a *second*—fantasized about Scarlett or Katie?"

Marty was momentarily stunned, even appalled at being put on the spot. He wasn't willing to admit that he'd fantasized—*a lot*—about Scarlett. "Do you *really* expect me to answer that?"

"You don't have to answer, Marty," C. Thomas said. "I already know the answer."

"This is far too much oversharing for me," Steve chimed in, a weak attempt to lighten the mood.

C. Thomas turned to him. "*You* stand the most to benefit from this, Steve-O. You're the best player here!"

"Then why even do it?" Steve asked.

"Because it will definitely improve *all* of our games. It's called motivation. Think about how much we'd all have at stake."

"This is puerile nonsense," Steve said, hoping to finally put the matter to bed.

"It sounds to me," Marty said, "that you doth protest too much."

"You'll probably win tonight, Steve," C. Thomas said. "Just think—you could choose another player to spend the night with. Who would you pick?"

All eyes suddenly were on Steve.

"This is crazy."

"Who would you pick?" Katie demanded, cutting him off.

"I'd pick you, of course."

"That wouldn't be allowed." C. Thomas attempted to clarify. "You'd have to pick someone *other* than your own partner. So try again. Who would you pick?"

"Yeah, Steve, who would you pick?" Katie repeated. She was watching Steve intently, and he didn't like it.

Steve shook his head and muttered something under his breath. He furtively glanced over at Scarlett. She returned his gaze, her eyes wide but her face expressionless. Then, ever so slightly, her lips parted and the corners of her mouth turned into, what Steve thought, was a subtle smile.

## 2

## STEVE AND KATIE

Contract: An agreement, upon sufficient consideration, to do or not to do a particular thing.

*One of the first things they teach you in law school are the elements of a contract: offer, acceptance, and consideration or value. Little did I realize that these three things underlie every conceivable human interaction.*

— STEVE KELLY

"Mr. Kelly. Brewster's coming up…Mr. Kelly? Mr. Kelly, time to get up."

Steve was lost in REM sleep and no doubt dreaming of something great and utterly forgettable when George, the train conductor, tapped him on the shoulder. He had heard his voice as if from the bottom of a deep, dark well beckoning him back to consciousness.

He opened his eyes to find George standing over him, liveried in his Metro North Railroad conductor's uniform. His stained white collar was bent upward, his worn, black tie askew, and tickets were sticking out of the rim of his beat-up conductor's hat. Steve swore he recognized the same brown amoeba-shaped spot on the breast pocket from the week before.

"You okay, Mr. Kelly?"

George had to be somewhere in his sixties with at least a good twenty years on Steve. It always seemed somewhat incongruous for George to be calling Steve "Mr. Kelly," but the caste system was still alive and well in America.

"You don't want to miss your stop again and end up in Southeast—or worse, Wassaic."

With his eyes barely open, he responded. "Thanks, George. You're a lifesaver. Mrs. Kelly wouldn't have been happy, I can tell you that." Steve roused himself and shook the sleep from his eyes. He stood up and grabbed his monogrammed leather litigation bag from the overhead bin and then made his way to the doors.

"You have a nice weekend now, Mr. Kelly," George said as he passed.

"Same to you," Steve said steadying himself against a seat as he walked the aisle toward the exit doors. "Except there isn't a nice weekend in sight," Steve grumbled under his breath.

No *nice* weekend started off with a four-hour, round-trip commute to the Manhattan office to prepare for a grueling trial. He now had nothing to look forward to but mowing the lawn and cleaning the pool. The unbelievably fertile green algae had been beating him in the perpetual war against clear blue water, no matter how much chlorine and shock Steve used. He'd tossed so much in the night before that he could still smell it in his nose hairs.

Not for the first time Steve questioned why he ever had become a lawyer.

The train pulled up to the Brewster Village station and the doors hissed open. Steve stepped out into the bright afternoon sunshine. It was a balmy July weekend with ridiculously high humidity and no reported relief in the forecast. Steve wiped the patina of perspiration that immediately formed above his brows, crossed over the platform, and headed to his paid parking space across the street on Railroad Avenue.

"Top of the morning to you, Mr. Kelly," Pat, the dispatcher, called out as Steve passed his cab stand.

"Hey, Pat, how is it going?"

"It's going pretty damn well as long as my Red Sox keep winning. They're going to take the Yankees for sure. We're on the road to another Series!" Pat, a quintessential Irish Catholic from Boston naturally assumed Steve was Irish with a name like Kelly and treated him as a "brother." Steve didn't have the heart to tell him that the amount of Irish in him wasn't enough to fill a shot glass of good Irish whiskey.

"Hope so," Steve said half-heartedly.

"Were you working today, Mr. Kelly?" As if the suit and briefcase weren't a dead giveaway.

"Yes, I sure was."

"Shame to be working on a Saturday, but I guess that's why they pay you the big bucks!"

Steve couldn't have agreed more. He also wanted to ask why Pat himself was working this stifling July Saturday. And speaking of big bucks, how could Pat afford the Lexus he tooled around in? Instead, he replied, "Yeah, sure."

"Well, if the Red Sox win you won't hold it against me, will ya, Mr. Kelly? You'll still let me take you to the airport for your next business trip?" Pat's Boston accent seemed to become heavier with each passing year, despite the fact that from Brewster it was a good three-hour drive to Beantown.

"Of course, Pat. You are my designated airport chauffeur."

Steve waved as he headed for his Audi. Two migrant workers were leaning against the car chatting in Spanish or Portuguese, Steve couldn't tell which. They immediately moved away as Steve approached, his keys wrapped around his fingers like brass knuckles. They'd stopped talking, and Steve could now feel their eyes boring into his back. They must have been two of the unlucky ones who weren't picked to do gardening or construction work today.

Steve pulled out of his parking spot and headed up the dilapidated Main Street to Route Twenty-Two for the twenty-minute drive home. Between the driving and the train, it was not the "hop, skip, and a jump" his Realtor had promised. No matter how you cut it, it was at least four hours of wasting his life. All that time to think did nothing for his mental state, not to mention his soul.

The sound of tractors and weed whackers filled the air as Steve crossed over the state line into Connecticut and navigated through the winding, sidewalk-less, private roads. Steve had always resisted hiring a landscaper or even a weekly lawn mowing service. Having been raised in an apartment most of his life, he'd vowed that if he ever had a house with a lawn he would plant flowers, trim shrubs, and mow the grass himself. It was a decade-old pledge that was weakening each season. At least Katie had taken over flower duty.

Just before he turned onto his block, Steve hoped beyond hope that Josh, his younger neighbor from across the street, may have mowed his lawn. Josh often did it as a courtesy, but usually not if he'd had a night of drinking and playing on-line poker. Steve was responsible for Josh's addiction to on-line poker, but hadn't played with him since the US tightened the on-line gambling laws.

Steve's hopes were dashed as he pulled up to his house. The grass was above-ankle height. Out of the corner of his eye, he noticed that one of the gutters was coming loose, and he couldn't be certain, but he thought there might be a hornet's nest under the eaves. It was beginning to look a little like the Addams Family home, despite the fact that the sprawling one-level ranch house was the largest on the block. It was going to be a long afternoon.

---

"I'M HOME," Steve announced, entering the kitchen and tossing his keys on the table. "Anyone here?" No answer.

"Hello??"

"In the bathroom," came a muted response.

Steve walked down the hallway and turned into the master bedroom. He approached the bathroom and knocked on the door: once, twice, then three times. On the fourth and loudest knock, the door finally opened. Steve was rudely assaulted with a blast of steam. When it cleared, an alien being was standing in front of him, complete with punctured bald cap through which wisps of hair jutted out in Eisenstein-like fashion. A gel-like substance from forehead to chin obscured most of what might have been soft, delicate features. The creature was clothed in a Beverly Hilton robe, two sizes too big, which hung open revealing a matching floral bra and panties. The alien definitely was female.

"I'm dying my hair," Katie said.

"Ahhh. I thought maybe you were practicing cryogenics."

"Rude. How was work?"

"Well, the brief is done. No thanks to my associate. I thought that once I made partner at the *oh-so-prestigious* Ashford, Stepford, and Simpson and had my very own associate to boss around, I wouldn't have to pull weekend duty. I need to fire my associate and hire one who actually has a work ethic."

"So why don't you?"

"Troy Ashford's nephew. Duh. Remember? He has a permanent hall pass. Unlike me, slaving over a pre-trial brief, he's having a grand old time on Fire Island."

Katie nodded. "I see. I guess that's why they pay you the big bucks."

Steve sighed. "That's the second time I heard that today—and it's still lame and tired."

"Ha. Anyway, I'll be done soon and then you can get in."

"What's the agenda? I was hoping to relax tonight."

"Jeez. Did you forget? It's the last Saturday of the month. *Duh*. We're playing cards tonight. I had to rush back from tutoring to hit the market and the liquor store. And that's why I'm coloring my hair."

"Hmm. Maybe you should paint my temples with some of that stuff."

"No way. I like your hair just the way it is. That pop of gray makes you look sexy and distinguished. My gray just makes me look *old*." Katie suddenly took on a seductive air. She looped her stained, gloved hands around Steve's neck. "Well—you know what we *could* do? The girls will be coming home from work soon and then heading right out to a party. If we cancel the game, we'll have the house all to ourselves. Are you up for a night of lust and wild abandon?"

Steve snickered. "Somehow I'm not feeling so lustful at the moment with this Bride of Frankenstein thing you have going on."

"Thanks." She turned away from him to face the mirror. "I may have to get my hair color from a bottle, but at least I don't have to get my passion from one—*Mr. Viagra*."

"That's a low blow."

"Ha. Maybe later—if you're lucky. You know, it is boldly unfair that women hit their prime in their forties just at a time when their men start to peter out."

Steve smiled and shook his head. "I'm not—I give up. I can't fence with you. We might as well play cards. If we cancel, the gang'll just want to do something tomorrow night. Sometimes I feel like the six of us are too joined at the hip—and not in a good way."

"Stop. They're our friends. Why don't you take a quick dip? I'll be done in about a half hour."

"Good idea. Anyway, I need to take something for this migraine."

Steve walked back down the hall to the kitchen. He opened the cupboard next to the sink which housed the gigantic bottle of acetaminophen and snickered at the Viagra bottle stashed behind it. The window above the sink overlooked his two acres of property. Spread across it were the girls' old cedar swing set that now was faded and worn, the shed which housed the dreaded lawn mower and weed whacker, and the massive in-ground swimming pool.

He fumbled with the tamper-proof pill bottle, finally freeing three capsules. He popped all three in his mouth. Maybe habit, but two never seemed to do the trick. As he ran cold water into a glass he caught a flurry of movement in the pool. Had Jamie and Anna come home already? No, Katie just said they weren't back. There it was again—a splash as someone dove under the water, bare feet momentarily visible before submerging into the blue. The pool water actually was clear.

He craned his neck and then he saw it. The Goddess had emerged, breaking through the surface of the water. Late afternoon sun behind and above bathed her in a photographer's coveted golden light. It played out surreally as in a movie scene. A blonde goddess, dripping wet and nearly naked—except for the bottom half of a very skimpy bikini—lifting herself out of the water. She was an exquisite specimen of female sensuality with round and full, symmetrical breasts with dark areolas that were unusual for natural blondes. She had a perfect waist-to-hip ratio, slender thighs with not a centimeter of cellulite anywhere, long legs, and dainty feet. Her shiny red toenail polish obviously had withstood the onslaught of the massive amounts of chlorine Steve had thrown into the pool.

Utterly flustered, Steve dropped the glass of water he'd been holding into the sink where it shattered into a thousand pieces.

"Shit!" Steve cried.

"What was that?" Katie called from the bathroom.

"Nothing. Just broke a glass."

The Goddess shook her long mane of hair, reached for a towel, laid it on the patio, then flopped down on her stomach, her barely-covered bottom half in Steve's direct line of sight.

As he fumbled to pick up the broken pieces of glass, his eyes remained riveted on the Goddess. Unfortunately multitasking never was one of Steve's strong points.

"Goddamn it!" He raised a bloody right hand and pulled a rather large shard out of his middle finger. He grabbed a dish towel and wrapped it around his injured digit.

"What's going on?" Katie called again.

"Nothing!" Steve, with his bloody finger still wrapped in the dishtowel, made his way around the family room to the French doors leading to the patio and the pool beyond. He quietly opened them and slid outside into the blazing sun.

Steve silently approached the Goddess from behind. When he was within a half dozen feet of her, he stopped to take in the sight. Her hair, swept back across the nape of her neck and left shoulder, already was beginning to dry from the summer heat. There were tiny beads of chlorinated pool water mixed with perspiration rolling off the center of her back to the curve of her breasts that poked out on either side of her perfectly tanned body. The bottom of her string bikini was slightly askew, exposing tan lines that cut across her smooth buttocks.

The Goddess suddenly stirred and opened her eyes. Steve seriously considered whether it was the pounding of his heart that might have roused her. Not wanting to be caught gaping at her, he walked around to face her.

"Scarlett?"

She smiled at him and lifted herself up slightly on her forearms, exposing her breasts. Was she doing that deliberately? Steve tried not to gawk. How could she not…know?

"Hi, Steve," she said, winking up at him, not conspiratorially, but rather from the bright sun. "I hope you don't mind. Katie said I could use the pool. They finally are going to pour the foundation for ours today."

"No, uh, no. I don't mind at all. You can use the pool—whenever. You know that. You're family." Steve tried to divert his eyes away from her nipples which were lightly scraping the threads of the towel as she moved. "I didn't see your car in the driveway."

"The Beamer's in the shop. Katie said I could use her car today, too, not that I'll need it necessarily. I hope it's okay."

"Of course it's okay. You know you can always borrow whatever you need." He felt like a bumbling adolescent.

"I'll keep that in mind." Another smile. Another wink. Was it conspiratorial this time? Steve couldn't be sure.

"What time is it?" she asked.

Steve looked at his wrist watch, a classic Rolex which used to belong to his late father. "Almost four."

"Um. Do you know you're bleeding?"

Finally, Steve tore his eyes away from her and looked down at the dish rag. Half of it now was a dark crimson.

"Broke a glass," he mumbled.

"That's a lot of blood. You better make sure you don't need stitches." She sighed. "I'd better get going. I have to get ready for the card game tonight."

"That's right. Yeah. We're playing tonight."

"I really look forward to the games. You're a good player."

"Nah. Fair to midland at best," Steve said deprecatingly.

"Not true. I've learned a lot from you."

Scarlett rose to her feet, taking the towel with her. Although she held the towel loosely in front of her, Steve still could see over it. Her nipples and areolas were framed within perfect white isosceles triangles; leftover imprints from her scanty bikini top. He fleetingly considered what Katie would say if she happened upon the scene.

"So is C. Thomas home?" Steve asked, grasping at anything to make conversation.

"No. He had another kiosk opening at a mall in Waterbury, I think. He dashed out early."

Steve nodded in understanding. Scarlett's long-term boyfriend, C. Thomas, was the owner of the first and largest, independent DVD kiosk chain in the country. They were in nearly every grocery store, discount store, and mall. To outsiders, this might have seemed like a great feat considering that C. Thomas was only in his twenties and dumb as dirt. To insiders like Steve, however, it was pure luck, happenstance, and genetics. C. Thomas inherited the business from his father who had built a fortune franchising video chain stores in the early eighties. When the video business dried up, his father capitalized on the DVD market and pioneered the self-service DVD kiosk empire. C. Thomas walked into it a few years after high school following his father's losing battle with pancreatic cancer.

"Impressive. What does that make it? A thousand or so?"

She shrugged, her breasts seductively rising and falling. "No clue. For every kiosk he opens these days, another closes. Everyone streams today, you know? Anyway, I believe there are still a few places he hasn't *penetrated* yet."

Did she purposely emphasize the word "penetrate" or was it Steve's imagination?

"I'm sure he will eventually obtain *full penetration*," Steve offered uncharacteristically, deliberately responding in kind.

She gave a sly smile. "I wouldn't count on it."

Steve was trying to think of a snappy comeback line but before he could, she said, "Can you hand me my top?"

"What?"

"My bikini top—it's on the chair." She motioned to one of two nearby poolside deck chaise longues.

"Of course." Steve turned and walked toward the chaise. He picked up the flimsy bikini by its string and walked it back to Scarlett. "Here you go. Um. Do you want to change inside?"

"No, it's okay."

She dropped the towel and turned her back to him. Although the movement was quick, Steve was able to take in the full breadth of her toplessness. This time Steve was certain she did it deliberately. They always had had a semi-flirtatious relationship, but Steve chalked it up to her and her outgoing, extroverted personality. He really never took any of their off-color banter seriously in the past. But surely, he thought, this had to be something different, something more. The crossing of a boundary perhaps?

She slipped the bikini around her neck with the part that she'd left tied, adjusted the triangles over her breasts, then reached behind her back with a loose string in each hand.

"Can you tie this for me?"

Steve was dumbstruck but quickly recovered. "Sure—uh, yes." He reached for the bikini strings, but not before shaking off the bloody dish towel. He again wondered what would happen if Katie suddenly appeared.

She chuckled. "Try not to get any blood on me, please." Before Steve could respond, however, she tilted her head toward him and said, "Although…that could be kind of *kinky*."

Now completely flabbergasted, Steve dropped both strings of the bikini. As it was, he wasn't very good at tying bikini strings or even shoes for that matter. He never quite got it down pat, a throwback to his youth when the cute little girl down the street used to tie his shoes for him every day. He scrambled to retrieve Scarlett's bikini strings to begin again, his hands brushing against her back.

"Not too tight," she instructed.

Steve obliged, completed a lopsided bow, and stepped back. She turned to face him and smiled.

"Thanks. I'm always a bit of a spaz when it comes to things like that. I'll see you later." She gave him a kiss on the very corner of his lips. Kisses and hugs generally were the norm when it came to greetings and farewells between them, but was this kiss different? A tad longer? A tad wetter? Was Steve a tad delirious?

Scarlett turned and sashayed away. Yes, that was the only way to describe it. He watched as the skimpy bikini bottom stretched and contorted as her buttocks moved from side to side. If Katie had come out at this moment she would have seen her husband standing with his mouth hanging open and a bulge in his pants which definitely was *not* his keys.

---

THE EGG TIMER went off and Katie clicked to save the file she was working on and then closed down her laptop. She'd been penning a self-help book for over a year, sneaking in a few paragraphs here, a few pages there, often between errands and other tasks, usually when some inspiration hit. She even had notes scrawled on multiple legal pads stashed in drawers around the house. But now she had to finish getting herself and the house ready for the game and she hated rushing.

She pulled off the cap and painted some hair dye on the strands of hair in the center of her part which were stubbornly still gray. She never could quite get the home coloring thing down, which was why she nearly always had it done in the salon. A last-minute cancellation by her stylist yesterday had left her with no choice.

Steve only told her after work Friday that he needed to go into the city early that morning, which meant all of the preparations for the night's game were left up to her. Saturdays were her tutoring days at the local community college. Katie's Master's degree in psychology was put to less than mediocre use with an occasional adjunct teaching position and some per diem tutoring. What she really wanted was to finish her licensure hours and hang out a shingle as a psychotherapist. Marrying Steve and accidentally becoming pregnant too soon put a bit of a crimp in her career plans. She'd wanted to go on for her Ph.D. but trying to go back to school now would be all but impossible. Steve worked too much and she'd become too set in her ways. Family was her priority but at least working part-time in the field kept her feeling productive and somewhat connected.

It was getting late and hair done or not, she had to shower. She hung up her bathrobe and was just about to jump in when Steve abruptly barged into the bathroom.

"Jeez. Are you okay?" she asked.

"Yeah. Why?

"I don't know. You look like a madman. Is anything wrong?"

"No."

Katie slipped off her bra and panties and let them drop to the floor. She reached into the shower, turned on the water and played with the dial for a moment. Satisfied with the temperature, she stepped inside and pulled the curtain around her.

Watching her through the semi-sheer fabric, Steve frenetically undressed in a matter of seconds, leaving his good work clothes in a rumpled pile in the middle of the damp tile floor. He pulled back the curtain and nearly leapt into the tub behind Katie.

"Hey, what are you doing?" Katie asked, just starting to soap up.

"What does it look like I'm doing? I'm joining you in the shower."

He reached around her body and grabbed both breasts.

Katie was both shocked and surprised. "Since when are you so frisky?" She reached around and felt his hardness. "Is this you? Without Viagra? What the hell happened to you?"

Steve didn't answer. The water and soap made the process so much easier. He pushed into her unaided. The initial thrust was so hard Katie almost fell against the wall of the shower. She braced herself as he took her from behind, holding a breast with one hand and her hair with the other. Hair dye and the dried blood from his hand trickled down their contorted bodies and flowed into the drain.

With his eyes closed tightly, Steve pushed harder and harder, his excitement driven not only by the act itself but the sudden full-blown fantasy that he was with *her*, the Goddess, Scarlett. Their neighbor. Their friend.

It was quick. But Steve and Katie climaxed together; an unusual event. Both of them collapsed into the bottom of the tub.

"Wow," Katie finally said, still breathing heavily. "We haven't done *that* since college."

## 3

## MARTY AND ERIN

"Henry James was a hack!" Sean Russo declared. "An utter hack. And yet he is revered by Hollywood as the Messiah. Do you know how many film versions of *The Turn of the Screw* there are?"

"No, I can't say that I do," Marty replied.

"Countless!" Sean exclaimed. "There are *countless* versions. And yet Anthony Trollope, who was a *god* compared to James, is barely known. There should be countless film versions of *The Eustace Diamonds*!"

"I agree," Marty said. But he really didn't. Or rather, it wasn't that he agreed or disagreed with his haughty, self-important student. It was that he simply didn't care. He didn't care about Henry James or Anthony Trollope or Sean Russo. All he cared about was that he was wasting a perfectly good Saturday in his office listening to a pontificating idiot.

As a tenured professor in the English Department at Colonial State University, Martin P. Fein, Ph.D. was given right of first refusal for course schedules. He chose to teach two summer classes; one three-hour seminar about Shakespeare, scheduled Monday afternoons, and another three-hour seminar about the Victorian novelists, offered Saturdays at eight a.m. Most professors shied away from Saturday classes, particularly in the summer, but Marty took this particular class because it was guaranteed to be jam-packed with hot coeds. On top of it, the classrooms were sweltering in the summer, and after the first class, they all showed up wearing little-to-nothing. Required to offer two mandatory office hours per class, he tacked them on right after each seminar, figuring that no student actually would take advantage of them, especially in the summer.

But Sean Russo did. Sean Russo, aka the biggest brownnoser in history. "*Barchester Towers* should be a series on the BBC, not the crap that they have now."

Marty spied his desk clock/paperweight out of the corner of his eye. Fifteen minutes left and his office hours would be over. Fifteen minutes to freedom. For a fleeting half second he wondered what would happen to a professor if he were to pummel a student to death with a paperweight.

He turned and glanced out his office window. It was a bright, hot day, probably the most brutal thus far this July. As he lazily scanned the campus, Marty thought about all of the things he could have been doing while Sean droned on in the background. Suddenly another of his students, Heather Pearlman, appeared as she crossed the quad. Heather was one of the primary reasons Marty looked forward to teaching at the college level. She wasn't necessarily *model material* as they say, but she had a rack to-die-for, and Marty would liberally avail himself of her décolletage every class. He told himself at least it was legal to ogle the over-eighteen set.

Marty's office was on the second floor of Brigham Hall. From his window, he had a perfect bird's eye view of the Student Union picnic area. He watched intently as Heather made her way through the wrought iron tables to the grass directly beneath Marty's window. He wondered if it was intentional. Looking more like she was going to the beach than to class, she was clad in a hot pink, low-cut tank top, tight, white cutoffs, flip-flops, and a pair of Lolita sunglasses.

Heather reached into her tote bag for a beach towel then tossed it on the ground in front of her. She positioned herself on it and turned to face the bright sun. She pulled a paperback from her bag, found her place in it, and casually tossing aside her bookmark, began reading. It was Trollope's *The Eustace Diamonds,* one of his later novels and one of his most celebrated. In it, Trollope explored the power of wealth and its influence on sexual relationships. Marty always assigned it whenever he taught the seminar. He favored it over Trollope's other books because of the sexual themes.

Even from the second floor, Marty could get a prime view of Heather's ample cleavage. He suddenly imagined what it would be like to be masturbating between her breasts.

"Don't you agree, Professor?" Russo asked, jolting Marty back to reality.

"What?"

"The Dickensian litigation fever effect—as exemplified in his *Bleak House*," Sean said. "Our judicial system is no better now than it was in Dickens' time. The only people who make any money are the lawyers."

"That is certainly true," Marty agreed. His best friend, Steve Kelly, was a senior partner at a big law firm in Manhattan and made money hand over fist.

For the second time during his office hours, Marty considered picking up the clock and bashing the crap out of Sean Russo. He'd lose his job for sure, but it would feel so damn good.

He glanced out the window again. Heather was still reading, her form now partly in silhouette as the afternoon sun hid behind a cloud. What I wouldn't give to have just one night with her, Marty thought.

Marty couldn't remember a time when he did not have such intense libidinous urges. In fact, as he'd gotten older, his libido seemed to increase with each passing year. Perhaps it was because he started his sexual career relatively late in life. He didn't lose his virginity until he was twenty-five. Needless to say, his segue into sexual manhood was not memorable or, for that matter, a pleasurable experience and set the stage for years of orgasmic dissatisfaction.

His first sexual partner was also a virgin in her twenties. She was a fellow grad student, average in the looks and intelligence departments, but more than willing to sacrifice her virginity to an eager taker. And Marty certainly *was* an eager taker. But that first experience was more problematic than Marty ever could have imagined and despite her discomfort, he insisted they keep trying. He always had thought that it would be a relatively quick process, momentarily painful for the woman, and then ultimately enjoyable for both partners. *Not!*

Every attempt at penetration had caused her such excruciating pain that they had to stop. Fortunately, mindful of his ejaculation point-of-no-return, she would gratuitously jerk him off after each failed coital attempt. Oral sex for her was "out of the question," however. Finally, after three weeks of push and pull, her hymen was history, although her pain—and complaints—

persisted. By then, both had decided the agonizing and unsatisfying sex was at least equal to their incompatibility and they just should move on.

His second sexual encounter was not much better. He was a newly appointed professor at Colonial State and attending a teaching conference in Charlotte, North Carolina. While at the conference he met an attractive fellow English professor who taught at the Queens University of Charlotte. They had dinner together after the conference where he learned she just had gone through a rather difficult break-up. Although she was way out of his league, they discovered a fairly solid core of compatibility as far as their teaching strategies were concerned and decided a trip back to Marty's hotel room was in order to check out other possible avenues of compatibility.

Marty was tentative at first, half expecting she was going to cry out in pain upon penetration since that had been his only previous experience. When she didn't, he became more confident and more aggressive. His excitement increased exponentially when it suddenly occurred to him mid-thrust that he was actually screwing a really good-looking woman.

"Easy cowboy," she'd said in an attempt to slow him down. "I like it slow and easy, big boy. If you don't you're going to blow your wad—"

And that's when Marty came.

Right afterward, she got up and quickly dressed, leaving visibly annoyed and unsatisfied. At the time, Marty was humiliated and deflated. In retrospect (and in an effort to soothe his bruised ego), although he knew he had been too quick on the draw, he considered that he actually got a few things out of it. Another notch on his bedpost and fodder for later masturbation fantasies.

A good deal of time would pass before his next conquest, but fortunately for Marty, the third time was a charm, or as close to a charm as there could be. Erin Stapleton was a young grad student pursuing a degree in education. She was assigned to Marty first as an observer and then later as a student teacher for a few of his classes. His job was to mentor and evaluate her, a role of authority he knew Erin found exciting, and he took full advantage of it.

Erin was cute as a button, as they say. Not gorgeous, but perky and sweet, and she was naive. Practically a country bumpkin from rural Pennsylvania, Marty could see her potential and he exploited it. He regaled her with stories of his many conquests, most of them fictional. He charmed her with rote memorization of Elizabethan poetry. And he explored new sexual ground with a near virgin who fell prey to his attempts at Svengali-like commands. It wasn't long before they were married.

The honeymoon period, however, wore off fairly quickly for Marty, probably due to the fact that they conceived while *on* their honeymoon. Erin was pregnant with twins, and it was no easy time, especially when she was on bed rest for the last two months before going into labor three weeks early. After the twins—later to become known by Marty as the "monsters"—were born, sex became somewhat of a distant memory. Life was too hectic, Erin was too busy, and Marty refused to beg. He was back to dry dock, and he didn't like it one bit. Teaching romantic poetry with classes mostly filled with sexy coeds didn't help. Thank goodness for porn and the internet.

"...and that is why our society is slowly sinking into Dickensian madness. Don't you agree, Professor? Professor?"

Marty didn't have the slightest idea what Sean Russo was rambling on about. All he knew is that he should agree.

"I agree completely," Marty said. He reached for the clock/paperweight, this time feeling that much closer to following through with his brutal fantasies. Then he realized what time it was and that his office hours finally were over.

"Time's up," Marty said, holding up the clock/paperweight so that Sean could see he was telling the truth. It was the only way to get rid of the ass-kisser. "I need to get going and start my weekend in earnest."

"Yes, sure. I understand, Professor. I can talk about this stuff all day."

"I see that," Marty said. He rose and began packing up his briefcase. It was obvious that Sean was thick as shit. Maybe if he guaranteed him an "A" for the course he could get rid of the brownnoser once and for all.

"I really enjoy our talks, Professor."

"Ditto," Marty said absently.

"So, next week? Same time, same station?"

"Yeah, sure," Marty said, not hearing him. Had he, he most certainly would not have responded in the affirmative. He glanced out his office window one last time. Heather was gone. Damn! He was hoping to stop and say hello and maybe flirt a little. It was all Sean's fault, stupid, ass-kissing prick!

MARTY TURNED into his driveway and pulled up to the garage. He had a three-bedroom cape, originally built in the 1960s, but substantially modified including the addition of a new master bedroom suite. It probably was his smartest investment, or more accurately, Erin's, since it was her brainchild to buy the house in the first place. The house had appreciated nicely despite the recent downturns in the real estate market and now was mortgage-free. That fact, coupled with Marty's solid position as a tenured professor, gave him a healthy cushion of financial security.

Although he hadn't even turned off the car, he could hear the screams of the monsters coming from inside the house. For a brief second he considered that maybe listening to Sean Russo might not have been that bad after all, not when you compared it to the shrieking banshees, otherwise known as his two, high-energy, indefatigable eight-year-old boys.

Reluctantly he killed the ignition, grabbed his case and empty travel mug, and headed into the house.

"I got you! I got you, asshole!" Devin, or was it Daniel, yelled, repeatedly shooting his marshmallow pump rifle at his near-mirror image. The boys most definitely were identical twins; few people other than Erin could tell them apart.

"Bullshit! You never touched me!" Daniel, or was it Devin, screamed in response. He raised his marshmallow crossbow and fired back.

"I heard that," Erin called from one of the bedrooms. "You boys are going to owe the swear jar!"

Marty closed the door behind him and stepped into the crossfire. Immediately he was riddled with dozens of mini and regular-sized white marshmallows. As he took a step further into the tile entry way, he felt a sudden resistance as he tried to lift his foot. "Jesus Christ, these monsters! Are they really mine?" he said to himself, a bit too loudly. Slipping off his left shoe, he turned it over and discovered that he had completely eviscerated several pieces of the dispensed ammunition. The marshmallows had congealed into a giant blob on the sole and up the side of his Topsiders. Dozens of marshmallows dotted the floor, walls, and ceiling. The boys must have mouthed them first, making them extra sticky. Marty was in a Jet-Puffed war zone.

"You boys are not supposed to shoot these things in the house!" Why had he ever thought these would make for an appropriate Christmas present?

The monsters responded by escalating the war and their animal-like vocalizations while totally ignoring their father's admonition. Devin or Daniel started jumping on the sofa as if it was a trampoline, reloading and firing in midair as his brother returned the fire from behind an overturned chair while holding up Marty and Erin's wedding photo as a shield.

Marty slipped off his other shoe, clutched both to his chest, careful not to get any gluey marshmallow on his Lacoste polo, and using his briefcase as his own shield, charged through the oncoming barrage of marshmallow bullets. He turned down the hall and headed for his study.

"Erin, where are you?" he called as he dodged the onslaught.

"I'm doing the laundry. I'm trying to hurry because I still have to get ready for tonight. We're playing cards, remember?"

That's right. It was card night. At least he would get to down a few while ogling Scarlett in all of her succulent buxomness.

He turned into his study, closing and locking the door behind him. He dropped his briefcase and shoes but not before flicking off the marshmallows, which now peppered his briefcase as well. He took a deep breath. Ahhh —peace—and—quiet, he thought. This was his sanctuary; his exclusive man cave. He made it a point to everyone that this was his private space, reserved only for work and off limits to everyone else.

He walked to his desk, flopped into his luxury leather, executive desk chair and powered on the MacBook. This was known to all as his "work" computer although in reality he did very little *work* on it. Only he knew the password. He logged in and went to one of his favorite "networking" sites: www.philanderers.com. Philanderers.com was touted as one of the most comprehensive, extramarital relationship information and destination sites for both married men and women.

He went to the sign-in link and typed his user name: *Naughty Professor* and his password: Trollope. Not very original, he knew. His profile popped up immediately:

Naughty Professor—*Attractive, well hung, mid-thirties professional. Intelligent and refined. Seeking single or married female 18 to 25 for fun-in-the-sun, no-strings-attached, casual relationship. Non-smoker. Disease-free: proof upon request. Favorite activities include theatre, movies, poetry, eating out, travel, and tennis. Photo upon request. Serious inquiries only.*

Marty had reviewed other profiles on Philanderers and used them to piece together his own. While some could have thought it was a stretch, Marty justified, at least in his own mind, the verisimilitude of his profile. For example, everyone called themselves attractive, and Marty was, in his own way, attractive. At least he believed so. He was a professional, and by all standards, he was refined. *Christ, I can quote everything from Emily Dickinson to John Milton*, he often told people—that is, anyone who would listen. His favorite activities really were the ones he listed although he enjoyed watching tennis rather than playing it; a slight misdirection at best.

He scrolled down to see if he received any comments or private messages on his profile. None! Damn!

There were two ways to meet people on the site. The first way, and the least expensive, was through comment threads or private messages from others with no ability to respond to said messages. These were VERY rare events, particularly because Marty did not post a photo of himself. In truth, he was not *that* confident of his looks. The second and more effective way was to pay for a first-level Premier Membership which gave users the ability to browse through the profiles of the site's other members and private message up to five of them. Once the five-member messaging limit was reached, one had to upgrade their membership status. So far, Marty had sent thirty messages to various women, he was about a hundred-fifty dollars in the hole, and not one of the women had responded. Needless to say, trying to meet a like-minded, would-be adulterer could be a very expensive proposition. In addition to site fees, Marty had to apply for a Visa card in his own name with the bills sent to a post office box in town. He paid the billing statements via untraceable postal money orders. Finally, he had to purchase a mobile pay-as-you-go phone which he kept in a special pocket in his locked briefcase. To date it had never been used, but Marty was ever the optimist. He knew, or at least hoped, that it just was a matter of time before he would indulge in the extramarital sex he so badly craved.

"Marty, did you get a chance to take lunch today?" Erin called from the other side of the study door. Engrossed in what he was doing, he didn't immediately respond. She tapped lightly on the door. "Marty?"

"I have to finish up a couple of things for work. I'll be out soon," he said trying to be casual. "Oh, and yeah. I grabbed something." He hadn't, but he had better things to do.

"Okay. But hurry up in there. The sitter will be here soon and I'm going to need a hand watching the boys so I can change."

"Sitter? I thought Jamie and Anna were coming."

"Katie called before you got home—the girls were invited to a party. I had to call Susie. Her daughter Mikayla—you know, the one who just graduated from Ithaca—hasn't gotten a job yet, so she's available."

"Yeah. Okay. Yeah." Marty remembered Mikayla from her graduation party in May. Mikayla was twenty-one, attractive and very personable. She didn't have much of a chest, but her Rockette-length legs and tight ass made up for any shortfalls upstairs. Besides, Marty always was of the mind that more than a handful goes to waste. She would make an excellent babysitter.

Hmmm…babysitter, he thought as he nodded to himself. He then signed out of Philanders and instead logged on to one of his many favorite porn sites. He clicked on the category *Banging Babysitters* and leaned back in the executive chair bought explicitly for this purpose. Then he unzipped his pants.

---

ERIN CONTINUED past Marty's study with an overflowing laundry basket in her arms and headed upstairs for the boys' room. Saturday was catch-up day. Why, she didn't know, because it was nearly impossible to *catch-up* with anything while Marty was at work and the boys were underfoot. It annoyed her that Marty always called the twins monsters. Devin and Daniel were the loves of her life. She couldn't remember a time without them and wouldn't want to. Despite their high energy levels, they really were wonderful children.

Since the boys were born, Erin really felt she had found her true purpose in being a mom. Most of the time she felt like a single mother though, yet she couldn't or wouldn't complain. Marty worked hard and provided them with a nice life so she was able to stay home with the boys. Originally planning to be a high school English teacher, she instead had taught second grade for a few years after getting her degree, around the time she and Marty became engaged and then married. She'd yearned for motherhood and had convinced Marty that he would love being a parent, too. He didn't have much choice when she had stopped taking her birth control pills three months before the wedding, unbeknownst to him. All of a sudden, she was practically an animal in bed on their honeymoon, and it turned him on. She knew just how to get to him. He'd always said he wanted her to be more aggressive. It was her perfect opportunity to both please him and to get herself pregnant.

If truth be told, Erin did not find Marty exceptionally attractive when she was working with him as a grad student, but she was shy and lacked experience. It was exciting to be the recipient of the attention of an "older man," too. What had begun purely as a teacher-student relationship, quickly turned sexual when he doggedly pursued her.

Erin was from a small town in Pennsylvania and did not have a lot of self-confidence. Until she began her college search, she never had crossed the state line. Even though she was cute and was a high school cheerleader, she never felt she could compete with the popular girls, so she never tried. She didn't see herself as others did. Always a wallflower, she wasn't asked out by the football players or the guys on student council. Those invitations were reserved for the outgoing bubbleheads with the low-cut shirts. Ultimately, she ended up dating a guy she worked with in the local grocery store. He was a nice guy, but there was no spark, at least not on her part.

Erin had hoped that college would be her opportunity to shine. She felt she was something of a changeling destined for greater things, which included moving out of *lame* Pennsylvania, she'd told her parents, with all of the *lame* people who never bothered to leave the state to take the under two-hour drive to New York City. She really hadn't meant to be insulting to her parents, but she was ready for something more and they knew it. Yet once she actually got out of Dodge, she was unable to shake off her shyness, and college turned into a great disappointment.

While those first four years weren't enough to bring her out of her shell, she threw her hat back in the ring and hoped that graduate school might be the turning point. Meeting Marty, then having him like her, really *like* her, was definitely an ego boost. She began to feel beautiful and confident. She wasn't a virgin when they'd met, but she'd had little experience in the sexual arena, and she was excited to be with a ladies' man who could show her what to do. Marty was experienced. He had told her about all of his conquests. She also was impressed by all of his career accomplishments and his recitation of poetry which he often did in their post-coital glow as he stroked her hair.

Erin was raised to be a doting wife, and she mostly was. Her mother and father had been married for forty years and still held hands wherever they went. She worked hard to make her life with Marty a reflection of that. She appreciated her husband. She loved her husband. But the nagging question remained. Was she *in love* with him? Had she ever been?

The bit of self-confidence Erin had gained after meeting Marty waned in the early years after the boys were born. It might have had to do with the fact that she'd never been a bigger girl—pudgy was a word Marty liked to use, but never about her. Cheerleaders weren't heavy. Her mom never was heavy. She had joined four different gyms over the years but never stuck with them. Her heart always was home with the boys.

Marty and she now often felt more like roommates than marriage partners or lovers. But that happens to everyone after so many years of marriage, right? She always questioned everything.

She really didn't miss sex, either. The schedule they maintained for their copulative efforts seemed to be enough for Marty and she managed to get through it without him ever knowing or caring that she got nothing out of it. She imagined most women faked it at least some of the time. The thing was she faked it *all* of the time.

"Mom!" Devin and Daniel screeched in unison. She was so lost in making sure their respective, coordinated clothing was stacked neatly in their identical bureaus, she jumped. "Mom!"

"What?" she called back.

*CRASH!*

Erin dropped a pile of shirts and went running for the stairs. When she neared the kitchen, she found her favorite terra cotta planter with the huge Peace Lily she'd been keeping alive since college, strewn from one end of the kitchen to the other. How it had gotten there, she couldn't be sure, as it had been strung from the ceiling in the corner from an unbreakable hook and chain.

"Boys, please get back!" Erin said as she shooed them out of the kitchen, concerned that they might step on the pieces in their bare feet. She got down on her hands and knees and began to clean up the mess, surveying the plant to see if at least part of it might be salvageable.

"He did it!" Devin shouted.

"No, I did not!" Daniel retorted. "You did it, you liar!"

"Now, now, boys," Erin tried to remain calm.

"This is bullshit!" Devin yelled. "You have to believe me, Mom!"

"Swear jar," Erin said as she pointed with a soil-covered finger to the oversized Mason jar on the kitchen counter, which right now was overflowing with quarters.

"No!" Devin said as he stomped past her. "Idiot!" he yelled to Daniel as they both ran out the front door into parts unknown.

"What the hell is going on?" Marty suddenly appeared in the kitchen, seeing Erin on the floor.

"Nothing, nothing. Just an accident. It's fine. I got it." She wiped a sudden burst of perspiration from her brow. "Are you going to get ready soon?"

Marty stood there scowling with no intention of lending a hand to Erin. "Yeah," he said. "I think I will." He walked over to the corner cabinet and pulled out a jug of Jack Daniels and a highball glass. Pouring himself a healthy drink, he walked out of the kitchen, leaving the bottle on the counter, cap off, and a brown puddle next to it. Erin heard him gulp, then belch loudly.

Erin stifled tears, hurrying to clean up the mess.

## 4

## SCARLETT AND C. THOMAS

Scarlett shimmied the covers up over her shoulders and shivered. The A/C was blasting, and she considered it was ironic that she could be so cold despite the sweltering July heat she literally could see sizzling through the open blinds of the bedroom window. She glanced at the clock. Ten thirty-six a.m. Damn. She'd wanted to be up earlier than this. She had so much to do–*Not*. They'd already called her off of work at the store today, supposedly because of some issue with the alarm system. She knew better. The dowdy owner of Lola's was intimidated having a young, attractive woman on staff—her husband was the one who had hired Scarlett. She was also sure that the women who shopped there realized Scarlett wouldn't be caught dead in the horrible, but expensive clothing she helped them purchase.

She pulled the blanket tightly around her, sat up, then yanked it from the corners of the king-sized bed as she trounced onto the carpet.

"Shit!" she screamed as she landed on a crimson studded stiletto in the middle of the floor. She sat back down and grabbed her foot to try and rub away the pain. It was then that she noticed the insanely huge bruise on her shin. It had to have been from the night before. God, heels were only meant to be worn on flat surfaces, she thought angrily.

She stood and snatched up the shoe, then its match. Gingerly padding over to the bureau, she grabbed the two other pairs of shoes that were strewn across the floor, piling them in her arms. She'd had on three different pairs last night before settling on the crimson ones. She didn't even remember why, but C. Thomas had preferred them over the others. She never could figure out why the hell he even cared.

"God damnit!" she said when she noticed the heel of her favorite Jimmy Choo stiletto booties had nearly snapped off. "Well, there goes another pair to the shoemaker." She was a regular customer at Alonso's Shoe Service over in Danbury. The cute little Portuguese owner and his wife must have thought she was quite the klutz. She probably was in there every other week. They should only know.

She headed into the walk-in closet with the pile of shoes and put the two good pairs and the one still-intact bootie on the sliding rack. She put the other in the bag by the mirror she usually used to tote the items for repair. She'd forgotten there already was another shoe in the bag—one of her exclusive and ridiculously priced, black patent leather Christian Louboutins.

"Oh, for God's sake!' she grumbled to herself. What she forked out for shoe repair in six months probably could pay a full-time minimum-wage earner's salary for a year.

She dropped the blanket for a moment and looked at herself in the mirror. The bruise was damn ugly. She inspected a similar one on the other leg, pale and yellowed now as it nearly was healed. She turned to the side and checked for the bruise that had been on the back of her arm but it finally was gone. One of these days someone might actually think C. Thomas was beating her.

Just call me the bruise collector, she thought. Scarlett couldn't stand him most of the time, but the one thing she could say was that C. Thomas had never hit her. She shook her tousled mane of blonde waves.

Catching her full reflection, she spun around checking out every inch, this time not for the bruises. Tight ass. Great legs. And her breasts. Oh, her breasts! She knew it had been the right decision to stop at a D-cup like Dr. Campone recommended. She was petite otherwise, and they were a perfect fit. Even back in the day at a B-cup she'd turned heads, but hooking up with C. Thomas meant having whatever she wanted, and she figured she should get it while she could. In her heart, she knew her relationship with C. Thomas wasn't going to last forever. He was a jerk. But a jerk with money, and it was what *Momma* wanted for her.

She again shivered in the cold of the A/C. She hoisted the blanket and headed for the shower. As long as she was going to take the shoes in to be fixed, she might as well drop off C. Thomas's shirts at the laundry and stop by the mall. What the hell else was there to do on a Saturday afternoon? C. Thomas had been up and out early for work, if you could call it that; a ribbon-cutting in Waterbury for the new video kiosk. Woo hoo. He was just the ditzy figurehead for a company his very intelligent father had started. His mother on the other hand, was a bimbo of the worst kind—obviously where C. Thomas's brain derived from. Scarlett wasn't even sure C. Thomas would have graduated from high school had all of the female teachers not passed him because he was so goddamn hot.

Scarlett let out a wide, loud yawn. Not very becoming for a lady, her mother would have told her. Momma was always in her head. But Scarlett was alone, as usual, so who cares? Somehow C. Thomas was always "working" leaving Scarlett to her own devices.

Just as she was about to turn on the shower, it dawned on her that the BMW was in the shop. She'd have to wait until C. Thomas got home to take her to get it. Screw it, the shoes could wait. Instead she limped down the stairs to make herself some coffee. Her foot and shin were killing her.

She popped a Starbucks K-cup into the Keurig and poured the water into the well then pushed the START button. Maybe she'd give Katie a call. She'd offered Scarlett their pool all summer since no one really was using it. Maybe Katie would want to have a few poolside drinks with her before the game tonight. Liquid lunch, perhaps? She and Katie only infrequently got together one-on-one and she really enjoyed hanging out with her. The two often would go back and forth psychologically sizing up the rest of the triptych. Katie could be a hoot, using a German accent like Freud and calling him Schlomo, his middle name.

*"Ja, ich bin Schlomo,"* Katie would start, nearly always putting Scarlett in stitches.

*"Marty ist ein…seething mass of ID,"* she'd once said, referring to Marty's all-too-obvious lecherous tendencies. He never tried to hide it when he eyed

their cleavage or "accidentally on purpose" brushed by their derrieres with an open palm. Katie therefore, rarely wore anything revealing around him and never allowed herself to get too close. Scarlett, on the other hand, didn't care.

*"Ja, mein Mann ist ein Schmerz im Arsch."* Katie would call Steve a pain in the ass on a regular basis, usually for not being home to help out with something or other. Katie's favorite psychology professor evidently had taught them German idioms when lecturing about Freud.

Scarlett grabbed her cell from the charger and fumbled for the number for the Kellys's landline. Katie almost never answered her cell. Scarlett was getting impatient waiting for the coffee to finish. She pressed "Kelly House" from her favorites then SEND.

"Hello?" It had taken five rings.

"Hi, Katie. It's Scarlett. What're you up to?"

"You know, my usual OCD stuff. Just trying to get the house ready for the game tonight—kitchen, bathroom, dining room, the floors. I still have to run to the market and the liquor store. Steve had to go into the city this morning, and he said he was going to help, but whatever. Thinking about mimosas for a change, what do you think? The girls went a little berserk with the new juicer yesterday and I have enough fresh-squeezed orange juice to fill a bathtub. Oh, then I have to color my hair—couldn't get an appointment with Ayanna today, and I am looking very OLD."

Scarlett had already stopped listening. Liquid lunch definitely was *not* going to happen. She was fairly certain Katie had rambled straight through without even taking a breath.

"Oh. Gotcha. Well, do you mind if I take you up on your offer to use the pool? They're only just pouring the foundation for ours today. C. Thomas is working late. Beamer's in for brakes, and I am stuck here without a car until he gets back."

"Sure, sure. Of course." Katie was distracted and Scarlett could hear scrubbing. Katie was probably on her hands and knees with a toothbrush at the bathroom grout like someone scouring evidence from a crime scene. Her "dirty" grout was always pristinely white. Katie had the kind of home where anyone could show up unannounced, yet she probably still would be apologizing up and down about some imaginary mess.

"Oh, and if you need a car for anything, just borrow mine. Jamie and

Anna hitched a ride to work so Jamie's car is here. I can just take hers to run my errands."

"Great. Thanks, Katie." Scarlett heard the gurgling of the Keurig stop. She really needed that cup of coffee. "Okay, then. I'll probably be by in a half hour or so. Oh, and you probably should give Steve a heads-up so he doesn't think you have another pool hopper like those crazy neighbor kids you had to call the cops on."

"Yeah. Okay." Katie said, still distracted.

Jeez, it's like talking to C. Thomas, she thought. "By the way, do you need anything for tonight?" Scarlett knew she wouldn't.

"No, no. Of course not. You took care of everything last time."

"Okay, then I'll see you in a bit."

"Just come right around the back. Gate's open."

"Great. Thanks, Katie. Bye."

"Bye."

Scarlett hung up and grabbed her fat free creamer from the Sub-Zero. She pulled the full cup from under the spigot, ditched the used K-cup, and immediately started another one. Instead of brewing a whole pot for herself in the big machine, she had convinced herself that she would drink less coffee if she had to brew a single cup at a time. But like a chain smoker, she'd brew another cup just as the previous one finished.

She headed to the laundry for her bikini, dropping the blanket to the floor. She wondered why she ever bought string bikinis anyway. They never fit right on top and she never could get the damn ties tied straight. Then again, the tiny suit barely covered anything and that's how it should be, right? She caught herself wondering what time Steve was getting home.

Brrrr. Even with a few swigs of coffee in her she was still cold. She grabbed the mug and the blanket again and went into the living room to adjust the air a little. C. Thomas always set it too low. She flopped onto the couch and reached under a cushion for her journal. It had been a few days since she'd written in it, something her therapist always was reminding her to do. He wanted her to address her "Mommy" issues or just write in it if she was feeling edgy. Today it was both.

*Dear Diary or MOM or WHOMever:*

She twisted her hair in her fingers. It was a nervous habit she'd started in her teens. She always felt that way when she started a diary entry, almost as if she was speaking directly to her mom. She picked up her coffee and took a big sip, then set it down and began again.

*I am bored. Bored. BORED! Whoever thought at twenty-five I'd be a bored HOUSEWIFE! Well, not exactly a wife. Not a WIFE at all!! God MOM! Money isn't everything!!! FUCK THIS! Yes, MOM, I KNOW LADIES DON'T SPEAK THAT WAY! I am sorry you lost Dad. I am sorry you had it so rough. But I DON'T NEED A MAN TO TAKE CARE OF ME!! At least not a dumb dick like C. Thomas. You tried so hard to find the right man after Dad. I know you did. But you never knew what that was like for me—or what some of them did to me…*

*Do you know what we did last night? No, I know you don't. Well, I can tell you what we DIDN'T do! Or what I didn't do! I didn't come. I didn't have an O R G A S M. In fact, I NEVER do. EVER! Not unless I do it by my—*

There was a knock at the door. Still wrapped in the blanket, Scarlett set the journal and pen on the table and went to answer it. Just a package for C. Thomas. Plain brown wrapping, unmarked, sitting on the front step. Weird. The third package like that this month. Maybe he was planning to surprise her with another pair of shoes. Or maybe it was something else. He had some strange "interests." She didn't even want to know.

She tossed the box on the floor by the entry and went to pack up to go to Katie's, taking her journal with her. She'd go back to it later. Right now she just wanted to head over to the pool—it was poker night so she needed to maintain her tan. Practically the only thing keeping her in the damn game was the thrill of seeing all five pairs of eyes on her throughout the night—even the women's. Scarlett knew that *a lot* of people got *a lot* of enjoyment out of ogling her, but lately she'd found herself inexplicably caring only about what Steve thought. In fact, she was thinking about Steve quite a bit, and she felt conflicted.

About a year before, Steve had helped her out when she was considering going to go back to school to study as a paralegal. He was the kind of man she dreamt her dad may have been. Her father had died in a car accident one winter when she was about two-and-a-half years old. Any memories she had probably were things she had just made up about him from the photo albums her mother kept, and of course from the stories her mother told. At least that's what her therapist said. He would ramble on about something called infantile amnesia. *We don't create memories when we are young because our brains aren't yet developed, blah, blah, blah.* What did he know anyway? Scarlett was sure she remembered her father and she was sure he was the best daddy ever.

Steve also had lost his father, but it was much later in life. He'd been raised by his, so it was different. But Steve was so caring when they'd talked about their fathers and supportive about her school work. He'd also told her that she reminded him of one of his law school friends, a woman from his study group. It made Scarlett feel more confident that she might really be able to knuckle back down with school and pursue a career as a paralegal. Maybe she'd even go to law school someday. Steve never made her feel like her looks were more important than her brains. Most men thought her brains were attached to her rib cage.

There wasn't anything more between them, right? Scarlett couldn't be sure. Besides, she really did like Katie, despite her quirks. Katie was like the big sister she'd never had. Scarlett would never want to ruin that.

---

SCARLETT TOSSED a towel and her Michael Kors tote bag onto a pool chaise. Wow—she hadn't seen Steve and Katie's pool ever looking so clear, but the smell of chlorine almost knocked her out. Scarlett had often seen Steve, beautifully shirtless and laboring over the massive basin summer after summer, wondering why he didn't just hire a pool guy. She knew C. Thomas would never take care of their pool. He was a pretty boy and never around. They already had a pool service on standby, and it wasn't even built. Mmmm, she thought as she briefly entertained what their "pool boy" might look like in his Speedos as he vacuumed their soon-to-be poured, equally lavish in-ground masterpiece.

She slipped out of her fishnet cover-up and kicked aside her flip-flops. As she did, her bikini top slid aside exposing a breast, and as she fumbled with it, the other flew out as well. Scarlett looked around. The Kellys's privacy fence kept out just about everything except the blazing sun overhead. Screw it, she thought as she untied the back of her top, lifted it over her head, and tossed it on the chaise with her bag. She grabbed her oversized Marilyn Monroe beach towel and whipped it out in front of her onto the concrete. She considered scrawling a few more entries in her journal, but her interest in doing so was waning. She figured it was better to work on the tan.

Scarlett lay down on her belly, burying the side of her face into Marilyn's blond locks. She always preferred tanning herself flat on the ground for more even tanning. Just as she was getting comfortable she glanced toward the house. Katie was looking out the window at her. Uh-oh, she thought. Would Katie care that she was topless? Katie smiled and waved a hand holding a bottle of hair dye as she pointed to her brown mane with the other. From the distance, Katie probably couldn't even see that she had taken her top off. She'd dodged that bullet. She closed her eyes. In no time, Scarlett began to drift off.

---

"OH. MY. GOD! Do you see that?! *Holy shit!!*" Doogie Perkins nearly fell out of the window of the treehouse. He had seen Scarlett take off her bikini top through his telescope and was almost eating dirt twenty feet beneath the canopy of the old maple.

The Perkins's home was next door to the Kellys's and in the vast wooded area behind it was a sizeable ligneous structure Hal Perkins had built for his children when they were small. Intended to be a place for make believe and youthful games, Doogie had done a bit of "redecorating" in the last year or so, and the treehouse was now referred to as *Recon DM*: "D" for Doogie and "M" for his BFF the Mole. Their pursuits were certainly no longer the stuff of childhood.

"Let me in there!" The Mole not-so-gently shoved Doogie out of the way, put his eye to the telescope and let out a yelp. "What? That isn't…it can't be! Jamie! Or Anna! *What the hell?!*"

Doogie was one of those classically over-privileged adolescents. An only child of a doctor mother and an engineer father, it was more than expected that he would have a lucrative, professional career someday. His father was a graduate of MIT and Doogie surely was going to follow in his footsteps, or so his parents thought. He was exceptionally good at convincing them. He knew how to say what they wanted to hear, all for the purpose of obtaining toys which he used for all the wrong reasons.

Take for example the high-tech Questar Birder Spotting Scope mounted on the window sill of the treehouse. On one of the few nights the family actually ate a meal together, Doogie had told his parents he wanted to attend MIT to major in astronomy. After all, he told them, "MIT's Haystack Observatory offers opportunities for research in interplanetary medium via radio propagation effects as well as probing the dusty interiors of colliding galaxy systems…" *Blah, blah, blah.* He'd read about it online. That was all it took to convince the pops to buy nearly the best scope on the market. What Daddy didn't know was that birders aren't ideal for scoping out the wild blue yonder due to the forty-five-degree diagonal and the limited field of view. However, it makes for a GREAT invasion of your teenaged neighbors' privacy. Especially when said teenagers not only are hot, but when they have their equally hot friends over on a regular basis.

He got them hook line and sinker. Doogie was not a dumb kid, but privilege meant too much freedom, too much time unsupervised, and too much money in his pockets to burn. After all, to alleviate their guilt for never being home, Mommy and Daddy gave Doogie a sizeable allowance, most of which he spent on weed.

The Mole was not quite as privileged. Actually, not privileged at all. He lived a few streets over in a more middle-class neighborhood, but he took full advantage of the perks Doogie received and Doogie didn't mind at all. They were perfect partners in crime.

"Did you get the camera hooked up right this time?" The Mole asked, not without a touch of frustration. He was fumbling for the camera's on button, hoping to snap a few shots before Scarlett laid down or turned her voluptuous breasts out of view. Through his Google pursuits about surveillance, Doogie had discovered the art of "digiscoping" which simply meant attaching an everyday camera to a spotting scope to get impeccable close-up photographs. *This* was definitely digiscope worthy.

"Yes, for Chrissakes!" Doogie shoved the Mole out of the way. "Let me do it!"

"Hurry!" the Mole nearly cried out. "Gotta put this on my Snap story!"

Flustered, Scarlett fumbled with her keys in the front door lock. As she was doing so, the door swung open. C. Thomas was home already. Scarlett wasn't up for dealing with him at all. Still on somewhat of a high from her little tête-à-tête with Steve, she didn't want to break the mood.

"You're home early," Scarlett spat. Sometimes it just was too difficult to hide her annoyance with him. He was so dense though, he usually didn't even pick up on it.

"Yeah, well the fanfare died out early. The Waterbury peeps just don't seem to be the big celebration types."

C. Thomas actually believes I really care about an explanation, she thought. Scarlett had already started for the stairs. She didn't think C. Thomas noticed that she'd walked away mid-sentence as she often did. When she walked in the house, he'd been standing there naked with his schlong in his hand. He had this odd habit of peeling off his clothes the minute he got home, and as always, left them in a crumpled pile just inside the entryway. Like a spoiled child, he just expected her to pick them up and put them away. Dutifully, usually she did.

Being naked twenty-four/seven was not his only odd proclivity. But that was another matter.

Scarlett groaned audibly as she neared the top of the stairs, realizing that C. Thomas was close at her heels. "So I had this brainstore today," he said.

"*Brainstorm?*" Scarlett spat again. She headed into the master bathroom for the shower. She really needed to wash out that chlorine from her hair before it turned green.

"Yeah, whatever. Brainstore. Brainstorm." C. Thomas said, seeming lost in thought. Not that C. Thomas could ever be lost in thought. Just lost.

He went on. "I feel all the grumblings from the powers-that-be. You know, the stuffed shirts at the company. I want to really wow them with *my* great ideas."

"Ha! Great ideas!" Scarlett mumbled under her breath too loudly.

"So, what do you think about user-generated content at the kiosks? I mean, wow! People can upload anything they want! The public will really eat that shit up, don't you think? It's a no-holes-barred situation!"

"Oh, my God. No *holds* barred," Scarlett quipped.

"Could you just *listen* to me for a sec?" C. Thomas was getting annoyed. "I think people would love to see what other people do in the *real* world, don't you?"

It wasn't a question he was actually expecting Scarlett to answer. He wouldn't have wanted to hear her response anyway.

"Think about it. You just walk in with your cell phone—you hook it up to the kiosk, and *BAM*! In return for your upload, you get a free movie!"

"Sounds to me like YouTube or Vimeo at a kiosk—that you have to pay for. Um…utterly novel." Scarlett was *utterly* unimpressed. His ideas were always ridiculous.

"C'mon, if I am going to stay alive, if this *business* is going to stay alive, we have to compete with Vudu, Hulu, Netflix, Amazon. You wanna keep getting those little piggies painted drop-dead red, don'cha?"

Scarlett had hoped if she just hopped into the shower, he'd get the message and go away. C. Thomas never got any message. But he did pick up on something.

"Hey, why are you just showering now?" C. Thomas queried. "And where the hell were you anyway without a car? You looked like a deer in the headlights when you walked in the door."

"Huh? I did not. What do you think I could possibly have been doing in the middle of a Saturday afternoon?"

"Knowing you, just about anything. Ah-haaa, I know where you were! You were over at the Kellys's pool, weren't you? I thought I smelled pool…or was it something else?"

And the prize goes to… Jeez, it didn't take rocket science to figure that out considering she had on a damn bathing suit.

"Hey, did you do a little skinny dipping with Katie—some bored housewife action going on? Or better yet, with Steve? I know—it was all three of you!" He actually may have been getting a hard on by the mere suggestion but she didn't want to look and egg him on.

"Shut up. I need to shower before the game tonight."

"You don't think I know you have it bad for Steve-O? I can see it. A little surrogate daddy action."

"Oh…my…God. Shut the hell up and get out of this bathroom! Go entertain your fantasies somewhere else!"

"You know, speaking of the game, I've been thinking about it a lot lately."

"Oh, yeah. How so?" Scarlett asked, as if she cared.

"Well, it *is* getting lame lately. I think we all know it."

"Yeah, so?"

"I think we need to spice it up. Make it spi-*ceyyy*," he said in an odd tone.

"Ok, C. Thomas. Whatever. Can I just shower, please?"

"What, you can't shower and have a conversation? What is it with you today?"

Maybe her annoyance with C. Thomas was more evident than usual. She admittedly had a very short fuse with him lately. "Sorry," she said. She didn't mean it.

"Well, I think I'm going to make a suggestion tonight. A real *good* suggestion."

"Okay, I give. What is your suggestion, C. Thomas?"

"It is a surprise. But do me a solid—okay?"

Scarlett was trying to be patient but she really just wanted to shower in peace. She also wanted to get a release after all of the sexual tension with Steve. The shower was a perfect place for an orgasm and C. Thomas was ruining her buzz. Plus, he'd more than love to watch, and she wasn't going to give him the satisfaction.

"What?!"

"Just promise me you'll go with it. Whatever I suggest. Okay?"

"Okay. I promise. Now will you let me finish?" She hoped he'd leave now.

"Yep."

She could hear something in his voice. Was it smugness? What was he up to?

She heard the toilet lid bang open. Through the shower door she saw him squat down on the bowl.

"C. Thomas! Don't tell me you're about to take a dump while I'm in the shower! Get out!"

"Fine. What the hell is with you today?" The lid banged shut.

Scarlett squeezed her eyes tightly and wished him away while she feverishly rinsed shampoo from her hair. Suddenly she heard the door slam and she looked around to scan the bathroom. He was gone. *Thank God!* She closed her eyes as the warm water ran down her body and she began to fantasize about what it would be like to be married to a man like Steve. Scarlett reached up to dismount the hand-held shower head and adjusted the spray setting to pulsating massage then she directed the water flow over her body and down.

## 5

## POST-GAME HIGHLIGHTS

It was two a.m. Sunday morning, and the Kelly house was locked down tighter than a drum and darker than a Hawking Black Hole. From the outside, there wasn't even the ambient glow of a bathroom night light or a digital clock.

To a casual observer, it might have appeared that the residents just simply had long since retired and they were safely ensconced in their beds, deep in slumber, with visions of sugar plums dancing in their heads. To an astute observer, however, the dark exterior may have served as but a superficial veneer. Things are not always as they seem. No one really knows what happens behind a closed door. To a true insider, someone privy to the events of the evening prior, it would be evident that chaos theory had begun to run amuck in the Kelly household. Events were building to a critical mass.

Steve and Katie were lying back-to-back in their canopied, king-size bed. There had been a time when Katie would fall asleep every night on Steve's shoulder, nestled under his chin. With her ear pressed to his chest, the rhythmic beating of his heart would lull her to sleep. But somewhere between the births of Jamie and Anna they became back-to-back sleepers, one blaming it on the other; Katie's restless leg syndrome or Steve's snoring. Neither wanted to admit that it was just more comfortable for each to occupy their own personal space, the intimacy of their former routine no longer needed nor desired to aid them in falling into their respective slumbers.

What the hell happened tonight? It had been like a runaway freight train.

That question was on Steve's mind. The very same was on Katie's mind. Not to mention Steve never did address the *other* critical question of whom he would choose if he'd won the game. He simply ignored the others' badgering until they had finally given up. The party came to an early end about fifteen minutes afterward, all of the players complaining of a sudden onset of exhaustion. Each guest delivered a perfunctory good-bye to their hosts, then made a hasty dash out the door leaving Steve and Katie alone. The air hung heavily in the Kelly home.

In a rare deviation from her routine compulsive behavior, Katie left cleanup for the morning and went straight to the bedroom. Steve followed soon after. Neither said a word to the other as they quietly undressed and slipped into bed.

Now both were wide awake, preoccupied with the game or, rather, the strange and disquieting direction the game had taken. The central air was on low, its steady hum of white noise offering no reassurance in the dark of this unsettling night.

Katie was just going to let go of the prospect of C. Thomas's ridiculous proposal. At first, she'd mulled it over but later stood firm. She wouldn't give it another thought. She shouldn't and she knew it. But she began to waver. What if? In retrospect, this choice, this decision to *not* let it go turned into one of those pivotal moments in which monumental and life-altering paths are taken, sometimes on the flimsiest of justifications. Hindsight can be twenty-twenty. Katie should have let it go. But ultimately, she didn't.

She turned onto her back and let out a fake cough, loud enough to have awakened Steve had he *actually* been asleep. Steve took the bait and turned onto his back. He was ready. He, too, wanted to put the whole C. Thomas thing to bed.

"Sorry," Katie said. "Did I wake you?"

"No."

"Oh, good. So, what do you think about what happened tonight?" she asked a little too eagerly.

"What do I think? I think C. Thomas is out of his mind! He obviously had too much to drink. His absurd proposal ruined the entire night. Don't you agree?"

"Yeah," Katie said, but after a brief pause she went on. "Um, no. I don't know. If truth be told, I thought it was kind of—*interesting.*"

Steve did a double take. "I can't believe you! You're actually *considering* it?" He reached over and turned on the lamp on the night table next to the bed.

"I didn't say I would go along with it. I just said that it was an interesting proposition to think about."

Steve propped his head on the heel of his hand so he could look directly into his wife's eyes. Although Steve didn't have Marty's encyclopedic knowledge of poetry and quotes, he did know that the saying "the eyes are the windows to the soul," was attributable to countless sources including the Bible and Shakespeare. He also knew from experience that it was true, especially where his wife was concerned. He could discern everything she was thinking or feeling just from the patterns in her irises. He studied her eyes now, searching for some truth.

"You are serious about this. I could tell from the way you were egging C. Thomas on. I can tell now from just looking into your eyes."

"That's nonsense," she said, but she averted her eyes nonetheless. "Plus you never answered any of us tonight. Who would you pick? I'm just curious."

"Do we have to do this now?"

"I won't be mad. I'm not the jealous type and you know it. I never have been. Physical attraction to other people is normal. It's biological. It's programmed into us, part of evolution."

"Stop with the psychobabble, Kate."

She hated it when he called her Kate. "You stop. Who would you pick? Just tell me and then we can go to sleep."

Steve sighed. "Christ. Who do you think I would pick?"

"I know exactly who you would choose. Scarlett, of course." It was Katie's turn to look into her husband's eyes for confirmation. Steve didn't look away. "I know it would be Scarlett."

Steve didn't respond. When he did finally look away, however, Katie had her proof. Every fiber in her body screamed out that it was true. Despite her earlier declaration, she felt a deep pang of jealousy with a side order of resentment.

She should have ended the conversation. At that point, there still had been no harm, no foul. No boundaries had yet been crossed. A point of no return had not been reached. She and Steve could have chalked up the whole incident to teasing, verbal fencing, and an overindulgence in silly parlor games. People often do not make the right choices, even when it is abundantly clear that they are making the wrong ones. It was Sigmund Freud who spoke of the dark side of human nature—those raging and unchecked, unconscious drives and desires which bleed over into our conscious decisions —Eros and Thanatos. Are we no better than the lower animals?

Katie just should have gone to sleep.

"Who would *you* pick?" Steve asked.

"C. Thomas," Katie said without hesitation.

Steve sat up in bed, shocked by his wife's answer. She'd been so blunt. He had expected his question to be rhetorical. He hadn't expected her to respond at all, much less to answer so quickly and so directly.

"C. Thomas! Are you joking?"

"You don't think I'd pick Marty, do you?" she asked matter-of-factly. "He's an id-ridden infantile pig."

"So tell me how you really feel about him."

"I just did!"

"But, but C. Thomas is a—jerk! A brainless buffoon!"

"Lower your voice. You'll wake up the girls."

"But you can't be serious!"

"All we are talking about is physical attraction," Katie said. "We aren't talking about an emotional attachment and, heaven forbid, love. This whole thing was proposed just to get us all excited. Mainly for each other—spice up our own lives. God knows we could use it."

"Unreal." Steve pulled the sheet over him, turned his back to Katie and lay back down in bed. "I'm going to sleep."

"Don't be an ass. I'm just being honest."

"That's a scary thought," Steve muttered. "Maybe you need to go back to work full-time, Kate. I think boredom is setting in, and it has nothing to do with me."

"Screw you, Steve. Like it's been that easy. Every time I even tried to go back to work *something* happened."

"You could have if you wanted to."

"How, pray tell? Let's see. First it was Jamie. Then it was Anna."

"So you're blaming it on the girls?"

"No! Of course not! But we both agreed I'd stay home while they were small. Then when Anna had all that trouble in kindergarten and first grade because of the dyslexia, how could I not have been around?"

"Well—"

"Well, nothing! And then you? What about when you broke your leg? I had just gotten things settled to finish my licensure hours and you're laid up for six months!"

"Fine, then, blame me. Blame the girls… I don't care. But after eighteen years of marriage you admit that you have the hots for a man-boy? And a dim, brainless one at that. Rich. Very rich."

"Oh! You are so infuriating. So you're honestly going to tell me that you've never lusted for another woman? Not even in your mind?"

"Never," Steve said. "Now go to sleep."

"You're so full of shit." Katie reached under the sheet and groped her husband.

"What are you doing?"

"What do you think I'm doing? I'm giving you a hand job."

"Get a hold of yourself," Steve said, still annoyed from their conversation, but now a bit thrown off his game as well. Steve could count on one hand the times Katie took the initiative in their sexual escapades. She rarely was aggressive and almost always followed Steve's lead. But now she had a hold of him and wasn't letting go, literally. Whatever residual annoyance Steve still had became overridden by a more powerful feeling—lust. He was hard for the second time within twenty-four hours without the aid of "Mr. V" as he would euphemistically refer to his regular Viagra prescription refills.

"Do you want me to stop?" Katie asked, a broad smile on her face.

Steve wanted to tell her to stop. He wanted to wipe that smug grin off of her face. He was the Alpha partner in this relationship, and he did not like relinquishing the upper hand. He wanted to say stop, but instead what came out was, "No, don't stop."

Now supremely smug, she did another rare thing, cementing her victory and asserting her new role as the sexual Top Dog she dove under the covers and went down on him. While both Katie and Steve enjoyed oral sex, it was far more prevalent in the old days, before kids and even more so before they were married. It gradually tapered off during their married years until it became a remnant reserved only for special occasions like anniversaries and Valentine's Day, that is, if they hadn't had too much to drink.

She had her mouth completely around him, and she felt him become even harder as her tongue grazed *that spot*. After twenty years, she knew exactly where and just how to get to him. He grabbed her by the hair and pushed her down even further. Usually she would object, complaining that he was smothering her, but not this time. She responded even more aggressively bringing him to a quick climax.

But the most exciting part of the escapade was not how aggressive she was, nor was it her decision to go down on him. It was the fantasy that Scarlett was the one performing fellatio on him, not his wife.

---

IT WAS TWO A.M. The Fein household, unlike the Kellys's, was lit up like a proverbial Christmas tree. After arriving home to an obviously frazzled and weary Mikayla, Erin was certain she'd never be able to ask her to babysit again. Although Mikayla thanked Marty for the payment she received for services rendered, offering a weak, "See you again" as she darted out the door to her car, both knew she'd probably never answer another phone call if caller ID showed Fein on the display.

Erin trudged up the stairs to the boys' room and after delivering a brief lecture, like most nights, she lay down with them for a bit until they drifted off. Ordinarily she would fall asleep herself, rousing a few hours later and dragging herself to bed, but tonight she was wound up, as tightly as a top. Finally sure that the boys were sound asleep, she headed to her and Marty's bedroom. Of course, little did she know that as soon as she closed the door behind her, the twins were tented under the sheets with their video controllers and flat screen, playing contraband mature games—ones their friends had stolen from older brothers and smuggled to them during school recess. The glow from the TV bled through the lightweight fabric and spilled out of the cracks between the sheets like a laser light show.

Nearly as bright as day in the master bedroom and in the study, Erin was alone in bed trying desperately to focus on the romance beach read she had started at the beginning of the summer. She really was only wasting time, waiting for Marty to finish up his work and come to bed. Somewhat out of character, she was hoping to get lucky tonight. C. Thomas's proposal had awakened something inside of her. She couldn't define or explain it, but she was titillated, even exhilarated, and she wanted to see it through.

Unbeknownst to Erin, Marty was not working, but instead seeking his own private release. He had checked the Philanderers website. Still no comments or private messages. He reluctantly charged his credit card for another level up on his membership and then proceeded to send out more solicitous messages to strange women with attractive headshots. He had nearly finished his last message when Erin showed up in the doorway. He'd forgotten to lock the door.

"The kids are finally asleep. Are you coming to bed?"

Marty frantically began punching keys to log out of the website and clear the browser history. He could feel his heart pounding but tried to remain calm as he wiped out the evidence of his lascivious activities.

"It's about time they settled down." Marty's attempt at nonchalance was paper thin.

"Poor Mikayala. Did you see the look on her face when she walked out the door? I don't think she'll be back."

"Um, no. But the monsters'll do it every time."

Whew, he thought. History deleted. He was in the clear.

"I'm exhausted," Erin said. "You coming to bed?" She stood, leaning on the door handle, attempting to look seductive. She'd actually put on a pretty, low-cut night gown instead of her usual old T-shirt and baggy pajama shorts. It was a bit snug, but she was hoping Marty might like that it left little to the imagination. It fell flat on him, however. He was only thinking about which website on his mental list of favorites he might log into as soon as he could get rid of her.

"I just have a couple more things I want to finish."

"It's the weekend, Marty."

"I said I'll be right in."

Erin shook her head. "They don't pay you enough to work twenty-four/seven," she said curtly. There was something else in Erin's face that made Marty flinch, but he turned away and pulled up the University's website as a cover should Erin have seen the screen. In a huff, she walked away, trudging toward the bedroom. He paused, listening as her footsteps became fainter then he got up and closed the door, turning the lock.

Marty closed down the browser and instead clicked to open a file on his desktop marked "Student Work." He hastily punched in the password: SCARLETT.

Two years ago, the triptych had decided to take the group vacation in Aruba. Marty's eyeballs were glued to Scarlett as she romped around in her barely-there bikinis, and he most enjoyed the occasional nipple slip like when she'd be caught by surprise in the lapping waves. One day, and quite by accident, Marty had stumbled upon Scarlett while she was getting changed behind the cabana at the private beach outside of their bungalow. Cell phone in hand, he surreptitiously managed to nab more than a few photos of her, in all of her glorious nakedness. There were some damn good shots.

He closed his eyes and quickly found himself back to earlier when Scarlett's feet were pressing against his crotch on the loveseat. He was hard.

---

IN THE BEDROOM, Erin wriggled out of her nightgown and yanked a tee and shorts out of the drawer and pulled them on. What a wasted friggin' night, she thought. She picked up the gown, folded it, and placed it back under the T-shirts in the bottom of the bureau drawer. She grabbed the book she had been reading off of the bed and tossed it onto the nightstand, then turned out the bedside lamp. She sat down for a moment on the edge of the bed as tears welled up in her eyes for the second time that day. She couldn't help but wonder how her life ended up here.

Erin stood up and as if turning her anger onto the neatly-made bed covers, she yanked them back, sending the pillows up into the air like popcorn. She couldn't take it. Something was not right about her relationship with Marty. She could feel it. She couldn't imagine how he couldn't have been turned on by what happened at Steve and Katie's. For a moment she considered what must be happening back at the Kellys's or with Scarlett and C. Thomas. She imagined at that very moment they all must be at it like rabbits, but here she was, alone in an empty bed. She tossed the decorative pillows onto the floor then flopped down on the bed. She pulled up the blanket tightly around her as she curled into a fetal position and wept.

---

THE DIM LIGHT of a dozen candles emanated from Scarlett and C. Thomas's open bedroom door, creating something of a pulsating glow throughout the entire upstairs of the house. From the outside, it created an eerie picture against the darkness of the night, like a haunted house at Halloween. Adding to it, Berlioz's Symphonie Fantastique fifth movement could be heard throughout the house; all of its provocative tempo changes playing like a witches' Sabbath with bubbling cauldrons and blasts of wind. It was C. Thomas's favorite piece, but it creeped Scarlett out.

"Oh, yes!" C. Thomas cried out. "You're killing me! Yes! More!"

"Shut up, Pissant!"

"Yes! God! We should have Marty massage your feet more often!"

"I said, shut up!"

Scarlett mashed her left stiletto into C. Thomas's back. She actually was enjoying it tonight, though not in a sexual way. Maybe for the first time she found something in the S&M palatable. She really couldn't stand C. Thomas. The desire for having actual sex with him had long since faded away. But inflicting pain gave her some smug satisfaction if only he wasn't aroused by it. That would have made it so much better.

C. Thomas lay naked on the floor, his erection pressing between his belly and the cool hardwood. Scarlett, donning a black leather dominatrix outfit, held onto one pole of their four-poster bed to keep herself from teetering over. She wasn't up for any more bruises. Tonight C. Thomas had chosen her highest stilettos: a cheap, neon pink, ankle-strap pair with bejeweled Lucite platforms and seven-inch heels. She'd hated them the day he brought them home, with that Cheshire Cat grin spread across his face, showing every overly laser-whitened tooth. He reminded her of Marty that day for some reason. The shoes looked like something a Barbie doll would wear. Prostitute Barbie, that is.

When Scarlett met C. Thomas, she was impressed by him, at least at first. His father had passed away years before, and he had become a very young president of a very successful company. They met at a friend's New Year's Eve party and he was so hot she couldn't keep her eyes off of him, even as they mingled, chatting with other people throughout the night. When he came over and planted a huge tongue-filled kiss on her as the clock struck midnight, she was done for. They barely made it back to his house in one piece, tearing off each other's clothes the entire drive home.

After pulling the Jaguar into his heated garage, C. Thomas had come around to the passenger side and scooped Scarlett out of the car and into his arms. All that remained on her was her thong and stilettos, but she was so overheated, that even the cool air from the opening and closing of the garage doors didn't faze her. Carrying her the whole time, C. Thomas practically bolted into the house and up the stairs to the bedroom.

Heady from too many cocktails and too much champagne at the party, Scarlett was ready to lose herself completely to C. Thomas. She was no virgin, but she usually was a bit discerning with regard to her choice of sexual partners, and truly, had not slept with nearly as many men as her friends had. There was something about C. Thomas though, she'd thought. Or maybe she was just drunk.

C. Thomas threw Scarlett onto the bed and yanked off her thong, keeping her stilettos still strapped to her ankles. She liked how aggressive he was, but found it odd that he said nothing the whole time. She couldn't recall him saying anything since before he'd kissed her at the party. Naked himself, he lay on top of her, his full weight pressing against her. She felt his erection. He reached down between her legs. She was wet.

The next thing Scarlett knew, C. Thomas had lifted himself off of her and had disappeared into the semi-darkness of the bedroom. She raised her head to scan the room and found him, his back against the wall directly across from her. She sat on the edge of bed, but as she reached down to undo one of the shoe straps, C. Thomas nearly shouted at her, "No. Lay back down!"

Taken aback, she let go of her stiletto and again lay on her back. Her eyes had finally adjusted to the darkness of the room, and she now could see what he was doing. Eyes wide open and staring intently at her, Scarlett could see he was jerking off.

The next morning, Scarlett awakened to feel C. Thomas spooning against her back. Her shoes were off. Had she dreamt the whole night? The whole sordid thing? She had a pounding headache and slithered out of bed to find her purse. After downing a handful of ibuprofen, she contemplated whether she just should leave. When she looked back toward the bed she saw that C. Thomas, head propped in his hand, was now staring at her and smiling.

"Morning, Sunshine," he'd said in the most velvety voice she had ever heard.

Scarlett couldn't help but smile back. He was gorgeous. Stunning, really. "Give me a sec."

Scarlett headed for the bathroom, closed the door and peed, then finding C. Thomas's toothbrush, she quickly brushed her teeth. She opened the door and saw C. Thomas with the sheet thrown back, laying there completely naked. For the first time, she could see how absolutely beautiful his cut body was. Plus he was hard. She nearly sprinted across the room and climbed on top of him, taking his full length inside of her. She moved slowly at first, then faster and faster until they both came. It was quick, but utterly satisfying. Scarlett slid off of him and lay with her head on his toned pecs. Any concerns she'd had about the night before vanished. She figured it had to have just been the alcohol.

Scarlett had begun to go over the events of the poker game in her head as she kneaded C. Thomas's back with her heels, right, left, right, left. The last image, and the one in which she could not let go, was of Steve, when he looked at her after Katie had been haranguing him about who he would pick if he won the game. Scarlett knew it would be her. It had to be her. I mean, who else would it be? Her heart had skipped a beat. She had felt the wetness between her legs at that very moment, and she couldn't help but smile at him. She was wet again now.

Just then Scarlett lost her balance and her hand slipped off the pole of the bed. She came crashing to the floor on her knee and let out a yelp. She was in for another bruise-filled night.

"For God's sake, C. Thomas, can't we just have *actual* sex?" She couldn't believe she'd let the words slip out of her mouth but she was hot now thinking about Steve and not up for digging out her vibrator.

"We are having sex, Scarlett. Get back on."

It was a very rare event when C. Thomas acquiesced to real intercourse. It made her feel like a dog begging for table scraps, which was why she didn't usually bother to request it.

"This isn't sex, and you know it!"

"What the hell are you talking about, Scarlett? What's gotten into you lately?" C. Thomas rolled over onto his back. He was still hard and looked beyond annoyed. "Is this about tonight? The game?"

"Fuck you, C. Thomas."

Scarlett took off the ridiculous stilettos and peeled off the leather get up, leaving them both in a pile on the floor. Grabbing her bathrobe off the closet door, she stomped out of the bedroom and downstairs to the living room. She flicked on the light and tossed herself onto the couch. She was pissed and so goddamn tired of C. Thomas and all of his wacked out bullshit.

"Scarlett!" She could hear C. Thomas calling. She wasn't going to placate him tonight. He could just as easily jerk off. When he didn't call again, she was sure he was already at it.

Scarlett reached under the cushion for her journal. Even though it was three a.m. she was wide awake. Anger will do that to a person. She pulled out the pen and opened to a clean page.

*Dear Diary, I mean MOM!*

*OH. MY. FUCKING. GOD!!! Make it STOP! I just can't keep this up anymore. This is not who I am. This is not who I want to be. I FUCKING HATE C. THOMAS! I'd even give my boobs back at this point just to be rid of him. WHAT AM I GOING TO DO?!?!?!*

*I don't care what anyone says, or what anyone wants for me anymore. This is MY LIFE. I am going to live it as I please. God, I pray that those prudish asses go for C. Thomas's proposal – the one bright idea that dumb dick has ever had. I am going to play, and I am going to play hard. And I'm going to win!*

*Watch out Steve, I'm coming for you, pun intended! (Sorry, Katie, but it's a game, right? It's ON!)*

# 6

## GOING VIRAL

Erin had hung up the phone with Katie, who only just before had hung up the phone with Scarlett. It was Monday morning. All the guys were at work. That was with the exception of Marty who was "working" in his home office until his afternoon class. He'd been holed up in the study since the wee hours, while Erin had showered, gotten the twins off to camp, done three loads of laundry, paid bills, and now was puttering around the house, tidying up things that did not need tidying. She was bored. It seemed pretty obvious that all three women were eager to discuss the events that went down at the poker game, but none admitted it. So they instead made plans to go swimming at Katie's and toss back a few cocktails while they were at it.

Erin bounded down the hall to the bedroom to find a bathing suit. A *dreaded* bathing suit. She felt a strange mix of excitement about the possibility of exploring C. Thomas's proposal, but absolute horror at having to don a bathing suit in front of Katie and Scarlett. It was no different than she'd felt in Aruba. But at the time, at least it had been fewer years since she'd given birth, and maybe, just *maybe* the baby fat excuse still worked. In any case, more than half the time she didn't even go to the beach.

She had started off the trip feigning that she'd gotten food poisoning from a sandwich at the airport café, so while everyone else hit the waves, she spent a lot of time alone in the group's bungalow with a pile of books intended to be beach reads. Then, her first day actually on the white sandy shores, she might have "accidentally on purpose" forgotten to put on sunscreen, which resulted in a nasty sunburn. For the rest of the trip she was forced to stay well-covered under an umbrella, a long beach cover-up she purchased at the resort's gift shop, and a wide-brimmed straw hat. It was uncomfortable, but not as uncomfortable as feeling like a beached whale compared to the others.

Erin yanked out the two suits she had purchased for that trip. The first, her Miraclesuit which promised to be slimming. While that may have accounted for all of her jiggly bits hiding under the suit, it did nothing for her thighs, her upper arms, or the bulging area near her armpits she not-so-lovingly referred to as her "chicken cutlets." She put it on and stood in front of the full-length mirror. It was hideous.

Her second suit she called her grandma suit. It was a slimming "swim-dress." No one under the age of fifty would be caught dead wearing one, but it was longer than a bathing suit by far since the skirt part of it nearly extended to mid-thigh. She looked away from her reflection—she couldn't stand seeing herself naked—and peeled off the first to put on the second. She looked ridiculous. She didn't know why she'd bought it in the first place. She put the first back on and quickly threw her cover-up over it before she could change her mind. She considered calling the girls and telling them she had another case of food poisoning.

Erin knew she shouldn't care and really, Katie and Scarlett were her friends, right? She could rationalize the whole thing, but still, those old insecurities crept back, wrapping around her psyche with the suffocating grip of a boa constrictor. Maybe she could join another gym. She slid into a pair of flip-flops and headed for the linen closet for a towel and her beach bag.

As she passed the study, Erin could hear Marty tapping away on the computer keys. *What the hell could he possibly do all day in there?* Erin thought disdainfully. *It's summer for God's sake!* She rapped on the door and Marty didn't immediately answer. She knocked harder and reached for the doorknob, but Marty called out, "What?"

"What?" Erin retorted. "Is that how you talk to me?"

"I'm in the middle of something. Sorry," he said.

She knew he didn't mean it. "You are *always* in the middle of something.

So many somethings. We should be living like royalty for all this *work* you seem to do around the clock."

"What's gotten into you?" Marty yelled from behind the door.

"Gotten into me? And why do we always have to talk with this two-inch piece of wood between us?"

"Oh, for Christ's sake!" Erin could hear Marty's chair creak and his footsteps approaching the door. He opened it. He was disheveled; he hadn't showered and was standing there in wrinkled boxers and a holey T-shirt.

"You're quite a sight, Marty. Glad you didn't dress up on my account."

"Well, beauty queen, what's with your get up? Hitting the camp pool with the boys today?"

"Yeah, sure, Marty. I'm suddenly eight again and need swimming lessons," she spat. "I am doing something for *me* today. I am going to Katie's to hang out with her and Scarlett."

It wasn't overt, but Erin noticed that Marty's visage changed when she said Scarlett's name. He stood taller and ran his fingers through his mop of hair. She figured he must be thinking about C. Thomas's proposal, too. She felt a pang of jealousy for what may have been the first time in their relationship. In spite of all of Marty's flaws, she never thought he was a cheat. Then again, how could she be upset about it when she was just as eager to explore the proposal?

"Whatever," he said. Marty noticed the same odd look on Erin's face. It was just like the one he'd seen the night of the poker game when Erin had caught him in the office at three a.m. He still couldn't put his finger on what it meant. But somehow he really didn't care.

Marty reached over and yanked aside Erin's cover-up to reveal part of her bathing suit. It was a little bit aggressive and made Erin take a step back. "Nice suit," he said in a surly tone.

"What is that supposed to mean?"

"Nothing. Hope it does the trick for ya. You need a miracle."

Erin turned beet red. Marty was not one for details. Did he even know this was her Miraclesuit? Was he insulting her? He had to be. Erin felt her eyes well up. All this time, in all these years, Marty had never said a word about her weight, but he *had* to be making a dig now.

"Asshole!" Erin nearly screeched as she turned on her heels. She stomped into the kitchen and opened Marty's favorite cabinet, grabbed a few bottles of liquor and some Solo cups and shoved it all hastily in her beach bag. She could hear the bottles clanking against one another as she pulled her keys from the wall hook and darted for the front door. At first heading toward the car, she changed her mind and decided to walk the block down to Katie's. She was so mad, but she knew she could use the exercise. A lot of good it would do.

---

SCARLETT WAS MAKING her third cup of coffee when Katie called. There was a strange tone to Katie's voice when she answered. Was it eagerness? Was it about C. Thomas's proposal? Katie animatedly invited Scarlett over to swim and for cocktails; for that liquid lunch Scarlett had been looking for on Saturday. Scarlett really hoped she was right—that it was in fact eagerness and that it wasn't only Katie who was ready to move forward with the new game rules. Katie told her she also was going to call Erin right afterward to invite her, too.

After downing the coffee in three gulps, Scarlett headed for the bedroom to get her suit. She still hadn't picked up her car yet. She was going to be marooned in the house yet again, so she was pleased to have something to do. She would have gone stir crazy just thinking about the proposal all day, too. She couldn't get it off her mind. She couldn't get Steve off her mind either.

Ransacking her drawer like some petty thief, she searched for her skimpiest bikini in hopes that maybe Steve might come home while they were at the pool. Finally finding it, she didn't even bother to pick up the mess she'd made before heading into the bathroom to put it on. She pulled off C. Thomas's company tee she had been wearing and tossed it in the hamper. She pulled on the bikini bottoms and then stood staring at her reflection. Goddamn, that new bruise! she thought angrily. The one she now had on her knee was twice as big and twice as ugly as the other one which had finally started to heal on her shin. Eyes moving upward, she couldn't help but smile when she got distracted by her tits. She cupped them for a moment, before reaching for her top. Men love these babies, she thought. She hoped Steve did, too.

After struggling to tie an always-lopsided bow across her back, Scarlett went back into the bedroom and pulled a pair of cutoffs out of a drawer. She wasn't going to bother with a shirt or a cover-up today. It was hot as hell. She was heading for the stairs when the phone rang again. Please tell me Katie's not cancelling. Checking the screen on her iPhone, she saw it was C. Thomas. Whew. She answered.

"What's up?"

"Hey, Babe. What are you up to?" C. Thomas often called in the day. He really had little to do when he was "working."

"Nothing. You know we never got my car, right?"

"Damn. Sorry. Do you want me to come now to take you?"

Scarlett could have cared less. She was far more interested in going to Katie's, but she was the one who brought it up. "No, don't worry. I'll find something to keep me busy here today. We can get it tomorrow."

"Okay. But when? I'll be tied up most of the day, and I have to leave early. You'll never be up. You know you need your beauty sleep."

Asshole. "Yeah, well, I guess I'll get up with you then come back to bed. Just make sure you call the garage and pay for it tonight. They won't be open that early. Tell them to put the keys under the mat."

"Okay, Baby."

She hated when he called her that. She was not a baby. Nor his baby. Not anymore. Scarlett said a weak goodbye and hung up even before C. Thomas had a chance to say it back. She just wanted to get to Katie's. She took the stairs two at a time like a little kid and when she reached the bottom, turned toward the dining room. Liquid lunch. Liquid lunch, she said over and over in her head. She and C. Thomas had a well-stocked liquor cabinet. Whenever C. Thomas felt he needed to impress the stuffed shirts at work, he had lavishly catered parties at the house, complete with every kind of booze and mixer available. She picked up an unopened bottle of Patron and a nearly full Ketel One. She wriggled them into the portable wine holder she had gotten from C. Thomas one Christmas for the picnics they'd never taken. Spotting her favorite—Gran Marnier, she grabbed it as well. Not exactly afternoon fare, but what the hell? She loved the burn she always felt in her esophagus as it went down.

Satisfied with her contributions, Scarlett headed out the door. She didn't bother to lock it or even to put on shoes. Her aching arches really needed a break. She padded down toward Katie's, careful to stay on neighbors' lawns whenever possible. The street and driveways were scorching. Scarlett bet that one actually *could* fry an egg on them today. It was several blocks, and she got more than a few whistles and honks as she walked, her breasts practically with a life of their own, bouncing almost completely out of her bikini.

---

KATIE WAS NEARLY JUMPING out of her skin as she got ready for Erin and Scarlett to arrive, so out of character for her since she had become such a reserved and fastidious person. She was the perfect *accessory* for a successful attorney, except she often felt like a Stepford wife. She'd forgotten what it was like to be impetuous and impulsive when she was younger like the summer after her freshman year in college when she and her girlfriends drove halfway across the country. That was until her car broke down and she had to call her parents to fly her back. But it was what made things work for her and Steve. They'd become birds of a feather. Or had they? No surprises, Steve would say. He didn't like surprises unless he was the one planning them.

Katie and the girls had intended a liquid lunch, but as the supreme hostess, she would never have anyone over without her usual special touches, which included making real food, all from scratch. She pulled out a wedge of brie, a tub of gourmet pesto, and a bunch of watercress from the fridge. She sliced a loaf of artisan ciabatta and assembled sandwiches. Earlier, she had made an exquisite fruit salad with perfectly-ripened mangoes, luscious, sweet pineapple, and the most beautiful, robust, red strawberries she had seen so far this season, with some fresh mint for color. Sunday afternoon she'd been to Whole Foods and had stocked up, with this very scenario in mind. When she was unpacking the groceries, both Steve and her daughters had asked what all the fancy food was for. Trying to appear casual, Katie responded simply that she just felt like something different to change up the family's weekday fare. Would they notice if it was all gone by the evening?

Katie was rushing and it irked her. She was usually ready for everything hours in advance, always with time to spare. Today was different—planned, yet not. She had hoped the girls would accept her invitation, but couldn't be certain, and she'd wanted it to appear casual. She was very pleased when both were available, and she didn't want to be wrong when she'd sensed that they really were looking forward to it, too.

Spritzing the counter and running the rag over it one final time for crumbs, Katie scooped the phantom ones which remained into her palm and shook them into the trash compactor. She headed for the bathroom to be sure everything still sparkled from her earlier once-over, even though no one else was home to have made a mess. She glanced at herself in the mirror above the sink and fluffed out her chestnut hair. She thought about whether she should get some caramel highlights. Her hairdresser often suggested it, but Katie was not one for trying new things before considering it, pondering it, mulling it over countless times. Anyway, Steve might not like it.

Katie turned around and looked at her figure. She still looked damn good, despite being over forty and having had two kids. She worked out almost every day on the elliptical in the basement, and she did the "Insanity Workout" at least four days a week. Thank God gravity had not yet taken hold. She was wearing a fabulous push-up bikini. Was she too old for Victoria's Secret?

Her cell phone rang from the charger on the counter. No one usually called her on it. She glanced over at the display and seeing that it was her sister, Alice, she let it go to voicemail. When the voicemail dinged, she saw that there were four unheard messages from her. She sighed. She'd have to call her eventually.

Katie carried the refreshments out to the pool. Years ago, she had convinced Steve to contract a designer to create an elaborate entertainment area complete with a poolside bar, grill, and refrigerator for entertaining, all housed under an elegant cabana. Just outside of it, there was even a stone fire pit and a backdrop waterfall. They didn't often entertain more than Jamie and Anna's friends. Occasionally Katie's brother and his family or Steve's sister and hers would come, or on rare occasion, colleagues of Steve's. Even when they used it themselves, Katie loved how the whole set-up turned out.

She busied herself setting out everything. She put all of the cold food in the refrigerator covered with plastic wrap until the girls arrived. Satisfied that everything was just right, Katie hurried back toward the house to make sure she'd not forgotten anything. Just as she pulled open the French door, she saw Scarlett and Erin coming around from the side of the house and she wondered if they had come together. For a moment she was rattled, thinking they might have discussed C. Thomas's proposal without her.

"Hey, girls!" she called out, shaking it off.

"I was an *animal* Saturday night!" Katie exclaimed with giddy delight. She already had downed two cocktails and was pouring her third from the pitcher. Scarlett had suggested margaritas even though she considered it a waste of Patrón and Gran Marnier, but she couldn't deny it was a great summer refresher. "Steve couldn't believe it!" She walked back over to her chaise longue, propped up the back of it and sat down to enjoy the drink.

"Oh, wow," Scarlett tried to keep the jealousy she was feeling out of her voice. It hit her like a ton of bricks. She really had been thinking she and Steve were connecting lately, but she never considered he was still a man with needs and could be flirting with her but still boffing his wife.

Erin, who usually was not a big drinker, was lying on her stomach on her chaise, already well into her third beverage and second sandwich. She had started out with margaritas but they kicked her ass, so she had switched to a light beer she'd found in the fridge, a leftover from Katie's brother-in-law from earlier in the summer. "I wish I could say the same. I went to bed with Mr. Xanax again."

"Xanax?" Katie responded inquisitively, leaning in toward Erin. "I didn't know you took any meds."

"I don't talk about it much." Erin flipped around and sat up, pulling her knees into her chest and wrapping her arms around them like a child. "I really don't take it that often. I've had prescriptions for it since I was a teenager. I suffered from a lot of anxiety through high school and college. It was better for a while, but sometimes it is the only way I can fall asleep—or start the day for that matter."

"Wow," Katie said, feeling the next margarita kicking in and unsuccessfully stifling a laugh. "Is it good stuff?" She hadn't meant to sound mocking.

Erin began to laugh as well. "It's a better bed companion than Marty!"

All three of them began cackling like hyenas. Spilling some of her margarita down the front of her bikini, Katie turned to Scarlett and said, "What about you, Scarlett? What about that bruise? Must have been a *damn* good time!"

Scarlett had been lying on the concrete on her Marilyn towel, mostly thinking about Steve. The thought of C. Thomas repulsed her. She didn't even bother to lift her head or open her eyes when she responded. "We just

# GOING ALL IN

conked out early," Scarlett lied. She wasn't going to get into her husband's lewd bullshit escapades.

"Really!" Katie nearly guffawed. She'd always imagined that Scarlett and C. Thomas must be wild in bed, attempting every crazy, hot sex move out there.

Changing the subject, or maybe not really, Erin asked Scarlett, "So, was C. Thomas really serious about this wife-swapping thing?"

All three women were simultaneously relieved that someone finally had brought it up.

"It's not wife-swapping!" Katie corrected. "It's choosing somebody else's spouse!" Katie had been thinking a lot about this, despite feeling somewhat conflicted at the same time. Nevertheless, she felt compelled to clarify it now as much as C. Thomas had Saturday night.

"Whatever," Erin said to Katie. For some reason, she felt a little bit defensive. She turned to Scarlett and asked again, "So was he serious?"

Scarlett felt the sun beating down on her. It had to be nearing one hundred degrees and the alcohol didn't help. She sat up and reached for the sunscreen, then responded, "I guess so." She knew damn well he was, but she was trying to appear casual.

"Have you guys ever done something like that before?" Erin asked with the wide-eyed curiosity of a young child. She took a swig of her beer. Then another. She needed to be brave for where this conversation was going.

"You mean, like with other couples?"

"Yeah," Erin said, feeling a bit more uninhibited. "You've never had an orgy, right?"

"Erin!" Katie said reprimandingly. She wanted to keep this conversation on the right track.

"Relax, Katie! I am sure if I get too personal with Scarlett she'll tell me to shut my pie hole." What was it with Katie today?

"No worries, girls," Scarlett began. She leaned back on her elbows and flipped her hair behind her with a quick toss of her head. She was turning the sunscreen bottle around in her hand. Both women's eyes were riveted on her.

God, she's gorgeous, Erin thought to herself.

"To be honest, we've never done it with other *couples*, but in the beginning, we did have a couple of threesomes."

"With other men?" Erin was becoming curiouser and curiouser; she felt like Alice in Wonderland sailing down the rabbit hole.

"Erin!" Katie again felt the need to chastise her. She wasn't a nice drunk today.

Scarlett actually was having fun with the conversation. Feeling like the leader of the pack, she was in the secure position of being able to direct and manipulate both Erin and Katie, ultimately, and hopefully, toward the goal of setting C. Thomas's proposal in motion.

"It's okay, Katie. I'm not embarrassed at all." She looked toward Erin. "No, not with men. With other women. What about you guys? Have you ever?"

Erin snorted. "Are you kidding? I'm lucky to have a twosome most of the time."

"Ditto, here," Katie said.

"But you guys have kids," Scarlett said in something of amazement. What happens after marriage? she considered nervously. She had hoped that in her next go-round, with the right man, she might actually have a *real* sex life. With Steve, perhaps?

"Ha!" both Erin and Katie chimed, almost at the exact same time.

Scarlett shook her head in bewilderment. "Well, it works if you are doing it with the right people." Were Erin and Katie catching on? Were they going to go for it?

Erin noticed how red Scarlett's shoulders were becoming. "Your shoulders are getting red, Hon."

Scarlett sat up and handed the sunscreen bottle over to Erin. "Can you put some on me?"

"Sure," Erin said as she got up off the chaise, first securing her towel around her waist, then walking over to Scarlett. She took the bottle and squeezed some into her palm then began to rub some onto Scarlett's shoulders. She was surprised to find it arousing.

"Thanks. That feels good."

Katie was watching the whole scene. She had done her best to shake off her annoyance with Erin and selfishly wanted to keep the conversation on track to ensure that the proposal remained on the table. "So, you wouldn't mind sharing C. Thomas?" she asked. Shit! Did I really say that? she thought. Did it sound too forward?

Scarlett shrugged from beneath Erin's caressing hands. "I guess not. I mean, it's only us. Besides, I think it would be a goof."

Erin and Katie looked at one another from behind Scarlett and both mouthed the word "goof" simultaneously. They silently laughed to one another. Katie shrugged a shoulder.

Scarlett scanned the pool area quickly. Erin's hands felt so good on her and she was mildly excited by it. She stood up and reached for her bikini top. With a pull of the string and in one quick motion she yanked it over her head, then said, "Since it's only us!" She slipped off her bottom, and in a swift, graceful leap, was in the pool.

"That girl has absolutely no inhibitions!" Katie squealed.

"With a body like that, I wouldn't either," Erin said, unable to hide the envy in her tone.

"Are you jealous or lustful?" Katie asked, this time not mocking, but rather straightforward.

"I think a little bit of both."

Katie stood and unhooked her own bikini top and tossed it at Erin. She began to slip off her bottom when Erin asked, "What are you doing, Katie?"

"What does it look like I'm doing? I'm going skinny dipping, too."

Erin froze. She'd have to be next.

"Come on! Take off your suit!" Katie said as she stood there completely naked.

Erin looked over at Scarlett in the pool, graceful as a dolphin, swimming and diving in and out of the water. I can't, Erin cried out in her head. "I'm too embarrassed. What if someone sees?"

"Jeez. The guys won't be home for hours. Your kids are at camp. Mine are working today. I have the privacy gate. What's the use in having a private pool if you can't do what you want in it?"

"Maybe what *you* want," Erin said. She was not happy about where this was going.

"Let's go! I want to see those tan lines!" Katie was practically giddy. She ran to the edge of the pool and jumped in like a child, splashing water on Erin.

"Hey!" Erin called out. She stood up and brought up a hand to her shoulder strap, but immediately reconsidered.

"Take it off!" Scarlett called out. Soon she and Katie both were chanting, "Take it off! Take it off!"

Erin just couldn't do it. She really wanted to, but she felt as insecure at that moment as she recalled feeling in the high school locker room getting changed next to all of the popular girls with their perfect bodies. But she wanted at least keep the conversation going, so she ran to the pool and did a whopper of a cannon ball between the women, splashing them both in the face. As she resurfaced, all three were in hysterics.

"Baby!" Scarlett called out.

"Coward!" Katie squealed.

Erin stuck out her tongue and swam away to the deep end. Scarlett swam over to a large inflatable swan raft that was drifting by the side of the pool and climbed up on it. Situating herself to sunbathe completely in the nude, she tied her hair up in a messy bun then paddled with her arms toward the edge by the area where they had been sitting. Leaning halfway off of the raft, she reached for her margarita, which now had a half inch of water on top from the melted ice. She took a long sip and placed it in the cup holder on the raft and lay back.

"Getting yours, Ladies?"

Katie swam over and reached across Scarlett's long legs for her own. It was almost empty.

"I think we need some fresh ones!" Katie said after she finished what was left. "Erin? Back to margaritas?"

Erin felt woozy. But she already had bailed on the skinny dipping so she figured she ought to keep up with the drinking, even if she just poured it out when they weren't looking. "Sure," she said.

Scarlett paddled over to Erin while Katie climbed out of the pool and went to mix more drinks. She slid off the raft. "What's up with the suit?" She playfully tugged at a shoulder strap.

"What do you mean?" Erin wasn't sure whether she was asking about the fact that it was a Miraclesuit or asking why she wouldn't take it off.

"C'mon, Erin. Why so uptight?"

Scarlett was leaning against the edge of the pool, back on her forearms, so that her bare breasts and her erect nipples were pointed toward the sun. It was hard for Erin not to stare. "Listen, Scarlett. You've never had kids. And

Katie, well, she's like some kind of Wonder Woman. God only knows how she looks like that after having *two* pregnancies."

"Stop." Scarlett cut her off. "You're being ridiculous. You have a great body."

"No I don't, Scarlett, and you know it."

"Listen, there are all kinds of bodies. Half of mine is paid for." Scarlett slid back into the water and cupped both breasts, one in each hand.

"What?" Erin said, shocked. She had no idea. What would she know? She was just a lonely housewife from bumfuck Pennsylvania. Fake boobs were the stuff of reality television and movie stars.

At that moment, Katie sauntered over, gracefully carrying three margaritas, despite being naked and with the hefty amount of alcohol already in her system. "What's paid for?" She had heard only the last part of the girls' conversation. She set all three drinks down at the edge of the pool

"My tits," Scarlett said, shaking them.

"Ha! I always thought so. But I never wanted to say anything."

"You did?" Erin couldn't believe Katie would have known.

"Want to feel them?" Scarlett asked Erin.

"No!" Erin thought Scarlett had to be joking.

"Why not?"

"Yeah, why not?" Katie asked. "I will."

Scarlett faced Katie and leaned in toward her. Katie cupped one, then the other. "Wow, they even feel real! C'mon Erin."

Erin really wanted to. She gingerly raised a finger and pressed Scarlett's left breast. Scarlett grabbed her hand and pressed Erin's palm against her whole breast, directly over the nipple.

"Oh, my God!" Erin said, laughing.

"You know you wanted to!" Scarlett said, reaching over and pulling off one side of Erin's bathing suit, exposing one of her breasts.

"Oh, my God!" Erin said again, louder, still laughing. "You're crazy!"

---

"DUDE! THIS IS REALLY GOOD SHIT!" the Mole said, after he took a long drag on what was left of a blunt. He passed it over to Doogie.

"No fake, Jake. My man only gets his ganja on the Lower East Side in Manhattan." He took a drag and passed it back.

As usual, Doogie and the Mole were hanging out in Recon DM, treehouse extraordinaire. Doogie was fiddling around with his telescope and camera, while the Mole, who was sitting on the floor, leaned back and closed his eyes.

Doogie put his eye to the scope and pointed it toward the Kellys's pool. He was having trouble adjusting the focus, when all of a sudden he hit pay dirt. He zoomed in on the three women in the pool. "Holy shit! Holy shit! Holy shit!"

The Mole nearly jumped out of his skin. He was so high, he'd almost been asleep. He was immediately on his feet. "What?"

"Oh, my...God!!"

"What the hell? Let me in there!" the Mole said as he shoved Doogie with an elbow and grabbed the scope.

"You have *no* idea, man!" Doogie stood next to the Mole. He was practically panting.

The Mole struggled in his state to focus and for it to register what was behind the lens. "What! Oh, my God is right!"

"Damn straight!"

The Mole pulled his head back from the scope. "Who the hell are they?"

"I'm not sure, but I think one of them is Mrs. Kelly! Now I see where Jamie and Anna get it from!"

"But what about that unbelievable specimen of hotness? That's the chick from the other day. She's got it *all* off today! I think I am going to blow my wad right here!"

"Oh, man. Puleeze!"

"Hey, I'd bone her."

"Lemme back in there!" Doogie grabbed the scope back from the Mole. "You know, now I remember. I think I've seen that chick hanging at the Kellys's for a while now. She and her asshole Jag-driving pretty boy come over sometimes. I've seen my dad with his tongue hanging out when she pulls up in their driveway." He turned on the camera. "I've gotta get pics of this shit!"

"I can't believe there're three of them! That one is still wearing her suit. WTF? I want to see some three-way action!"

"I'm not into soccer moms." Doogie was taking pictures mainly of Scarlett although he caught one of Scarlett pulling off Erin's bathing suit top.

Doogie continued snapping away on the birder cam while the Mole pulled his cell out and tried to get some photos on it. "Damn! Shit! Hell!" he cursed, getting frustrated because the zoom on the phone wasn't good enough to get a decent shot.

"What are you worried about, Dipshit? I got all the goods we need right here. These pics will be all over cyberspace by tonight!"

## 7

## MEN FROM MARS

*How to win at Texas Hold'em:*
   Be prepared to fold most of the time. In order to be in for the long haul, you cannot afford to take risks. Don't chase the cards. Wait for the good hands. They will come. You need patience. Play your cards and not your ego. Most importantly, ride your luck.

MARTY WAS SITTING in his office at Colonial, feet up on the desk, lost in thought with the book *How to Win at Texas Hold'em* spread open on his chest. On this particular day, he was experiencing a rare and quite enjoyable solitude during his office hours. Sean Russo was home sick with a bad stomach bug, otherwise he would have been sitting across from Marty, pontificating about some new Dickensian atrocity which had befallen modern society. As it was, he had texted Marty no less than three times to ensure that he had not missed anything significant in class. Out of all the students he had ever taught during his entire teaching career, Sean Russo took the prize for the most bombastic, annoying, brown-nosing windbag imaginable. That's why Marty was certain that someday Sean Russo would be at the top of the pyramid either as a tyrannical CEO or as President of the

United States. Marty also was certain that at that time, he would likely be begging Russo for some kind of favor.

But for now, Russo was just a pest who could be swatted like a bug from Marty's thoughts, so that he could focus on more important things like poker and what had become known in his inner circle as the "C. Thomas Proposal."

He could not stop thinking about it.

Never in his wildest imagination would he have believed he would have had a shot at shagging Scarlett. Indeed, he thought the closest he ever would get was jerking off over the clandestine photos he had of her from Aruba.

How times had changed. The worm had turned. The fates may have shifted into his corner after all. If C. Thomas's proposal could be put into play, then all things were possible, including him screwing Scarlett six ways to Sunday. Of course, he knew it required that he win the game. No easy task given his present poker skills.

Marty picked up the book from his chest and started to read again when he heard someone knocking. His door had an opaque window preventing anyone from seeing through it. His first thought was that Sean miraculously had recovered from his stomach virus and had made his way to the campus to kill Marty's blissful solitude and waste the remainder of his office hours with arcane and useless trivia. He looked at the clock/paperweight, the thought of bashing in Sean's head with it still alive and well. Maybe Sean would go away if he just ignored the interruption.

But the knock came again, harder and more insistent this time.

"Oy," Marty muttered. "Door's open," he said, giving up.

The door opened and Heather stuck in her pretty head. "Hi, Professor. I hope I'm not disturbing you."

If Heather was as perceptive as she seemed, she noticed the immediate transformation in Marty's countenance and posture. Marty's face brightened, his color changing from an ashen hue to a bright red, his lips curling into a welcoming smile. He quickly closed the poker book, tossed it in his top drawer and sat up in his chair. His hand went instinctively to his hair, sweeping it back then patting it down.

"Hello, Heather. Please come in."

In a move which reminded Marty of Scarlet O'Hara, Heather swept into his room. She was wearing a pastel sundress and flip flops, her hair pulled up into a loose ponytail. Her mere presence brightened his dingy little office. She pulled up one of Marty's guest chairs and sat across from him.

"You look busy. I hope I'm not interrupting you."

"Don't be silly. Office hours are for students." He wanted to add *with the exception of Sean Russo*. "Besides, I look forward to the company." *Especially your company.* "The campus can be like a ghost town in the summer."

"For sure," she said, flashing him a brilliant smile.

"What can I do for you?"

"I wanted to discuss the topic for my term paper. I thought it would be really cool if I could do a comparison between the English authors we've been studying and the themes in Pirandello's work. That would make a nice cross-pollination between your class and my Italian literature class."

"Wow!" Marty whistled his appreciation. "That is an immense undertaking!"

"I was thinking of narrowing it somewhat. Maybe do a comparison of the themes expressed in Shakespeare's *As You Like It* and Pirandello's *Cosi e (se vi pare)*?"

"Which one?" Marty had taken Latin in high school, thinking it could help him in his study of the classics. All it did do, however, was bring down his overall GPA and leave him with an immense distaste for foreign languages.

"The English translation," Heather said, "is *Right you are, if you think so*."

"Of course," Marty said. "I am familiar with it." Marty wasn't familiar with the work, but he couldn't let Heather know it. "I still think it's a herculean task."

Heather flashed him another brilliant smile. "That's okay. I'm up for the challenge."

Marty shook his head in appreciation. Nothing sexier than a pretty girl with a big rack and big brains to match, he thought.

"Well, young lady, if you are up for the challenge, then I am up for reading it." Marty would be *up* for any number of things where Heather was concerned.

"Thanks!" Heather stood to leave. "Oh, by the way, before I forget, are you going to be at the summer mixer at the Rathskeller next Saturday night?"

"I'm not sure. This is the first I've heard of it."

"You have to come! It's the first one of summer break. Everyone will be there."

"Are faculty members invited?"

"Pretty sure. Anyway, who cares? I'm inviting you. You can be my guest."

Is she flirting with me? he considered.

"I'll check my schedule and let you know."

"Sounds good. I hope you can make it. Bye." One last dazzling smile for the road and she was gone, the closing of the opaque-windowed door cutting off his view of her flouncing down the hall.

Marty sat for a long time staring at the closed door, drumming his fingers on his desk, taking in the lingering smell of the floral notes of her perfume.

---

SIXTY MILES AWAY, Steve was also drumming his fingers. He was sitting at the mahogany table in the fishbowl conference room at his firm, a stack of Redweld expandable file folders in front of him, impatiently waiting for his associate, Troy Ashford. It was time to begin their weekly case review. Every week Steve was assigned new cases by the managing partner of the firm, and every week, as the partner in charge, Steve would set up a weekly meeting to review those cases with Troy. Then every week, without fail, Troy would keep him waiting.

The notion that an associate could keep a partner waiting for anything is anathema in the legal world. Under normal circumstances, if this situation occurred, the associate would be quickly dispatched with walking papers and a referral to ambulance chasing and solo practitionerhood.

But these weren't normal circumstances. Troy Ashford was the nephew of Johnathan Ashford, Jr., the leading named partner of the firm. As such, Troy had carte blanche at the firm as far as his behavior was concerned. Apart from egregious moral turpitude that could mean disbarment, young Troy could do just about whatever he wanted, much to the chagrin of the other associates and partners, including Steve, and get away with it.

Steve was about to text Troy yet again when he bounded into the conference room, with not a care in the world, humming some familiar pop song

Steve had heard on the radio but couldn't name. He pulled out the chair next to Steve and plopped himself down.

"You're late...again," Steve said.

"Yeah, Captain, sorry about that. My Pilates class ran over."

Steve hated when Troy called him Captain. He expressed his disapproval several times to Troy, but it was to no avail. Troy did as Troy wanted, knowing that he had a permanent *Get Out of Jail Free* card. Steve knew that Troy did things just to annoy him, like calling him Captain. Being forever tardy was number two on the list. No matter what time Steve scheduled their weekly meetings, Troy would be late and armed with myriad excuses—everything from Tai Chi classes and late brunches to early lunches, tennis matches, doctor and dentist appointments, and now Pilates. Steve didn't believe any of them.

"Did you review the new cases?" Steve asked.

"Yessiree," Troy said, leaning way back with his arms behind his head and crossing his ankle over his knee like he was watching a ballgame. He nodded toward the first Redweld. "That's the Kramer case. Shelly Kramer, age five, was on a school bus. One of the seats had a loose metal hinge sticking up. She cut her face on it—right cheek to be exact—four inch gash. We represent the bus line of course. Plaintiff is claiming permanent disfigurement, scarring, physical and emotional pain and suffering. Demands five million. Want to see the pics? There are some real gruesome, Technicolor ones."

Steve shook his head. "Solo practitioner?"

"Two-man firm. Chambers and Garibaldi, LLC. Ambulance chasers. Slip and falls mostly."

"Any stitches?"

"None. The girl never went to the hospital for treatment."

Despite his loathing of Troy's preferred position in the pecking order of the firm, Steve was impressed with his ability to manage cases. He was a quick study with a sharp memory and could recite facts from the case record verbatim after only a casual perusal of the file. While Steve could find fault with Troy on any number of behavioral issues, his work product was, unfortunately, impeccable. Sometimes Steve felt he was Troy's Salieri, his envious and less-talented mentor.

Steve's cell phone vibrated in his pocket. He pulled it out, checked it, saw that it was Marty calling, and clicked to decline. He left it on the table.

"Stall the case," he said to Troy. "Delay, delay, delay. Get as many adjournments to answer the complaint as you can. When you do finally have to answer, hit them with the usual onerous discovery requests. Drag the case out for a year. The kid's face will be healed by that time and we'll settle for five hundred. Next case."

Troy sat forward and picked up the next Redweld, tossing it toward Steve. "Miller, Rita. She went to a chiropractor—our client—claims he herniated her disc with a manipulation he did. He said he merely performed a routine adjustment. He even did it on me."

"You let him?" Steve asked, surprised.

"I didn't want him to. He grabbed my neck and before I could object he twisted it."

"You survived unharmed."

"I did. Seems this Rita Miller is quite litigious. Five lawsuits within the past seven years, two against doctors, two against municipalities, and one against her neighbor for a dog bite."

"I guess she didn't know about the law that every dog is entitled to one free bite. Sounds like a scammer. Put a PI on her for a week. Try to get Matt Banacek on it. Tell him we need stills and video, fortune-cookie style. He'll get the movie reference and know what we want."

"Will do."

Steve was not annoyed that Troy never took notes, rather, he was annoyed that Troy never needed to and that he always followed through with Steve's directions.

"Next case," Steve said. The table started vibrating as Steve's phone went off again. He checked it, saw that it was Marty *again*, and clicked to decline the call for the second time.

Troy made a circle with his index finger and thumb and flicked a third folder into the center of the table. "The best for last. Jasmine Russell goes into the New York State Medical Center for a tubal ligation. They take out a vein instead of her fallopian tube. She gets pregnant, has to abort. She asks the hospital what gives. They tell her it's called "recanalization" which is a low statistical possibility of the fallopian tube growing back. Later on down the road she's talking to another attorney about another matter entirely, mentions the incident and he is all over it. Gets a doctor in Atlanta to say it's clear malpractice. She files a lawsuit in the Court of Claims, but the ninety-day notice of claim provision has run out. The Court of Claims allows the complaint in its discretion."

In New York State, one has ninety days from the time of an incident to notify a municipality that he or she intends to sue. If the ninety days pass, the Court of Claims, which hears suits against municipalities, can decide to allow the claim in its discretion. As long as the claim is brought within the statute of limitations of one year and ninety days from the time of occurrence, it is not considered time-barred.

"I presume the claim was made within the statute of limitations." Steve's cell phone went off again. He looked down and could not believe that it was Marty...for the third time.

"Maybe you should get that, Captain."

Steve clicked decline. "That's okay. Where were we?"

"The claim was brought within the statutorily prescribed period but outside the discretionary ninety-day notice provision," Troy said without missing a beat.

"Let's do an interlocutory appeal from the Court of Claims' allowance of the claim after the ninety days."

Troy rubbed his chin, deep in thought. "Tough one to win," he finally said. "We would have to argue it was an abuse of the discretion of the Court of Claims to allow it."

"Who cares if we win? The appeal will be pending nine months to year. That will slow up the ambulance chasers on the other side. What's our mantra?"

"Delay, delay, delay," Troy replied in a mock sing-songy tone. "You do realize that there was clear malpractice in this case. Not to mention fraud in trying to cover it up with that recanalization bullshit."

"That's not our problem. We do not have these problems. Our clients do. We took an oath when we were sworn in as officers of the court to provide the best representation and advocacy we can to our clients. Everyone is entitled to a defense, even the guilty."

"A defense is one thing. Innocent by subterfuge and manipulation is another," Troy rambled.

"When children get in the way of the First Amendment, the Supreme Court says, 'Too bad. Collateral damage.' That's just the way the law works."

"Aye, Captain, you are a shark!"

"Maybe you should share your views with your uncle. He's the one who built this firm. See if he agrees with you."

Troy was thoughtful for a moment. "You know, Steve," he finally said, "I take that back. You aren't a shark. At least with a shark you know what to expect. You are worse than a shark. You're one of those chameleon-like predators who makes people think you're one of them. Then when they are at ease you go in for the kill. On the surface, you seem like a cool, reserved, straight-arrow kind of guy. But beneath the surface, there is a very cold, dark soul."

Steve was about to tell the puissant, smug, trust-fund brat to go fuck himself, uncle or no uncle, when his cell phone started vibrating. It was Marty...*again*! This time Steve picked it up.

"Jesus Christ, Marty!" Steve yelled into the phone, suddenly oblivious of Troy's presence. "I'm in a goddamn meeting! What do you want?"

"It's really important," Marty replied. "We need to talk. What time will you be at the train station?"

"What's going on? Can't this wait till I get home?"

"No. It's imperative that I talk to you before you get home. Tell me what time to be at the station."

"This better be good! I'll be there at six forty-five."

"It is. I promise. See you then."

Steve clicked off and tossed the phone on the table. "Putz," he muttered under his breath. He became acutely aware that Troy was staring—no, more like studying him.

"It's my neighbor," Steve said dismissively. "He needs some help with landscaping."

"Sure," Troy said, but he continued to stare.

---

AT SIX FORTY-FIVE P.M. SHARP, the train from Grand Central pulled into the Brewster Village Station. Steve exited with the rest of the rush hour cattle, climbed the stairs on the departing platform, crossed over the tracks, and then descended to the northbound platform. He spotted Marty's Honda next to Pat's cab stand.

"This better be good," Steve said, sliding into the passenger seat. "What in the world could be so important that you had to meet me in person at the train?"

Marty was on his third cup of coffee. He was so anxious to talk to Steve that he had arrived at the train station an hour early. To kill time, he grabbed a Reuben and fries at Bob's Diner, the local hangout next to the station. Afterward, he sat in his car making run after run back to Bob's for take-out coffee and to use the john. He had a fourth, as yet untouched cup in the center console cup holder. He offered it to Steve.

"No thanks," Steve said. "Now will you kindly tell me what the hell is going on?"

"C. Thomas was serious."

Steve washed his face in his hands. "Are you whacked? This is what couldn't wait until tonight? This is what you couldn't talk to me about over the phone?"

Marty nodded emphatically. "Yes! I wanted to talk to you before you went home. I want to do this. So do you. So don't give me any of your shit-don't-stink, pompous, self-righteous attitude."

"You don't care if I sleep with your wife. Is that what you are telling me?"

Marty shrugged. "If that's what you want, why not? I'm sure Erin would enjoy it. She's always had a thing for you. I can tell."

"You're crazy."

"This is me you're talking to. We've known each other for a lot of years. You can't bullshit me. There is a lot of flirting going on when we are all together. You *cannot* tell me you've never fantasized about being with anyone else—Erin *or* Scarlett."

Steve sighed. Frankly, he'd never fantasized about being with Erin, but Scarlett was quite another story. "Even if that was true, it's just harmless flirting. Do we really want to cross a line?"

"Did I ever tell you about my Uncle Bill?"

"No," Steve said. "I didn't know you had an Uncle Bill."

"He was from the South," Marty said. "An old codger—Korean War Vet. He lived way into his nineties. When he was ninety-five he once told me what the most important thing in the world to him was at that age. You know what he said?"

"I have no idea," Steve said annoyed by Marty's dissertation but nevertheless somewhat intrigued.

"Pussy," Marty said. "That's what he said. This was a man who could barely walk, barely think, who couldn't remember what he had for breakfast that morning. But he remembered in acute detail all the women he'd had. I don't want to get to ninety-five and regret the women I *could* have had."

"Your ancestors were Ashkenazi Jews and the furthest south you've ever been is D.C."

Marty chuckled. "Yeah, you're right. But it was a great story, wasn't it?"

Steve had to laugh in spite of himself. Marty could turn on the charm and humor when he wanted something.

"Massaging Scarlett's feet," Steve said, "must have gone to your head, and I don't mean the one on the top of your neck. Does your wife know how gung-ho you are about all of this?"

"Of course not! I told her you were the one with the hots for the idea."

"Jesus Christ. That will get back to Katie. Are you out of your fucking mind?" Steve was more than annoyed now and he rarely cursed. The last thing he needed was Marty meddling with his marriage.

"Calm down. I wouldn't just throw you to the wolves. Besides, Katie really wants to do it."

Steve momentarily blanched but he recovered quickly. "Bullshit," he spat back.

"No bullshit. The girls talked about it today. Erin told me. Katie is hot on the idea. Go home and ask her if you don't believe me."

"I will." Marty's statement was like a hard slap in the face. Steve's ire was transforming into something else, something darker. Something foreboding. After his conversation with Katie in bed after the game, he knew that Marty probably was telling the truth.

"This is better than a hall pass," Marty said. "We have an opportunity that few couples ever get—dropped right into our laps. The ability to live out fantasies without blame, remorse, guilt, or consequences."

"There'll be consequences, Marty. Believe me." Steve opened the car door.

"Go home and talk to your wife," Marty said in summation. "Don't blow this for us."

Marty's last line was lost as Steve exited the car, slamming the door behind him.

## 8

## WOMEN FROM VENUS

Katie was busy in the kitchen making dinner. She had in her earbuds and was dancing around while she cooked. She'd decided to use the leftover fruit salad from her little pool party and make a fruit salsa to go with the swordfish steaks she'd gotten the day before. She had taken a nap after the girls left so she was feeling pretty refreshed between that and the cool shower she'd taken to soothe her sunburn. Maybe I should have had Erin put sunscreen on me, too, she thought when she caught her reflection in the oven glass. She'd even had time to pen a few more pages of her book.

She heard the front door open and close then glanced at the clock over the stove. It was nearly eight. Footsteps grew louder as Steve's oxfords clacked against the entry tile. He walked into the kitchen looking weary with his Brooks Brothers suit jacket hanging over a shoulder from his index finger. After tossing the jacket and his briefcase on a stool by the center island, he slumped into a kitchen chair.

"I thought you were going to be home early," Katie said questioningly.

"Got a little held up at the train." He wasn't exactly lying. "So what's up?"

"Nothing. Just making dinner."

"Where are the girls?"

"Jamie's working at Eagle tonight and Anna is sleeping over at Madison's."

"Jeez. Do we even have kids anymore?"

Katie laughed. He hadn't seen her laugh in a while. He used to love the way her right cheek dimpled and her eyes crinkled when she did. "Sometimes I wonder. You remember when you were young and—"

"Innocent and free," Steve interrupted.

Katie raised an eyebrow wondering what he meant. She opted not to find out. Instead she asked, "Is everything okay?"

"You tell me." He was being intentionally coy and evasive. "So what did you do today?"

"Hung out," she said in an attempt to appear casual. "Actually, Scarlett and Erin came over. We were in the pool."

"Ah. What did you talk about?" Clearly, he was indicating talk of the game.

"Okay, Steve. Knock it off. I'm not being deposed here." She was used to this tone from him when he was trying to get something out of her. It was the lawyer in him. "If you have something to say, say it. If you want to ask something, ask it. I am not a mind reader. I hate it when you do this."

Steve rubbed his forehead against the heel of his hand. He had a headache. "All right. I heard you talked about the game and the potential new *rules* with the girls today."

Katie actually felt a bit relieved. "Ha! I guess Marty got to you. Is that what the 'hold-up' was at the train?" She snickered and used air quotes. "Yeah, so what? We discussed it."

"Are you saying you want to do it? Is that the bottom line?" Steve got up to get some acetaminophen out of the cabinet. He unscrewed the cap and palmed four—he didn't bother to put the extra one back nor did he bother to get a glass, but instead reached for the retractable faucet at the sink, tossed the pills into his mouth, and took a hearty gulp of water.

Katie watched Steve the whole time. She felt distanced from him; maybe now more than she could ever remember before. What was once passion now seemed to be something more like tepid indifference. What was worse was neither seemed bothered by it.

"Look, Steve, you and I were college sweethearts. We've been married a long time." She walked over to him, still with a few feet between them. "I only had one serious boyfriend before you. I wouldn't be honest if I said that this whole thing wasn't a bit exciting or titillating."

"Hmmmff. Titillating," he growled.

"It's just—"

Steve cut her off. "I don't believe this. I feel like I'm in the bizarro world! My wife of eighteen years wants an open marriage!"

"Stop it, Steve. That's not true." She looked upset. "If push came to shove, I don't know what I'd actually do. All I said was that I find it exciting and would keep an open mind. These people are our close friends. It's not like we're going to a swinger's party with strangers."

Steve began pacing back and forth. He had been thinking a lot about the game, and the new rules, and Scarlett, but that was him. The idea that Katie might want to sleep with another man, especially that man-boy C. Thomas, repulsed him, and it clearly was not right.

"Why am I the only one who is having a hard time with this?"

"I don't know," Katie began softly. She was filling a pot of water at the sink and carried it over to the stove. "Maybe it's because you've always had a hard time expressing your real emotions."

"What is that supposed to mean?"

"You know what I mean. You've never worn your heart on your sleeve. You've never opened up. You always keep a wall around your true feelings. I don't know. When we were first married, I thought maybe I could break it down. Now I just tolerate it." She had gone to the refrigerator and pulled out a bag of summer squash then returned to the counter with them. She pulled out a cutting board from a cabinet below and slid a carving knife out of the butcher block, then began slicing.

He'd been watching her intently. "Are you done? This is just psychobabble bullshit. Is this what you and the ladies talked about today? *My* private life?"

"No. Not at all. Come on, Steve. I know you better than you know yourself. I know you have desires just like everyone else."

"That doesn't mean I have to act on them."

Katie stopped what she was doing and waved the knife at him. "Oh, yeah, only selective ones."

Steve did a double-take. "What is that supposed to mean?"

Katie turned to face him, looking him square in the eye. "I know about the office Christmas party three years ago."

Steve stopped dead in his tracks. "What do you think you know?"

"Please, Steve. Don't insult me. I know quite a bit about how firms operate, you know." She still had the knife in her hand. "I *know* why party policy has the 'no spouse' rule, and it has *nothing* to do with the finances."

Steve began pacing again. He looked nervous. "This is ridiculous, Kate. I don't know what the hell you are talking about."

Katie interrupted before he could slather on more lies. "For once—*just once*—I wish you could be honest with me. That's all I'm asking." She put down the knife and walked over into his line of sight. He stopped pacing. "What if I invited Scarlett into our bed? The three of us. No repercussions, no guilt—my idea totally. Would you still be so upset and indignant? Would you not participate?"

"Katie—"

She again interrupted. "Can you really stand there and look me in the eyes and tell me that the possibility doesn't excite you?"

Steve was defeated. Katie always could read him. He flopped back into the kitchen chair. "I give up. Yes, it does excite me. You happy now?"

Katie's heart fluttered with a mixture of both excitement and jealousy. She'd gotten what she wanted. "I'm happy you were at least honest with me."

Steve's cell phone vibrated in his pocket. He'd forgotten to put on the volume after getting off the train. He pulled it out and looked at the caller ID. "It's Marty."

Katie looked at him with a blank stare. For once, despite looking into her eyes, he couldn't tell at all what was in her head. He looked away and accepted the call. "Marty, meet me at the corner." He pressed END and walked out of the kitchen.

"Where are you going?" Katie called after him. "We weren't finished."

Steve opened the front door and just before closing it behind him said, "Yes, I think we were."

---

FROM TWO HOUSES AWAY, Steve saw Marty approaching the stop sign just a moment ahead of him. Like the cat who swallowed the canary, Marty looked like a kid with ADHD—he was bouncing up and down as if he had springs in his shoes.

"Well?!" he practically screeched.

In stark contrast, Steve responded with defeat, his voice just barely above a whisper. "You were right. Set up the card game."

Marty nearly fell over his own feet as he leapt into the air. "Yes! Yes! Yes!"

"Jeez, Marty. What will the neighbors think?"

"I don't give a crap! Woo hoo!"

Steve rolled his eyes and slapped his forehead. He pulled his shirt collar away from his neck. He was sweating profusely in the heat, still wearing his clothes from the office. "I have a feeling we're going to regret this. Or I will."

Marty slugged Steve in the bicep. It hurt.

"C'mon! We're not going to a funeral here! We're standing on the precipice of something *grand*!"

"Marty—I think you're overstating things quite a bit. Once we open this door, we can't close it. We don't know what could be behind it."

"Are you kidding me? Why would I want to close it? I'm not letting this mood of yours bring me down. I'm outta here. I'm going to go home to tell Erin and call C. Thomas. Sayonara, baby!" Marty spun around toward his house. His walk quickened until he was nearly sprinting. Steve had never seen him move so fast.

Steve stood for a moment against the stop sign. He was dreading going home to face Katie again, but something stirred inside of him. *Scarlett. Scarlett.* He kept saying her name over and over in his head. All of a sudden, he felt light-headed. He turned down the street and began to walk home, his pace slowly quickening to match the beating of his heart.

---

ERIN WAS JUST PUTTING dinner on the kitchen table and serving the twins their regular fare of chicken nuggets and macaroni and cheese. She'd gotten tired of fighting with them about trying new things. She rationalized it with the fact that she at least could get them to eat veggies from time to time. Devin and Daniel were having a sword fight with broccoli stalks when one of them knocked over a cup of milk. It began to spill all over the table and onto the floor.

"Boys!" She was short with them and it was unlike her. Marty had run out the door and hadn't told her where he was going, and she was feeling a bit tired and hungover. She went to the counter to grab the roll of paper towels and began mopping up the mess.

It was then that Marty burst through the door. He was covered in perspiration and nearly panting. By this point, Erin was on her hands and knees cleaning up the floor. She took one look at him and scowled. "What's going on?"

Marty was grinning from ear-to-ear. He looked as if his cheeks were about to explode; Erin found it disconcerting. "Steve wants to have a card game as soon as possible!"

Erin stopped what she was doing, hand in mid-air, paper towels dripping milk back onto the floor. "You're kidding!"

"It's the truth. I just got back from the corner with him. He called me. He told me to set it up."

Erin couldn't believe it. Conservative Steve? Reserved, no-nonsense Steve? It sounded more like Marty. "That's so unlike him."

Finishing up with the mess, Erin threw out the towels then went to the refrigerator for the gallon of milk and refilled the empty cup.

"Well, he said so." Marty still wore the grin as he was wiping the sweat from his head with a kitchen dishtowel. Erin made a face at him then turned back to the boys. She reached over to take the cup away from Devin, who had been blowing bubbles over the sides of his cup with a straw, making more of a mess on the table.

"Devin, stop blowing bubbles! Daniel, get going on that chicken!"

She sized Marty up and down. What was he not telling her? "Where are we going to play? You know my parents are on vacation so we can't do it here."

"I guess at Steve and Katie's."

"And Katie can get the girls to come over and babysit? They're willing to give up a Saturday night so soon? It's not as if I can get any other sitters after the last fiasco."

"I guess so. We didn't discuss it. That's a woman's arena. You call Katie and confirm it."

What a sexist asshole. "Fine. One of these days we're going to be stuck for double pay, you know. I don't think we can keep getting away with twofers. The boys are a lot of work." She paused a moment, then said, "You know, I still can't believe Steve went for it."

"Steve may seem calm on the surface but there's a lot of passion and emotion underneath."

Erin raised an eyebrow thinking what an odd remark that was. "We'll find out."

Marty pulled his cell phone out the pocket of his baggy shorts, unlocked it, and punched up C. Thomas's number as he walked out of the kitchen. Erin gave him one last long look as he disappeared down the hall toward his study. She turned back to the boys who, surprisingly, were eating without incident.

---

C. THOMAS WAS in the den. It was where he puttered around surfing the internet for ideas about ways to improve the company. He never really did any work there or anywhere, but he called it his home office and he had plenty of company logo-emblazoned swag all over his desk. He was sitting in his high-back executive chair swiveling around like a child. He was talking to Marty when Scarlett entered.

"So, it's all set. We'll see you Saturday night!" He punched END and set the phone on the desk blotter.

"Who was that?" Scarlett asked as she felt her heart skip, hoping that it had been about the game.

"That," he said enthusiastically, "was Marty. They all want to do it."

"Even Steve and Katie?" Scarlett responded, with just a hint of worry in her voice.

"That's what he said and they want to play *this* Saturday night." C. Thomas paused a moment, looking out the window at a passing group of kids on bicycles. "You know, I was only half-serious when I brought it up."

"What do you mean? You'd been thinking about it all that day." Scarlett was momentarily concerned again. "Don't you want to do it?"

C. Thomas shrugged. Things usually didn't run too deeply with him. He just wasn't wired that way. He looked toward her and smirked. "I think it will be a goof."

"That's what I think," Scarlett responded, smiling weakly. As she stood there looking at him, it hit home hard that there really was little between them anymore. She couldn't blame him because it was her, not him who had changed. She'd known what she was getting into when she decided to move in with him. She'd done it for all the wrong reasons, or the *one* wrong reason —because her mother wanted her to be taken care of by a wealthy man. Her mother didn't want her to struggle as she had. But Scarlett had realized over the years that there was so much she was missing out on in the loveless relationship.

"Of course, it will change everything," C. Thomas said, looking back toward the window.

Scarlett felt the hairs on the back of her neck prickle. Truer words may never have been spoken.

## 9

## GAME DAY

It finally was Game Day or Game *Night* to be exact. There was a palpable atmosphere of electricity that filled the room as the players assembled for their inaugural game. Each had prepared in their own way. Marty's overuse of cologne hung in the air as the others' olfactory bulbs were ready to explode. Thankfully they eventually acclimated to the smell. He had traded in his sad, plaid thrift-store shorts and sorry graphic tees—among his favorites were: "I'm a Poker Player—I don't even fold laundry" and "I'm all in—Bitches!"— for a polo shirt and pressed cargo shorts. C. Thomas was looking sharp in a white satin shirt and skinny black shorts that accentuated his muscular thighs and ass. Steve wore a Brooks Brothers button down, sleeves rolled up, shirttails out over a new pair of jean shorts; a departure from his usual card-playing uniform consisting of a V-neck tee with bleach spots and faded swim trunks he'd still be wearing from cleaning the pool.

The women were noticeably less casual as well. Katie, usually rather conservative and looking as if she'd walked out of an ad for Talbot's, instead had on a short, flirty sundress she'd gotten in Aruba. It was low-cut and showed off her curves. Erin abandoned her soccer mom garb and donned a casual patterned maxi dress she'd picked up at the mall earlier that day. With clothes on that actually fit her, she looked about ten pounds lighter and five years younger. She was not as heavy or dowdy as she either thought or appeared when she took some time to pull herself together. Both women had quite a healthy glow from their pool romp and needed little makeup, but each had punched it up a few notches with eye makeup and lip gloss.

Scarlett always looked hot and tonight was no different. Her skin was a gorgeous bronze and the white swingy keyhole camisole she wore hugged tightly against her full breasts and accentuated her clavicles. She had on a pair of embellished short shorts that made each sinewy, well-toned muscle stand out as she moved. Often abandoning makeup in the summer, she only wore mascara, which created the look of a dark butterfly's wing with each blink of her eyes.

The group dispensed with their customary chit-chat as they took their seats around the table. C. Thomas broke the charged silence when he opened a new deck of cards and peeled off the cellophane, broke the stamp, popped the lid, and slid out the cards. He had purchased them that afternoon. The others watched intently as he skillfully shuffled the plastic-coated cards, a growing realization sinking in that their destiny now resided within fifty-two fickle fates of chance.

Little did the players realize, but the Fates indeed were minding the game, intent to ensure that individual destinies be fulfilled. The triptych was about to embark on a one-way trip from which there would be no return, no refund, and no do-over.

C. Thomas finished shuffling the cards and placed them to his left for Katie to cut.

"Run them," Katie said, sounding like a poker pro. Steve shot her a quizzical look. She had flipped to the poker channel on television earlier in the week, hoping to pick up a few tips in case the proposal had been a go. Just as she had settled down to watch, Steve had come home so she clicked off before he could catch her.

C. Thomas picked up the deck. "Okay, people, just so we are all on the same page. Instead of money, we are playing for something far more valuable." He reached into his pocket with his free hand and removed a key ring with a single gold key attached to it. He tossed it to the center of the table. "Here's the key to my father's cabin. For one night, it will belong to the winner of the game."

The remaining players stared at it in silence. Katie was the first to break it. "We don't have to do anything we don't want to, right?"

"It's all consensual," Marty chimed in, "but we should give great deference to the winner's wishes. Right, C. Thomas?"

"That's right," C. Thomas agreed.

"And we can't ask what happened," Erin stated.

"Don't ask, don't tell," C. Thomas said. "Whatever happens at my father's cabin stays at the cabin or anywhere else for that matter."

"Enough questions," Marty barked. "We all know the rules. Deal the cards."

So it began.

---

Two hours later there only were two players left in the game, Steve and Marty. For the most part, the game chatter, which during most games was usually raucous, flirtatious, and downright distracting, was held to a bare minimum. Each player totally focused on his or her hand. The only real interruptions were the groans and curses that erupted when players made blunders and mistakes. Poker tells be damned.

Erin was the first to go bust. Her all-in on three of a kind was soundly trounced by Steve's full house. Katie was the next player out. Her straight beaten by Marty's flush. C. Thomas tried a bluff and was rewarded by losing all of his remaining chips to Steve. Scarlett survived the longest against the two men holding her own until her all-in on a full house was beaten by the rare and usually royalty-paying event of four-of-a-kind held by Marty.

Going into the third hour, Steve and Marty were matched evenly with chips. Steve was both surprised and impressed at the much improved caliber of Marty's card playing this evening. He had to make a conscious effort to step up his own game. He wondered whether this just was a lucky night for Marty or had he been hustling them all along.

One thing was certain, Steve knew that Marty was wound as tightly as a drum and could explode at any moment. He had been drinking heavily all night, though the liquor hadn't adversely affected his level of play. He rapped his fingers nervously on the table. Even though the central air was running, Marty was sweating profusely. They both waited for C. Thomas, the appointed dealer for the evening, to deal the next round. The other players sat around the table in rapt attention. Regardless of the winner, *everyone* had a stake in the final outcome.

"You look nervous, Marty," Steve said. "It's only a game."

"It's no longer just a game," C. Thomas corrected. He dealt two hole cards to both Steve and Marty. Marty was about to pick them up when Steve reached out to stop him.

"What do you say we call it a tie?" Steve asked, hoping that he could somehow stop the runaway train from barreling down the tracks. "No winner tonight and we all go home. To our own homes."

Marty shook off Steve's hand and picked up his hole cards. He had a pair of sevens. "Play your cards, Steve." His tone was so completely emotionless, it was almost disconcerting.

Steve sighed and picked up his hole cards. He had a pair of aces; a strong hand, especially before any of the community cards were played.

"I'm all-in," Marty said, pushing his chips to the center of the table.

Steve should have gone all-in. He had the stronger hand with a pair of aces. It was beyond unlikely that Marty had the other pair of aces. The odds were with Steve. It was the right play. He later would think back on this moment countless times and try to understand why he did what he did next. He tossed in his cards leaving Marty to rake in the blinds. Steve was certain that had he met Marty's bet, he would have won the game.

"What did you have, Steve?" Marty asked. In a professional game, no one reveals what they had if they had folded. It was not proper poker etiquette. In the friendly, neighborly games of the triptych's past, however, the couples often would show their hole cards or discuss what they had and what they should have done. But that was the past. The stakes were much higher now.

"I had garbage," Steve said, lying smoothly.

C. Thomas shuffled the cards and dealt two new hole cards to each player. This time Steve had a seven and a deuce—known as the worst hand in poker. Marty looked at his hole cards and almost cried out with joy. He had a pair of queens.

"All-in," Marty said and, for the second time in a row, pushed all of his chips into the center of the table.

"Call," Steve said. He picked up his stacks of chips and added them next to Marty's. His stood neatly in their pristine columns, towering over Marty's disordered heap.

They turned over their cards. There was a collective gasp from the onlookers at seeing Steve's hand.

"Why did you call with that hand?" Katie asked Steve. Even with her limited knowledge of poker, she knew that the seven-two combination usually meant certain death in Texas Hold'em.

Steve shrugged. "I had a feeling."

"You had a feeling?" C. Thomas asked, incredulous.

"He had a feeling," Marty said, rapping the table impatiently with the heel of his hand. "So what? Deal the cards."

C. Thomas dutifully dealt the three card flop: king of clubs, four of diamonds, seven of spades. No help to Marty, but Steve now had a pair of sevens.

"Well, looky there, Steve-O," C. Thomas said. "You caught a pair. Didn't somebody win the WSOP championship with a seven-two combination?"

"Who cares?" Marty asked.

"Joe Hachem won the WSOP in 2005 with a seven-three combination," Steve shot back.

"Stop with the trivia and deal the cards!" Marty demanded. He was apoplectic at this point, his face beet red, eyes bugging out, sweat rolling down his forehead and dripping on the table in front of him. He was quite a sight.

"Easy, boy," C. Thomas said mockingly. "You're gonna have a heart attack."

"Just deal."

C. Thomas flicked the next card off the deck and held it up into the air so that only he could see it. With agonizing and exaggerated slowness, he placed the "turn" or "fourth" card as it is known, on the table with the other community cards. It was a jack of diamonds. No help for either player.

"One more, baby!" Marty yelled, unable to contain himself any longer.

For the first time during the game Steve was sweating.

C. Thomas flicked off the next card from the deck and held it up in the air, again positioning it so that only his eyes could see it. He was intentionally taunting Steve and Marty.

"Well, will you look at that!" C. Thomas exclaimed, a broad smile stretching across his face. "We have our first winner!"

"Stop fucking around!" Marty screamed.

C. Thomas placed this last card, the "river" or "fifth street" next to the others. It was a five of spades.

"I did it! I won!" Marty stood up so quickly that his chair toppled over. Oblivious, Marty danced up and down. "I can't believe I won!"

"It was a bogus win," Scarlett said unable to conceal her anger. "Steve deliberately threw the game. Nobody would go all-in with a seven and a deuce."

She shot Steve a look of pure fury. Steve averted his eyes, but he could still feel her gaze boring into him, reaching down into his very soul. He realized then that he had committed a fateful mistake.

"That's bullshit," Marty said, finally recovering his composure enough to retrieve the chair and sit back down at the table. "This is poker. Any two cards can win."

"You're the winner," C. Thomas said. "Here's the key to the cabin." He slid the key across the table to Marty. "Now all you have to do is pick who you want to take."

Marty picked up the key ring and held it up to the light. He felt like he had won the gold ring on the carousel ride. This indeed was a first for Marty. He'd never won anything in his entire life, much less the key to the woman of his dreams and fantasies. Euphoria washed over him in gigantic waves. His trademark Cheshire Cat grin plastered on his face like it was drawn on with permanent marker.

"It's up to you, Marty," C. Thomas urged. "Who do you want to spend the night with?"

All three women looked uncomfortable, especially Scarlett. She continued to stare at Steve, fire in her eyes, her body rigid, every fiber seething with disdain and rage.

"Well, since I can't pick my wife—"

"That's against the rules," C. Thomas interrupted.

"It's really a tough decision." Marty made a pretense of looking at Katie, but his eyes finally settled on Scarlett. "My decision is Scarlett."

Katie exhaled a sigh of relief. Steve turned away, unable to look at Scarlett or Marty.

"We will see both of you tomorrow morning," C. Thomas said.

Marty rose to his feet and walked to the doorway. He motioned for Scarlett to do the same. Scarlett reluctantly stood up and approached him. Her movements were slow and stilted. One easily could have mistaken her for one of the walking dead. For all intents and purposes, she felt like a zombie; an unfeeling, uncaring piece of dead meat. Unfortunately, her mind still worked and she could think—about what was to come. Pun intended.

The losers, with the exception of Steve, watched in silence as Marty and Scarlett walked out the door. Steve didn't look. He couldn't. The silence continued as they heard Marty start his car and pull out of the driveway.

"Too bad we can't have consolation prizes for the losers," Erin said, breaking the silence and trying to make light of the situation. She turned to Katie. "Will you lend me Steve for the night?"

"That's against the rules," C. Thomas interjected as if Erin had been serious.

"So now what do we do?" Steve asked, trying to hide his anger over the outcome. "Play poker all night?" He began collecting the cards.

"I'm beat," C. Thomas said. "I'm going home and crashing." He stood up and walked to the door.

"This doesn't bother you at all?" Steve asked, disconcerted by C. Thomas's apparent lack of concern.

C. Thomas stopped then turned to face him. "We are all consenting adults, Steve-O. We all agreed to this. 'All-in,' right?"

"I guess," Steve said. "But we didn't know how it would turn out."

"We still don't. The only thing that bothers me is that I didn't win. Good night, everyone."

C. Thomas headed for the door leaving the others staring blankly in his wake.

"What a weird guy," Steve finally said after the front door closed behind C. Thomas.

"He's right, Steve," Katie said. "We agreed to this. It could have been any one of us. That is, any *two* of us."

"That's true, Katie," Erin nodded. "We have no one to blame but ourselves. We all went into this thing with our eyes wide open."

Katie turned to Erin. "Why don't you stay here tonight? I can't give you Steve, but I can give you the spare room and company. We can stay up and watch the classics. I can tell my girls to just crash at your place with the twins. They don't have camp tomorrow."

"Thanks, Katie, but I really should get home. I'm sure the twins have worn them out. Besides, C. Thomas isn't worried about Scarlett. Why should I be worried about Marty? Anyway, I think my husband's bark is worse than his bite. For all his bravado, I bet he ends up watching television all night."

Steve raised an eyebrow. It was obvious that Erin didn't know her husband at all.

# 10

## THE MORNING AFTER

Marty drove up in front of his house. It read six-seventeen a.m. on the dashboard clock. He contemplated closing his eyes and conking out for a while before going into the house. He was afraid if he went in now, he'd either get the third degree from Erin, or worse, risk waking the monsters. Either way, he wanted to take a nap and continue riding the sexual high he was on. As exhilarated as he was feeling about the night, he also was hungover—badly.

While he mulled over what to do, he watched as his next door neighbor's garage door went up. Greg was an avid fisherman and was heading out early to nearby Squantz Pond. He did so nearly every weekend, or so he told Marty. Marty wouldn't know, since this was an ungodly hour on a Sunday to be up if you didn't have to be. He watched Greg walk out of the garage with several rods and a large tackle box, placing them in the back of his pickup which was parked on his driveway. As he did, he caught a glimpse of Marty in his car watching him. A look of surprise was followed by a smile and a hearty wave.

Shit, I'm spotted, Marty thought. It was then that he decided he had better go in the house. It would have looked mighty strange if he was still in the car sleeping when Greg returned home. Marty opened the car door and got out, then waved back. "Pulling for walleyes or bass today?"

"Whatever takes my bait," he said as he shook a brown paper bag, surely filled with dozens of disgusting nightcrawlers.

Marty nodded, although he could have cared less.

"Late night there, Marty?" he said with a throaty chuckle. Greg was a smoker and always sounded like he'd swallowed a bullfrog.

"Yeah, something like that. Well, good luck." Now Marty just wanted to get inside. He certainly was not up for chit chat this time of the morning, and he didn't like Greg much anyway. He closed the car door and headed for the house.

Marty was careful not to let his keys jingle as he approached the door. Knowing Erin, she could be sleeping on the couch in the living room and since having the boys, she was a very light sleeper. He slid the key in carefully and turned the lock. The door creaked a bit when he opened it. Damn! He kept meaning to oil it. He stepped in and closed it quickly as if it wouldn't creak again, which it did.

Marty paused a minute to listen for any signs of life. Satisfied that everyone must be asleep, he kicked off his Topsiders, leaving them on the mat by the door and then gently laid his keys on the entryway table. As he walked past the living room, he could see Erin curled up on the couch under a throw blanket with the table lamp still on beside her. Was she planning to ambush him when he got home? He quietly rushed past and headed for the kitchen, unbuttoning his shirt as he went. He slipped off the polo and turned it around so that he could inspect it. Scarlett really did a number on this! he thought triumphantly. It looked as if it had claw marks up and down the back of it. Like another notch on his bedpost, he considered keeping the tattered garment as a souvenir, but instead thought better of it and shoved it as far down in the garbage can as he could. How could he explain that to Erin?

Marty, now shirtless, hurried upstairs to the master bathroom. With Erin on the couch, he was relieved he'd be able to shower and change quickly, then jump into bed without interrogation. He stood with his back to the mirror, craning his neck so that he could see the marks Scarlett had made. He smiled. What a tiger she had been! He turned on the water and unbuttoned his shorts, letting them drop to his ankles then lifted the toilet seat.

"You're home."

Marty spun around to see Erin standing in the doorway, and as he did, he sprayed urine on the floor like a child with bad aim.

"You scared the shit out of me!"

"Sorry," Erin began. "I thought you might be home early. I waited up for you as long as I could. So how was everything?"

"Can I finish taking a piss?" Even though he'd had to struggle to stop mid-stream, he remained facing her so that she wouldn't see his back.

"I can't ask how it was?"

"Fine. It was fine. *Now* can I finish? I need to take a shower."

"Was it—" she started again.

Marty interrupted. "No more questions, Erin. We all talked about this. You know the rules!" He was annoyed. He was always annoyed.

"I know. I'm sorry. Do you want some breakfast when you're done? Before the boys get up?"

"Yeah. Yeah. Fine." He lied. He'd be sawing wood before she'd even have the bacon fried. He'd just eat it later if he was in the mood.

Erin closed the door behind her and headed to the kitchen. Halfway down the hall, she stopped and leaned against the wall. She had her head in her hands. She was shocked. When she first went into the bathroom, she'd seen the scratches up and down Marty's back. She'd also noticed his shorts in the bathroom, but no shirt. She was afraid to ask what happened to it or to him. Maybe it wasn't that she was afraid to ask but because she already knew.

---

MARTY HAD DRIVEN Scarlett home and after she said a weak good bye and closed the passenger side door, she took the walkway steps two at a time. Some gentleman, she thought. He didn't even come around to open the door for her. She was clutching her shoes in one hand and with the other, holding a blanket around her that she'd taken from the cabin. It already was at least seventy-five degrees outside, but she felt chilled to the bone. Home never looked so good.

The front door was unlocked. Scarlett figured it would be and she was grateful. She didn't have her keys since she and C. Thomas had driven together to the game the night before. She was too damn tired to have to walk around to the patio to fish the spare house key out of the muddy planter by the backdoor. As expected, when she got inside, the house was lit up like a ballpark, and C. Thomas was at the kitchen table, butt naked, perusing the sports section of the local Sunday paper. It was the only section he ever read. In truth, he only scanned for game scores and player trash talk.

"You're home!" he nearly yelled. Scarlett sensed he was far too excited. She didn't want this to become more fodder for his fantasies. She couldn't take that.

"Without breaking any rules," he continued, "how was it?"

"A little rough."

"Oh, poor baby, just the way you like it!" he chortled.

"Um. Yeah. Sure. He's a little too needy," Scarlett felt compelled to explain. She wasn't up for being jabbed.

"You want breakfast?" C. Thomas asked as he held up a bag of preservative-laden grocery store powdered mini donuts. *His* idea of breakfast. Those things would last through a zombie apocalypse.

"Uh, no thanks." Scarlett couldn't think of a snarky comeback although she wanted to make a dig about the donuts. Her head was pounding. "I'm beat. I'm going to go lie down."

"M'kay," he responded, already with his nose back in the paper.

Scarlett was tired, but she was wired at the same time. She hurried out of the kitchen and started up the stairs to the master bedroom. She hoped that C. Thomas wouldn't follow her. She just wanted to be alone. She knew she had no right to complain. She'd wanted everyone to go for his proposal to fire up the lame poker games, but now she felt violated. In truth, she'd rather have spent the night with just about anyone on the planet than with Marty.

Halfway up the stairs, Scarlett turned back down and went into the living room. She found her journal under the couch cushion and hugged it to her chest then headed back upstairs to the bedroom and closed the door. Not that it would keep C. Thomas out, but she wanted to, *needed* to feel safe. This was her only space. She set the journal down on her nightstand then went over to the bureau. She fumbled around in a drawer for a pair of comfy sweats and an old long-sleeved shirt from her high school cross country days then headed for the shower—she had to scour away Marty's filth.

She stood motionless under the hot water a long time. Her headache was getting worse by the minute. Finally she soaped up, aggressively scrubbing every inch of her skin as hard as she could. She turned off the water and grabbed a towel, wrapping it tightly around her as she fell into a crumpled heap on the bathroom floor. After a time she dragged herself up and reached for the shirt and sweats, attempting to avoid her reflection in the foggy mirror. When she caught sight of the marks on her breasts and wrists she quickly looked away.

Scarlett climbed into the center of the bed and pulled the covers up all around her, then reached for her journal, taking out the pen and finding a clean page she began:

*Dear Diary:*

*What a hellish night. But I guess you get what you ask for. I wanted C. Thomas's proposal to be a go. I wished on stars and even prayed for it. I did NOT ask for that pig Marty to maul me, and he did – MAUL ME! I feel completely and totally violated.*

*I admit at first I was doing my usual cock-tease stuff. That ass drinks so much, I thought maybe he wouldn't even be able to do the job, but reality hit me like a ton of bricks when that bastard slobbered all over me and grabbed me like a common whore. Thank God C. Thomas had the sense to stock the bar at the cabin. I think the only thing that saved me was getting him to down two doubles of Jack Daniels after we got there. That on top of what he drank during the game only gave him enough stamina for about ten minutes and it was over.*

*I have bruises and bite marks on my breasts. He was holding my wrists so tight that I have bruises there, too. I had to literally claw my way out from under him just to stop him from doing worse. I think I drew blood, multiple times. The sad part was, I think he liked it. Poor Erin, how does she STAND HIM??*

*I only had to deal with one, torturous poke, and he crashed for the rest of the night. I made him wear a condom. Dick thought he was getting me without it. Then he was fumbling so much to get it in, and I was dry as hell—I've never been dry. That speaks volumes, doesn't it? At one point, he had his hands around my throat. What do they call that shit? Autoerotic asphyxiation? Yeah, real sexy. I was screaming for a full thirty seconds before he got the hint. He was so excited though, he pumped harder and harder. Then it was done. He fell asleep on top of me, and I was afraid to move for fear he'd wake up and want round two. He finally moved off and I got up and slept on the couch. When he woke up the asshole was hugging a pillow and thought we slept together all night.*

*This must be what prostitutes feel like, but I am a grown-up and put myself there, didn't I? Thank you, dear therapist. See, I'm taking responsibility for my actions.*

*I've got to win this fucking game. How did Marty, the biggest loser of all time, manage to win last night anyway?! Well, if he can, I surely can! I won't ever be in that position again!! The only time I want to find myself back in that cabin again is with Steve. Save me, Steve.*

---

IT WAS NINE A.M. Steve was sitting at the kitchen table with a cup of coffee and *The New York Times*. No one except for Katie knew, but he rarely read anything more than the Book Review and the Art and Leisure sections. He'd become more conservative over the years, and the liberal slant of *The Times* was of little interest to him anymore. When he and Katie first were married, they used to sit in bed, paper splayed out all over the comforter, and he'd read it cover to cover. Katie usually ended up with the crossword that the two eventually would work on together, going back and forth to get through the tougher questions. It was like a game to see if they could finish it. How times had changed.

Steve was staring off into space, holding the cup close to his lips, but not drinking. Katie walked into the kitchen and stopped short. "Steve, are you okay?"

"Huh?" She'd startled him. He spilled coffee on his leg, just missing his shorts. He reached for a napkin.

"What's wrong?"

"Nothing. Just thinking."

"You're thinking that it could have been you."

He twisted uncomfortably in his seat. God, how is Katie always right? "What are you talking about?" he asked softly, setting down his coffee mug. It was ironic that he'd been using the one he'd gotten from last year's office Christmas party. It read: "I see guilty people."

"You know what I'm talking about. You threw the game last night. I know it. *Everyone* knows it."

Steve's cell phone buzzed from the counter where it was charging. He was saved from immediately having to answer Katie's queries. She could be relentless. He checked the display. There was a text message from Marty. He unlocked the screen and read in all caps:

*MEET ME AT THE SQUARE ASAP!*

"Anything up?" Katie asked.

"Just my associate checking in."

"On Sunday? He's not on a beach somewhere?"

"Not this weekend." Steve stood up. "I'm in the mood for bagels this morning. Be right back."

As he was about to leave, Jamie and Anna both walked into the kitchen, groggy with sleep. Jamie climbed up onto a stool at the center island, and Anna sat at the table next to where Steve stood. She crossed her arms on the table and set her head down on them as if to sleep.

"Morning, Ladies. You're up early."

No answer.

"You look like the boys must have given you a rough time last night." Steve knew how difficult Erin and Marty's boys were. It was why they usually lost babysitter after babysitter; Jamie and Anna had little choice, but it necessitated hiring the two of them, tag-team style.

Neither of the girls answered him. Teenagers, he thought. He remembered when they'd been Daddy's girls. Now seventeen and fifteen, they looked at him like some kind of alien with three heads just about every time he spoke. Or they pretended he wasn't there at all. That is, unless they wanted something from him.

"Mom, can I take the Jeep and pick up Gabby to go to the mall?" Jamie asked.

"You said you'd take me, too," Anna said into her folded arms.

"Why can't you take your car?" Katie asked.

"Gas, Mom. I don't get paid 'til next week."

"Um, but you're going *shopping* at the mall?" Katie laughed. "I guess so. But it's a beautiful day. I thought you were going to hang out at the pool."

"There's a sale at Hollister and I need a new bikini. Plus I need to pick up my schedule." In addition to the part-time summer camp counselor position, Jamie had been working at American Eagle since she turned sixteen. It was where most of her paychecks went. "We'll be right back after the mall. Anyway, you owe me after last night!"

"God, they were *horrible*! My head is still pounding," Anna grumbled, still with her head on the table. "What is *wrong* with those kids? Did Marty drop them on their heads when they were babies?"

"Okay, okay," Katie acquiesced. "But if I catch you texting while you're driving again, Jamie, that's the last time you use my car or *any* car this summer."

Anna perked up and lifted her head. The girls looked at each other and rolled their eyes. They both rose and began walking out of the kitchen. Anna stopped abruptly and turned to Steve with her hand out, obviously expecting money to be deposited in it.

"You heard your mother, right?" he called to Jamie as she trudged down the hall. Turning to Anna he gave her a quizzical look. These girls made his head spin. Jamie didn't answer and Anna still stood there.

"Money?" she said. When Steve didn't immediately reply, she clarified, "Um, I don't *work*. They don't *pay* the junior counselors."

"Yes, but you babysat," Steve said.

"That's hardly enough. Plus Jamie and I have to split what we get between us," Anna pleaded.

Steve pulled out his wallet and handed her two twenties. Anna kept her hand out. He shook his head and gave her two more. "That's it." Anna smiled and folded the bills as she skipped out of the kitchen.

"All righty then." Steve gave Katie a look of defeat. "My pocket is a bit lighter now but I guess I still have enough for bagels."

Katie didn't respond. She was making a fresh pot of coffee after dumping out the pot Steve had made. She liked it stronger than he did so she usually tried to get to the kitchen before he could start the machine. He had been restless this morning and was up earlier than usual.

Steve grabbed his keys and walked out the door toward his car. Katie went to the living room window and watched as Steve pulled out of the driveway. She shook her head. The phone rang and she returned to the kitchen. It was Erin on the caller ID. She reached for the phone and answered. "Hello?"

"Hey, Katie. It's me. Is Steve there?"

"No. He just ran out for some bagels."

"Hmm. Marty just left, too. Errands, he said. Such bull. He *never* runs errands."

"Hmm," Katie responded. "The two of them are quite the pair."

"Meet me at the corner in five," Erin said and hung up.

Katie returned the phone to the charging base. She called down the hallway to the girls, "I'm running down to the corner to talk to Erin for a sec."

"Okay," someone responded, she wasn't sure if it was Jamie or Anna. She heard the shower going, too. It was nice having older kids who were self-sufficient most of the time, but she also missed their little girl ways and the feeling of being needed.

Katie slid into a pair of sandals and headed out the front door. She walked the half-block to the corner, mid-distance to Erin and Marty's house. Erin already was there, leaning against the stop sign.

"What's going on?" she said as she approached Erin.

"I think he *did* it! I think he had *sex* with *Scarlett*!"

"Did he say anything?"

"Of course not. Are you kidding? Marty? Mr. Covert Activity Marty? Pffttt!" Erin was upset. "Anyway, I could tell. He got home early. I caught him tiptoeing through the house like a cat burglar, trying not to wake anyone."

"That doesn't mean he did anything."

"I walked in on him in the bathroom. His back was all scratched up!"

Katie was shocked. "Scratches? Really!?" she screeched.

"I mean, he couldn't have made those scratches himself!"

"Wow, I'm stunned."

"So am I." Erin looked distraught.

"Well, we knew this could happen when we all agreed to play the game." She wasn't making Erin feel any better. "Does it really bother you?"

"I'm not sure. On the one hand, I feel jealous and pissed. Really pissed," she said. Then her face softened and one corner of her mouth turned up into something of a smirk. "But on the other, I'm *horny* thinking about him with another woman. I don't know what came over me, but it took all I had not to jump him in the shower this morning!"

"Maybe you should have," Katie said with a laugh.

"I actually was afraid we might wake up the kids. No, that's a lie. The real reason is because I was afraid he wouldn't be up for it, that he wouldn't want me after being with *her*."

Katie nodded, knowingly. She'd wondered about that herself had Steve been the winner and spent the night with Scarlett. "So what are you going to do?"

"Ha! I'm going to get revenge! I'm taking poker lessons! I've been trying to find somewhere to go. Want to take them with me?"

Katie weakly shook her head.

Erin pulled out her cell phone and looked at the time. "I have to get back. The boys can't be trusted being alone and I've been gone too long as it is. I have to make breakfast. Plus, Marty will probably be home any minute."

"Okay."

"I'm really serious about the poker lessons. I think you should take them with me. What do you say?"

Erin is far too excited about this, Katie thought to herself. "I'll think about it. Let me know what you find out." She paused a second, then asked, "Just wondering. If you win, who would you pick?"

Erin responded too quickly. "C. Thomas, of course." She saw Katie grimace, but wasn't sure why. "C'mon. Same as you, right? Nothing against Steve, but I'd love to know how it feels to be with a younger man."

"I hear that."

"And, it would be too weird between us, don't you think? Choosing each other's husbands?"

Katie couldn't tell her the truth, but the idea of being with Marty was just too repulsive to consider. Anyway, C. Thomas was so damn hot and while she wasn't exactly a cougar (was she?) it would be a thrill to be with someone that much younger.

"Yeah. Definitely," she said. Dodged that bullet.

---

STEVE PULLED up in front of the luncheonette in the small shopping center in the town square. It was a hopping place for the local yokels and usually extra busy on weekend mornings. It was a good place to talk. From the window, Steve could see Marty already was sitting in a booth, drinking a cup of coffee. He waved when he saw Steve get out of the car. Steve pulled open the door of the restaurant and headed for the table.

"What's up?" he asked as he slid in across from Marty.

"It was incredible. *Fucking incredible!*" he nearly yelled.

"Shh!" Steve said. Even though it was loud, Marty was louder. This town was well-known for its thriving gossip mill. "I hope you didn't bring me all the way down here to brag about the gory details."

"Don't you want to know?" Marty sneered. Was he gloating? "It could have been *you*, you know!"

"What about the game rules?" Steve knew rules were meant to be broken. After all, he was a lawyer.

"Screw the rules! This is just between you and me. It was—hands down—the best sex I've *ever* had!"

Steve shook his head. He wished Marty just would shut the hell up. He knew he wouldn't be able to keep listening to him go on about Scarlett. It was then that the waitress came by the table with a full pot of coffee in her hand and asked Steve if he wanted some. She was about fifty and had a pleasant smile. Steve was worried she might have heard their conversation.

"Yes, coffee, thanks." She filled the empty cup sitting on the paper placemat in front of him.

Marty turned to watch her walk away. As soon as she was out of earshot, he continued. "I have *scratch marks* all up and down my back! She's a wildcat! She likes it very rough—if you know what I mean!" Marty turned in his seat and reached to lift up his T-shirt. "I'll show you!"

"Not here!" Steve hissed. He was doing the best he could to tolerate Marty's blathering. "What did Erin say?" It was a weak attempt at changing the subject.

"Not a word. Well, she did try to ask, but I cut her off. What could she say? We all agreed."

"I don't know, Marty." Steve was tearing at the corners of his placemat.

"What don't you know? Why are you always such a downer?"

"I'm a realist. Besides, once you let the genie out of the bottle, there's no putting her back."

"Who would want to put her back?! I can't wait until we play cards again."

Steve shook his head. "Can we just stop?"

"What do you think I called you here for? I *need* to talk about this. I wanted this. I wanted her. *Bad!* And I want more. So does Scarlett."

"What do you mean, so does Scarlett?"

"I told you. She was all over me. She loved every minute of it."

"How could you tell?"

"C'mon. A man knows! We went for God, I can't even remember. Three, four rounds. Maybe more. That's why I am so exhausted. Look at me." He tugged at his eyes.

"You look fine, Marty."

"I even offered to use a condom but she wouldn't let me."

"Wow. I hope she is on the pill." Was Marty for real? Steve was getting edgy. He was downright sick imagining Marty with Scarlett. The idea that she also enjoyed it upset him. He hoped it wasn't obvious. Then again, Marty was so into himself, Steve was certain he wouldn't notice a thing.

"Of course she is. At least I think…" Marty trailed off. He had a strange expression on his face then. Steve couldn't put his finger on it.

"Really, Marty, enough. There was a no-kiss-and-tell rule for a reason."

"Steve, you're being ridiculous. I already said it's just you and me here. I would want to know when it's your turn." He lied. If he had his way, it would not ever be Steve's turn, at least not with Scarlett.

Steve's cell phone buzzed on the table in front of him. He glanced down and saw it was a text from Katie, but he didn't open it. He lowered his head to the table and banged his forehead against it several times. When he looked back up, the waitress had arrived to refill their coffee cups again. He smiled meekly at her.

"Are you gentlemen ready to order?" she asked, holding up her pad and pen.

"Yes, I'm starved!" Marty said emphatically.

He picked up the menu and put it down almost immediately. "Give me the deluxe breakfast with three eggs over easy and double bacon. Hash browns and white toast with extra butter. Oh, and a corn muffin, too. With butter." He looked over at Steve and said, "I really worked up an appetite!"

"Very healthy," Steve said condescendingly as he shook his head at him. He'd have called him an asshole if the waitress hadn't been standing there.

The waitress turned to Steve. "And for you?"

"Nothing else for me, thank you." The waitress nodded and left to place Marty's order.

"What the hell, Steve?"

"Look, I told Katie I was going for bagels. I'm going to need to come back with something and actually have breakfast with her, or she'll wonder what I was doing all this time."

Marty shrugged and shook his head. "Well, I'm telling you, you wouldn't believe *where* we did it and *how* we did it. I mean, that girl can bend herself into a pretzel. We barely made it in the front door. We were on the floor. She was on top. Then we were up against the wall. We even ended up in the shower. And what a mouth—those teeth left marks on my—"

Steve cut him off. "Jesus Christ, Marty. You sound like you're in a damn high school locker room. Could you keep your voice down? I think that is my next door neighbor behind you!" It was. It was Hal Perkins. He was something of an oddball, always outside, always looking into Steve's yard. Nosey. God only knew what he'd heard of their conversation.

"Whatever, Steve. When did you become such a stuffed shirt? I thought you'd eat this shit up. You could be next, you know."

"Yeah, well. I'm not so sure this whole thing was such a good idea."

"Of course it was. Are you jealous? Is that what this is about?"

"You're incorrigible, Marty." He downed the last dregs of his coffee and stood to leave. "Look, I have to go. Katie already texted me."

"You're just going to leave me? I haven't even gotten my breakfast yet."

"You're a big boy, Marty."

Just then the waitress arrived with Marty's plate and the coffee pot. She looked at Steve and motioned toward his cup. "Another refill?"

"No, thanks. I'm leaving." He pulled a five out of his wallet and handed it to her. "Have a nice day."

"Thank you, sir. You, too." She poured more coffee into Marty's cup. "Enjoy your meal." She turned to leave.

"Sorry, Marty. Maybe I'm just tired. I did toss back a few last night."

"Sure, Steve."

"I gotta run. I have to make it next door to the bakery before they're out of bagels. Otherwise I'll end up at Dunkin'. Katie will be furious. She hates the bagels from there."

"No prob, Steve," Marty said through a mouthful of potatoes. He didn't look up.

Steve knew Marty was annoyed, but he didn't care. This was a shitty morning and he just wanted to get home. On top of it, it was nearing ninety degrees already and he had to vacuum the pool before Jamie and Anna got back with their friends. "All right. Talk to you later."

Marty grunted then dismissed him by picking up his cell to check for messages. He actually had been hoping Scarlett might have texted him.

Steve walked out of the luncheonette, turned next door and went into the bakery. Whew, he thought, thank God they still have bagels.

## 11

## REFLECTIONS

Marty was sitting with his feet up on his desk in his office daydreaming. Again, no Sean during his office hours. He'd caught another break. For the past hour he had been trying to study more poker strategies but was having difficulty concentrating. He couldn't get Scarlett off of his mind. He was reliving their Saturday evening romp over and over like a looped video. A knock at his office door pulled him from his reverie. Since he'd only had Sean and Heather in there thus far this summer, he was hopeful it would be the latter. He pulled down his feet and tossed the book into his top drawer.

"Come in."

The door opened and Heather took a tentative step across the threshold. She was holding a pink zebra-striped folder. "Hi, Professor. I hope I'm not disturbing you."

Marty straightened. "Not at all. What's up?"

Heather approached his desk with her flip-flops clacking as she walked. Even though Marty's mind was on Scarlett, he couldn't help but take in the full view of Heather's breasts, nearly bursting out of her V-neck tee shirt. He could see the straps of a bikini peeking out from around her neck. She'd obviously been out sunning on the campus green like most of the coeds who were at the college in the summer.

"I wanted to drop off a draft of my paper. I didn't want to wait until class Saturday, because I wanted time to clean it up more for you by then. I was hoping you could give me some initial thoughts."

"Sure, I'll take a look at it." He reached over his desk to take it from her. As she leaned in to pass it, he took in more of the buxom view.

"I didn't see you at the mixer Saturday night." Was she pouting?

"No. I, um, had some friends over." He had completely forgotten about the mixer, not that it would have mattered. The game would have trumped everything including a visit from the President of the United States.

"There's going to be another one in a few weeks," Heather began hesitantly, as if she was concerned about being stood up again. "Maybe you'll be able to make that one. They're a real blast. I know you'll have a good time. You can be my 'date'." She emphasized the word "date" with air quotes.

Marty was staring down at the pink folder, his fingers lightly drumming it. He was really only half-listening to Heather. Weakly, he responded, "I'll certainly try."

"Are you okay, Professor?" she asked with a fair amount of concern in her voice. She was used to his more ebullient banter. The nearly permanent smile was gone from her face as she reached out and put her hand over his. It pulled him out of his trance and he reached over with his other hand and placed it on top of hers.

"I'm sorry, Heather. Yes, I'm fine. I just have a few things on my mind today."

"Oh, I hope everything is okay."

"Nothing serious," he said, forcing a chuckle.

"Okay, then. Great. So you'll let me know what you think of my paper? You can just email me any comments." She removed her hand from between his two and took a step back from the desk. The smile had returned. "Oh, and I'll let you know about the date of that next mixer."

Marty, realizing his two hands were now one on top of the other, instead folded them together. Forcing himself not to appear so detached, he smiled back and said enthusiastically, "Yes, please do."

Heather then went bouncing out the door, which she'd left wide open. As she turned down the hall she waved at him and flashed another beaming smile. "Kay! Bye!"

Marty leaned back in his chair as it groaned beneath him. He was lost in thought again. Scarlett. Scarlett. Scarlett. He pulled his cell phone from his pocket and searched for Scarlett's number. After he pulled it up, he got up to close his office door. As he headed back to his chair, he hit SEND and listened while it rang.

Damn, he thought as the voicemail kicked in. He had rehearsed in his head a few times what he would say when she answered. He'd just assumed she would. Why wouldn't she? He hadn't thought about getting her voicemail. As the recording began, he sat down.

"Hey, Scarlett. It's me, um Marty. I, um, just wanted to let you know that I had a great…um… time Saturday night. I can't wait until the next, uh, game. Uh, give me a call on my cell." He pressed END. He was used to sounding far more literate. In his message, he sounded like an awkward adolescent. Back to being sixteen again.

He had broken out into something of a sweat. He glanced up at his clock and saw that his office hours had ended five minutes earlier. Instead of packing up for home, he leaned back in his chair again and returned to his thoughts. Home wasn't where he wanted to be.

Just then the telephone buzzed. Scarlett! Marty reached out to grab it, but realizing it was Erin, dejectedly flopped back and watched her name across the display until the call went dead. She was the last person he wanted to speak to right now. A moment later, the voicemail tone jingled. Damn, what now? Begrudgingly, Marty opened the voicemail and set it on speaker.

"Hey, Marty, I know your office hours are just about over. Did you forget what this Saturday is? I can't believe I almost did! It is the boys' birthday party! We still have so much to do. I've been on the phone all morning pulling together last-minute arrangements. Thank God I was still able to get a bouncy house on such late notice…"

Marty started packing up his bag while Erin rambled on. He suddenly had the image of a dozen or so of those monsters running around his backyard, and it made him wonder why he'd ever even had kids. Then it dawned on him that Scarlett would be there! Undoubtedly wearing less than nothing, maybe even in his pool! It was the sound of the twins' screeching in the background on the voicemail that knocked him from his reverie. He froze, unnerved, because this meant there would be no game this weekend.

"…so please stop on your way, okay? We'll figure out the rest when you get home. Love you." She always said "Love you." It wasn't exactly insincere, but it came off as casually as ending a call with good-bye or see ya. As for Marty, he never said it at all.

Damn, he'd missed whatever Erin had said in the middle of her rant and it was obvious she'd asked him to do something. Now he'd have to listen to the whole message again. Marty threw his bag over his shoulder and pulled his keys out of his pocket. Locking the office door behind him, he punched up her voicemail and walked down the hallway with the phone to his ear.

---

LIKE SHIPS PASSING in the night, C. Thomas and Scarlett were becoming more and more like roommates with opposite work schedules. There was something unsettling about living in a home with someone with whom you didn't want to even share the same breathing space. It was already Thursday and they'd hardly spoken about the previous game or any upcoming ones. It was as if they were avoiding the subject entirely. After C. Thomas had gotten home from work that afternoon, he headed out the backdoor and Scarlett out the front.

C. Thomas had gone to inspect the beginnings of their new in-ground pool. Never one for baggy swim trunks, just for the occasion, he had pulled on a pair of Hugo Boss tight black swim briefs and his Tom Ford aviator sunglasses. Quite the metrosexual, C. Thomas was a fan of manscaping, and his bulging pecs and six-pack were smooth and well-oiled.

Even though only the foundation for the pool had been poured, he wanted to put himself in the mood. He and Scarlett had chosen a custom, natural stone design with accent lighting. He walked around the whole area, hopping over wires and avoiding piles of materials. As he approached the stone steps he climbed down into the bottom of what was to become the deep-end. The foundation was cool, as the sun already had moved behind the house. He lay down in the empty pool.

While he lounged there, C. Thomas was thinking about a conversation he'd overheard at work earlier in the day. One of the women in the office was worried that her husband was cheating on her. The day before she evidently had found a receipt from a florist, and she complained to her cubicle-mate that she hadn't received any flowers, therefore he must have bought them for someone else. She was rambling on and on. In the middle of her diatribe, a delivery man walked in with flowers for her and placed them on her desk.

She'd looked like an ass, C. Thomas thought. What did it matter if he was sleeping with someone else? We have all kinds of relationships with all kinds of people. Who cares who we have sex with? It's just physical. Isn't it about who we come home to at the end of the day that's the important thing?

C. Thomas had been with a lot of women. He thought back to his first time. It was prom night. He was a sophomore, and Jessica was a senior so she had asked him. So had a few other girls, but this girl was hot, really hot. She had long blonde hair, the most stunning blue eyes, and full, round breasts. C. Thomas was an early bloomer and looked much older. He already was six-feet. This girl was petite. She'd worn four-inch stilettos just to come close enough to be able to kiss him while they danced. Her gown had a slit nearly up to the top of her thigh and he could see her shoes with every step she took.

After prom, he and Jessica went to his father's cabin, even though his parents would have grounded him for a month had they known. He knew where his father kept the spare key. They went inside with the plan to fool around first, change their clothes, then meet up with a larger group who had a few kegs and a bonfire down by the lake. C. Thomas was nervous. He knew Jessica had a reputation and he felt intimidated. They made out a long time before they got undressed. She never took off her shoes.

Jessica started out giving C. Thomas a hand job and he'd been really hard. He remembered as she got on top of him that one of her heels grazed his thigh, leaving a nasty scrape. She started to ride him, but all of a sudden, he went soft. He was humiliated. Jessica was sweet though. She climbed off and lay down next to him with her head on his chest. She'd told him they'd try again in a while but it was already one a.m. She barely got the words out when she fell asleep and that was it. They never made it to the bonfire.

But C. Thomas couldn't sleep. When Jessica rolled off of him, he climbed out of bed. He looked down at her as she lay there. She was so beautiful and still wearing nothing but her stilettos. He was hard almost right away. He backed away into the shadows of the room and jerked off. Jessica never awoke until the morning, but C. Thomas pleasured himself a few more times into the daylight hours.

Now C. Thomas had Scarlett. In fact, Scarlett and Jessica bore quite a resemblance to one another. Even though C. Thomas never dated Jessica again, they remained friends for the next few years. Whether she ever spoke of his failed execution that night, he would never know, but he still thought of her often. Scarlett, on the other hand, had been bringing up her dissatisfaction with their sex life a great deal lately and he couldn't understand why.

---

AROUND THE OTHER side of the house, Scarlett sat with her legs curled under her on the chair swing on the wrap-around porch. She had her journal beside her, but she was paging through the most recent issue of Cosmopolitan, sipping a glass of iced tea. Her cell phone had buzzed a few times with calls and text messages, but she hadn't bothered to look at the display. She just turned off the volume and continued to rock back and forth in the swing. For the first time in weeks, there was a cool breeze as the sun played hide-and-seek behind the few clouds which dotted the early evening sky, and she was enjoying the solitude.

Scarlett looked up from the magazine as her elderly neighbors walked by, hand-in-hand. She was a sap for romantic movies and always imagined someday she'd find that one perfect person to grow old with. They'd be slapping their gums together as they pushed their walkers side-by-side. She watched the couple chatting away, swinging their arms, and laughing at their own private jokes. The sun was starting to set, and the sky looked like something Monet would have created. As the two faded into the distance, she could see their silhouettes against the beautiful pastels of orange, pink, and blue.

The phone vibrated next to her yet again. She finally looked down to see who had been calling. Marty! What the hell? Didn't he remember the rules? Or could it be about something else? Maybe Erin was using his phone. Maybe it was about the next game. She clicked to answer. "Hello?"

"Finally got you! I've been leaving messages and texting you. I actually called you earlier in the week, too. Um, it's Marty, by the way."

"Yeah, sorry. I was busy. Working. So, anyway, Marty. What's up?"

"Um...I, uh, just wanted to tell you that I had a really good time Saturday night."

Scarlett wasn't sure how to respond. "Uh, I'm glad?" It came out almost like a question.

"Yeah. So, I'm really looking forward to our next, uh, card game." Scarlett could tell what he really meant was their next tryst.

"I'm looking forward to the next game, too." Scarlett rolled her eyes.

"Oh, and Scarlett, I'll be seeing you Saturday at the monsters—I mean the boys'—party, right?"

"Yeah, yeah," Scarlett said. She just wanted him off the phone. "Erin called to remind me earlier in the week."

"Great! It will be a great time. For the kids, I mean."

"Oh, Marty? Yeah, um, C. Thomas just came home. I have to run. I'll talk to you later."

"Yeah, sure," he said.

She thought she sensed a hint of annoyance in his tone. "M'kay. Bye." She hung up, put down the phone next to her on the swing, and flipped back to the page in her magazine. She shook her head. She was the one who should be annoyed. God, what had she done? Maybe it started when she'd had Marty rub her feet. She was enjoying torturing him, but in retrospect, she never should have. She had a bad feeling that she'd set something in motion that night, something that couldn't be stopped.

---

ACROSS THE STREET from Scarlett's house was a construction site for a new home. There was a bulldozer and an excavator, among other large vehicles, and loads of building materials. Scarlett had no idea that Marty had been parked there for nearly an hour. He'd driven by the house and when he spotted her on the porch swing, he pulled in behind one of the trucks. He thought—hoped—perhaps Scarlett might actually have asked him to come over. He was getting frustrated by the minute each time he called or texted and she didn't pick up or respond.

"Bitch!" he yelled as he slammed down the phone on the passenger seat. He started the car and pulled out of the graveled driveway, skidding onto the street. He drove past Scarlett as she read her magazine and sipped her iced tea, glaring at her as he went.

Steve had just finished mowing the lawn and weed whacking, and now was cleaning the pool. It was nearing 8 p.m. on Friday night, and even though it had been a long and grueling week at work, he was restless, and he was agitated. He simply didn't want to be home. Being outside the house was the next best thing. Katie would be thrilled anyway. He was doing his chores like a dutiful husband.

Since Saturday night, Steve couldn't shake the darkness that had overtaken him. To add insult to injury, Marty had called him early this morning while he was on the train to the city, going on about some encounter he'd had with Scarlett the evening before. Marty, always the violator, had called her to reignite their cabin escapades, game rules be damned. Evidently Scarlett was still hot from their big night as well, and the two came close to phone sex while Marty was in his car and Scarlett was outside on the porch swing. Marty was certain he was going to win the next game, too.

Steve wondered what he had up his sleeve.

Steve tried again and again to go over the events of last Saturday's game, wishing he could understand what had possessed him to throw it. What was worse had been the look on Scarlett's face when he lost. She looked like an innocent found guilty at sentencing. Off with your head. Fifty years in the slammer. He'd instantaneously wished he could take it back, but they all unanimously had established and agreed upon the new rules of the game. No refund, no do-overs.

Steve lamented over his entire life history of bad decisions both personal and career.

"Steve, it's late. You coming in to eat?" Katie pulled him from his rumination. She was standing at the back door, her hands on her hips.

"No," he grumbled. "Not hungry."

"What's with you? You sound like a monosyllabic caveman."

"Nothing, sorry. I'm just tired and hot." He lied.

"You sure you don't want anything to eat?" Katie pressed. "I have to run out and get to the mall before it closes. I totally forgot about the twins' birthday party tomorrow."

Steve didn't answer. He froze, standing there with the pool skimmer in his hand looking like the Tin Man in the *Wizard of Oz*. The next words out of his mouth might well have been "Oil can."

"Steve?"

No answer.

"Steve!"

"What?"

"Did you hear what I said? I have to run to the mall."

"Yes. Okay." The very last thing on earth Steve wanted to do was go to the twins' party, but knew he'd have no choice, barring the contraction of a deadly disease between then and tomorrow. "Uh, what time is the party?"

"Two to six, I think. I have to check the invitation again."

What about the game? Steve suddenly felt uneasy. How can we just mill around and make small talk when we are in the middle of all of this insanity? "Aren't we playing cards tomorrow?"

"Yes. Erin is certain the party will be over in plenty of time."

"Uh, okay." Steve felt very out of it. He needed to lie down. He put down the skimmer and walked over to one of the chaise longues. He sat for a moment.

"What are you doing, Steve?" He hadn't realized Katie still was standing in the doorway.

"Just taking a break."

"Okay, well I left you a plate in the microwave in case you change your mind about dinner. I'll be back in an hour."

"'Kay."

Katie sighed and closed the French doors behind her. In a few minutes, Steve heard the Jeep start up then pull out of the driveway. He was still sitting motionless on the chaise. If one good thing could come out of the party, at least he'd get to be near Scarlett. The smell of her. Her very presence. He just hoped that she and Marty wouldn't be flirting. That would be intolerable. Utterly intolerable.

## 12

## MONSTER MASH

It was more than three months until Halloween, but for Marty, it had already arrived. Along with his two monsters, all he could see were trolls and ghouls and hobgoblins screeching and racing through the yard, the deck, in and out of their above-ground pool, and in and out of the house. Had it not been for the last-minute locking of his study door, they'd have been in there, too. He shook his head as he wiped the dripping sweat from his brow with the back of his hand. He reached for the rolling Coleman cooler of hot dogs and hamburgers Erin had set outside for him and begrudgingly pulled it over to the grill. He was in no rush to stand over the unbearably hot flames while the external thermometer reached into the high nineties. The sun was blazing today. He surveyed the melee and took a swig from his soda can, the one he'd surreptitiously opened, dumped out more than half of the cola, and filled to the top with vodka.

Erin had nearly threatened him within an inch of his life if he didn't help her today. The poker game had so completely consumed the two of them in these past weeks, that all of the preparations for Devin and Daniel's ninth birthday party had been pushed to the last minute, almost forgotten. Erin was already out of bed and frosting the cake while Marty was getting ready for class. As soon as he'd arrived home, he darted for the study, but right after he logged into Philanderers.com she was banging on the door.

"Get out here now!" she'd shrieked, practically knocking his diplomas from the wall.

She always got stressed at the holidays or when she was entertaining. Marty knew it, but it never prompted him to offer to lend a hand, his apathy just fueling her stress that much more. He couldn't avoid it today though, because it was for the boys. He came out of the study and she'd put him to work.

It was a quarter past two and most of the guests had arrived except for Steve and Katie, and Scarlett and C. Thomas. Katie had run to the party store to get the balloons that Marty had forgotten to order Friday. Scarlett and C. Thomas were getting bags of ice and cheese for the burgers at Stop & Shop, the things Marty had forgotten to purchase on the way home from work that morning. Erin was furious, but figured she could afford to pawn off a few little jobs on her friends in order to keep track of her husband and have him help with things at the house. She made him set out the folding chairs and tables and skim the top of the pool for leaves and bugs. Erin had vacuumed it at six-thirty a.m. after she'd vacuumed the entire house, cleaned the bathrooms, and washed the kitchen floor. Since Marty didn't get home from class until twenty past one or so, mostly everything else was done, including the tent Erin assembled in the backyard—a weak attempt to prevent her guests from getting heat stroke. Erin nearly hit the roof when Marty tried to change out of his work polo into one of his offensive poker tees proclaiming: "Poker Players do it with their own hand."

Erin was frazzled; she still was running around setting up, decorating, and putting out snacks, despite the fact there were about forty guests already at the house. A few mothers she knew from the boys' school had offered to help and were putting Batman tablecloths on the tables and watching the kids at the pool for her. Now where was Marty? He was supposed to be grilling. And where was the bouncy house?

Amid all of the other goings-on, it had finally occurred to Erin that the delivery company had not come to put up the bouncy house. They were supposed to arrive two hours before the party's start time. She called out for Marty. There was no answer. She called out again, louder. One of the children's fathers heard her and asked her if she needed a hand. She didn't remember his name, but recalled seeing him often at school as one of those fathers who attended *every* school function, did drop-offs and pick-ups at least half of the time, held down a good job, and still looked adoringly at his wife. How was that even possible?

Erin did need a hand, but it was Marty's she was looking for. He was nowhere to be found. Erin flew into the house to look up the number for the inflatable service, but just as she hit SEND, out of the front window she could see the company truck pull up outside. Despite her usual non-confrontational, wishy-washy demeanor, she went charging out to give the driver a piece of her mind. She wanted a hefty discount for the time lost—it was now almost two forty-five—and for the intrusion in the middle of the party. As she passed the study, she saw Marty in there, the door opened just a crack.

"What the hell are you doing, Marty?"

"Nothing. I just need a break for a minute."

"A break?! Are you serious? You haven't done a damn thing!"

"I worked this morning!"

"Oh, yeah. Mr. Professor. You work so damn hard. Get off that fucking computer and start those burgers!" Erin never used the f-word which made Marty do a double-take. He shut down the computer and left the study with his tail between his legs. Erin flew out the front door to ream out the inflatable man and Marty detoured into the kitchen for another fill-up of vodka. He didn't bother with another can of soda, he just filled the empty one he had all the way to the top with twelve ounces of Absolut.

Marty walked out into the backyard and stopped short. The Goddess had arrived. Wearing a flimsy, nearly see-through sundress over a bathing suit and bare feet, sandals dangling from her delicate fingertips, Scarlett was chatting with Katie; her long blonde locks bouncing around her bare shoulders. Katie was dressed in her usual conservative style, perfectly coiffed. C. Thomas was around the corner filling up the empty coolers with the ice, and Steve was tying balloons to the poles of the tent. Marty darted over to Steve, spilling vodka down the front of his shirt as he nearly tripped over a boisterous and screaming eight-year-old. "Where the holy hell are the parents?" he grumbled under his breath.

After he recovered, he looked over at Steve then at Scarlett. "Steve! Holy Christ! Do you see her?"

"Yes, of course, Marty. We all walked in together."

"I don't think I can handle this today. I'm going to blow my wad."

"Listen, Marty. This is your sons' birthday party. Get a hold of yourself."

Scarlett noticed the two men staring at her. She glanced at Steve with what he thought was a sly smile. She turned away quickly, however, and resumed her conversation with Katie. She couldn't shake the uneasy feeling that Marty was gawking at her like a dog slobbering over a piece of raw meat. She excused herself from Katie and walked over to help C. Thomas. In an uncharacteristic public display of affection, she leaned over, kissed him on the cheek, and put a hand on his hip, reaching down to help him shake the remaining ice out of a bag. He responded with a playful slap on her ass. Though not exactly what she was hoping for, it was enough to make Marty look away.

"Oh, my God! Did you see that?" Marty nearly screeched at Steve.

"What?" Steve had been tying the balloons and actually hadn't noticed the exchange between Scarlett and C. Thomas. He was struggling to tie three balloons while holding on to the larger bunch. "Can you hold these?" He extended the majority of the balloons to Marty, who just ignored him.

"Steve! I have to do something!"

"Marty, what the hell are you talking about? You and Scarlett—that was part of a *game*. Not real life! Don't you get it? Scarlett is with C. Thomas. *With C. Thomas!* You are with *Erin*, and you are at your *sons' party!*"

Completely disregarding Steve's admonition, Marty took a huge swig of the vodka and charged over to Scarlett and C. Thomas. Before he approached them, he took a final swig, emptying the can. He tossed it on the ground.

"Scarlett, may I speak with you for a moment?"

Scarlett looked up at Marty, then at C. Thomas. She pleaded with her eyes to C. Thomas, hoping he'd understand that she was in distress. She did not want to be alone with Marty at all today. She'd told C. Thomas in the car on the way. Marty had texted her at least a dozen times already this morning. Suddenly she was relieved when she spotted Erin from across the lawn, piling the packages of hot dogs and hamburgers from the cooler onto the side tray of the grill. "I'm sorry, Marty, but Erin asked for my help," she lied.

"Scarlett…" Marty began as Scarlett nearly sprinted over to Erin. He stood in front of C. Thomas who had just finished emptying the last of the ice bags and was holding six very wet and dripping pieces of plastic.

"Where's the garbage, Marty?" C. Thomas asked.

"Uh, over there," Marty pointed toward the back door at the big black can. "I need a drink. Join me?"

"Sure, but isn't this is a kids' party? You have booze?"

"Ha! I always have booze. Come with me." C. Thomas followed Marty into the house.

Thick as shit, this guy is, Marty thought, and he doesn't have a clue what I am going to do to his girlfriend when I win the game tonight!

When Scarlett approached Erin she could see she was flushed from the heat of the grill and the soaring temperatures outside. Even her eyes were watering. Or was it tears?

"Erin, are you okay? Can I help?"

Erin looked at Scarlett and wiped her eyes with the dishrag she had draped over her shoulder. "Thanks, Scarlett. I'm fine."

Scarlett could now see that she had in fact been crying. "What can I do?"

"I think you've done enough!" Erin snapped. She hadn't meant to. Scarlett just stood there, frozen.

"Erin, um…" she stammered.

"Oh, my God, Scarlett. I'm so sorry. I didn't mean it." Erin reached over to hug Scarlett. She was a pile of perspiration.

"Listen, Erin. Why don't you go take a break? Go inside and cool off a bit and clean up. I'll take care of this." She motioned toward the grill.

Erin's face softened. She looked at Scarlett and immediately felt horrible for what she'd said. Scarlett was her friend, and they'd all gone into the game with their eyes wide open. But Marty had become so goddamn awful since the night with Scarlett. And those scratches! Or maybe he'd always been awful. It just seemed that lately things really had become worse. He seemed more difficult than ever, and if it was possible, more covert.

"Thank you, Scarlett. I am a mess. You look beautiful, though." Erin gave Scarlett a half smile and handed her the spatula. "I really appreciate it."

"No problem, Erin." Scarlett took the spatula and set it next to the grill as Erin headed for the house. She had just begun opening the packages of hotdogs and burgers and putting them on the grill when she felt someone come up behind her; she shuddered. It had to be Marty. As she spun around to face him, she said, "Leave me alone, Marty!"

Scarlett was shocked. It was Steve.

"Huh?" he said.

"Oh, thank God it's you!"

"Um, okay." Steve was confused.

"That pig just won't leave me alone," Scarlett was distraught.

"Scarlett, I have no idea what you're talking about."

"I cannot begin to tell you. Marty isn't even a pig. He's an oozing pimple on a pig's ass. He makes me sick when I even think about him!"

"I thought. Um, I thought..." Steve stammered.

"Look, I don't know what you thought—wait a minute! What has he been telling you?" It dawned on Scarlett that Marty may have been lying about their night at the cabin. She had a frantic look in her eyes.

"Well, to begin with, he said things went mighty, um, *well* the other night at the cabin."

"Are you fucking kidding me?!"

"No, I'm not. In fact, he said you are just as interested as he is in keeping things going between you."

"There is *nothing* between us! I was so sick to my stomach at even the thought of having to go with him that *one* time! He has been harassing me ever since!"

Steve reached out and put a hand on Scarlett's petite shoulder. She turned her face toward it. He then moved his hand to caress her cheek, and she sank into it. "Scarlett, I'm so sorry. I didn't know. Have you told C. Thomas?"

"That's a joke. He thinks this whole thing is a thrill. He gets off on it." She paused a moment. "I do think he gets it though that Marty is after me. That he's not following the rules. But he is so thick, he hasn't done anything to help. I have no clue where he even is right now."

Both Scarlett and Steve looked around the yard for C. Thomas. Steve hadn't seen much of Katie since they'd arrived, either. They froze when they saw Katie standing only a few yards away. It registered that she must have seen their whole exchange; she was watching them, fixated.

"Uh-oh. I better go talk to Katie," Steve said.

"Shit! And double shit!" Scarlett said both about Katie as well as the fact that some of burgers were burning as the flames lapped up fiercely, grease dripping into them.

Steve crossed the lawn. Katie stood alone with her arms crossed. She looked pissed.

"What's up?" Steve asked in a lame attempt to sound casual. He was unsuccessful.

"What's up? What's up you ask me? Bullshit!"

"Listen, Scarlett just told me that Marty has been harassing her since last weekend. And I know he has been. He's told me. But he made it seem like it was mutual."

"Well, that isn't your problem, is it, Steve? Scarlett's a big girl. She has C. Thomas. She doesn't need you."

"Look, all I'm saying is that she was telling me what's been going on. I know it's not my business." He reached over and put a hand on Katie's still-crossed arms. She flung it off, arms folded more tightly against her chest.

"Katie," he began, his tone calm and soft. "I knew this whole thing was a bad idea. I said it from the beginning."

"Oh, no! No, you don't! You can stop this right now, Steve. You're not pulling the plug on this! You're not ruining it for everyone. *Poor Scarlett!*" she said mockingly. "She went into this the same way we all did. I'm sure she can handle Marty. Anyway, I have plans to win this thing!"

"What the hell is that supposed to mean?"

"Forget it. Just stay away from that woman. We are here for the boys and for Erin anyway. In fact, I'm sure she needs help. Let's go find her. You're coming with me." She reached down for his hand and practically dragged him across the backyard into the house.

Katie's head was spinning. She was going to tell Erin to schedule the poker lessons. She was fighting fire with fire now. This may just be a game, but she could play, too. Katie and Steve got into the house to find Erin on her way back from the bedroom, walking into the kitchen. She'd freshened up and changed her dowdy blouse to a loose, but flattering tank top. She'd pulled her hair back into a ponytail and actually had a smile on her face.

"Hey, guys," she said when she saw them.

"The troops are here. Do you need any help?" Katie asked.

"Sure." With the efficiency of a factory worker on an assembly line, she opened the refrigerator and started pulling out dish after dish covered in plastic wrap and placed them side-by-side on the kitchen table. She pulled out a watermelon boat with the Batman logo carved into the side of it. She opened the pantry and picked up a half dozen unopened multi-packs of juice boxes and plopped them on the table next to the food. She turned around, headed into the dining room and came back with a huge box filled with countless hand-decorated Batman-themed goody bags, placing them on the table as well. Lastly, she went back to the dining room for the birthday cake, returning with a massive frosting and fondant-laden Batmobile. She stood there, cake in hand and announced, "Okay, let's do this!"

"Oh, my God, Erin! How did you do all of this?" Katie was flabbergasted. The supreme hostess, even she was impressed.

"Ha! Call it therapy! I'm exhausted though. I went to bed at two and was up at four-thirty. I couldn't sleep because I had so much on my mind. I had all this to do and Marty has been such a dick."

"Where do you want everything?" Steve asked, the cartons of juice boxes already stacked in his arms. Now that there was room on the table, Erin set down the cake.

"I'm going to leave the cake inside so it doesn't melt in the heat. You can put those in the coolers with the ice, Steve. Just separate it from the soda. I don't want the kids with any more sugar than is necessary." Erin said. "Thanks."

Steve headed out the door. As soon as he was out of earshot, Katie nearly shouted, "I'm in!"

"You're in?" Erin asked.

"The tutoring. Poker. I'm in."

Erin laughed. "I had no idea what you meant! If you don't mind, let's talk about it a little later? I have to get this shit outside before those creepy kids out there bust down the walls." She felt bad. She sounded a little like Marty. "But what made you decide?"

"Scarlett."

"Huh?"

"I don't know if both of our husbands have the hots for her or what, but all I know is that I've gotta win this. I'm going to see to it that I have a damn good time of my own!"

"Ahhh. I see." Erin nodded as she picked up the huge bowls of macaroni salad and potato salad, one in each arm.

"It's high time I take my life in my own hands. I love Steve, but for Christ's sake, I've been the Stepford wife for too damn long." Katie picked up the watermelon boat.

"Well, then. Here's to us!" Erin exclaimed, clinking a bowl lightly against the watermelon.

"Yes!" she said, teetering from the weight of the massive fruit. "Oh, my God. I don't want to drop this! It's beautiful."

Steve was heading back in for more and held the door as the two women walked outside. Katie kissed Steve on the cheek as she passed. He was taken aback at first but regrouped and trudged outside with another arm's load of party goods.

---

ERIN HAD JUST FINISHED CLEANING up all of the juice boxes, soda cans, cups, and discarded plates, many filled with half-eaten burgers and salads, and tossed it all into the garbage pail that Marty had been pulling along behind her. She'd had to drag him over to help. He was so drunk it was sickening. Thank God he had spent the last hour under the tent rambling on to C. Thomas so none of the other guests really noticed. She'd figured the two of them had to have been drinking when they kept going in and out of the house with soda cans that never left their hands. Marty rarely ever drank soda.

"Change the garbage bag before you put that back over by the door, please," she said, nodding toward the overflowing pail as she headed back to the table where she had been sitting. She had spent most of the afternoon chatting with some of the mothers from Devin and Daniel's classes. She knew nearly all of the parents and kids since the school district insisted the twins be in separate classrooms after kindergarten. It was impossible not to invite a cast of thousands to the boys' parties without offending anyone living in such a small town. But the twins loved tearing through their presents, and they had received loads of them. Between that and with all of their gift cards, they'd own Toys 'R' Us before they were done. She had no idea where they were going to put it all.

Katie and Steve had been standing by the fence talking and laughing for a long while. Erin noticed how close they'd looked. Really cozy; in fact, they hardly socialized with anyone after they finished helping her set up. She felt a pang of jealousy. Katie seemed to be handling the whole game thing really well. Better than she was. Maybe she was wrong about Marty. Maybe Marty was just being *Marty*. It could have had nothing to do with his night with Scarlett. She considered that if the idea of spicing up the game was working to spice up Steve and Katie's relationship, there still could be hope for her and Marty.

Scarlett, on the other hand, was in the pool with the kids. She looked like a big kid herself, with three little girls hanging on her; one around her neck and two she was pushing on a floating raft. She was wearing a pink bandeau bikini with ruffles; a little more covered up than the ones Erin had seen her wear before. One of the girls had put a plastic tiara from a goody bag on Scarlett's head. She looked like a princess, a princess with big boobs that is.

"Who does Aidan have for a teacher next year?" Erin asked mom number one, who was sitting across from her.

"Mrs. Berger. What about your boys?"

"Devin has Mrs. Simmons and Daniel has Mr. Roberts. I wish they both had male teachers. They could use the discipline!"

Mom number two laughed. "Don't I know it! My Dylan has Mrs. Joseph, and I think that is going to be a bad match! She's just too easy with the kids and they run slipshod over her."

Mom number three chimed in. "Well, my girls have no issues with any of the teachers. Sarah is such a good student she could have the worst teacher there and do fine. And my Chayce is off to middle school this year. I can't believe what a smart and capable young lady she's becoming!"

Erin looked at mom one and mom two and mock frowned. They mirrored her expression. Mothers like number three nauseated her. "That's great," she said neutrally. "Can you excuse me a minute? I am going to go get the cake."

When Erin approached the pool, she called out to Scarlett, "Hey, Scarlett! Would you mind rounding up the troops for birthday cake?"

"Sure!" Scarlett called out. She had been doing handstands in the water with the girls whose numbers had at least doubled since earlier. Several of the dads were standing by the pool trying to appear casual, but their tongues were practically hanging out of their mouths. It was suddenly funny to Erin.

Scarlett couldn't help who she was. She felt even worse about the way she'd snapped at her earlier.

On her way into the house, Erin spotted Katie who was leaning with her back against Steve's chest, his chin rubbing against the side of her head. "Hey, Katie. Want to come help me with the cake?"

Katie turned to Steve and planted a huge kiss on his mouth. She looked more like she was planting a flag in the name of the queen. She turned back around and walked toward Erin, shooting her a sly wink.

As the duo neared the house, Erin asked, "What's up with all that?"

"What's mine is mine. I just want to make it clear."

"Well, at least you have something worth keeping." Erin pointed toward Marty who had returned to the tent and was sitting at the table with C. Thomas. "Look at him. He's disgusting." Marty was shaking his man boobs and laughing at some private joke with C. Thomas, who was laughing so hard he spit out his drink on Marty. The two of them pounded their fists on the table.

Erin snarled as they passed the still-overflowing garbage can, tilting against the house by the backdoor. The two went inside and Erin headed for a kitchen drawer for a box of candles. She tossed them to Katie. "Can you put in ten on each side? Nine for their years and one for good luck. There are just enough."

"Sure," Katie said. She began pushing candles around the Batmobile. "This really is gorgeous, Erin. I don't know how you pulled it off."

"I did have a little help from you—and Scarlett."

"Hardly. All I did was pick up balloons. I told you I'd have done more."

Erin turned around and reached up into Marty's liquor cabinet where she kept the matches. There were two empty bottles, one Absolut and one Cuervo right in the front. Erin knew they had both been fairly new.

"Uggh," she grumbled out loud. Turning back to Katie she said, "So you really want to get poker tutoring?"

"Yes! I am glad you are ready to revisit that one. I was thinking though, what about going to Foxwoods casino? I bet we can pick up some great tips from watching some of the players there. I hear they get some pros."

"Hmm," Erin responded thoughtfully. "That might be a good idea."

Just then, Scarlett walked through the backdoor to the kitchen with a green towel around her waist. She looked like a mermaid. She was still wearing the tiara and her blonde hair was curling every which way around her shoulders and cascading down her back. "Hi, girls. What's up?"

"Oh, we were just talking about going—" Erin began.

"Going for cocktails after the party!" Katie cut in. She didn't want Scarlett joining them at Foxwoods. This was something she wanted to keep between her and Erin. Erin was no competition to Katie even though both of them wanted to sleep with C. Thomas if they won the game. For damn sure, they didn't need Scarlett getting any better at the game, then getting to choose either of their husbands. It was bad enough the guys would choose her.

"Cocktails? I thought we were playing cards?" Scarlett asked, surprised.

"Oh, well, um—I am not sure we're going to be able to play tonight," Erin said. She was not entirely lying. It was getting late, and it didn't look like anyone was itching to leave. The only people who had left were one family whose daughter had another party to attend.

"Oh." Scarlett looked disappointed.

"Well, we all can go out for a few drinks. Steve was saying in *bed* last night how he wanted to check out the new club in Danbury. He and I used to go dancing all the time—pre-kids. He's been *dying* to take me for a whirl on the dance floor." She did a little spin.

"Oh, well, maybe," Scarlett said, all of a sudden feeling a bit uncomfortable. Or was she feeling sick to her stomach? She'd caught more than just a glimpse of Katie and Steve's coziness and PDAs several times throughout the afternoon. Katie had even been feeding him strawberries with her fingers.

Erin had lit almost all of the candles on the cake. She motioned to a stack of small party plates and a box of plastic forks. "Scarlett, can you be a dear and carry those out for me? Oh, and Katie, can you grab the big carving knife? I think I'm going to need it to get through all this fondant."

Almost at the same time both women said, "Sure." Katie sauntered over to the butcher block and grabbed the knife. She twirled around again, walked past Scarlett with the knife, and headed for the door, holding it open for the other two.

"Can you start the singing ahead of me, Scarlett?" Erin asked, struggling to carry the cake. It had to weigh twenty pounds with the wooden board she had underneath it. She needed far more cake than she anticipated once she started building the thing, and it took two five-pound boxes of fondant to cover it.

After Scarlett headed out, Erin whispered to Katie, "What's up? You don't want Scarlett coming with us?"

"No way! Are you kidding me? This is just a you-and-me thing! It will be a *goof*." Both women broke into hysterics.

"Stop!" Erin said. "You are going to make me drop the cake!"

Just ahead of the others, Scarlett walked past Steve. He looked away from her. Was it her imagination, or hadn't he seen her? Did he do it deliberately? She felt her face turn red, likely unnoticeable to anyone since she'd gotten a bit of a sunburn in the pool. Shaking it off, Scarlett saw that Erin and Katie were just behind her so she began to sing, "Happy birthday, to you…"

---

It was well after eight o'clock, and all of the guests finally had gone home. Two errant boys wouldn't get out of the bouncy house for over half an hour, despite their mothers' coaxing, then bribing them with ice cream. Exasperated, the two women climbed into the BatHouse and dragged their boys out by their arms. One of them looked embarrassed. The other just looked angry. They hurriedly said good-bye and thank you, and were in their matching minivans and speeding down the block in no time flat.

"Phew," Erin said, plopping down on a lawn chair next to Katie and Scarlett. She pulled her cell phone out of her pocket and looked at the time. "Shit, no poker tonight."

"Still want to go out for those cocktails?" Scarlett asked, not really meaning it. She was bone tired from playing with the kids in the pool and from helping with the clean-up.

"God, I'd have to shower again and Marty's already passed out inside. He was piss drunk," Erin said.

"We could have a few here, if you want," Katie offered. "What have you got inside?" She stood up.

Where does she get her energy? Scarlett thought.

"Let's go see what Marty *didn't* drink," Erin said, getting up to head in the house. "You coming?" she asked Scarlett.

Scarlett shook her head. She wasn't just tired. She was upset. Steve had been ignoring her for the entire party. Maybe she pushed too far telling him about Marty, after all the two of them were friends. Maybe she was misinterpreting all the signals and he wasn't interested. He was a nice guy. That she knew. What she thought was interest was probably just Steve being Steve.

"No, girls. Thanks. I'm really tired all of a sudden. I think I'll just head home."

"Oh, all right. Thanks for coming," Erin said as she leaned over to hug Scarlett.

Katie stepped over to hug her, too. "Bye."

"Night," Scarlett said. She watched the two of them walk away, arm-in-arm, toward the house.

She stood up and looked around for C. Thomas. It still was light out, but the sun was behind the house and it was harder to spot him. She finally did see him sitting on the raised deck at the edge of the pool, his feet dangling in the water.

"C. Thomas, you ready?" He didn't answer.

She walked over to him and asked again. She could see he was drunk, like Marty. He and Marty were a strange pair, but they'd been tossing them back together all afternoon.

"Why the hella people bother withaa bathtub like thisss?" he spit in the direction of Erin and Marty's above-ground pool. "Ya cann't even swimm'n it." He was slurring and he was being mean.

"Come on, C. Thomas," Scarlett said as she pulled on his arm for him to stand up. "Let's go home."

C. Thomas stood up and walked around the deck to the stairs. He stumbled down the first two and righted himself to safely make it to the bottom. Scarlett had his loafers in her hand and offered them to him. He sat down on the last step to put them on. Abruptly, something hit him like a bolt of lightning, and his head spun around to her. "What about the game?"

"No game tonight, C. Thomas. It got too late."

"Damn!" He was shaking his head. "An' I was hoping for a little sumthin' sumthin'."

"Yeah, sure. In your condition." She helped C. Thomas to his feet and started walking toward the car when out of the corner of her eye she saw Steve through the window. He was in the kitchen standing next to Katie, brushing her hair from her neck with his hand. He leaned in to kiss her by her ear. Scarlett quickly turned away before she could see his look of shock when he caught Scarlett staring at him.

"C. Thomas, are you really up for fooling around?" she asked.

He grabbed her hand and pulled her toward him. His breath stank of tequila. "Sure, Babyyy!" he slurred. "Did ya get those booties back from the shoemaker yet?"

## 13

## POKER SMARTS

"This place is massive!" Erin said for the umpteenth time since they'd arrived at Foxwoods Resort Casino. "Can you imagine what it takes to heat this place in the winter?"

Katie chuckled. "There are a lot of things I can imagine about this place, but that wasn't one of them."

The ladies perused the hodgepodge of clientele, those obvious regulars clad in track suits and sneakers; the ones still hanging out past the morning check-out, wrinkled, overdressed and visibly hung over; and of course, other wide-eyed new arrivals, the greenest of which were Katie and Erin.

"Thank goodness you talked me out of getting dressed up." Never having been to a casino, Erin was prepared to go all the way. Luckily, Katie convinced her otherwise. She was pretty certain it was casual dress, especially during the day.

Foxwoods was a two-hour drive east of New Fairfield. However, it took Katie and Erin almost three hours to get to Ledyard since they made two critical wrong turns even with the GPS. They had taken Katie's Jeep and left rather furtively after their spouses departed for work.

Katie had convinced Erin that Foxwoods was the way to go after Erin's failed tutoring research. It only had turned up a few questionable posts on Craig's List that may or may not have led to the two of them ending up bound and gagged and at the bottom of Lake Candlewood. Resourceful Katie found out that the really good players go to Foxwoods. She thought perhaps they could watch the tables and pick up some pointers.

It was time to pull out all the stops. The triptych's game was beginning to feel cutthroat, even bloodthirsty. On the heels of the twins' birthday party, Katie had a nagging suspicion that Steve and Scarlett were the ones who next might be headed for the cabin, and she was going to do everything to avoid that, including thwarting either of their wins at the table. Of course it was at her insistence that she and Erin elected not to invite Scarlett for their foray into the aggressive world of casino poker. Sometimes Katie's relationship with Scarlett felt like her relationship with her sister, Alice; the two of whom hardly spoke anymore.

Neither Erin nor Katie had ever had been to Foxwoods or any other casino for that matter. Needless to say, both "virgins" had been a bit overwhelmed by the sheer enormity of the place and the vast array of gaming tables.

"There are the poker tables," Katie said pointing across the room. "Are you ready to go down the rabbit hole?"

"Let's do it, Alice."

Katie did a double-take hearing her sister's name.

They advanced to the entrance of the poker area and immediately were approached by the poker host, a pert, twenty-something redhead uniformed in Foxwoods attire. A black and gold nameplate on the lapel of her jacket said KYLIE. "Good morning, ladies. What kind of poker game would you like to play?"

"Hi, Kylie. Um, well, um, actually we would like to watch, maybe," Erin started.

"Texas Hold'em," Katie said, cutting off Erin's inarticulate stammering. It was clear that Erin was flustered and the last thing they needed was to be perceived as two bumble-fucks from Podunk City.

"Well," Kylie said, "there is a forty-five dollar no-limit buy-in tournament waiting for two more people. Shall I show you to the table? You can begin immediately."

Katie wondered how she was able to talk and still wear that plastic Foxwood's smile at the same time. She looked like a ventriloquist. "No, I don't think we would be interested in a tournament," Katie said.

Still smiling, Kylie said, "There are several limit and no-limit tables waiting for players. You will not have to sign in on the electronic queue."

Erin turned to Katie and mumbled under her breath, "What in the hell are we doing here?" It was obvious she felt in way over her head.

Katie sighed. There was no way around the bumble-fuck perception now. "Actually, Kylie, we are novices."

Kylie's smile became even broader. "There are players here at all different levels and calibers from novice to expert. What monetary limits are you interested in playing?"

"We just want to watch," Katie said. She couldn't help thinking that her response sounded as hollow as the trademarked line from the movie *Being There*.

Kylie's smile finally faded. "That's not possible. Unlike other gaming areas, poker players do not like people standing around them watching them play."

"I understand," Katie said. She turned to Erin.

"Let's just go," Erin replied.

"Hang on a sec," Katie recovered. "Kylie, this may sound like a weird request, but do you know where we can take poker lessons, maybe from a tutor?"

Kylie flashed the casino work smile again. "No, I'm sorry. I'm sure there are books or courses for which you can register."

"I'm sure there are," Katie said. "But this is kind of an emergency. We need help right away. Thank you, anyway."

They turned and were about to leave when Kylie stopped them.

"Wait a minute," Kylie said." She pulled back the cuff of her Foxwoods shirt sleeve and checked the time on her wristwatch. In something of a muted tone, she continued, "I'm on break in twenty minutes. If you have some time, can you wait for me in The Scorpion Bar? I may be able to help you."

---

KATIE AND ERIN were on their second round of mimosas when Kylie entered the restaurant. They waved her over to their table.

"I couldn't really talk before," Kylie said as she sat down. "We're not supposed to make recommendations or endorsements to players about anything."

"We understand," Katie said. "Can we buy you a drink? Lunch?"

"That's a no-no, too, I'm afraid. We aren't supposed to get chummy with the players or fraternize with them. Besides, I have to be back on duty in a half an hour."

"Well, we appreciate whatever you can do for us," Erin said.

"I do know someone who may be able to help you. He's a player—actually a high roller here. He plays every Monday and Friday night. He's somewhat of an area celebrity. He's won the WPT and was a runner-up at the WSOP a few years back. He usually has dinner right here in this restaurant and then heads to the tables around eight."

"Who is he?" Katie asked.

"Zack Braun."

Katie and Erin looked at each other and shrugged in unison. "Never heard of him," Katie said.

"He's mostly known in gambling and poker circles. He's been in the local press a lot. We need to keep this on the down-low. I could get in trouble for suggesting this."

"We'll keep it confidential," Katie said. "Do you think he would really help us?"

"I'm not sure. I know he has helped other beginners. But he's a strange bird. You have to find a way to approach him on your own and convince him to help you."

"I think we can do that," Erin said.

"It may not be that easy. Like I said, he can be a very strange bird. He's a professional gambler. This is what he does for a living. Professional gamblers are pretty eclectic types to say the least. Some are downright weirdos."

"What do you suggest?" Katie asked. "Should we try approaching him at dinner?"

"No. I would recommend trying to play at his table. You'll have to wait for him to be seated and then sign in on the electronic queue if the room is busy. His table doesn't always get filled quickly. A lot of players won't play with him because he's so good."

"How will we know him?" Erin asked.

"Google him. Like I said, he's a celebrity of sorts. I'm sure you can find plenty of pictures of him online. He's good-looking, but not in a classic way —if you know what I mean. Hot in a roguish, bad-boy type of way. Think Daryl of *The Walking Dead*. You'll get it when you see him."

"Okay. We'll check him out when we get home," Katie said.

"I would dress more appropriately for tonight. What you're wearing is fine for the day, but will not do at night, especially at Zack Braun's table. You don't have to dress to the nines, but wear something trendy and sexy. I heard he has an eye for the ladies even though I think he has a girlfriend."

Katie and Erin exchanged looks. If Kylie was a mind reader, she would have known that both women were asking themselves the same exact question: What in the hell were they getting themselves into? But their thoughts were left unvoiced.

Instead Katie said, "We will figure it out."

"One more thing," Kylie said. "I hope this isn't a deal breaker for you."

"We're listening," Katie responded.

"He's a high roller."

"So you've said," Katie said. "What does that mean to us?"

"He only plays at the higher-limit tables. On Monday nights, he sometimes plays on the twenty-to-forty no-limit tables. But if they open one hundred or higher, he'll be there. He plays the hundred-fifty-to-three-hundred no-limit tables on Friday nights."

"Yikes," was all that Erin could muster.

"Like I said, Kylie, we'll figure it out," Katie said, but she couldn't hide the anxiety she felt. She picked up her napkin and wiped the perspiration from her forehead.

"Are you sure we can't treat you to something?" Erin asked.

"No, I really can't. I've already risked a lot."

"Why did you?" Katie asked, wondering why this girl took them under her wing when she didn't even know them.

Kylie flashed her casino smile. "You two looked so crestfallen and desperate when I said I couldn't help you. I don't know why playing poker is so important to you—and even though I'm curious as hell—I really don't want to know. I just hope it all goes well for both of you." Kylie stood and looked at her wristwatch again. "I have to get back. Make sure you try the stuffed chicken and corn taquitos. They are excellent here. Good luck." She turned and hurried out of the restaurant.

"Well, this was all very interesting," Erin said after Kylie was gone. "Too bad it's all a bust."

"What are you talking about?" Katie shot back. "We *have* to do this."

"How are you even going to get out tonight? It's a Monday night in the dead of summer."

"I'll say I have to do something for my family. We can't let this opportunity go by the wayside. What about you?" Katie asked.

Erin thought a moment. "I could say some people on Facebook that I know from high school want to get together for drinks. There's always someone proposing some sort of get together. My parents were picking up the kids from camp. Maybe I can convince them to keep them overnight. Marty will be relieved—he can get into trouble all alone at the house. God only knows what he does in that study."

"Won't Marty want to go?"

"No way. He hates my friends, that is, except for you guys. He'll be on his computer all night, *working*."

"Then that settles it. Let's order something to eat and we'll head back."

"There is one other problem," Erin said. "The money. We're going to need a lot."

Katie frowned. "That's right. At least a grand, maybe more."

"Marty controls all the money. There's no way I can finagle that much by tonight."

Katie rubbed her forehead, trying to erase the beginning of a headache. "I have my own credit cards, but Steve pays the bills. I may be able to take out a cash advance on one for a thousand and pay it off before he gets the bill. I can lend you half."

"From the way Kylie was talking, that's still not going to be enough," Erin said.

Katie rubbed her forehead again, this time trying to soothe the now full-blown throbbing migraine. "I can take another thousand out of the girls' savings accounts."

"No! I can't let you!"

"It's okay. I'll replace it before anyone knows it's missing."

"How far are we going down this rabbit hole?" Erin asked.

"All the way. We can't stop now."

"You still don't think we should tell Scarlett? I'm feeling a little bit guilty about leaving her out."

"Look, Scarlett is a good player. She doesn't need poker lessons. She also has the greatest chance of seeing action even if she *loses* the game. Besides, the last thing we need is for this Zack Braun guy to be distracted by Scarlett."

Erin nodded. "You're right, on all counts. Now what?"

"Let's eat. I think I'll take Kylie up on the stuffed chicken and corn taquitos."

---

AT SEVEN-FIFTY P.M., Katie and Erin entered the Rainmaker Casino for the second time that day. The Casino was a great deal busier than it had been earlier. There also was an entirely different vibe. Katie couldn't put her finger on it, but there was an air of anticipation and excitement that was missing just eight hours before. The lights around the gaming tables were brighter; the drinks more plentiful, and the overall noise level was several decibels higher. Much of the evening crowd was better attired as well. Even though the casino was filled with people in everything from shorts and tees to jackets and ties, it appeared that the high-roller types were serious. They looked and played the parts. Kylie was right.

Katie had thrown on a classic little black dress. She always made looking fabulous seem effortless. She had told Steve that her sister called her out of the blue and needed back-up at one of those girly home lingerie parties and that the invitation said the hostess was giving out prizes to the best black dress. Katie was one of those fortunate ones who was quick on the draw. She could concoct great stories on the fly.

Steve knew Katie and Alice were on the outs, but Katie told him this was a good opportunity for them to mend fences. He had bought it hook, line, and sinker. When she left, he was watching movies with the girls, quite an unusual event, but when he acquiesced to renting chick flicks at one of C. Thomas's kiosks and picking up fifty-dollars' worth of Chinese take-out, the girls were happy campers.

Erin was wearing a flattering knee-length ombré dress she'd gotten for a wedding the previous summer. She had left the house in the clothing she'd worn to the casino earlier, but had stuffed her dress into a duffel bag and put it in the trunk of her car while Marty was in the study. She also brought along her rarely-used makeup bag. Marty would have been suspicious had she put on the dress or makeup at home, knowing that these reunions usually take place over a couple of six-packs and a few bowls of chips. She felt like a teenager who changes in the school lavatory so her parents don't know what she's up to. She stopped at a McDonald's along the way to the casino where she dolled herself up in the bathroom, with Katie's help of course.

The two lingered at the entrance to the poker room. While there were women at some of the tables, the vast majority of players were men. It was intense.

They didn't have long to wait. At precisely eight p.m., Zack Braun made his way past Katie and Erin and entered the poker room. He was immediately ushered to a table mid-center. He passed so close to Katie and Erin that they got full whiffs of his pungent cologne. Both women recognized him immediately and they felt giddy.

Erin had googled Braun on her phone on the way home and found several photos of him. Kylie had been right. He was a local celebrity. She also was right about his ruggedly-handsome-in-a-roguish-way looks. His photos, however, did not do him justice. Erin and Katie immediately turned to one another with the same look on their faces. Their jaws dropped and their eyes grew wide. He was much better looking in person. He was wearing a brown silk button down tucked into dress jeans, a blazer, and loafers sans socks. A matching brown hankie folded neatly into a triangle poked out of the breast pocket of his blazer.

"I think my heart skipped a beat when he passed us," Erin whispered. "I might hyperventilate!"

"He does have presence," Katie admitted.

"Presence! Oh…my…God. He's so fucking hot!"

Katie laughed. She'd never heard Erin speak like that. "You're right. I think mine skipped two beats. He looks like something out of a movie—bad boy with all of the girls panting after him."

"You mean dropping their panties! At this point I don't even care about the poker. I could just stand here looking at him."

"Um, Erin, we are here for the poker. Don't forget that. Just don't get *your* panties in a bunch." She turned to look at Erin who was practically drooling. "Erin! You're too obvious!"

"Katie, when all you've had to look at for over a decade is *Marty* can you blame me?"

Katie laughed again. "I guess not! But let's get back on track here, okay?"

"Okay, okay. You're right." Erin pulled herself together. "Oh, we're in luck! He's at the twenty-to-forty no-limit table." Suddenly realizing he'd caught them staring, she added, "He's looking at us. Maybe he thinks *you're* hot."

"He probably thinks we're stalkers—and we are. Let's go sign in."

They were about to sign into the electronic queue when a poker host approached them. He was young, mid-twenties, dark good looks more appropriate for modeling than casino hosting. His name tag said BRADY.

"Excuse me, ladies, but you don't have to sign in," Brady said. "There are a few open tables."

"Can we sit at Mr. Braun's table?"

Brady raised an eyebrow. "Mr. Braun's table? Yes, I think that can be arranged. Follow me."

Katie and Erin fell into Brady's wake as he navigated through the crowded poker room to Zack Braun's table. He stopped at the table and politely held the two remaining chairs out for Katie and Erin to be seated. "It's now a full table. Good luck everyone."

Brady was about to leave when Erin stopped him. "Wait a sec," she said. She rummaged through her clutch looking for a tip.

"That's okay, ma'am," he said. He looked at the dealer and winked. "Take care of these ladies, Wyatt." Wyatt was a fairly good-looking man, somewhere between Erin and Katie's ages.

"Absolutely," Wyatt responded, extending a welcoming smile to them.

Both women pulled out matching envelopes each containing ten crisp one hundred dollar bills.

"A thousand in chips," Katie said.

"Me, too," Erin said.

"How would you like them?" Wyatt asked.

The women exchanged dumbfounded looks. Katie felt the eyes of the other players bore into her, especially those of Zack Braun. This was not how she wanted to start off her professional poker career.

157

"What denominations would you like?" Wyatt asked, trying to be helpful.

"Oh, I guess one hundred dollar chips," Katie said.

"Me, too," Erin echoed.

Wyatt counted out twenty one hundred dollar chips, split them into two stacks and slid them over to Katie and Erin.

"I'm going to take a break," Zack Braun said. Was he snarling? He stood up, pocketing his stacks of chips. He tossed a chip to Wyatt.

"Thank you, Mr. Braun. Will you be returning?"

"Maybe."

The women watched Braun leave.

"Now what?" Erin asked.

"I guess it's a bust," Katie said, suddenly feeling exasperated.

"So what do we do now? Play poker?"

Katie shook her head. "We can't afford to play poker. I suggest we go and drink heavily. That we can afford to do."

The two women stood up in unison. "Sorry," Katie said to Wyatt. Wyatt nodded sans casino smile, clearly disappointed in another game delay and no tip.

"Thank Christ," Katie overheard one of the players at the table say as they were leaving. "I hate newbies."

"Jeez," Erin muttered. "I could really use a drink."

---

THE WOMEN SAW Zack Braun as soon as they entered The Scorpion Bar. He was sitting by himself at a table in the back of the restaurant nursing a tall drink. Erin spotted him first and immediately jabbed Katie in her side.

"It's him!" Erin exclaimed.

"Easy, girl. You almost broke my rib. Calm down, we have to look natural. Let's go see if we can talk to him."

Katie led the way to Braun's table. He saw them coming and deliberately averted his gaze.

"Excuse me, Mr. Braun," Katie began, "I was hoping we could—"

Braun held up a hand. "Let me just end this right now. I don't give autographs and I definitely don't appreciate poker groupies," Braun said. His tone was icy, bordering on positively frigid. "So if you will, let me enjoy my drink in peace."

Erin chuckled. "Poker groupies? Is that what you think we are?"

"We're not here for your autograph and we are not groupies," Katie said.

"Then why are you stalking me? You watched me go to my table today and then followed me over to it. Now you're here yet again."

"You were recommended to us by an employee of the casino. We were hoping you could teach us some strategies for winning at poker."

"Please inform me as to the name of the employee who recommended me so I can have him or her fired." His tone was now thirty below and dropping.

Katie and Erin exchanged perplexed looks. This was not what either of them had anticipated or expected.

"I'm afraid you don't understand," Katie said.

"No, ladies, you are the ones who do not understand. I am a professional. I am not a teacher. I do not teach people to play poker. As soon as I saw you two, I knew there was going to be trouble."

A waitress approached the table. "Can I get anyone anything?"

"No, thanks," Braun volunteered. "I'm good and they were just leaving."

The waitress nodded and hurried off to a more welcoming table. The wait staff always had to endure Braun's curt and quirky ways. Their jobs depended upon it, but he tipped handsomely, so at the end of the day it was worth the aggravation.

"We need your help," Katie persisted.

"We need to beat our husbands," Erin offered. Katie shot her a look of dismay. That was not the thing to say at this juncture.

"I would suggest marriage counseling rather than poker," Braun said, sipping his drink. "I will be past the point of rude and into the realm of enraged very soon unless you leave me alone. Be forewarned. I can become quite aggressive in that state."

"We're sorry to bother you," Erin backed down. She took Katie by the elbow and tried to pull her away but Katie stood her ground.

"We are playing for *very* high stakes," Katie said, unwavering and straight-faced.

"Really? What kind of high stakes would two bored housewives from

Connecticut be playing for? The stash inside your respective cookie jars?" He was coolly rude.

"We're more than just housewives, for your information. And it is for the right to spend the night with another player of my choosing, *other* than my husband." Katie figured it was worth it at this point to lay all the cards on the table, pun intended. Obviously, she had nothing to lose since it looked like Braun's stonewall was impenetrable.

To her surprise, the gambit worked. Zack Braun blinked.

"Now you have my undivided attention," he said in a tone that finally had risen above freezing. He leaned back, draped an arm behind him, and with the other, gestured to the remaining seats at the table. "Please, have a seat."

Katie and Erin exchanged quick smiles and pulled up chairs. The waitress appeared seemingly out of nowhere with order pad in hand. "Can I get you anything now?" she asked.

Speaking on behalf of Erin, Katie said, "We'll have what Mr. Braun is drinking."

The waitress smirked. "Two Diet Cokes," she said. "Coming right up." She turned and disappeared.

"Diet Coke?" Erin asked.

"I don't drink while I'm working. I like to have a very clear head. Now, ladies, why don't you tell me about your, um, *situation*."

The waitress returned with the sodas. Katie waited until she was gone before launching into the explanation of, as Braun phrased it, their situation. She described everything in great detail, including the events leading up to the first game and the results. Erin filled in the gaps and even told Braun about Marty's scratches the following morning. Braun remained impassive throughout the diatribe, quietly sipping his soda, looking from one woman to the other.

"So?" Katie asked when she was finished.

"So?" Braun volleyed back.

"So will you help us? Our next game is this coming Saturday."

Braun reached into his jacket pocket and pulled out a card. He handed it to Katie. It was a miniature playing card; the jack of diamonds. Superimposed over the jack was Zack's name and address.

"I live in Roxbury," he said. "Be at my place at seven a.m. Your training begins then. The cost will be the two thousand dollars you brought with you tonight."

"Whoa!" Katie said. "That's a bit steep."

"You were prepared to lose it at the tables. At least now you will actually get something out of it."

"We have to wait until our husbands leave for work," Katie said.

"And I'll have to arrange for someone to get my kids on the camp bus," Erin said. "That's not going to be an easy task that early in the morning."

"Are you serious about poker training or not?" Braun asked.

"We are serious, but we do have certain issues. We don't want our husbands to know. Besides, this is poker training, right? It's not going to be a wax on, wax off regimen, is it? We have limited time for bullshit." Erin was uncharacteristically fiery all of a sudden.

Braun smiled for the first time. It was a captivating, engaging smile. "*Touché, mon ami.* You passed the first test. Be firm. Do not accept bullshit from anyone. Be at my place at ten a.m. sharp. Now, if you'll excuse me, I really must get back to work."

## 14

## SVENGALI

*Whether he likes it or not, a man's character is stripped at the poker table; if the other players read him better than he does, he has only himself to blame. Unless he is both able and prepared to see himself as others do, flaws and all, he will be a loser in cards, as in life.*

— ANTHONY HOLDEN

*Tuesday*

ERIN WASN'T ENTIRELY sure that Marty believed her but she made up a whopper of a story that she had to help an old high school friend pack up to move out of her boyfriend's house this week. She said she'd been asked Monday night at the bar. Since Marty didn't work at the college except for Mondays and Saturdays, he was home during the week, and he'd have expected Erin to be there to make him lunch and clean up after him. Thankfully the boys were at camp, so he couldn't complain *that* much. Katie, on the other hand, was free as a bird with Steve in the city and her teen girls who weren't around much, so she jumped in the Jeep after he left for the train and darted over to collect Erin.

"I can't believe we are doing this!" Erin said through sips of her coffee after Katie pulled out onto the street from the drive-thru.

"We're on our way!" Katie exclaimed as she gunned it onto Route Thirty-Seven.

Like teenagers on Spring Break, the two chattered the whole way making the forty-minute drive to Roxbury seem far shorter. Despite having lived in Connecticut for some time, neither Katie nor Erin ever had been to Roxbury; an historic, private twenty-six square miles tucked away in the Litchfield Hills. They'd never had a reason to go until now.

Guided by the GPS, they made it to Zack Braun's house several minutes earlier than expected. It might have been Katie's lead foot, however. She was giddy with excitement, only slowing with each glimpse of a cop. Braun's house was off the beaten track and the women gasped when they saw it.

"Oh, my God, Katie! Is this it?!"

"It has to be. That's the address. It must be six-thousand square feet!"

"This has to be the biggest house we've seen so far. I wonder if this belonged to someone famous before Braun bought it!"

"Could be. A lot of celebrities hide out here from what I understand."

Erin and Katie sat, mouths gaping open, staring at what only could be described as a compound. The house was a ginormous three-story contemporary with a natural stone front and a barn off to the side with numerous horses grazing freely. It was classic New England at its finest. The property was immaculately landscaped with sculpted shrubs and topiary spirals. Mixed in among traditional designs were shrubs in hearts, diamonds, spades, and clubs. There were flowers everywhere planted in stunning designs. There also were ornamental grasses and raised turf in slate structures.

"This looks like something out of *Edward Scissorhands*!" Erin exclaimed

"How does one man need this much space?" Katie said as she exhaled. She hadn't even realized she had been holding her breath.

"I can only imagine what's around back! Or inside!" Erin was acting like a little child, waiting for the candy store to open. She literally was bouncing up and down in her seat. Katie half expected her to be frothing at the mouth.

It was nine fifty-five. They were early, so they decided to sit outside in the car. Katie was determined to knock on the front door at precisely ten a.m.

"You okay, Erin?" Katie asked. "You look nervous."

"I am nervous! What are we getting into? Do you realize how different our lives are now? Who would have thought six months ago that you and I would be sitting outside a stranger's house after hooking up with him at a casino no less, begging for poker lessons so that we can sleep with men other than our husbands? We have truly crossed the line into the bizarro world!"

Katie smiled. "Isn't it exciting?"

Erin returned a sly smile. "Yes, it is," she admitted.

Both women broke down into gales of laughter. It became infectious; every time one would stop, the other would start again and continue until both were belly laughing all over again.

"This guy could be a serial killer for all we know," Erin said, finally quelling her urge to laugh and wiping the tears from her eyes.

"He could be a lot of things," Katie replied, also wiping tears from her own. She pulled down the visor to make sure she hadn't ruined her eye makeup. "But I'm certain serial killer is not one of them. He is so unbelievably sexy."

"There's something dark, almost dangerous about him. But you're right. He is sexy."

"Well, don't get any ideas," Katie said. "Remember Kylie said she thinks he has a girlfriend."

"Guess that means we can't invite him to play in our game," Erin said laughing again.

Katie chuckled in response. "I think that would depend on his girlfriend. Don't get me started. We need to pull it together. The last thing Zack Braun needs is trying to mentor two giggling house fraus on the dos and don'ts of Texas Hold'em. We need to get serious here."

She glanced down at the car clock. "It's nine-fifty-nine. Let's go."

Katie and Erin both reached for their doors and climbed out of the Jeep at the same time, looking like it had been choreographed. They approached the front door which was adorned with a custom-designed brass knocker with a carved jack from a deck of playing cards. The knocker extended from each side of the jack's handlebar moustache and ended in a diamond shaped knob. With some trepidation, Katie reached for the knocker and rapped several times on the door.

Almost immediately they heard footsteps from within. The door opened and both women involuntarily blanched. The last thing that either had anticipated seeing was a young, strikingly beautiful Asian woman on the other side of the door. She looked like someone out of the pages of a magazine. But she had an edge so different than one might have expected of someone so classically and exotically gorgeous. She had a half-sleeve tribal tattoo which extended from her left shoulder partway down her upper arm and over much of her back shoulder blade. It was visible due to the one-shoulder camisole she was wearing which hugged her fit upper body. She did not have large breasts, but they were perfectly round and youthful. She wore a pair of embroidered shorts which looked terribly expensive. She also had a number of piercings; nothing too off-putting, but more than just a few in her ear, including her cartilage, rook, and tragus. She also had a diamond stud in her neck a few inches below her ear. She was barefoot with perfectly-painted black toenails.

They heard Braun call out in an Asian language they couldn't identify. The woman turned and responded in the same language. She faced Erin and Katie and in perfect English said, "Zack is expecting you. Please come in."

She held open the door and ushered them into the foyer. "He will be down in a few minutes. Can I get you something to eat or drink?"

Katie and Erin both shook their heads. "No, thank you," Katie said. "We ate on the way."

"Okay, then. Let me know if you change your minds, will you?"

Both women nodded, dumbfounded.

"Right this way, then," the woman said as she walked through the entry to a room off to the side. Erin and Katie looked at one another wide-eyed, then followed at the woman's heels.

"You can wait in here," she said as she entered Braun's study. "Please, make yourself at home. The bathroom is down the hall should you need it." The walls were flanked with floor-to-ceiling, fully-stocked bookshelves and next to them, a roll-top mahogany desk and matching swivel chair. The tones were brown, warm, and very masculine. There was no question that the room belonged to an Alpha male. The only things missing were animal heads on the wall or a bear skin rug.

"If you need anything at all, just call," the Asian woman said.

"Before you go," Katie ventured. "If you don't mind my asking, where are you from?"

"I'm Cambodian," the woman said. "My name is Savan."

"Nice to meet you, Savan," Katie said.

"Yes, nice to meet you," Erin echoed. "Mr. Braun speaks Cambodian?"

"He speaks seven languages including fluent Cambodian. He should be here momentarily." She turned and disappeared into the bowels of the house.

"Seven languages!" Erin whispered after she was gone.

"Apparently our Mr. Braun has a number of eclectic pursuits. I'm amazed at the titles and authors of some of these books!"

"I don't even know what most of these are."

"I don't know all of them, but I am familiar with a few. In college I learned quite a bit about quantum physics and a few other oddball topics."

The two perused the shelves. They were filled with books about black holes, theories about God and the universe, super string theory, chaos theory, existentialism, quantum physics, time travel, telekinesis, and countless other obscure and esoteric subjects. Authors included Steven Hawking, Carl Sagan, Tolstoy, Nietzsche, Camus, Sartre, and Teilhard de Chardin. There also were books in foreign languages which both Erin and Katie could not identify.

"O M G!" Erin exclaimed. "Will you look at that!"

Katie followed Erin's line of sight to a spot on the wall above the roll top. There was a framed Ph.D. from Yale University. "He has a doctorate from Yale!"

"Then why in the hell is he playing poker?"

"Because it's lucrative and pays the bills," Braun said, making the women jump. "The degree ain't worth the paper it's printed on."

Both women turned to find him standing in the doorway. He could have walked off a page from Brooks Brothers' summer look book. He was wearing an untucked military sport shirt and slim navy shorts. He had wayfarers hanging from the top of his open shirt collar and his hair was casually tousled. He also was barefoot.

"I trust Savan has attended to your needs?" Braun asked.

"Yes," Katie said.

"She is beautiful," Erin said.

"You're a lucky man, Mr. Braun," Katie continued.

"I am indeed," Braun said, "but it's not because of what I presume that you're thinking."

"What pray tell am I thinking?" Katie asked.

"That Savan is my girlfriend—or my concubine. She's actually my housekeeper."

Katie blushed. "I knew that," she said, trying to recover.

"I hope you can bluff more effectively when you play poker."

"We'll find out," Katie said.

"Follow me," Braun said. "It's time for your training."

He led them out of the study and down the hall to a closed door.

"Where are we going?" Erin asked.

"To the basement," Braun replied. He pulled a key ring from his pocket and unlocked the door.

Katie looked at Erin and raised an eyebrow. Erin mouthed the words, "Serial killer." Katie smiled and shook her head, silently stifling a laugh.

He led them down carpeted steps to a dark basement. He flicked on a light and the finished room came to life. Both women stared in awe at the scene before them.

"Welcome to the *Inner Sanctum*," he said.

"I think this basement alone could fit both of our houses in it!" Erin said, taking it all in.

"I thought you only played poker?" Katie asked.

"While I do enjoy poker the most from a player's perspective, I also play blackjack and craps." He led them to the poker table and waved an arm. "Have a seat, ladies."

Katie and Erin pulled up chairs on the players's side of the table. Braun moved around to the dealer's side and took a seat. He picked up a new deck of cards from the built-in rack on the table, broke the seal, and dumped out the cards. He deftly picked out the Jokers and the information card and tossed them aside.

"What are we going to learn today?" Erin asked.

"Nothing today," he said.

"What?" Katie asked.

"Today is the day I learn about both of you. I will learn how good each of you are at poker. I will learn what you need to know to become better. I will ascertain your present skills, thoughts, intuitions, and develop a plan for your improvement."

"I thought this wasn't going to be a wax on/wax off lesson," Katie said.

"It's not. It's poker boot camp. I am your drill sergeant and you are my recruits. This isn't a democracy. If you don't like the way I am proceeding or running things, you are free to leave at any time. Any questions?"

"When do we learn about you?" Erin asked.

"This isn't about me, ladies."

"Deal," Katie said.

Braun smiled. "That's what I like. Cut right to the chase." Braun finished shuffling and made a one-handed cut with his left hand, his movements smooth as silk.

*Wednesday*

"So what's the lesson for today?" Erin asked.

Katie and Erin were sitting in the same seats as the day before. Braun was in the dealer chair shuffling a new deck of cards. More casual than the day before, he was wearing a silk Hawaiian shirt with the top four buttons opened.

"We are going to learn about rhythm," Braun said.

"I didn't know a poker game had rhythm," Erin said.

"Poker is so much more than just a game. To illustrate, just look at how much you have riding on your 'game' as you say."

"Touché," Katie said.

"Poker is both a philosophical and a psychological journey. It's something of a microcosm of life itself. The thrill of winning, the despair in losing. Risking it all or playing it safe and risking nothing. It's anticipation, anxiety, luck, timing, skill, competition. A competent player who can apply effective poker strategies will be—"

Erin interrupted. "A success in life."

Braun smirked. "I was going to say a well-rounded individual."

"Is that what they taught you at Yale?" Katie asked.

"No. I learned that when I was playing poker at the homeless shelter where I once lived."

Katie raised an eyebrow and exchanged a quick look with Erin. "So what did you learn about our style of playing from yesterday's game?"

Braun dealt the down cards for the first round. "I learned that both of you are fish."

"Fish?" Erin asked.

"Food for the sharks," Braun said. "Bad poker players are generally known as fish."

"We know that," Katie said. "That's why we're here—to get better. I was hoping for a bit more insight."

"You are both passive-aggressive players. You want to win, at least you think you do. But you are tentative players. You are reactors. You play at the whim of the other players. You let them control you. You let them lead you through the dance. I would imagine you approach life in the same manner."

Katie looked annoyed. He might have been right, but she was not going to give him the satisfaction.

Erin smiled and shook her head. "I don't think you can get all that from a card game. You hardly know us."

"But it's not just a game now, is it?" Katie asked.

It was Braun's turn to smile. "Touché," he offered.

"Would you care to elaborate further on this psychological profile of the two of us?" Katie asked.

Braun put the deck on the table and folded his hands. After a pause he said, "You two also are *ritualists*."

"Ritualists?" Erin asked.

"What the hell is a ritualist?" Katie demanded. She wasn't sure she liked where this was going.

"It's one who rejects successful outcomes even though he or she still believes in the means or route to achieving those outcomes. For example, I am sure you both believe that in a democratic country like America anyone who works hard and persists can be President. But you just don't believe that *you* could become President. You two ladies are sleepwalkers. You know what you want, you know how to get it, but you don't believe you personally are entitled to it. So you wear your masks of false happiness and play the parts of dutiful wives and mothers."

There was a long silence which Katie finally broke. "You're a smug bastard. You think you know everything."

Erin stifled a gasp.

"Tell me where I'm wrong," Braun said.

"We're here, and we were able to convince you to help us get what we want. Deal the cards and let's get going."

A sly grin spread across Braun's face. "I guess there's hope for you ladies after all. This has already proven to be the start of a successful lesson."

*Thursday*

"So, Sensei, what's our lesson for today?" Erin asked as they sat down for their next session.

Braun followed the precedent he had established with each prior lesson by opening a new deck of cards. "Today we are going to learn about tells," he said as he shuffled.

"Ah! Finally, something I know about!" Erin said.

"You think you understand tells?" Braun asked.

"I can always tell when my husband has a good hand. His eyes bulge like he's just seen a ghost. It's almost as if he can't believe he was dealt such a good hand."

"Is that so?"

"Yes," Katie agreed, chuckling. "Please don't get mad at me, Erin, but when Marty gets a good hand he looks like one of those giant blowfish."

"I know!" Erin said, laughing. "It's so true!"

"What about the other players?" Braun asked.

"Well," Katie said, "Scarlett may be the easiest and hardest to read at the same time. She can be a ditzy player. At times she appears to be completely transparent, and at other times she is as dense as a brick shithouse."

"She's built like one too!" Erin said through laughter.

Braun flashed a rare smile. "Does she win a lot?"

"She holds her own with the men," Katie said.

"Then maybe she's not at ditzy as you think," Braun said. "Maybe it's her strategy; to deflect and keep everyone guessing."

"It's hard to believe she would actually have a strategy," Erin said. "I mean, up until the recent rule changes, it was just a friendly game."

"I'm not so sure about that," Katie said. "Scarlett is competitive about everything. I have a lot of experience with people like that. She's a lot like my sister."

"Hmm. I take it that Scarlett is attractive?"

"Oh, yeah," Erin said. "She's a head turner. Not a whole lot upstairs, but what a staircase."

"Really. Well, maybe she has more on the ball than you think," Braun suggested. "What does she wear at your games?"

"Casual," Erin said. "We all dress casually, at least until very recently."

"I don't think that's what he means," Katie said. "I think he wants to know how distracting she can be. Isn't that right, Mr. Braun?"

"Yes, as a matter of fact, that's precisely what I was getting at."

Erin said, "in that case, she makes it a point of wearing low-cut tops."

"Come on, Erin. *Low-cut* is being generous. On game nights, she shows so much cleavage you can drive a Hummer between her fake tits. Christ, when she wins a pot and leans over to rake in her chips, her nipples practically scrape the table."

Braun raised a solitary eyebrow. "I imagine she's quite a distracting player. How do the male players react?"

Katie exchanged a look with Erin. She noticed that Erin was suddenly perspiring.

"Um," Erin began, a bit flustered, "we're all friends."

"But now you're friends with *benefits*." Braun said matter-of-factly. "Do you think your husbands are distracted by this woman?"

"I guess," Erin said tentatively.

"Come on, Erin, your husband's eyes are Krazy Glued to Scarlett's boobs."

Erin flushed. "So are your husband's," she said barely above a whisper.

Katie took a deep breath before responding. "My husband is a man like any other. If a beautiful buxom woman flaunts her tits in his face, he's going to look. Anyway, I know he intends to pick Scarlett if he wins."

"This woman knows precisely what she's doing," Braun said. "We all know what we are doing. At times I'm sure you wear certain items of clothing that you believe will create a desired effect on the part of your audience, wherever you happen to be. After all, if people only wore things to please themselves, we'd all be in sweats and sneakers. Obviously, this woman knows how to work her assets and titillate, pun intended, your husbands. It's also quite obvious that she is threatening to both of you."

"Why do you say that?" Erin asked.

"She's not here," Braun said. "If you weren't threatened by her, if you weren't afraid she would win, she'd be right here sitting next to you. You said you are all *friends*."

Katie ignored Braun's last comment. "So what can we do about her?"

"You can use the knowledge of her manipulation to your advantage. If your husbands' eyes are glued to her breasts, they probably have weak hands. They're not going to take the time for cheap thrills if they have strong hands and are intent on winning the round."

"That's a helluva tell," Erin said.

Braun nodded. "Tells come in two varieties of conscious and unconscious. You need to be aware of both."

"Steve is obsessive about stacking his chips and playing with them before he bets," Katie noted.

"Obsessively stacking and sorting chips generally are signs of a conservative player," Braun said. "If someone keeps their chips disorganized, it usually means they're a looser player; one who is subject to bluffing and risk-taking. Does anyone smoke while they play?"

"No," Katie replied.

"Too bad," Braun said. "A player's pattern of respiration during play can be a great tell. Shallow breathing is usually a sign of a weak hand. Strong exhalation, on the other hand, generally is an indication of a strong hand. That's why is easier to tell someone's breathing pattern if they're a smoker."

"Wow!" Erin said.

"You can learn a lot about someone from the way they play," Katie said.

Braun smiled. "Now you're connecting the dots. It's all body language." He picked up the deck of cards and dealt the opening hand. He waited until they looked at their hole cards before continuing. "But in order to discern someone else's tells, you need to know your own. So, what tells do you two have?"

Both Katie and Erin shrugged in unison.

"So I guess you two have no tells?"

Katie shook her head. "I can't think of any."

"Me, either," Erin said. "I try not to give anything away."

Braun chuckled. "I guess I was mistaken when I saw your eyes widen, Katie, when I dealt you the pair of bullets. Not to mention the fact that you have been keeping your hand over your cards. Protecting your cards often is a sign of a strong hand."

Katie turned over her aces. "How did you do that?"

Braun turned to Erin. "You covering your mouth and avoiding my gaze told me you had a very weak hand."

Erin turned over a seven and a two. "You knew!"

"You're also a card shark," Katie said.

"Just a little sleight of hand while you weren't looking." Braun turned over the next three cards. They were all kings. "So much for card tricks. Let's get down to business and find out more of your individual tells." Braun picked up the cards and shuffled them.

*Friday*

IT WAS the last day of their tutelage. Braun was unusually quiet, curbing even his usual sarcastic wit and haughty attitude. Maybe he was upset that this was their last meeting together, Katie thought—hoped—wistfully. He was at his most casual in a black V-neck tee and stonewashed slim jeans. Poking out from his left sleeve was the bottom of a tattoo with the Latin phrase *Semper fi*. Katie didn't need to see the rest of the tattoo to know that it was the Marine Corps emblem. Her grandfather had been in the Third Marine Division, had fought on Iwo Jima during World War II, and had had the same exact tattoo. It was a rite of passage, her grandfather explained, that most, if not all, marines obtained the tattoo upon the completion of their tour of duty. Katie wondered, not for the first time, was there anything that Zack Braun didn't do in his lifetime?

Braun opened yet another new deck of cards and began shuffling.

"What's the agenda today?" Erin asked.

"A few things you're not going to find in books about poker," Braun said. "First, let's talk about bluffing. There are lots of theories and strategies about bluffing. I follow my daddy's rule, and it has served me well. In poker and in life one should bluff strong and hard."

"I never bluff," Erin said.

"Then you may never get what you want in poker or in life. Sometimes you must bluff. But first, you have to know your opponent. Some people can be bluffed and some cannot. For example, if you want a raise at your job, you may be able to get one by bluffing to quit. Knowing your employer and his appreciation of your work is critical to whether your bluff succeeds."

"I never win when I bluff," Katie said. "I never know when to bluff and I'm always so tentative."

"It is sound judgment to put on a bold face and play your hand for a hundred times what it is worth. Forty-nine times out of fifty nobody dares to call it and you roll in the chips."

"Did you just make that up?" Katie asked.

"No. Mark Twain said it, and what he said is valid and applies equally to a game of chance as well as to life. Just remember this. You can bluff, but once you're called on it, you cannot bluff again. Someone will always call you after that to keep you honest."

"When do you bluff?" Erin asked.

"That brings us to our next lesson," Braun said. "Luck and timing."

"Neither of which have been strong points for me, and I'm not just talking about poker," Erin said.

"Then you have to change your mindset."

"Are you saying you can learn to be lucky?" Katie asked.

"Yes. You can change your luck. There have been scientific studies done about lucky people, and it was discovered that they all share certain principles. First, lucky people tend to maximize the chance opportunities in their lives. Chance favors the prepared." Braun paused, shuffling the cards. The women stared at him intently through his dissertation.

"Second, you need to follow your gut feelings and hunches. It is intuition—that feeling that something is right even when you don't know or can't explain why."

The women nodded like two little birds, hanging on his every word.

"Third, you need to expect and anticipate that you will win. This is more than just being an optimist or the power of positive thinking. It's a mindset. As Tennessee Williams once said, 'Luck is believing you're lucky.' And, finally, and this may sound trite, you need to make lemonade out of lemons when bad luck does strike."

"Yeah. Don't I know that one? I make lots of lemonade being married to Marty," Erin frowned.

"Sounds easier said than done," Katie said.

"Maybe," Braun said. "It is a commitment to a change one's mental outlook. In order to see if we can do this, I thought it might be helpful to change the game. Let's play five-card showdown poker. This will give you a chance to work on your hunches."

Braun started dealing. "Ante up."

---

"That's it for today, ladies," Braun said, raking in the chips and the cards.

It was four o'clock, and the tutelage had ended. Both women looked dejected.

"Do you think we're ready?" Katie asked.

"As ready as you'll ever be," Braun replied.

"I feel like you taught us everything there is to know about poker," Erin said.

"I'm not so sure about that," Braun said. "But since you came with less than zero knowledge, I am sure I've taught you quite a bit." Braun's sarcasm and haughtiness was back in full force. "Everything *you* might now know about poker, but not everything *I* know. Unfortunately it would take far more than a week and two grand to teach you everything I know."

"I guess that's it then," Katie said.

"Yes. I'll walk you out. Then I have to get ready for the casino tonight."

"That's okay, Mr. Braun. I'm sure we can find our own way out," Katie said, reaching out to shake his hand. He surprised her by suddenly taking her hand in both of his. His hands were strong, his long fingers cupping and supporting hers.

"There's one more lesson, Katie, that I think you need to learn. It's the ability to let go and move on, in poker and in life. This is the hardest lesson of all."

His eyes bore penetratingly into hers; it was as if he was looking into her very soul—and then it was gone. All of a sudden, his eyes seemed to glaze over as the intensity drained out of them. He let go of her hand. Did her heart flip-flop? She suddenly felt like a teenager and wondered for a moment if she would ever wash her hand again. Was she blushing? Did Erin see that she was flustered? Katie didn't want to chance looking at her. What was worse? Did the Master know what she was feeling?

"Good luck tonight, Zack," she said.

Braun flashed one of his trademarked engaging smiles. "Thank you, my dear. But I do expect to win. One *always* must expect to win." To them both, he said, "Good luck to both of you, as well. I'll be thinking of you tomorrow night."

## 15

## BLUFFING

*Life is not always a matter of holding good cards, but sometimes, playing a poor hand well.*

— JACK LONDON

It was Saturday and once again, game night at the Kellys's. Everyone agreed that since C. Thomas's proposal, the games should be played there. It ensured that Steve and Katie's girls would not be home and that Marty and Erin's boys would have babysitters. The familiarity of the routine helped calm the intensity of the new game twist.

It was only about half an hour into the game, and Marty already was pacing back and forth in the dining room while the others played cards.

"Marty, can you sit down? You're distracting. I can't focus," Steve requested.

"Yeah," C. Thomas agreed. "Where do you think you are?—On a submarine? Go make yourself a drink."

"He's already had too much to drink," Erin said curtly.

Marty stopped pacing and took a step toward Katie, glaring at her. Throwing up his hands he spat, "I just don't believe how you can go all in with nothing! Talk about fishing expeditions!"

Katie glared back at him. "Calm down, Marty. I had four clubs and a pair of threes. I had a lot of outs. Besides, I got pot odds."

Everyone but Erin turned to her in disbelief. Erin buried her face in her hand trying to hide her smug smile.

"Wow!" C. Thomas exclaimed. "Someone has been doing her homework. Have you been tutoring her, Steve?"

Steve shook his head. "Not guilty. I'd like to know, though, who *has* been coaching her." He turned to his wife. "Care to tell us?"

Erin drummed her fingers on the table and averted her eyes. She wondered what her co-conspirator was going to say.

"This is poker," Katie began, "not rocket science."

"But you're playing very differently tonight," C. Thomas said. "I think we are *all* wondering what is responsible for this new level of playing style."

"I'm going with my gut and my hunches," Katie said. "A little bit of luck and a little bit of timing."

"A lot of luck," Scarlett said.

"I'm just focusing on the game tonight. I can't help it if Marty is a sore loser."

"I'm not a sore loser!" Marty rubbed his forehead so hard Katie thought he was going to remove some skin. "If I'm going to get beat, it's one thing. It's quite another to be the first one knocked out, especially when I was holding a pair of aces in the hole." He returned to pacing.

"That's why they call it gambling," Steve said.

"Yeah," Erin agreed. "Suck it up. You won last time."

"Can we stop arguing and get on with the game?" C. Thomas asked. "Katie, I believe it's your play."

Katie was about to look at her hole cards again, but then thought better of it. "All in," she announced.

Steve sighed. "Fold."

"Out," C. Thomas said.

Now it was Scarlett's turn. All eyes were riveted on her. She looked at her hole cards and then at the pot. Katie knew from her tells that she wasn't confident about her hand. Scarlett looked at Katie and for a long moment they held each other's gaze.

"Is this a poker game or a staring contest?" C. Thomas asked, finally breaking the silence and the contest. "What's your play, Scarlett?"

"All in." Scarlett pushed her chips into the pot and turned over an ace and a queen.

Katie overturned her hole cards; a pair of tens.

"Here we go," C. Thomas said. "May the best hand win." C. Thomas dealt the flop, allowing Scarlett to pair her aces.

"This suddenly became more interesting," Marty said, returning to the table and leaning in close to Scarlett. She shivered.

C. Thomas dealt the fourth community card. It was a four; no help to anyone. Scarlett smiled, feeling secure with the highest hand and only one more card to go. Katie sat back and took a deep breath. Braun's words came back to her: *Expect to win.*

C. Thomas turned over the river card. It was a ten, giving Katie a set and the game.

Katie let out a long sigh of relief.

"You're on fire tonight, Katie," C. Thomas said.

Scarlett's disappointment in losing the hand was palpable. She tossed her cards into the center of the table, rose, and took a seat on the sofa.

"That was great," Erin said.

"Thanks," Katie said, "but I was lucky."

Erin winked at her. "You know what the pros say. 'You have to go with your hunches.'"

Marty sauntered over to the sofa and plopped down next to Scarlett. "I was pulling for you," he said.

She could smell the sour scent of his breath and it nearly made her gag. "Thanks," she said, "but Katie's on a streak."

He leaned over to her and not only could she smell the alcohol, but a more pervasive, underlying *stank* like rank, dirty gym socks. She had noticed it the night they had been together at the cabin.

"Do you want your feet massaged?"

"Um, no, thanks. I'm good." She looked away, taking a deep breath downwind of Marty's foul stench.

Scarlett got up off the sofa making an excuse merely to get the hell away from Marty. "I think I'm going to go make myself a mimosa. Anybody want one?"

Erin was paying more attention to what was going on at the poker table, responding only with "Mmhmm," while C. Thomas held up a hand and nodded.

"Gotcha," she said as she hurried to the kitchen in hopes that Marty wouldn't follow. The puppy dog thing was getting old.

"I'll see if she needs any help," Marty announced after a pause, trying not to look obvious. Erin looked up and watched him disappear into the kitchen.

Scarlett was standing at the counter pouring champagne into three glasses when Marty came up behind her, slipping his arms around her waist and nuzzling her neck.

It took just a nanosecond for her to realize who it was as the stink hit her nasal passages like a semi-truck. She wriggled out of Marty's grip, slapping his forearm. "Don't be fresh."

"I was hoping that you and I could pick up from last time."

"Yeah, well. It just wasn't in the cards." Scarlett turned to hand him one of the mimosas. "Give this to your wife."

"What the fuck, Scarlett?"

"Marty, keep to the game, okay?"

Marty tried softening. "C'mon, Scarlett. We can play our own game. Just the two of us." He moved closer, and Scarlett could again smell his breath. She detected a hint of bourbon despite the fact they'd all been drinking mimosas.

"Look, I really don't know how to say this any clearer. We played the game. You won. We had a night. That was it. We are both out of the game tonight, so nothing is going to happen."

Marty's face reddened. "Scarlett."

"Marty, please, don't do this." She pointed to the mimosa in his hand. "And your wife is waiting for her drink."

"Fuck the drink and fuck Erin."

"Oh, my God, Marty. And you *should* be fucking Erin! Maybe that's your problem."

Marty slammed the mimosa down on the counter, spilling half of it on his hand and on the counter. He licked off the remnants first and with the same hand reached over and grabbed Scarlett's left breast, pulling aside her tank top and exposing her bra.

"Stop!" Scarlett said in a muffled yell, not wanting to upset or alert the others. She grabbed his hand with both of hers and dug her fingernails into the back, leaving scratch marks, then picked up the half-empty mimosa and threw the rest down the front of his shorts. "You're an asshole!" She turned and picked up the other drinks and stomped out of the kitchen.

Marty looked down at his crumpled and now drenched khaki cargos. "What the fuck am I going to do now?" He reached into his pocket and pulled out a flask of Jack Daniels and took a swig, then grabbed a dishtowel from the hook and mopped himself dry the best he could. He put the flask away and hurriedly filled up the mimosa glass, taking a long swig from it before leaving the kitchen.

"Here you go, C. Thomas," Scarlett said putting a mimosa in front of him at the table. As she looked down she realized her top was askew and adjusted it quickly. It did not go unnoticed by Steve. She walked over to the sofa with her own drink.

Erin was now occupying the spot on the sofa where Scarlett previously had been sitting. "What happened to you?" she asked before taking a sip from her glass.

"Ask Killer Katie," Erin said. "Hey, where's my mimosa?"

"I think Marty's making you a special one," Scarlett said sitting down and intentionally hip bumping Erin. "Scoot over, Hon."

"Oh. Looks like he got lost. C. Thomas is out, too, by the way. He's just dealing."

"She took us both out with a full boat," C. Thomas called over.

"So that means—" Scarlett began.

"One of the Kellys is going to be a winner," Marty said as he appeared and headed over to Erin with the now half-filled glass, handing it to her.

"Real *special*, Marty," Erin said seeing the less-than-full drink. He gave her a quizzical look.

"Did you have yourself a little accident there, Marty?" Erin asked, pointing to the front of his shorts.

"Very funny. Yes, I pissed myself. For Christ's sake, Erin. I spilled some of your drink on the way in here." She rolled her eyes in response. Marty was an ugly drunk.

C. Thomas dealt a new hand. Katie looked at her hole cards and found a pair of jacks. Steve was holding a pair of kings and let out a not-so-subtle smile, as he cupped his other hand around them. Marty, who now was standing behind an empty seat and watching the exchange, started drumming his fingers on the back of the chair.

"Be careful, Katie. Your husband has the worst tells for a lawyer."

Steve glared at Marty. "No help from the peanut gallery, *thank you*."

"That's okay, Marty. I think I can hold my own." She fumbled with her chips for a moment then said, "I raise," as she pushed two big stacks into the center of the table. Steve matched her chips.

"I raise you," he said pushing in another two stacks. Katie matched his without hesitation.

"Call," Katie said.

C. Thomas turned over the flop; an ace, a ten, and a king. Steve now had three kings. All Katie needed was a queen for a straight.

"All in," Steve announced, pushing the remainder of his chips to the center of the table, careful to keep them standing tall.

Marty was watching impatiently as the whole hand was played. The last thing he could take as the alcohol continued to muddle his brain was seeing Steve walk out of there with Scarlett, cabin key in hand. He mouthed "fold" to Katie. She ignored him, pushing in the rest of her chips, which cascaded down like dominoes.

"Let's do it," Katie said neutrally.

Both Steve and Katie turned over their cards simultaneously. Steve smiled.

"I told you to fold, Katie," Marty slurred.

"It's not over yet," she said, maintaining the same neutral tone, hiding the fact that her heart felt as if it was going to beat right out of her chest.

C. Thomas dealt the turn card: a three of hearts.

"Damn!" Marty shouted.

C. Thomas then turned over the river card. It was a queen, completing Katie's straight. Steve was visibly stunned.

"Gotcha!" Katie exclaimed.

"Wow! What a play!" Marty was just as stunned, but relieved.

Katie grinned ear-to-ear. "All you have to do is *expect to win*."

Steve was about to respond, in fact he opened his mouth, but words failed him. C. Thomas pulled the key to the cabin from his shorts pocket and slid it across the table to Katie.

"Your choice, Katie," he said, winking at her.

Katie picked up the key and tossed it up and down in her palm. She looked first at Steve, who immediately averted his eyes.

"So, who's it going to be?" Marty asked.

"It's a tough decision," she said, looking directly at C. Thomas. Without more than a second's hesitation she said, "Let's go," sliding the key back toward him.

C. Thomas picked up the key and stood. "See y'all tomorrow. *Sayonara*."

Katie took a step toward Steve and pecked him on the temple before triumphantly strutting toward the door where C. Thomas waited. He leaned in close and whispered, "Bring the highest heels you have. Stilettos, preferably."

Katie raised an eyebrow. Did he want to go out dancing first? She wondered what he had in mind, but she just shrugged and headed to the bedroom to get them. It had been a very long time since she'd been anywhere with another man. She returned with a sexy, strappy pair of four-inch heels and her toothbrush, looking one last time over her shoulder at Steve. He didn't notice. He was turned away and looking out the back window.

The remaining players sat in silence for a moment. Marty was pacing; Erin sat smiling smugly at Katie's powerful win. Scarlett was filled with glee that C. Thomas was not going to be home for the night. She contemplated what she might actually do with a night off. Then it hit her. She got up from the couch and sauntered over to Steve who appeared to be pouting.

"Maybe you should have some company tonight," she whispered.

Steve hardly had time to consider a response before Marty was on them. "Break it up, you guys. No consolation prizes in the game. That would be against the *rules*," he said, with more than a hint of sarcasm in his tone.

"Marty, was I speaking to you?'

"Just keeping things fair and above board around here, Scar-*lett*," Marty said in a drunken tone.

"So what about it, Steve?" Scarlett redirected her attention back to him. He didn't look up as he collected the cards and placed the deck back in the box.

"No thanks, I'm fine."

"You sure? I could hang a bit and help clean up." She really wanted to stay and see where things might go if they were alone.

"Really, I'm good," he said, still without looking at her.

Scarlett's heart sank. What had gone wrong? She'd once thought they were on the same page. Now, Steve was hardly giving her the time of day.

"Too bad," Scarlett said, trying not to look dejected and smirking at Marty. She pulled her purse from the back of her chair before heading for the door. "Anyway, tell Katie thanks, Steve. G'night."

After Scarlett left, Erin got up from the couch and walked over to the table. "You want us to keep you company for a while, Steve? Maybe we could go to the tavern for a drink?"

"You two can go. I'm going home," Marty spat.

Erin shook her head as Marty stormed out. Erin and Steve were alone.

"I can't believe she did it," Steve said, washing his face in his hands.

"Why not, Steve? We all agreed to the game."

"Still, I just didn't think that when push came to shove, she'd actually pick him. That she'd actually go through with it."

"C'mon Steve. Wouldn't you have picked Scarlett if you had won?"

Steve busied himself collecting and stacking all the poker chips. He stopped, looking up at Erin with a surprised expression. "You think I would have picked Scarlett and not you?"

"Please, Steve. We've known each other a long time. I know that you would have picked Scarlett for the same reason that I would have chosen C. Thomas. You think you're projecting this mysterious, private persona. Meanwhile, you are as transparent as those ice cubes," Erin said pointing to his nearly-drained mimosa.

Steve smiled. "Maybe we should go for that drink."

"Really?"

"Or we could just have another here. At least until the girls get back from your house. I imagine Marty will be sending them home."

"Okay. I'll go mix us a few while you finish in here?"

"Sure," Steve said.

Erin headed for the kitchen while Steve continued putting all of the poker chips into the rack. "Hey Erin, make mine *all* champagne. I think I need it. On second thought, make it a screwdriver—sans OJ."

"Got it," Erin called back with a laugh.

Steve finished putting the poker chips away then collected the dirty plates and trays and carried them into the kitchen.

"So Erin, you must know how Katie managed to win tonight."

Erin was not about to "tell" Steve anything; she didn't turn around. "Huh?"

"Come on, Erin. You two discuss everything."

"Steve, I don't know what you're talking about." Erin turned around and handed Steve a glass of vodka on the rocks.

"Mmmhmm."

"Listen, Katie and I are friends, but we don't do *everything* together."

"All right. I see I'm getting nothing out of you."

Erin put her hand on his forearm. After a moment, she took the dirty dishes over to the sink and began washing them. They both were quiet.

"Erin, did you ever think—"

"We'd find ourselves here?" Erin finished his sentence. She shut off the water and turned away from the sink, leaning against it.

"Yeah. Something like that."

"Honestly, no, but when I look back, I guess I can say I should have seen certain things coming. I mean, I know Marty and I haven't been on the same page for a very long while. I don't know where his head is a lot of the time. I'm just hoping we can get back somehow."

"Yes. But, here? I mean *here*? This is crazy stuff we're all doing."

"Well," Erin laughed. "I don't think anyone could have predicted we'd be exactly right *here*, in *this* level of insanity."

"It is pretty insane, isn't it? I mean, my wife is having sex with another man as we speak."

"Um, Steve. Am I detecting a double standard?"

"What are you talking about?"

"For Christ's sake. Where is your head? Has it *always* been with Katie?"

"Again, I ask, what are you talking about?"

"I think you know."

"No, Erin, I really don't."

"There is so much about all of us that just isn't what it seems."

Steve scratched his head. He wondered what Erin might know.

"And, as long as we're talking about all this, what about the fact that my husband slept with another woman just last week? Or that, whether you admit it or not, you would have slept with Scarlett, too, had you won?"

Steve shook his head. "Erin, like I said before, what makes you think I wouldn't have picked you? You are a beautiful and desirable woman."

Steve looked right at her, maybe through her. Marty hadn't looked at her like that in a very long time. Maybe he never had. Her stomach did a flip. She looked down at the floor, shaking her head. When she finally looked up, Anna and Jamie walked through the door.

"Hey, Dad. Hey, Erin," Jamie said, flopping into a kitchen chair, Anna into another.

Erin collected herself. "Hi, girls. How were the boys tonight?"

Both girls looked at each other and broke out into hysterics. Erin followed suit.

"Well, I guess that answers your question, Erin." Steve laughed, too.

"Marty paid you?"

"Yeah. He went a little overboard though. I'm not sure he even counted. Do you want some of it back?" Anna asked reaching for her pocket.

"Nah, I am sure whatever he gave you was well deserved. We really appreciate you two doing all this babysitting."

"No problem," Anna said.

"Got any snacks left, Dad?" Jamie asked.

"Sure. I think there are still chips in the bowls, and Mom left some of the extra appetizers in a plastic container in the fridge."

"Oh, okay. Where's Mom, by the way?" Jamie asked.

"Uh, yeah. Um, she went over to Scarlett's for a little bit. I think she needed help with something—for work maybe."

"Oh, but it's late."

"Yeah, but Mom was going to be too busy tomorrow."

"'Kay," Jamie said, her head already in the refrigerator. She pulled out a rectangular container and turned to Anna. "Wanna go finish that movie? The DVD has to go back tomorrow."

"Sure," she said and both girls left for the living room.

"I better head out, Steve," Erin said, spilling out the last of her mimosa into the sink.

"Okay. Thanks for your help cleaning up. Anal Katie would have had it done already. I'm sure she'll appreciate not having to do all of it tomorrow. I'm not exactly the best at doing these things to her standards."

"Sure, no problem."

"You know, Erin, I meant what I said before," Steve said.

"What? Oh, yeah. Well—"

"Marty doesn't deserve you, you know."

"Yeah, well tell him that. I am sure he sees things as completely the other way around."

"He's more bark than bite I think."

"Well, his bark is annoying as all get out."

Erin took a step toward Steve and gave him a quick hug and peck on the cheek. "Try to have a good rest of the night, Steve. Remember, I've been there." She picked up her purse and headed for the door.

"Thanks, Erin. 'Night."

## 16

## BLINKING

Scarlett adjusted the volume on the radio then pranced away from it, humming to herself as she took off her clothes and tossed them one-by-one into the hamper.

"Score!" she shouted as she landed her panties in the basket. She hadn't missed even once. She genuinely felt lighthearted. C. Thomas was somebody else's problem tonight. She paused a moment to wonder whether he'd really go for the stilettos or if he'd save face and actually *perform* with Katie. After all, Katie was the winner, and it would be up to her what they did, wouldn't it?

Scarlett headed for the bathroom with a paperback under her arm. Even though it was late, she had a sudden surge of energy. She wanted to take a long, hot, relaxing bath, something she rarely did. She dug out a bottle of aromatic oils then turned on the faucet, adding a few drops of the rose oil into the water stream. She immediately felt a sense of calm, adding to her already good mood, sans C. Thomas.

Facing the mirror, she pulled her hair up into a messy topknot. She glanced down at her reflection and noticed the faded remnants of her last and only bruise, then chuckled at the idea that maybe Katie might end up with one—or ten. The tub only was about half full, but the water was steamy; just as she had swung one leg in, she heard the doorbell ring.

"Damn! Who the hell could that be?" she said out loud. It wasn't as if C. Thomas couldn't have let himself in. Could it be Steve? Scarlett pulled her foot out of the water and quickly rubbed it on the bathmat to dry. She grabbed her bathrobe and headed toward the stairs putting it on and tying it as she took the steps two at a time.

She took a deep breath before she slid the security chain into place and opened the door. It was after midnight, and while she was hoping Steve might have taken her up on her offer, she wasn't taking any chances. Plus, she didn't want to look too eager. She pulled open the door against the chain and found Marty standing on the doorstep. Her mood instantly fell.

"Marty? What are you doing here? Where's Erin? Is everything okay?"

"Yeah, yeah. She's with Steve. I guess she felt he needed some *comforting*. How about you? Do you need *comforting*?" Marty was staring right at her cleavage. She pulled her robe tighter.

"It's late, Marty, and I'm really tired," she said, a wave of panic washing over her, although she couldn't put her finger on exactly why.

"You're going to *bed*?"

"Yes, Marty. I was just getting ready to go to bed. See you—later?" Scarlett responded almost as a question, closing the door as she spoke. Marty blocked it with his foot.

"Bed. Yeah. Bed. Scarlett, I really want to be with you. I thought we had a good time."

"We did, Marty, but it was part of the game. C'mon. You're breaking the rules." Scarlett could tell from his expression that he wasn't budging, nor did he care about any game rules. "Can you please move your foot so I can go to sleep?"

"Scarlett. I know you want this as much as I do. C. Thomas is gone for the whole night. It's a perfect opportunity."

Scarlett attempted to fake a yawn. "Marty, really, I'm tired and I already said it was fun, but—"

"Yeah. You said it. I got it. The *rules!*" he said, his tone quickly aggressive. He pulled his foot away.

"Good night, Marty," Scarlett said as she closed the door. Her hands were shaking as she slid the deadbolt into place and turned to set the security system to ON. She hadn't planned to arm it, figuring it would be less of a hassle when C. Thomas got home, but she wasn't taking any chances after this. Now she was hoping—*praying*—that C. Thomas would come strolling through the door.

Scarlett headed into the living room and sat down on the couch, careful not to turn on any more lights in case Marty returned. She pulled a throw blanket over herself and tucked her feet under her. She hugged her knees to her chest and tried to take long, deep, focused breaths, the kind her therapist had taught her to use whenever she became upset. If it wasn't so late, she might actually have called her mother.

After a few moments, she began to feel calmer. She reached into the cushions for her journal. She hadn't written in it for a while and really needed a cathartic release. This actually was the first time she'd looked forward to being alone. But now she was scared. Why? This is just Marty being Marty, she thought to herself. Right?

---

UNBEKNOWNST TO SCARLETT, after she had closed the door, Marty planted himself on her WELCOME mat. Half an hour later he still was sitting there, cursing under his breath and thinking about what to do next. Erin had gone to bed right after she came home, and he certainly didn't feel like going back there.

He pulled the flask out of his pocket and unscrewed the cap. There wasn't much in it so he emptied it. He rose, turning toward the door and contemplated whether he should knock again. Maybe Scarlett was still up. He peered through the living room window but there was only the faint glow from the hallway light. He wondered for a moment if the back door might be open.

---

STEVE WAS LYING on his bed, still dressed and watching the digital clock change from two-thirty-six to two-thirty-seven to two-thirty-eight. He'd been doing the same thing for the entire two hours since Erin had left, while mindlessly tossing playing cards from a deck into a baseball cap sitting at the end of the bed. There were three empty beer bottles on the nightstand. He'd considered calling Katie, but thought better of it. He also had considered calling or even stopping by Scarlett's, but thought better of that as well.

His thoughts were racing about what happened in the game. How had Katie won? How could she bed C. Thomas? He wrestled with the fact that he, too, would have elected to sleep with someone else—Scarlett. But double standards be damned. Somehow the idea of Katie doing it was wrong. Just plain wrong.

Steve got up, knocking cards to the floor. He walked down the hallway, looking into each of the girls's rooms as they slept. He was feeling the alcohol. He shook his head, muttering to himself. "How did we get here? Oh, my God. How the hell do we get back?"

He made his way to the kitchen for some acetaminophen, pouring four from the bottle into his palm. He pulled the spigot out of the faucet and took a long swig after downing the pills. He looked out the window at the pool as the moon reflected on it.

"Scarlett," he said out loud. He surprised himself. After a few minutes, he grabbed another beer out of the refrigerator. He didn't want to go to sleep. He couldn't. Instead he headed for the den.

Steve rarely used the den which was something of a makeshift home office. He spent enough time in New York preparing and litigating cases so he really hated working from home and only did so when absolutely necessary. But he did keep older files in there which he often used when some burning issue kept him up late and he needed to ferret out something for a case. Tonight was one of those nights, but it wasn't about a case. Not exactly.

He knew precisely where to find the folder. He pulled open the middle drawer and about a third of the way from the back, he yanked out a blue-tabbed file. Flopping down on the leather sofa, he took a long swig before setting his beer bottle on the floor beside him. He opened the case and flipped through a few pages until he found her photograph. *Michele*.

Michele was an attorney whom he supervised on a case in Georgia almost a decade back. She was sharp as a tack and had a great sense of humor. She was a beauty, young, slim, and with a mane of deep red curls. She and Steve had a lot in common and spent a good deal of time together during the nearly two weeks he'd consulted with her firm. He paged through the file, looking at the notes and the copies of the receipts—a few restaurants, the hotel, a gallery. A drawing of a stick figure fell out into Steve's lap.

He looked at it for a long moment then put it into one of the pockets of the folder. He took a deep breath.

Steve closed the file and laid it back against his chest. His head was spinning, but his eyes were becoming heavy, and he needed to go to the bathroom. The last beer had hit him almost immediately, and he didn't want Katie to find him like that, so he dragged himself from the couch to put away the file. He staggered to the bedroom, detouring into the master bathroom and then headed to the bed. He collected most of the playing cards then lay back down. After a few missed tosses into the ball cap, he was out like a light.

---

"Thank you for a great night, Katie," C. Thomas said, reaching out of the driver's side window to take Katie's hand as she stood next to his Jag. He planted a long kiss in the middle of her palm.

"You're welcome," Katie replied, smiling weakly.

It was almost ten o'clock and already stiflingly hot outside. Katie said good-bye over her shoulder and waved as she walked toward the house.

"Katie! Hey! You forgot something!" C. Thomas said smiling wide, dangling her shoes from the tips of his fingers out of the car's open window.

"Ahh, thanks." Katie walked back as C. Thomas opened the door to stand to hand them to her. He leaned in to give her a hug. She awkwardly hugged him back then headed again toward the front door.

C. Thomas waved good-bye, but Katie hadn't turned around, instead quickly closing the door behind her as she shivered from the chill of the A/C in contrast to the quickly climbing July temperatures. Expecting to see Steve in the kitchen sitting over a cup of weak coffee, she was surprised not to find him there. She walked down the hallway toward the bedrooms. The girls were still asleep.

"Did you sleep all night like this?" Katie said as she barged into the master bedroom. Steve was lying on his back snoring loudly and covered in playing cards.

When he didn't answer, she shook him and called out louder, "Steve?"

Steve nearly jumped. The alcohol and broken-up sleep left him ragged and ornery. "Jeez! What time is it?"

"Ten."

"You just got home?!"

"Yup. The girls are still asleep. No surprise there. You want to go out for breakfast? I could really use some coffee."

Steve stumbled out of bed and made a beeline for the bathroom. He fumbled for the faucet to wash his face. From the mirror, he could see Katie was leaning against the doorway watching him.

"So I guess you're not going to say anything about last night?" Steve asked. He reached around behind for a towel off the rack but Katie pulled it off and handed it to him.

"That's against the rules, Steve."

Steve turned to face her. "What about the rules of our *marriage*?"

"Are you *kidding* me? Don't try to guilt me. You agreed to this just like I did." Katie was annoyed. "If you *really* didn't want to do it, you should have said so. No one twisted your arm."

Steve stood looking blankly at Katie.

"That's the problem, Steve. You always say what you think others want to hear. Or else you say nothing and let everyone else do the talking, that way you're never to blame." She waited for a response but none came. Katie turned on her heels and grabbed a tank dress and a pair of sandals from the closet then headed out of the bedroom. "Forget it. You can make your own breakfast. I'm going out."

Steve turned back to the mirror and stared at his reflection. He could hear the hallway bathroom door close. He continued to look into his own eyes, not certain what he was seeing. Unlike when he looked into Katie's eyes, he couldn't read his own, or he wouldn't admit to what might have been behind them. He soon heard the sound of Katie's footsteps down the hall. The jingling of her keys and the slamming of the front door made him jump.

---

Katie got into her car and immediately called Erin. She picked up before the first ring even ended.

"Katie!"

"Yeah. It's me."

"Oh, my God! How did it go?!"

"I'll tell you all about it. Can you meet?"

"Um. I guess so. Hold on." Katie could hear her call to Marty that she was going out. She couldn't hear Marty's response, but she could discern from his tone that it was not an agreeable one.

"Fuck it," Erin said. "I'm outta here. Where should we meet?"

Katie laughed. Hearing Erin curse always struck her as funny. "The luncheonette is fine. See you there. I'm already on my way."

"Okay. Me, too."

---

"So let me get this straight," Erin said, setting down her coffee cup. "You never actually had *sex* with C. Thomas?"

"Not even a French kiss. All I did was spank his naked ass with a ruler while he masturbated. It was so sick! After that he collapsed in bed and was out for the entire night." Katie's expression was more than glum.

"Ewww," Erin said, grimacing. "Remind me never to shake his hand."

"Who would've ever thought? What a waste of a hot specimen. I ended up watching movies all night—alone."

"So what was that talk about the heels before you left? I thought maybe you two were going to go out somewhere first."

"You have no idea! Oh, my God. At first, he wanted me to walk on his back! I said no goddamned way. Can you imagine?"

"Are you serious?"

"Um, yes. Spanking was the—at least something that I—sort of enjoyed. I guess the idea of inflicting pain was a good way to make him pay for ruining my night! Sad part is, he enjoyed it—of course for the wrong reasons."

"Unbelievable!" Erin was laughing into her cup and spit out her coffee. "No wonder Scarlett is so sex starved all the time."

"Well, it does explain some things about them. Ha! Probably explains those bruises. Who the hell could walk on a person's back in stilettos? And you should see his back."

"No thanks. You've ruined any interest I have in seeing that body ever again."

"Me, too."

"What did Steve say about all this? Did you tell him?"

"Are you kidding? It's against the rules anyway. Let him think what he wants. He should get jealous once in a while. He's being a real ass about things lately anyway."

Erin looked away and stared out the window, suddenly appearing lost in thought.

"What's wrong, Erin?"

"Nobody's going to pick me," she said, still looking out the window.

"What are you talking about?"

Erin turned to Katie. "Let's face it, Katie, if Steve wins he'll choose Scarlett. After hearing this, I wouldn't want C. Thomas to pick me, not that he would."

"Well, C. Thomas's—what should we say? His *predilections*? They do narrow the field somewhat."

"I have to be honest with you, Katie. If I win, I'll have to choose Steve."

Katie paused, about to take a bite of her omelet, her fork in mid-air.

"What's the matter?" Erin asked.

Katie put down her silverware. "There's something just a little weird about my best friend telling me that she intends to sleep with my husband."

"We knew this was a possibility."

"But we both talked about choosing C. Thomas. All along that was our plan, wasn't it? I never imagined it would come to *this*."

"So what are you saying? That if I win, you don't want me to pick Steve? That you won't let me?"

Katie began pushing her breakfast around her plate, and she was becoming increasingly agitated. "No, you do what you want."

"Katie—"

"You're a big girl, Erin. Steve is a big boy. You realize of course that this means the next time *I* win I'm going to have to choose Marty."

Katie thought she saw a hint of a smirk cross Erin's lips before she responded. "I know. That's your choice. I won't be upset."

"Are you kidding me? I don't *have* a choice anymore. And the problem is I am simply not attracted to your husband."

The smirk disappeared instantly. "That's a terrible thing to say. What's wrong with my husband?" Erin said defensively, her voice growing louder. An older woman at the table behind her turned around.

"Puleeze! He's hardly my type!"

"Listen, *dear*, Steve is no prize, either. The only reason I'd pick him now is that it's all I can do *not* to spank in my own home with the twins."

Katie took her wallet from her purse on the seat next to her. She rifled through it for a twenty and tossed it on the table. She stood. "I have to get back now. The girls will be up."

"You're upset. Don't leave like this—please. Let's talk about it. Finish your breakfast."

"I'm sorry. I really have to go."

---

KATIE PULLED into the driveway with her car loaded with groceries. She really hadn't needed much but she was hungry and that's a dangerous way to shop. In fact, shopping could have waited, but she didn't want to go home to deal with Steve. She was upset about her altercation with Erin, too. She had mindlessly strolled the aisles and before she knew it, she had a full grocery cart. Steve was sitting on the patio. He looked up when he saw her get out of the car.

She went around to the back of the Jeep for the bags; as she did, Erin drove by.

"Katie!" she called out. She pulled up against the edge of the driveway.

Katie didn't respond and walked toward the house with both arms laden with bags. Steve stood and reached to take the bags from her, but Katie ignored him and headed for the door. As she opened it, she said over her shoulder, "There're more in the car."

"Okay." Steve headed for the Jeep and saw Erin's car idling on the street. He shrugged at her questioningly.

Erin shook her head and shrugged back. She waved and drove off.

Steve's cell phone rang in his pocket. It was Marty, the last person he wanted to speak with. Begrudgingly he answered.

"Yeah? What's up, Marty?"

"She's playing hard to get."

"Who is?"

"Scarlett."

"I don't have time for this right now, Marty."

---

*Dear Mom:*

*You were right. I am a cock tease. What was I thinking? There is something really wrong with that man. Marty scares me.*

*I know you wanted me to be taken care of. C. Thomas does that—he buys me things—but he and I are so—NOT compatible. He might as well be with a blow-up doll. A blow-up doll with stilettos. He doesn't need me. He doesn't love me. Not really.*

*I am so tired of not being seen. By anyone. Well, that is, maybe except for Steve. But that could be my imagination. Does he see me? He seems to see me, but sometimes I'm not so sure. He's married anyway. God. Katie. I'm sorry. Or maybe I'm not.*

*But Marty sees me in ALL the wrong ways. I feel like a piece of meat, and I think I must have caused it. You remember when you told me all I had was my looks, and I'd better use them? That was wrong, Mom. So wrong. I have a brain, and I should be using that. I need to go back to school. I need a man who loves me for what I have on the inside, too.*

*What should I do about Marty? I need to tell him to leave me the hell alone once and for all. I haven't slept all night. I'm afraid to. What if he comes back?! Mommy…*

## 17

### REMATCH

Katie always had been intrigued and somewhat baffled by the concept of time. In college, for the sake of sleeping late Mondays and Wednesdays, she took a three-credit physics course in the evening to satisfy her science requirement. Professor Leo was up for tenure and, consequently, was a madman in class; somewhere to the right of Einstein in his own personal theories, but a bit left of Hawking. As a result, he steered away from the classic curriculum and included new and, at the time, rather avant-garde notions of time and space based on quantum physics and quantum mechanics.

The course became her undoing. Katie, always an "A" student, had to work her tail off just to get a "B" in the class. Her final grade ended up bringing down her GPA and while she still graduated magna cum laude, it knocked her out of the running for valedictorian. But what she did take away from the class was the notion that time may not be linear at all. Past, present, and future all may be happening spontaneously in the *now*. She learned that even Einstein believed it. In writing to the family of a departed friend, he'd said that even though his friend had preceded him in death, it was of no consequence. "...for us physicists believe the separation between past, present, and future is only an illusion, although a convincing one."

On this particular Saturday night, she thought once again about the nature of time and how strangely it seemed to pass. Somehow it was already August. Where did the summer go? The weeks had become a blur; time merging onto itself, indistinguishable, and frankly, totally forgettable. Lately, the only things that stood out from the miasma were Saturday nights and the game. It became both habit and ritual. Katie wondered whether it was an addictive habit as well. Would they all need to go to Gamblers' Anonymous? Or worse, Sex Addicts' Anonymous?

Katie was done with it. Really done. It was nine-thirty, and she and Erin were sitting on opposite ends of the sofa. Katie was toggling back and forth between playing word games on her cell and attempting to craft a text to her sister, the latter of which she was having trouble. Erin was mindlessly paging through a fashion magazine. Both had busted early in the game. Katie couldn't speak for Erin, but she was not following Braun's advice and *expecting to win* this evening. In fact, she did the opposite of what Braun told her and went all-in on a weak hand with very few outs, hoping to lose. Why would she want to win at this point? For another night of playing Dominatrix to a boy toy? Not! For a night with the drunken turd Marty? Certainly not! Where did that leave her? A night with her own husband—that not only was against the rules, but she had that every night anyway. Yippee. She and Steve had been at odds since this whole game change-up started. Maybe it truly was all a slippery slope, one that they never should have started down.

On the other hand, if she were playing for a night with Zack Braun...hmm.

She could not stop thinking about Braun. She actually toyed with the idea of calling him and telling him about her poker progress. But that also would mean having to tell him that she had in fact won and consequently about her night with C. Thomas. The idea of revisiting *that* experience, especially with Braun, was nauseating. Maybe they could talk about quantum physics.

"I'm going to go make a drink," Erin said as she stood, tossing aside the magazine. "Does anyone want anything?" She avoided Katie's gaze. When no one answered, she disappeared into the kitchen.

Katie had contemplated responding. She really wanted to air things out but not in front of the others. She got up from the sofa and walked into the kitchen unnoticed. Erin turned around, surprised to see her. The two stared at each other for a moment when Katie broke the silence.

"Erin. About the other day—"

"You don't have to say anything. Things got a little—weird, I know."

"Yeah. I'm so sorry. I don't know about you, but I'm just not into this game tonight."

"God, me either." Erin took a step toward Katie, and they hugged for a moment.

"I never want this nonsense affecting our friendship. Good friends are too hard to come by," Katie said.

"I know."

"You are always the one I can turn to, you know? Like sisters…" she trailed off.

The two women turned toward the mock bar Katie always had set up on the island. "Wine tonight?" Katie asked.

"Sure, chick juice. We can drown our sorrows."

"You know, when I think about it, I haven't had any really good friends since college. Once I met Steve that was it." Katie poured two glasses and walked over to the kitchen table with them. Erin joined her and they both sat down.

"That's right. You guys got married not long after, right?"

"Yeah. Well, I was almost done with licensure, then along came Jamie." She gestured to her stomach. "I'd wanted to get my Ph.D. in clinical psychology. Maybe I'll go back. I've been thinking a lot about it lately."

"Well, with chasing after the boys all these years, I sometimes wonder about going back to corralling someone else's rambunctious kids five days a week. But I did really love teaching. Then again, I could pursue another career path. Maybe professional poker?"

Both women broke into laughter.

"Did I ever tell you I'm writing a book?"

"Really? No! What about?"

"Sort of a self-help, psychology book. More or less about getting what you want out of life."

"Wow! When do you write?"

"Just here and there. Whenever I can. I'm more than halfway done. I'm trying to make good use of my education until I can get back out there and practice as a psychotherapist, you know?"

"That's great, Katie."

"And I've finally decided it's time to mend fences with Alice. I just don't know how to go about it."

"I know that'll be tough for you. I'm glad though."

"Yeah." Katie turned away.

"Well, if you need a sounding board, I'm here." Erin leaned over and put her hand on Katie's.

They chatted for a short while longer before Katie realized that they might be missing some interesting action in the other room.

"Let's head in and see what mischief the other four have gotten into."

Katie and Erin entered the playing area at a critical moment. Scarlett, C. Thomas, and Marty had gone all-in on the same hand. C. Thomas dealt the flop, fourth street, and the river in quick succession. There was a pregnant pause as everyone assessed their hands. Marty was the first to react.

"What the fuck!" He jumped up, slamming his chair into the table, knocking over his empty glass in the process. "How the hell can you go all-in with a pair of deuces and three people left in the game?"

Scarlett ended up beating the two of them with a full house. "I guess I just felt lucky," Scarlett said, raking in her chips.

Katie and Erin navigated to the sofa, arm-in-arm and drinks in hand. Now there was no distance between them. "We're gone for a few minutes," Erin said, "and the game goes to shit."

"Apparently so," Katie said, sipping her wine. "It's just Scarlett and my *hubby*"

"I need some air," Marty blurted. He turned and stormed into the kitchen.

"Sore loser," Scarlett muttered, barely above a whisper.

C. Thomas picked up the deck of cards. "I guess I'll deal until there's a winner." He shuffled and dealt the opening hand. Steve got an ace and a ten; Scarlett a pair of fours.

"All-in," Scarlett said without hesitation. She pushed her pile of chips into the center of the table. Marty returned and stood in the doorway with a fresh drink in his hand.

Steve silently considered his next move, one hand pressed against his jaw, the other holding a stack of chips inches above the table and letting them fall and restack in front of him.

"Your play, Steve-O," C. Thomas coaxed.

Katie could tell from his body language that he was insecure about his hand, but didn't want to let it go. Braun's parting words came back to her: *You have to know when to let go…*

"Call me," Scarlett said, challenging him. "I want to go head to head with you." She looked at Marty to see if he caught the double entendre. She could tell from his caustic look that he had.

"All-in," Steve finally said. He pushed his stacks into Scarlett's pile and turned over his cards. No surprise from the peanut gallery when Steve's cards were revealed. It was a fairly strong hand for an all-in call with two players left in the game. There was a collective gasp, however, when Scarlett revealed her pair of fours. Even Steve breathed a sigh of relief when he saw Scarlett's cards.

"Scarlett, what are you doing going all-in on that shit?" Marty asked.

"I'll let you know when I need your advice, Marty."

"Let's play nice, children," C. Thomas admonished.

"Just deal the damn cards," Marty barked.

"Yassir, Masser Boss Man," C. Thomas responded sarcastically. With exaggerated slowness just to piss off Marty, C. Thomas dealt the next three cards in the flop, an ace, a ten, and a three.

Steve smiled and leaned back in his chair. The flop had been good to him giving him two pairs, aces over tens.

"Told you," Marty said, needling Scarlett.

"Shut-up, turd," Scarlett fired back. She gave a sidelong glance to see if Erin had heard her latest ad hominem attack on her husband, but she was engaged in an animated conversation with Katie. Scarlett took the opportunity stick her tongue out at Marty. The exchange was not lost on Steve.

"Are you ever going to deal the fucking cards?" Marty asked, almost hyperventilating.

"When I'm good and ready," C. Thomas said. He turned over the fourth street card. It was a jack.

"Looking good, Steve-O," C. Thomas teased.

The girls had caught on to the intensity, and both Katie and Erin rose to their feet to watch. Marty wiped sweat from his forehead with the back of his hand.

C. Thomas turned over the river card. It was a four, giving Scarlett a set and the game.

"Yes!" Scarlett screamed, stood up and began twerking.

Marty nearly swallowed his tongue. When he regained his composure, he said, "I don't fucking believe it!"

Even C. Thomas was rendered speechless.

Steve leaned back in his chair, deflated. "Damned river. Gets me all the friggin' time."

"I told you I felt lucky," Scarlett said. She collapsed into her chair, picked up her drink and downed it in a gulp.

"This is going to be interesting," Erin whispered to Katie.

"Very," Katie responded.

"Congratulations, Babe," C. Thomas said. "The river was very kind to you." He took out the key to his father's cabin and pushed it across the table toward her. "Here you go. You're the winner. Now all you have to do is pick who you want to spend the night with."

Scarlett picked up the key and held it up to the light. All eyes were on her.

"Who are you going to pick?" C. Thomas asked.

Scarlett deliberately took her time, looking from one face to the other. She had decided long ago whom she was going to choose if she'd won. Now that she had the chance, she was determined not to waste it.

She looked at Steve and smiled, but as she did, he averted his gaze and turned away. The rebuff was clear, the rejection palpable and painful. Scarlett felt as if she was stabbed in the heart. She glanced at Katie and thought she noticed a trace of a smug smile. Her own smile and decision faded like the morning mist.

"So who is it going to be?" C. Thomas urged.

Scarlett stood up. "It's a really tough decision." She noticed that Steve was still turned away. The bastard! If he only knew what he could have had tonight. Indeed, she was prepared to give him everything she had and more.

But not now.

She walked to Marty who was still skulking in the doorway. He brightened when she approached and stood up straight, a broad smile stretching across his face.

Do you really think I would pick a drunken perv like you? she screamed in her head, half hoping he could read her thoughts. Obviously, he hadn't, because he reached out to her, as if accepting a trophy, victorious and gloating.

She turned abruptly, brushing aside his outstretched fingers. "I choose—Erin," she announced to the group.

The words couldn't have been more impactful if they had been emblazoned on stone tablets by the fiery tendrils of God's fingernails. Marty almost fell over and had to steady himself by grasping the doorway molding with both hands. Both Katie and Erin collapsed simultaneously onto the sofa. Steve had her full attention now. Even C. Thomas was taken back, dropping the deck of cards and almost spilling his drink.

"You can't pick *her*," Marty said, breaking the hitherto silence.

"Why not?" Scarlett asked.

"Because it's against the rules," Marty said, slurring most of his words, his face beet red.

"That's ridiculous," Scarlett fired back. She turned to C. Thomas, the rule maker. "What do you say?"

C. Thomas shrugged. "It's your choice. You can pick anyone but me. Those are the rules. Erin is fair game."

Erin giggled more out of awkwardness than amusement. "I don't know about this."

"Erin's my choice," Scarlett said. "What we do is our business."

Erin looked at Katie, searching for some sign or reaction from her. Katie winked and gave her a slight nod. "Go for it," she mouthed silently.

"This isn't how it's supposed to be," Marty said. He turned to Erin. "You're not going."

"You can't tell her not to go," Scarlett said.

"I can tell my wife anything I damn well please!"

"No, you can't!" Erin said defiantly. "I'm a big girl, and I'll decide what I do." She stood up and turned to Scarlett. "I'm going to the powder room to freshen up. I'll meet you outside."

Erin headed for the bathroom, deliberately shoving her husband out of the way as she passed through the doorway.

Scarlett looked at Marty and rolled her tongue seductively over her lips. "Don't wait up for her, Marty." She picked up her purse and headed for the door. Like Erin had, she bumped Marty on the way out; this time he almost lost his balance and fell over. He slumped against the doorway like a man having a heart attack. He clutched his heaving chest with one hand while his other tried to steady himself against the wall. His shirttail had come out of his shorts and was soaked in perspiration.

"Have a good evening," Scarlett said to the others over her shoulder.

"I can't believe this," Marty grumbled more to himself than anyone else.

"Don't worry, Marty," C. Thomas said, with his usual over-the-top toothy grin. "Erin will have a good time. Scarlett will make sure of that."

Marty grimaced, then turned and stumbled after Scarlett.

Steve was as devastated as Marty by the turn of events, but the devastation was not as publicly visible. He really had thought, believed, that Scarlett was going to choose him. Did he blow it somehow? Lately he was being deliberately aloof, even distant with Scarlett, but surely she understood why. She must know how he felt about her and that he must act otherwise for appearance sake. He could have been wrong. Maybe he misgauged her understanding of the way things had to be or, worse, her feelings for him.

His head was spinning. He could feel his heart thundering in his chest. What was he to do? He considered whether now might be the right time for him to throw caution to the wind and to show his true feelings; to go after what he truly wanted in life for once instead of merely being a passive matchstick swirling to and fro at the behest of life's fickle seas.

He looked over at Katie. She was staring back at him, an all-knowing, all-seeing expression on her face. For one awkward, jarring instant, he felt as if she had just read his thoughts.

Outside, Marty made a beeline for Scarlett while she waited for Erin in C. Thomas's car on the darkened street. There were no streetlights and the house was far enough back that only a little light from the moon was cast upon the Jaguar which Scarlett was using to primp in the visor mirror. She didn't notice when Marty approached the car, despite his bumbling, drunken gait.

"Are you doing this to torment me?" Marty barked, punching his fist against the driver's side window, fury filling his eyes.

Scarlett screeched, nearly jumping through the roof. Catching her breath, she rolled down the window partway and spat, "Marty, go home!"

"How dare you do this to me!"

"Do what to you?! What is it that you think I owe you?!"

"Are you kidding me?!" he slurred. "We had a night like nothing you've ever had! You've never had a lover like me!"

"You're kidding me, right?"

"I am most certainly not kidding you," he slurred. "You know it, and I know it!"

"Marty, leave me alone. Erin will be out soon. There is nothing between us."

"You know you want me," Marty softened a moment, surely believing that a different tack would get through to her. "C'mon, I'll come around the other side, and you and me—we can just head to the cabin."

"Marty, I picked Erin. I want to go to the cabin with her—not *you*."

"What are you? A lesbo?" he asked, slurring more than before.

"I am not even going to dignify that with an answer. You are a pig, Marty."

"Well, maybe that's the reason for all this. I am too much man for you!" he bellowed, grabbing his crotch, but he lost his footing and fell against the car.

"You flatter yourself. The simple truth of the matter is that I'd rather sleep with your wife than with a whiny, needy little perv like you."

"You bitch!" Marty began, reaching into the partly opened window to grab at Scarlett. She pulled herself away just in time. Before he could do anything else, Erin bounded out of the house and approached the passenger side door.

"Don't wait up for me," she called over the roof to Marty, oblivious to what had been going on. She opened the door, slid in, and slammed the door—hard.

Scarlett was doing her best to compose herself, in an effort not to upset Erin. Why the fuck did she ever marry such a prick? Why did she stay with him? Shaking it off, she turned to Erin with a smile and asked, "Ready?"

Erin nodded, smiling back. "Let's do this!"

They pulled away, leaving Marty stumbling after them in the street.

## 18

"L"

"Do you want to watch movies?" Erin asked Scarlett. The two women were sitting on the edge of the bed in C. Thomas's cabin. The car ride there had been quiet and despite her show for Marty, Erin felt awkward.

Scarlett shook her head. She reached over and placed her hand on top of Erin's. "I didn't come here to watch TV."

"C'mon, Scarlett. We both know this was just some kind of joke. What is it you like to call it? A goof?"

"Erin, it isn't a joke at all. Why do you think that?"

"Because. It's us. You and me. Two women."

"Erin," Scarlett began softly. "Yes, it is you and me."

"I don't think—I don't know if I—if I can."

"Have you ever been with a woman?"

"No, never."

"Really?" Scarlett sounded surprised.

"Never sex. I mean, in high school I made out with my best friend Lila on a dare."

Scarlett was looking at her wide-eyed. It really hadn't been a big deal, Erin thought.

"That was the extent of my lesbian experiences."

"Did you enjoy it?"

"Um. There was really nothing to it."

"Really?" Scarlett was looking right into Erin's eyes.

"Yeah. Really."

Scarlett paused for a minute before saying anything else. She leaned closer to Erin and finally said, "I know you want to."

Hearing Scarlett say those five words had made her heart flutter; Erin was taken aback by her own body's—what was it, betrayal? She didn't know what she was feeling, but she did know she was confused and her head was spinning. "How do you know that? How could you know what I want?"

"I've seen the way you look at me."

Erin shook her head in response. "Scarlett."

"I could tell that day when you rubbed sunscreen on my back. You have great hands. They felt great on me."

Scarlett took Erin's hand which was now curled into a fist in her lap and pulled open her fingers. She began stroking her palm. Erin's breathing began to quicken. "You know you wanted to touch these," Scarlett said as she pressed Erin's hand against her breast.

Erin tried weakly to pull her hand away, but Scarlett pressed it more firmly against her breast and with the other hand, pulled her tank top away, exposing her fullness. Erin stopped resisting, and Scarlett leaned in to kiss her. Erin willingly responded. After about twenty seconds, Erin suddenly broke free and stood up.

"I can't. I just can't do it." She ran to the bathroom and closed the door.

Scarlett rose and walked over to the bathroom and leaned against the doorway. "Erin," she said.

"What?" Erin asked weakly.

"I find you very attractive, Erin. I know this may seem weird, but I really want this. I think we both—need this."

"I—"

"Listen. We can go slow. As slow as you want. Or if you really don't want to, we don't have to do anything at all. I don't want to push you. It's up to you."

Scarlett walked over to the bed and sat down with her back against the headboard. She heard the water running in the bathroom and closed her eyes. She just really wanted companionship tonight. There was something about being with a woman that felt so genuinely appealing. Lately all men sucked. C. Thomas could care less about real sex or whether she ever had an orgasm. Marty, well, he just scared the living shit out of her. Then there was Steve. He couldn't be any colder than if he was on a slab in a morgue.

Scarlett looked toward the bathroom and considered going back over to cajole Erin to come out, but thought better of it. She didn't want to force Erin to do anything. That would be awful. Instead, she reached for the remote and flipped on the television. A *Honeymooners* marathon came on, and she didn't care enough to change it. After a while her eyelids began to flutter and she struggled to keep them open.

When the bathroom door finally opened, Erin emerged wearing only her panties and bra. It was a pretty, lacy magenta set. It was obvious that Erin was prepared should she either have won the game or been chosen. Scarlett sat up and faced her. Erin held her arms over her belly, almost hugging herself as she stood in the doorway. Scarlett smiled and stood up. As she did, she clicked off the TV and tossed the remote into the basket on the nightstand.

Erin smiled back as Scarlett approached her. She pulled the straps down on Erin's bra, but before she could release her breasts from their constraints, Erin put her hands up to stop her.

"What's the matter, Erin?"

Erin hung her head. "You have such a beautiful body, Scarlett. Mine is—I'm embarrassed."

"Stop, Erin. You shouldn't be."

"That's easy for you to say," Erin whispered.

"Trust me." Scarlett reached behind Erin's back and unclasped her bra, then removed it and let it drop to the floor. Erin's hands immediately rose to cover her breasts, but Scarlett pulled them away and leaned in to brush her cheek against Erin's. Erin let out a soft moan.

"I'm not—"

"Shhhhh," Scarlett said as she moved her face down toward Erin's breasts. Taking one in her mouth, she traced the nipple with her tongue. Erin moaned louder but she was shaking.

"Trust me, please," Scarlett said softly, pulling her mouth from Erin's breast.

Scarlett knelt down and pulled down Erin's panties, kissing the top of each thigh as she rose. She pulled off her own tank top then unbuttoned her shorts. She shimmied out of them, finally pressing herself against Erin. Erin was panting.

"You have a beautiful body, Erin. You are such a silly rabbit." She took Erin's hand and led her to the bed. "Come here."

Erin lay back on the bed and Scarlett slid in beside her, propping her head up with her hand.

"Do I? Do I really? I know I don't. Marty doesn't even look at me anymore."

"Marty's an ass."

"You're right." Erin laughed. "You know, we hardly have sex anymore."

"I don't know why you'd want to. And I would know." Scarlett was stroking Erin's breasts.

"That's right. You would." Erin looked away.

Scarlett gently pulled Erin's face back toward her. "Believe me, Erin, it was nothing. Nothing."

"But I saw—"

"Shhhh," Scarlett said as she laid a finger lightly over Erin's lips. "It's about us tonight. You and me." She leaned over and kissed Erin with a full, open mouth. Their tongues danced around each other.

Propping her head up again, Scarlett asked, "So was this like your high school make out session? What did you say her name was? Lila?"

"Oh, no. Nothing like this." Erin drew Scarlett's face to meet hers, and they kissed again, this time longer, more intensely.

Erin finally pulled away and looked directly into Scarlett's eyes. "I really want to do this," she said, reaching up and twirling a blonde curl around her finger.

"I know. So do I." She kissed Erin again. "Touch me."

"But, I don't know—I don't know how—or what to do."

"Erin, you know how it feels. You're a woman. I mean, you know what you like. So you need to imagine that when you are with another woman. Let your own feelings—your own wants and needs—guide you. I'll tell you if there's something else I like."

Erin reached over and traced Scarlett's nipple with her finger tip. She lifted her head off the pillow and took it in her mouth and nudged Scarlett onto her back. Scarlett moaned.

"Like this?" Erin asked, lifting her head up to look at Scarlett.

"Mmm hmm and this," Scarlett said as she took Erin's hand and pressed it down between her legs. Erin resisted for a second, but then allowed Scarlett to bring her hand to her mound. Erin could feel her heart racing.

"Taste it," Scarlett said.

Erin pulled her hand away and again, paused tentatively. Scarlett cupped Erin's hand and pushed it toward Erin's mouth. Erin sucked on her finger, closing her eyes. Scarlett sat up and pushed Erin back down on the pillow. She climbed between Erin's knees and pulled her hair to one side, then bent forward, burying her face between Erin's legs. Erin let out a nearly primal scream.

"Oh, my God!"

Without lifting her head, Scarlett asked, "How does this feel?"

Erin responded only with the same, "Oh, my God!" but louder this time. She moved her hips rhythmically against Scarlett's tongue. Scarlett reached up with her fingers and pressed two inside Erin who let out another scream.

"Okay, slow down, Erin," Scarlett said. "We want to take our time."

"It's been so long, Scarlett," Erin said, panting.

"I know, honey. Believe me, I know," Scarlett said, pulling herself up to kiss Erin. Erin could taste her own saltiness on Scarlett's mouth. They kissed a long while, hands all over one another's bodies.

"Can I?" Erin asked, looking down between Scarlett's legs.

"Um, are you kidding me? You think you need to ask?"

Scarlett laid back, her head nearly off the end of the bed as she spread her knees apart. Erin was not tentative this time. She pressed her mouth against Scarlett. Scarlett moaned and moved with every flick of Erin's tongue.

---

THE SUN WAS STREAMING in through the blinds of the cabin window. Erin was awake and contentedly lying alongside Scarlett. A light sheet barely covering her bedmate, Scarlett was beyond beautiful. She was going over in her head what had happened between them. She wondered what it meant that she enjoyed the experience so much. She knew it wouldn't ever happen again and, in a way, wouldn't want for it to. Like losing her virginity, though, she felt that it changed her, and it was a change she felt wonderful about.

Scarlett stirred and opened her eyes. She looked up at Erin and smiled. Erin smiled back and brushed the stray blonde hairs from Scarlett's cheek. "Morning."

"Morning, beautiful," Scarlett responded. "What time is it?"

"After seven. I better get going. Marty won't be able to handle the boys for long." She slid out of bed and picked up her bra and panties from the floor, taking them with her to the bathroom where she'd left her clothing the night before. "I'll just be a few minutes."

"Okay," Scarlett said, sitting up in bed. Even though she loved being with men, she hadn't felt this good, this satisfied, in a very long time. She watched Erin get dressed through the partly open door, wondering how Erin didn't know how beautiful she was. It had been an amazing evening.

Lying back, Scarlett thought about the times she and C. Thomas had had threesomes. They were the only times in the years since the two had been together that she actually got something out of sex. But it was sex for sex's sake. She and the women got the job done. Of course, while C. Thomas watched and masturbated. But those times didn't compare to the closeness and real sensuality she and Erin had shared last night. Knowing first-hand what kind of sex partner Marty was, Scarlett was sure that Erin both needed it and enjoyed it as much as she had.

While Erin finished up in the bathroom, Scarlett scooted off the bed and found her clothing. Erin's phone began to vibrate on the table.

"Erin, your phone is ringing."

"Can you check who it is—I'm sure it's got to be Marty."

Scarlett went over to the table and glanced down at the phone. Marty's picture had come up and she felt her stomach turn. "Yep, sure is."

"Uggh. I'm coming right out. Just let it go to voicemail."

"Okay." Scarlett drew her hair up into a ponytail and pulled a hair elastic from her wrist to secure it. Erin walked out of the bathroom and teasingly tugged at Scarlett's hair before picking up her cell phone.

"My turn," Scarlett said, smiling as she headed for the bathroom.

"God, it's the boys. They said they don't know where Marty is," Erin said as she pressed END on the screen. "Shit, I better get back."

"Yup, almost done," Scarlett said through a mouthful of toothpaste. She spit and quickly rinsed out the sink. She came out, stepped into her flip flops, grabbed the cabin and car keys off the nightstand, and her purse off the back of a chair. "Let's roll."

The two headed out the door and straight for C. Thomas's Jag.

"It's a shame we couldn't sit out back and have coffee," Erin said as she opened the car door. The lake views were tremendous and the temperature was only about seventy-five at this hour. The smell of the summer flowers around the cabin was intoxicating.

"I know. C. Thomas and I never really use the cabin."

Scarlett started the car and pulled out onto the windy road. The ride to Erin's was fairly uneventful. Both women were quietly content and said little. As Scarlett entered Erin's driveway, Erin leaned over to give her a peck on the cheek.

"Thanks for dropping me off."

"I had a great time, Erin."

"Me, too," Erin smiled and reached for the door handle. "Uggh. Here goes."

"Just ignore his shit." Scarlett knew that Erin was dreading what was to come, and Scarlett felt partly responsible, but it had been well worth it to both of them.

---

ERIN PULLED out her keys to open the front door but found it unlocked. Was Marty that drunk last night that he hadn't locked it? Erin thought as she closed it behind her. She looked in the living room, then the kitchen, finally heading for the study. She was surprised to find the door closed, but unlocked. Marty was passed out with his head on the desk next to his computer. It was no wonder the boys couldn't find him. When the office door was closed, locked or not, it was a no entry zone. In his obvious state, Marty wouldn't have heard them call.

Erin walked in and saw an empty bottle of Jack Daniels on the floor next to the desk as well as his flask and several wadded up tissues. With a groan, she leaned over to pick up the mess and noticed that the computer was on. She tapped a key to switch it out of stand-by mode when a website popped up featuring several nude teenaged girls in various sexual poses. She noticed there were several tabs open and clicked on one. Instagram popped up with a hashtag "NewFairfieldBabes" at the top and there were multiple photos of Katie and Scarlett skinny dipping at Katie's pool, including one with Erin's breast exposed.

Her hand flew up to her mouth and she dropped the bottle to the hardwood floor, shattering it. Marty lifted up his still-drunk head and with only one eye open said, "What?" then laid it back down.

Erin frantically tapped at the keys to close out the websites, careful not to wake Marty. She backed out of the study avoiding the shards of glass. She could have cared less at that point if Marty ground it into his bare feet. She was disgusted, horrified, and angry. Had he been getting off on imagining Scarlett and her together? Who had taken those photos? How had they gotten online? What would the people in town or at the twins's school say?

She headed upstairs to the boys's room to see what kind of trouble they'd gotten themselves into. When she didn't find them there, she heard the television on in her bedroom and was surprised to see them under her covers watching cartoons.

"Hi, boys."

"Hi, Mom."

"Hi, Mom."

"How long have you been in here?"

"We slept in here," Devin said.

"Oh? How did that happen?"

"Jamie and Anna told us we could." Devin answered.

"Really? What time was that?"

The boys looked each other, knowing that the truth might get them into trouble. "Ten," Daniel said.

"Um, ten-something," Devin corrected, even though it had been well after midnight.

"Oh, okay. What about Daddy?"

"I don't know. We couldn't find him or you this morning. We found Daddy's phone on the kitchen counter though, so we called you," Daniel said.

"That was a good idea. Did you eat anything?"

Daniel pulled out a box of Honeycomb from under the covers, revealing a huge pile of cereal and crumbs. They both broke into gales of laughter.

She teasingly chided them. "I'm not even going to ask who did that!"

At the same time, both boys pointed at the other and said, "He did it!" and the cackles became louder.

"Okay. Well, I have to run a quick errand, okay? I expect you are going to keep the TV on this channel. No rated-R movies, you hear?"

"Okay, Mom," they both responded.

"Daddy's in his study if you need something. Be back soon. Love you." Erin leaned over and kissed both boys on the top of the head as each tried to duck away.

Erin headed for the stairs, dialing Katie as she went.

"Breakfast?" Katie asked as soon as she picked up.

"Yes," Erin said laughing. "I just need to scream into the dungeon that I'm going."

"Okay, see you at the luncheonette."

Erin headed to the study and flung open the door letting it hit the wall with a bang. Marty nearly fell out of his seat.

"I'm going out."

"What the hell, Erin?" Marty stumbled to his feet.

"Watch the glass," Erin said as she turned on her heels, "or don't." She disappeared down the hall, slamming the front door behind her.

---

"I can't believe you two actually *did* it!"

"Believe. And it was incredible. You should try it."

"I don't think I could. Wow. I'm shocked."

Erin was grinning and tucking her hair behind her ears. "That's what I thought. You'd be amazed how quickly you get by any—uh, uncertainties."

"I still don't think I could."

"Listen. I'm not switching teams or anything. I still like sex with men better—a real man, I mean. But when you're with a man, it's all hair and rough skin and smelly armpits."

"Yeah," Katie responded with a laugh, enraptured by the conversation.

"But when you're with a woman. Wow. It's way different. It's soft skin, curves, the smell of shampoo and perfume, and—it's just so—feminine. It's exhilarating, even hypnotizing."

"Wow."

"I'll be honest with you. I never felt so uninhibited. So self-assured. Like I didn't care about the little rolls and bagels," she said with a snicker as she pinched her waistline.

"C'mon Erin. You have a great body."

"Funny, that's just what Scarlett said." Katie raised an eyebrow.

"What did Marty say when you got home? The girls said he was a real piece of work when he paid them last night."

"He was passed out drunk as a skunk with his face smushed against his laptop. He was obviously still sleeping it off."

"Uggh."

"When I went in to try to wake him he had goddamn porn on his computer! I can't believe it! Porn! We have kids in the house! Eww, Katie," she teased. "Oh, my God. Oh! I can't even believe that I almost forgot something else. There were pictures of *us*—from that day at the pool."

"What day?"

"*The* day. The day you and Scarlett went skinny dipping."

"How?!"

"I have no idea. It couldn't have been Marty. He was at school!"

"We better find out!"

"I know. How about the nosy rosies around here? We'll be the talk of the town."

"Are you going to ask Marty?"

"Honestly, he was so drunk, I'd bet he thought he hallucinated! I closed it all out and deleted the history before I left him there snoring and drooling on the desk. I'll have to see if I can find them myself. They were on Instagram."

"Let me know, God. What'll Steve say? And my girls are all over Instagram."

"Ha! He'll probably think it's sexy. You're so beautiful. Anyway, I don't think anyone would even be able to tell it's us. You really couldn't see our faces."

Katie shook her head and let out a snicker. "So what was up with your boys when you got back?"

"I found them in my bed with a box of cereal dumped out all over the place. Shocked that was the only mess they'd gotten into. God knows it will be worse by the time I get back home now."

"Oy."

"You know, I had hoped this summer would've been good for Marty and me. The first summer with the boys in camp. Marty is only working Mondays and Saturdays. I thought *maybe* we'd finally be able to reconnect. What was I thinking?"

Katie shook her head again. She and Steve were faring no better these days.

---

"Hey, Steve!" Marty called out from the street. Steve was pulling weeds from the mulch around the walkway and looked up, surprised. Marty was following behind the twins, trying desperately to keep up with them on their bicycles as they repeatedly rammed into each other.

"Quit it!" one of them yelled out, yanking his handlebars to one side to ram the other right back.

"Boys! I said I'd take you out, but you have to behave! You see that red mailbox down there?" Marty was pointing to a box several driveways down.

"Yeah?"

"What about it?"

"That's as far as you can go. Back and forth to here," Marty said pointing to Steve's elaborate stone-encased box. He wasn't even certain the boys had heard him because they were already well past the red mailbox, still ramming each other but with more speed and aggression than before.

"Jesus Christ, Steve. Can they really be mine?" He was shaking his head, trudging and limping toward Steve who was piling the pulled weeds into a wheelbarrow.

"Marty, my God, you look like shit."

"Yeah. Well, I feel like shit. I fell asleep at my desk last night. I have a stiff neck like you wouldn't believe."

"Why are you limping?"

"Must have knocked over the bottle of J.D. Glass everywhere. I pulled out a whopper of a piece from the bottom of my foot."

"Is Erin home?"

"Here and gone in a flash. I barely saw her. I expect she's having breakfast with your wife. Did Katie go out?"

"She's not here. They could be together. Katie and I haven't exactly been in sync lately—if you know what I mean."

"Yeah, I know *just* what you mean. It's this stupid game."

"Finally, someone who agrees with me."

"Look, Steve. I need a favor. Man to man."

"What?" Steve said, now trimming the shrubs.

"I need you to help me win the next game." He sounded desperate.

Steve did a double-take. The boys began screeching. "Boys! Settle down!" Marty yelled.

"You just called it a *stupid* game, Marty."

"So? I still want to *win* it."

Steve paused with the hedge trimmers in mid-air. "What are you saying? You want me to *throw* the game?"

"Well, no. Yes. Sort of. If it comes down to just you and me in a hand, I need you to throw me your chips."

"You're kidding me, right?"

"I *need* to win, Steve. I need to get with Scarlett again."

"You're obsessed, Marty. This was supposed to be a game."

"I have to."

"I don't think that's a good idea." Steve turned back to the shrubs.

"I didn't ask for your opinion. I just need for you to help me."

"I can't."

"Why not?!"

"Because it's against the rules. *And* it's cheating. *And* your kids are about to mow down my flower beds."

"Boys!" Marty yelled to the twins. "This is bullshit, Steve. You just want to save her for yourself. Admit it. That's what this is about."

"Marty, calm down. You're actually beginning to scare me."

Marty was nearly frothing at the mouth. "Okay, forget about helping me win. Just agree now that if you win, you won't pick Scarlett."

"I'm not doing that. Are you really telling me you'd rather have me sleep with your wife than our friend? Is that what you are saying?"

"I don't care who you choose. Take C. Thomas if that floats your boat. As long as it's not Scarlett."

"This is ridiculous. I'm not agreeing to anything." Steve tossed the hedge trimmers on top of the weeds in the wheelbarrow and started to push it toward the side of the house. Marty grabbed him by the arm and tried to pull him back before Steve broke away from his grip.

"Get your hands off me. You need help, Marty. Some serious help." Steve pushed the wheelbarrow, quickening his pace, leaving Marty standing on the walkway as he rounded the side of the house.

"You're a fucking liar!" Marty screamed. He turned to see Devin and Daniel standing behind him on the driveway, straddling their bicycles.

In unison they said, "Swear jar, Daddy."

---

*Dear Diary,*

*Obviously, I'm not writing Mom about this one. She'd never understand.*

*I was with a woman last night. Just a woman. Not a threesome like with C. Thomas, but a woman. A soft, warm, loving woman.*

*No, I'm not gay. But I have to tell you, the pickings these days have been horrible. And Erin, well, it was just beautiful. She is beautiful. You know what? I think I'm pretty beautiful, too.*

*I realize now how very, very lonely I have been. Being with Erin was just something we both needed. But now, more than ever, I know I need someone for real. An actual relationship. Is there such a thing as a soulmate? Is there really just one person on this earth who is perfect for each of us?*

*I have made a decision. I am leaving C. Thomas. I am not entirely sure what's next, but I am finally putting myself first. Maybe for the first time ever. I am going back to school, and focusing on one thing – ME.*

## 19

## GAME BALL

THE HEADLIGHTS CUT INTO THE ALL-ENCOMPASSING DARKNESS, BUT visibility was limited to only a few hundred feet. The dirt roads leading to the cabin ordinarily had little traffic, even at peak times during the day, but at night they were eerily deserted, void of streetlights, road signs, or traffic lights. It had rained earlier, the remnants of which had settled into a fine mist, giving the road ahead a ghostly sheen.

Steve, try as he might, could not focus on the travels or his destination; instead his mind was totally consumed with his passenger. He watched her peripherally, her profile in partial silhouette by the backwash of the headlights and the full moon that darted between the still-pregnant rain clouds. Her bare legs were crossed, and she had her hands tightly clasped in her lap. She stared straight ahead into the darkness. Neither had said a word since they left the house.

"We don't have to do this," Scarlett said, finally breaking the cone of silence that was hanging over them.

"I want to do this," Steve said matter-of-factly. "Why are you saying that? You don't want to?"

"You could have fooled me. I thought you were going to throw the game to Marty—*again*. Then wasn't that quite the move when you almost took him up on his offer to call it a tie."

"Maybe I was just afraid of losing to him."

"Come off it. You're the better player, and you know it. Plus, you had the stronger hand."

Steve just shook his head and continued driving. This night was not starting out like he'd hoped.

"And when you won, I didn't even think you were going to choose me."

"Who else would I have picked? Marty?"

"Ugh! Just the thought of him lately is so repulsive. There is something very, very wrong with that man."

"Something's going on with him, that's for sure. He seems desperate lately."

"And needy. Too needy. It's like the game has unleashed some dark and feral beast."

Steve shrugged. "Maybe. But I think the game has had an impact on all of us."

"Or maybe we've been like this all along, and the game has become some convenient excuse to finally let our true colors show."

"I'm not sure I even want to entertain that notion," Steve said. "You make it sound like we're all a bunch of libidinous animals, and the only thing stopping us from acting on our urges is some—I don't know, societal pressure."

"Hmm. Sounds very Freudian. I guess Katie has rubbed off on you all these years," she jabbed.

Steve rolled his eyes.

"But isn't it true?" Scarlett continued.

Steve sighed. "This conversation is getting too deep for me. We're on our way to have—a—wild fling tonight, aren't we? I don't think it's a good time to discuss social mores and taboos, or anyone's moral compass for that matter. We tossed out morality weeks ago."

"Which brings us back to my initial comment," Scarlett said. "I didn't think you were going to choose me at all. You could have chosen Erin. She's attractive. It's obvious there has always been something between you two anyway."

Steve did a double take. "Not!"

"I've seen it, at least on her part. She's into you. Women notice that kind of thing in other women."

"Really?" Steve asked, more amused than serious.

"Yes, definitely," she said patently, although she wasn't actually as sure about her assertions as she was about trying to needle Steve. "So you've never fantasized about being with Erin?"

"No, never," Steve said flatly.

"How about me? Have you ever fantasized about being with me?"

Steve squirmed. "Can I plead the fifth?"

"Honestly, Steve, I don't get you sometimes. Hopefully we'll be at the cabin soon, and shortly after you will be fucking me, but you won't even let your guard down for a second beforehand. God! Sometimes you play things too close to the vest. I'm warning you now that if you keep this up, you'll be fucking yourself."

Steve was about to answer when he lost it completely. He pulled the car to the shoulder, slamming on the brakes so hard that even with their seatbelts, they were both thrown forward.

"What the fu—" Scarlett started.

He was out of his seatbelt and on top of her before she could finish her sentence. His mouth was all over hers. He found her tongue and sucked on it while his hands ripped open her top and dug into her bra to massage her breasts. His mouth slid down her neck to her nipples, and he sucked on each one while his hands fumbled with undoing her zipper and pulling off her shorts.

Scarlett was taken by surprise at first, but she quickly recovered and responded in kind. She pulled up his shirt and began to suck relentlessly on his neck giving him a hickey like a schoolgirl. Fleetingly, she thought about what Katie would say. Her hands moved down to his button and zipper.

"Commando!" she exclaimed between passion-laden gasps. "You remembered!"

He sat back in his seat and pulled her forward. She went down on him, her tongue finding him through his open fly. He was hard, but continued to swell to twice his size in her mouth. He was over the moon.

Tonight, there was no need for any purple pills. Steve was hard as a rock. Scarlett was able to deep throat him completely while rhythmically working her tongue and teeth at the same time, alternately licking, biting, and sucking. His pain/pleasure barometer was through the roof, and he was close to climaxing within minutes. As his point of no return rapidly approached, he wondered vaguely if he should give her a heads up—no pun intended—that he was going to come at any second. He also wondered how she would feel about him filling her mouth.

He never got the opportunity to find out. Seconds before he was about to lose control and ejaculate, she pulled away, leaving him exposed and throbbing. The abrupt withdrawal of stimulation made him cry out. But the discomfort was fleeting as Scarlett climbed on top of him and, with her back braced against the steering wheel, slid onto him. He held onto her for dear life as she gyrated over him in the cramped space. He met her halfway, thrusting with as much pelvic force as he could muster given his position.

He climaxed inside her, but he refused to give up. The last thing he wanted was to leave her unsatisfied. So he kept pushing, moving in sync with her as she pogoed over him. Just when he thought he couldn't go any further, her body became rigid as she fell forward, her hands gripping his back, her fingernails digging into his flesh. She screamed with pleasure. She found his mouth and forced her tongue inside it, panting and huffing as her body continued to shudder in orgasmic spasms. He held her until she finally went limp and collapsed back onto the passenger seat, totally spent.

"Wow!" She said between breaths. "That was incredible."

"Now do you believe that I wanted to be with you?"

---

SATURDAY'S GAME night had been more like a wake than a social event. Little did the players realize, but the death knell had indeed sounded, and this would be the triptych's very last poker game. Both Katie and Erin were already done with the game, at least from a mental and emotional standpoint, and their lack of interest was evident in their early busts with weak all-in calls. C. Thomas was the next early evacuee, the victim of a bluff gone terribly wrong. Scarlett could not afford to have Marty win, so she was playing conservatively; more conservatively than usual, especially for her. Even her posture was stiff. Hardly any cleavage was visible the entire night. She patiently waited for the right cards, but her strong hands ended up being second best and she finally ended up losing her all-in call on a straight to Marty no less, who had beaten her with a flush.

Katie and Erin retired to drinking on the sofa. C. Thomas continued in his role as official dealer. Scarlett remained riveted to the cards on the table, praying that Steve would win. It wasn't just that she wanted for Steve to win and for him to choose her, but of greater importance was she wanted Marty to lose so she never would have to spend another night with that lecherous creep. She decided at that moment that the game was over for her. If Marty won she would flat out refuse to go with him.

Fuck him, she thought. Fuck him and the game. She was finished with compromising herself anymore.

C. Thomas dealt the down cards for a new hand. Marty had an ace and a king; Steve had an ace and a nine. Marty's eyes were bulging as always. Both Steve and Scarlett were certain that Marty had a strong hand. He proved it seconds later when he raised twice the big blind.

Easy, Steve, Scarlett thought. Be careful, my love.

"Your play, Steve-O," C. Thomas urged.

Steve was playing with his chips, which was never a good sign. "I'll call," he said finally, tossing in the majority of them.

"Here we go," C. Thomas said.

The flop turned up an ace, a king, and a nine. Marty now had two pairs, aces over kings. He raised again.

Steve had two pairs as well, but he had to figure Marty for equal or better based on the way he was betting. It's do or die, he thought. If he went out now he would suffer a staggering loss. If he went in, he would have to stick by the hand for better or for worse. It would be awful to fall second to Marty.

"Up to you, Steve-O," C. Thomas coaxed again.

Steve decided he had to commit. There was no turning back. "I call," he said, and tossed in his chips.

Fourth Street turned up another nine giving Steve a full house. Steve was relieved, but couldn't show it. He looked at Marty who was sitting on the edge of his seat, protecting his hole cards and sweating profusely, a stench permeating the tense room.

"Your play, Marty," C. Thomas urged.

Marty looked at Steve. "What do you think I should do, Steve? Should I go all-in?"

"You should do what you think is best."

Marty smirked. "Bastard. You wouldn't tell me the truth no matter what."

"Come on, Marty," C. Thomas said. "Stop being a bully and play cards."

Marty sighed. "All-in."

Steve smiled. It was at that point that Marty knew he had lost for certain.

"Call," Steve said. He was about to push in his chips when Marty stopped him.

"What do you say we call it a tie? No winners tonight. Would you do that? Would you do that for me?"

Steve shook off his hand. "Maybe we should."

Marty beamed.

"On second thought," Steve considered, tossing in his chips, "let's play it out."

"At least I finally know where you stand," Marty said snarkily, turning over his cards.

"Yes, you do," Steve said. He turned over his cards revealing his full house.

Marty squeezed his glass so tightly that it cracked, slicing his finger. "Shit!" Marty muttered.

"You cut your hand, honey," Erin said patronizingly.

"Shut up," he barked.

Erin gave him the finger behind his back, making Katie giggle and spill her drink in her lap.

C. Thomas turned over the river card. It was a four. Scarlett breathed a sigh of relief. Marty leaned back in his chair with a snort, defeated.

"Can't believe it took this long for the master to prevail. Here you go, Steve-O. *Your* choice," C. Thomas said with the delivery of a game show host. He slid the cabin key across the table. All eyes were on Steve as he rose to his feet and pocketed the key.

"Let's go, Scarlett."

Katie collapsed against the sofa, crestfallen. Even though she had expected it, it burned. Steve hadn't even dragged it out or pretended it was a difficult decision.

"No surprise there," Erin said, barely above a whisper, reaching over and putting her hand on top of Katie's.

Marty stormed out, deliberately ramming into Steve as he passed.

Scarlett almost jumped for joy but tried not to show it. She picked up her purse and followed Steve. Neither of them said another word nor looked back.

"And then there were two," Katie said to Erin after C. Thomas followed them out.

---

STEVE AND SCARLETT couldn't get into the cabin fast enough. He pulled up in the driveway and they both jumped out and raced to the door. He French kissed her as he fumbled in his pocket for the key. She was undoing his zipper on the porch as he fished it out; he managed to open the door just as his shorts fell around his ankles.

They stumbled through the doorway together, a mass of arms and legs flailing in the air, with Steve's shorts still wrapped around his feet. The scene was as comical as it was erotic.

Steve kicked his shorts across the room and slipped out of his Topsiders. He was naked from the waist down and had another huge hard on. Scarlett had been the aggressor in the car, but now Steve was determined to dominate her this round.

He continued to kiss her as he led her into the bedroom. He had her top and bra off by the time they reached the bed and then he collapsed on top of her. His mouth moved down her neck to her nipples. He sucked each one again as he had done in the car, but now he took his time. His tongue danced around each areola, pulling her nipples erect. He moved to center of her breasts and sucked as hard as he could. Now was his opportunity to mark *his* territory. She groaned with pleasure, holding him tightly against her breasts.

Satisfied with the hickey he'd produced, he continued his journey down her naked torso to her shorts. In one fluid motion, he removed and flung them over his shoulder. He moved his head between her legs, entering her with his tongue, tasting her moistness. She screamed out as she arched her body. He found her clitoris and deftly massaged it with the tip of his tongue. She moaned and writhed and squirmed, and there were moments when he wasn't sure if she was in the throes of passion or on the verge of quitting. But

Steve refused to stop despite her intermittent efforts to push him away. When he believed the time was right he slipped his finger into her, finding her G-spot. Holding her across the stomach, he continued to tongue and finger her until her body went rigid.

"Oh, my God!" she screamed. Her body convulsed several times. "Stop! Please! I can't take it anymore!"

This time he allowed her to push him away, but before she could relax, he climbed on top and entered her. He pinned her arms to the bed and drove into her, each thrust deeper and more powerful than the one before. She continued to scream and convulse, as he took her, pulling her legs up so that they wrapped around his back. She continued to come multiple times. It was only when her body finally went limp with exhaustion that he allowed himself to climax inside of her. He collapsed next to her, out of breath and exhausted, his arm draped over her. Soon they both were asleep, more soundly than either had slept in years.

---

KATIE SAT on the edge of her bed flipping through cable channels. She could find nothing to watch but romantic movies, something she just couldn't stomach. "An elderly man recalls his courtship with his Alzheimer's-stricken wife." "A widowed man finds true love because his son calls into a radio program." "The tempestuous love-hate relationship between Clark Gable and Vivien Leigh." She shut off the television. She'd had enough.

She lay back in bed and picked up her cell phone from the bedside table. She unlocked it and clicked on her word game app, scrolling down to one of the current rounds she was playing. Mid-game, the battery died, and the phone shut off. She looked up at the digital clock. One-thirty-two a.m. She knew she just should go to sleep but expected nothing but an insomnia-filled night or worse, a nightmare-filled one. She got up and sat at her ornate leather-topped desk and opened her laptop, turned it on and opened the file for her book. She stared blankly at the screen for a full five minutes before she finally shut it down.

She stood up and began to pace. She never paced—it was a practice of Steve's. She stopped short. *What am I doing?*

She glanced at her reflection in the mirror. "When in hell did I start to look like my mother?" she said out loud. She peered in closer and inspected the wrinkles around her mouth and then those around her eyes. She tugged at her temples and surveyed the creases on her forehead.

Should I get Botox? she considered. She'd once priced it. It didn't seem so bad, but she wasn't too sure about the needles.

Is my jawline drooping? She placed her finger tips at her cheekbones and pulled the skin back, stretching against her mouth, then let go.

God, it's time to color my hair again. She clutched at the hair on either side of her head, pulling apart the thin grey stripe now noticeable down the line of her part.

It was then that Katie noticed her wedding photo had fallen over on the bureau. How had that happened? When she picked it up, she saw that there was a hefty crack in the glass. She set the picture back, face down and began to heave, sobbing hard and uncontrollably.

---

STEVE LOOKED OVER AT SCARLETT, the light of the full moon streaming in through the window. He could hardly believe how beautiful the sleeping Goddess was or that she was there, next to him. He'd awakened from a dream and his heart still was racing. The only pieces he could recall from his unnerving nocturnal reverie were of Katie and his girls on a boat and he and Scarlett waving from an island. He thought he recalled Marty was there somewhere, but it all was fading quickly. Thank God. He lifted his head and squinted his eyes to focus so that he could see the time on the digital clock. It was one-forty one a.m.

Scarlett opened her eyes and smiled up at Steve. He stroked her cheek. "Hello, beautiful."

"Mmm," she said.

"So, did the night turn out the way you wanted?"

"I can honestly say it is far better than I'd ever have hoped or expected."

"I undeniably agree."

"I could stay here forever. With you," Scarlett said, a strangely shy look crossing her face.

"Mmm," Steve said, pulling her close. "Me, too."

"Really?"

Steve looked down at her. "I wouldn't have said it if I didn't mean it."

"But, I mean, what about Katie?"

Steve didn't immediately respond but he continued to hold Scarlett close, stroking her shoulder with his fingertips.

"Katie and I, well, we haven't been right for a long time," he finally said.

"Well, I can certainly relate to that."

"Oh?"

"C'mon, Steve. I mean, C. Thomas is far from the sharpest knife in the drawer."

"Yeah, but—"

"No buts. He is not normal. I mean, sexually he is a freak. He has more fetishes than I can count. But that's not even the reason. We just have nothing between us. Nothing at all. Never really did."

"Then why have you been with him?"

"I could ask you the same thing."

"We have kids, Scarlett. It changes the whole ball game. Plus, we're married. I can't just walk away so easily. There is a lot to a divorce. The house, everything. And the worst thing a litigator can do is be involved in personal litigation."

"Yeah. Well, it is supposed to be about happiness though, isn't it?"

"Yes. So answer my question then. Why are you still with C. Thomas?"

"Where else am I going to go?"

"That's ridiculous, Scarlett. You are an intelligent, beautiful woman. You could do anything you want with your life. You could have anyone you want."

"Tell my mom that."

"Huh?"

"My mom always told me to find a man to take care of me, looks were all I had, and they weren't going to pay any bills. Then of course, there were a number of other things her male 'friends' told me…"

"What!" Steve pulled himself up. "What are you talking about?"

"Nothing. Really. Forget I mentioned anything."

"No, Scarlett, I really want to know."

Scarlett looked away. After a moment she turned back, but couldn't bring herself to look him in the eyes. She couldn't bear to see his expression as she began. "Look. It wasn't my mom's fault. She wanted to find someone to replace my dad, maybe as much for me as for her. I'm sure she thought she was doing the right thing. It would kill her if she ever knew…"

"Yes," Steve said. "Go on." He stroked her hair.

"Anyway, there were several live-in boyfriends. Well, more than *several* to be exact and a few of them seemed to be more—I don't know—interested in *me* than my mother."

"Did any of them—" Steve felt himself getting angry.

"Not all of them. Only one went as far as—sex, if that's what you're asking. I was fifteen. God, I was so scared. The next time I heard him coming down the hall I was ready. I kicked and screamed and clawed him so badly he moved out the next day. It devastated my mother. I could never tell her, and she never knew why he left."

"Oh, my God."

"It was my fault. My therapist says no, but …" She looked away. "My mom—she was so upset…"

"Scarlett! How can you say that? You were a child!"

Scarlett's eyes filled with tears. "I was a tease. I guess maybe I still am."

"That's crazy talk!"

"Maybe. Maybe not." Scarlett turned toward the window and after a moment or two, changed the subject. "Do you think you and Katie could go to counseling or something? Maybe do some more, I don't know, date nights to—uh, reconnect? You can't be that far gone."

Steve laughed out loud.

"What?" Scarlett said, mildly insulted.

"I'm sorry. But that's just not even in the realm of possibility anymore. So much has happened over the years. We've just been going through the motions for a very, very long time."

The idea that Steve really could be available, that he could be hers, quickly restored her mood. "In that case, I can think of some other *motions*," she said as she reached under the covers.

"Mmmm, I like those motions," Steve said, pulling her on top of him.

## 20

## ENTROPY

"Professor! You made it!" Heather exclaimed when she saw Marty coming up the walkway to the entrance of the Rathskeller Pub. It had gotten late after he left Steve and Katie's, but he'd texted her, and as the young set usually do, they start their evenings when most grown-ups are going to bed. He was relieved. After the game fiasco, he wanted to go out and have some sort of release. Heather was standing out front with several other young college coeds. They were clad in typical club attire of tight-fitting and low-cut dresses, and they all were giggling and chattering until Marty came upon them.

"Hi, Heather. Girls," he said, nodding toward the others.

Heather bounced over to him and planted a kiss on his cheek to Marty's instant pleasure. He was a bit out of his element, however, as hanging with students outside of the classroom was only the stuff of his fantasies. She took his hand and guided him to face her friends. She bounced up and down.

"I'm really glad you came. I want to introduce you to my friend Abby. Oh, and this is Lisa who you know from class."

They exchanged perfunctory "hellos" before Marty tugged Heather away. "I need to talk to you about something. Maybe we can go somewhere?" His hushed voice displayed a fair amount of urgency and Heather was instantly rattled.

"Um. I guess so. Girls, I'll be right back? Don't get too hammered without me, 'kay?"

Abby and Lisa laughed and headed into the Rathskeller. Marty led Heather around the building onto a darkened side street. He was intense and didn't speak the whole time until Heather finally broke the silence.

"What's the matter, Professor? Is everything okay?"

"Yeah, fine. I was just hoping that we could spend some time together."

"Sure. I'd like that, too. I'm really glad you could make it."

"I don't often go out like this with students. In fact, this is the first time."

"Wow! You've never gone to any student-faculty events, ever?"

"No. Busy man, I am."

Heather chuckled. "I'm sure, Master Yoda! Well, it's summer! We all get to let loose."

"Mmm. Yeah."

Marty put his hand on Heather's shoulder. He pulled her close and kissed her gently on the mouth. She tentatively responded but pulled away quickly.

"That was sweet. Um, I'm really glad you came." Heather smiled, taking a few steps back. The alcohol she could now smell on his breath made her wince.

Marty leaned in again to kiss her, this time harder and more demandingly. He reached up to cup one of her breasts.

"No, Professor! Please—" Heather pleaded as she squirmed out of his grasp.

Marty reached around her with both arms and forcefully pulled her against him, again pushing his mouth against her now unwilling, pursed lips.

"Stop it!" she yelled loudly, wrestling out of his grip, punching against his biceps with both fists.

"I thought—I thought you said you wanted—"

"Wanted what? You to grope me? How could you think that?"

"Heather—"

"I'm going back to my friends. You are officially *un*invited. Don't follow me." Heather turned on her heels and stormed off, looking once over her shoulder

Marty leaned against the brick wall with his head in his hands. "Women," he muttered under his breath. "What the fuck?!"

Two students walked by him shaking their heads. One of them said, "Asshole," as he passed.

"Yeah, same to you, Dickwad," Marty spat. He dug into his pocket for his keys and headed for his car.

Heather darted into the Rathskeller and quickly found Abby and Lisa. The club was nearly full to capacity and there was a band playing loudly in the back. She looked frazzled which did not go unnoticed.

"What's going on, Heather? Are you okay? Where's the professor?" Lisa asked.

"Hopefully about to get into a massive car accident. Do you believe that loser came on to me?"

"No! Oh, my God! What did he do?" Abby asked.

"I don't even want to talk about it. Did you guys get me a drink? I need one."

"Men! They're all the same," Lisa said. "And no, we were just about to get something. Let's go."

"I don't even know how I can go back to his class now," Heather said as they walked over to the bar.

"Three drafts?" Lisa asked the other two. When both nodded, she signaled to the bartender and ordered their beers.

"Do you think it's going to affect your grade?" Abby asked.

"It better not. That's all I can say. I may have to go public with this. I really liked him, too."

"Maybe we should report it," Lisa said as she handed two of the beers to Heather and Abby. They walked over and stood by an empty cocktail table.

"I don't know. I mean, I stopped him, and he did leave. Plus, I know he has kids. Can you imagine what that would do to his family?"

"Yes, but that's not your problem," Lisa said.

"Maybe it was my fault. I invited him here. Maybe I gave off some kind of vibe."

"Stop it," Abby said. "You are not the one at fault. He is."

"Well, I need to think about it. But not right now. Let's just enjoy the evening. Did the guys make it?"

"Yeah," Lisa said. "I saw Nate when we first came in. He said Sam and Jonah were here, too."

"Let's go find them. I need to be around *normal* guys," Heather said, grabbing her beer from the cocktail table and heading straight into the massive group of students encircling the band.

---

STEVE AND SCARLETT were enjoying their post-coital glow following round three. Scarlett had her head against Steve's bicep and her body molded against his. She was tracing his chest hairs with her fingers.

"That was so amazing. The best I've ever—"

"Sure it was," Steve teasingly scoffed.

"I'm serious," she said, gently pulling a chest hair.

"Ow! Why do I find that hard to believe?" Steve chuckled, pulling her hand away and holding it tightly in his.

"Look. I've had sex with other people. Even Erin as you know. But honestly, there haven't been *that* many. The girls I was hanging out with in my early twenties were *really* promiscuous. But this is the first time—and I mean the *first* time—anyone has ever *made love* to me." She lifted her head up to meet his and kissed him for a long time. "I'm really glad you picked me," she said, laying her head back down.

"Mmm. So am I."

"Wow! It must have cost you to say that!"

"You'll never know how much," Steve chuckled, stroking her hair.

"You know, I've always had a thing for you."

"Yeah, right. I'll bet you say that to all the winners."

"That's not true at all. As soon as C. Thomas proposed this, all I could think about was this was the way for me to finally get to be with you. In fact, I steered the girls to accept his proposal that day at the pool for my own selfish gain."

Steve was silent a moment. "You do realize that I am practically old enough to be your father?"

"Give me a break. Maybe if you were a teen dad. A very *young* teen dad," she said. "And anyway, who says maybe I didn't have a thing for my father?"

"You're incorrigible!" Steve said with a laugh, tickling Scarlett in the ribs.

"So what about you? I imagine you've had a pretty colorful past."

"What do you mean? It's been just me and Katie for a very *long* time."

"What about before Katie?"

"Just the usual kid stuff," Steve said, turning away.

Scarlett reached over and pulled his face back toward hers. "C'mon, Steve. Everyone has a past."

"This isn't the kind of pillow talk I was hoping for," Steve said, pulling Scarlett up to him for a kiss.

"You don't get out of it that easy. I really want to know."

"It's honestly not that interesting. I mean, I messed around a little in high school. Junior year mostly. Then in my senior year I was working at a local garden center. This woman used to come in—a lot. One day it would be for mulch. Another day for flowers. She'd come back to ask questions and advice. I didn't make the connection at first that she always made a beeline for me."

"Ahh. I see," Scarlett chided. "Mrs. Robinson."

"Ha. Very good. Except her name was Lori Thompson."

"Was she married?"

"No, no. She was about thirty, I think. Very attractive. But at that age, it didn't matter. I just couldn't believe my luck. This older woman was showing interest in me."

"Yeah, I'll bet she showed you a lot of things."

"This is where a gentleman draws the line, Miss Scarlett."

"Then it was Katie?"

"Well, there were a few girls before her in my freshman year of college. Nothing serious."

"So that's it?"

Steve was silent.

"Steve?"

"There was one more girl."

"Before Katie?"

"No. After her."

"Oh," Scarlett couldn't hide the surprise on her face. But Steve again was looking away. "So what happened with that?"

Steve rubbed his palm against his forehead several times before he spoke. "It was in law school. Third year. Katie and I had been engaged since senior year of college. We knew we were going to have a long engagement because I needed to graduate first. She was just finishing getting her Masters and stressed out trying to do her licensure hours and find a job—so we weren't together a lot."

"Mmhmm."

Steve looked right at Scarlett. "I know this sounds trite, but we weren't *connecting*. We were young. Our parents were like runaway stallions with the wedding planning. I was losing sight of what I wanted. What I wanted for myself. *My* life." He grew silent a moment before finishing. "Maybe I was being selfish."

"So what about the girl?"

"Well, she was in my law class. She was part of my study group. The whole bunch of us met up a few times a week. Lots of late nights. Sometimes Elaine and I would find ourselves the last ones in the library, in a café, in the student center. We had so much in common. We really understood each other. I often imagined what it might be like to be with her forever."

"Then what happened? Why did you break it off? Or did she?"

Steve shook his head and closed his eyes. When he opened them, he said, "I did. I had to. I felt I had no choice."

"So you didn't follow your heart?"

Steve shook his head. "It was a long time before I stopped beating myself up over that decision. But the wedding became quite a distraction. In the beginning, the newness of everything helped me forget."

Scarlett froze. "Steve, can I ask you something?"

"Of course."

"You once told me that I reminded you of someone from law school. It wasn't—I mean—oh, hell. Was it—Elaine?"

Steve was silent for a moment. "Yes."

Scarlett stroked Steve's face with her fingers, tracing his jawline. Steve took her hand and kissed each fingertip.

Scarlett pulled her hand away and lifted herself up onto her palms on either side of Steve and pulled a leg around him to straddle him. She leaned down to kiss him as she rubbed her pubic bone against his groin.

"Okay, I've needled you enough. You ready to go again, Old Man?"

"There's a bad moon arising—" Steve began before Scarlett pushed her tongue into his mouth. She reached down and pulled his now erect penis into her wetness and sat up, riding him. Steve reached up, cupping a breast in each hand then pinching her nipples.

They moved as one until Steve reached behind her, holding her buttocks and flipping her over on her back. He continued to move in and out until they both climaxed.

Steve started to move off of her when Scarlett stopped him. "Stay a minute. I love the feel of you on top of me."

Steve leaned slightly to one side, holding his head in his hand so that he could look down at her. "God, you're beautiful."

"So are you," she replied.

Steve finally slid off and laid his head on Scarlett's breast. They both were exhausted. Within minutes, they were asleep.

---

DEEP IN SLUMBER, the sound of Steve's cell phone pulled both Steve and Scarlett out of some very sexy dreams. Steve fumbled around on the bedside table trying to find it.

"Who is it?" Scarlett asked.

"Not sure."

"You know, it's against the rules if it's anyone from the gang. It better be important."

"You're right."

"Don't answer it," Scarlett scolded gently.

"I have to. It could be the kids. Maybe it is an emergency." Steve finally reached for the table lamp so that he could see. He looked at the display. "It's Marty."

"Don't answer it! He's just jealous that we're together." The phone stopped ringing.

"Well, he's gone."

Almost immediately the phone began to ring again. "Jesus! This is ridiculous!" Scarlett said.

"Maybe, but it is the middle of the night. I think I should answer it." Steve picked up.

"What's going on?—Marty?—Marty!—Slow down!—What?—What happened?" He sat up on the edge of the bed and paused a moment or two, nodding silently while Marty spoke. "Oh, my God. Okay. Okay. All right,

I'll be there as soon as I can." He pressed END and placed the phone gently on the nightstand.

"What's the matter? You look like you just saw a ghost."

Steve laid back with the back of his hand against his forehead. Scarlett began running her fingers through his hair. After a moment he flipped around and kissed her gently on the mouth.

"Something's happened. I'm so sorry. The last thing in the world I want to do is to leave here, but I have to go help out Marty." He reached up and stroked her cheek.

"Can you tell me what's going on?"

"No, I really can't. —Oh, hell. Just come with me."

"Right now?"

"Yes, I'm afraid so. We have to get dressed."

"Okay," Scarlett said, sliding out of bed and taking the sheet with her. She began picking up her clothes from the floor. Steve already was getting dressed.

"Do you see my bra?"

Steve spotted it and handed it to her. He was quiet.

"Steve," Scarlett said, coming over to him and putting her arms around his waist. "I really wish you would tell me what's going on."

"Marty's in trouble. *Serious* trouble."

---

"I THOUGHT SHE WAS A HOOKER! How did I know she was an undercover vice cop?" Marty said as he and Steve walked out of the Danbury police station. Steve was shoving his wallet in his back pocket.

"You and a zillion other guys. That's no excuse! What the hell, Marty? What were you thinking? How could you do something like this?!"

"I was drunk."

"No goddamned excuse. You're always drunk. Doesn't mean you go around soliciting whores."

"You don't know what I have been going through, Steve. Oh, ye of the ivory tower."

"Oh, yeah, Marty, my life is fucking perfect."

"Sure seems that way to me," Marty spat.

"What about Erin? How could you do this to her? To your boys?" Steve crossed the parking lot to where his car was parked in the visitors' area.

"I just need this squashed. Do me a solid. If this gets out, I could lose my tenure at school. Erin can't find out either."

"I already told you, this is not my field. I don't do this kind of work. I'll have to have one of my partners call you tomorrow. He'll know what to do."

As they approached Steve's car, Marty spotted Scarlett sitting in the front passenger seat. He stopped short.

"What the hell is *she* doing here?"

"I came right after you called. You know where we were. I had to bring her."

"Great! Fucking great! Thanks for bailing me out, Steve-O," he said sounding like C. Thomas. "I'll find my own way home!"

"Stop acting like a child, Marty. Just get in the damn car."

"No fucking way," Marty said, turning away and walking in the opposite direction.

"I don't think this is a good idea after all that's happened, Marty," Steve called after him. Marty didn't turn around. He disappeared behind a K-9 truck. Steve climbed back in the driver's seat with Scarlett.

"He looked pissed to see me," Scarlett said after Steve closed the door.

"He's just pissed in general. I don't know what the hell is wrong with him lately."

"I do or at least I think I do. It's me."

"You? How could it be you?"

"It's the game. He doesn't see it as a game at all."

"C'mon, really, Scarlett? He gets his rocks off once, and now he's a crazed maniac?"

"I don't know. Maybe I'm wrong, but I don't think so. He's—obsessed. Anyway, are you going to tell me what happened here?"

"Guy code. Sorry. I really can't. Just suffice it to say, Marty's been a bad boy. A *very* bad boy." Steve started the ignition and pulled out of the parking space, headed back to New Fairfield.

"Should you just take me home?"

Steve stopped the car at the stop sign just before exiting the parking lot. "Is that what you want?"

Scarlett reached over and took his hand, entwining her fingers through his. Steve looked down at her beautiful slender fingers.

"No, that is not what I want *at all*."

"Okay, then. Then I hope you're ready for round four—or is it five?" The street lights reflected off of her face, and her smile was brilliant.

"You betcha."

---

It was midweek and Katie and Erin had gone to the mall with Jamie and Anna. They were poking around in Macy's while the girls had taken off to parts unknown. They'd all planned to have some girl time, do some back-to-school shopping, and then grab dinner.

Katie picked up a blouse and held it against her as she looked in the mirror. Cocking her head to the side, she liked what she saw, threw it over her arm and continued browsing.

"I don't know why I bother," Erin said sifting through the clothing racks. "I have nowhere to wear this stuff and it all looks terrible on me anyway."

"Don't be ridiculous, Erin. You look great in everything."

"So not true. Anyway, did I tell you I'm applying for some teaching positions? I think it's time I got back out there now that the kids are going into fourth grade. My parents said that if I need them to, they'll get the kids after school for a few hours depending on Marty's semester schedule. Thankfully, he can get them on the bus in the mornings."

"Wow! That's great! Well, then, maybe you should buy *this* dress!" Katie said, pulling a slim-fitting blue one she'd been looking at and tossing it at Erin.

"Not exactly my size, Katie! And not exactly work wear, either. By the way, how are things on the home front?"

"Chilly, bordering on frigid. We've hardly spoken since Steve came home Sunday morning. I'll bet more went on with Scarlett than the nonsense I endured with C. Thomas. Ahhh, then again, *you* would know."

"Stop!" Erin looked a bit embarrassed.

"We are ships passing in the night. Gives me more time to work on the book. I feel really focused all of a sudden. How about you? How are things with Marty?"

"Pretty much same as you. He was really strange all day Sunday. He slept half the day. Then again, he's always strange. He called in sick to school Monday, too, and it was his last class for the summer seminar. He never came out of the study."

"You know, I'm sorry we ever started that stupid game."

"So am I," Erin nodded, perusing some other dresses while she spoke.

"I think we need a break from it."

"Why don't we have a girls' night out this weekend? Let the men fend for themselves." Erin held up a dress for Katie to see. "What do you think about this?"

"I think it will look beautiful on you. You know, a girls' night would be great. Sounds like a plan. Do you think we should ask Scarlett?"

"I think we have to, don't you?"

"I guess you're right. I mean, she never did anything to us we didn't all ask for."

"Let's get something new to wear," Erin said. "Make it a real special night. A *new beginning* of sorts."

"I'm all in," Katie said, and they both started laughing.

---

"He's going to talk to the District Attorney next week," Marty began, taking a swig from his beer. "Maybe I can plea bargain down, and they can seal my file. If the University finds out, I'm history."

Steve and Marty were sitting on longue chairs while Marty's boys were in the Kellys's pool. They were spraying each other in the faces with squirt guns, alternately laughing and screaming at each other to stop.

"Boys, if you can't behave, I'm taking the guns away!" Marty called out. "Why don't you find something else to play?"

"You bought them for us," one of them said. They continued the battle.

"Paul is an excellent criminal defense attorney. If anyone can help you sidestep this mess, he can," Steve told Marty.

"Well, man. I really appreciate you setting me up with him. You came through."

"Yeah, no problem."

Marty looked away. Steve thought he may have seen remorse, but that would be odd for Marty. He marched to the beat of his own drummer and apologized for nothing.

"I wish we never started playing the stupid game," Marty said, drawing out the last of the ale before swapping it out for the full one he'd already opened on the side table. Steve didn't respond. Marty looked over at him, as he sat in silent thought.

"You know a week ago you agreed. Are you telling me you've changed your mind now?" Marty was beet red, and it wasn't because of the sun, which was starting to move behind the house. "It's because of *her*, isn't it? You slept with her. Now you *know*."

"Now I know what, Marty? What are you talking about?" Steve picked up his own beer and took a sip, before turning to face him dead on.

"I can see it in your face. You're hung up on her."

"This is ridiculous, Marty."

Before Marty could respond, they heard the doorbell ring from the wireless extender mounted on the back of the house. Steve stood up. "Someone's at the front door."

"Fine! We were leaving anyway." Marty stood and grabbed his beer. "Come on boys, we have to get home. It's dinner time!"

"No!"

"We're not leaving!" They continued to splash in the pool, diving back under the water.

"Let's go pick up pizza at Augie's." Marty had said the magic word.

"Pizza! Pizza!" they both called out as their heads resurfaced. They quickly scrambled out of the pool. With their limited palates, the word pizza always did the trick.

"Grab your towels. I don't want you getting the car seats wet."

The boys complied, although they began squirting one another again as they ran around the side of the house to the driveway. By the time they got to the car, the towels were as drenched as their bodies.

Steve had already headed in the house. He couldn't take Marty right now. He couldn't take him much at all anymore. When he reached for the front door, he was surprised to find Scarlett on the other side, and he felt his heart jump inside his chest like a bullfrog on steroids. She was wearing a see-through sarong which outlined her incredible curves, and she was seductively leaning against the doorway. At her feet was a tote bag with her signature

Marilyn Monroe towel folded on top. Marilyn looked like she was coyly smiling up at them as if part of their little secret.

"Scarlett?" Steve looked furtively behind him toward the window to the back of the house, spying Marty downing the last of his beer. He wasn't taking any chances that he might spot Scarlett when he came around to the driveway. He pulled her gently by the arm and closed the door behind them.

"Hi, Steve," she said, draping her arms over his shoulders and kissing him.

"Mmmm. Katie's out with Erin and the girls. I'm hoping you just missed Marty."

"Holy crap! Is his car out there? I walked over and didn't even notice! All I was thinking about was you."

"Yes, but he's around back and leaving with the boys. He's pissed at me anyway."

"Uggh. Well, your wife did give me carte blanche to use your pool, remember? We can tell her there were a few hang-ups with our installation, so it could be a bust for the rest of the summer," she said, batting her eyelashes at him.

"Uh, yeah. So, uh, help yourself if that's why you came."

Scarlett untied her sarong and let it drop to the floor. She was wearing a bikini beneath that couldn't have been made from any less material. It looked more like pasties and a G-string. "I'd rather help myself to Katie's husband." She pressed herself against him and kissed him passionately.

Steve locked the front door and picked Scarlett up in his arms, carrying her to the bedroom. He stopped short in the doorway.

"Oh, are you okay with this?" he asked, nodding toward Katie's and his bed.

"I don't stand on ceremony, Steve. I just want to be with you."

With that, Steve practically bolted for the bed, tossing Scarlett onto it before pulling off his swim trunks. Scarlett was frantically pulling off her bikini top when Steve bent over to pull off her bottom. He dove face first between her legs as she flung her top onto the floor and let out a primal scream.

STEVE AND SCARLETT were lying in bed facing each other, each with their heads propped in their hands. The comforter was splayed off the side of the bed, leaving them covered only in a twisted sheet.

"I don't want to play the game anymore," Scarlett said, a slightly authoritative tone to her voice.

"I don't either," Steve said.

"But I'm glad we did. I'm glad it brought us together."

"Me, too."

"You know, Katie and Erin are planning a girls' night out. They called me from the mall earlier. Didn't you wonder how I knew it was safe to come by?"

"I just thought you were really coming to use the pool to taunt me like you did last month."

"Taunt you? Is that what I was doing?" Scarlett said with a chuckle. "You mean taunting you like this?" she asked, pulling the covers down, exposing her breasts.

"Yeah, like that," Steve said, pressing his mouth over her right nipple.

"You know, they asked me to go with them," Scarlett said, her back arching to allow Steve to take in more of her areola.

He pulled away. "What did you say?"

"C. Thomas is going to Chicago for one of those ridiculous video conventions. I just don't get how he can't see these kiosks are dinosaurs already. It's all streaming video. Anyway, he's hopeless. He won't be back until Sunday."

"You didn't answer my question."

Scarlett reached under the covers between Steve's legs. "So, I actually was hoping I'd have other plans—that something else would come up in the meantime."

"Yeah, well, something just did come up," Steve said, feeling his erection under Scarlett's dancing fingers.

"Ah, yes. I think it has."

Steve pressed his mouth over Scarlett's, forcing his tongue in as far as it would go. He reached under the covers and felt for her wetness. He climbed on top of her and entered her.

"Harder!" Scarlett insisted.

Steve pulled her legs up over his forearms to penetrate deeper and thrust harder. Then he released her legs and flipped her over so that she was on top of him. With one hand he held her hip and with the other, he reached down and with his thumb began rubbing her clitoris in a circular motion. She sat, gyrating against him. He could tell she was close, and he rubbed more urgently. Her breathing quickened, and her body tensed until she exploded in deep orgasm.

"Turn over," Steve said.

Scarlett complied. She turned onto her stomach as Steve pulled her feet to the floor. He placed his hands on either side of her round bottom and guided himself from behind into her drenched vagina, thrusting over and over until she cried out, her body shuddering in waves of pleasure. When he was sure she was done, he finally came, filling her completely.

Scarlett crawled slowly across the bed toward the pillow, utterly spent. Steve climbed in beside her and lifted her head onto his chest.

"That…was…incredible," Scarlett said, catching her breath.

"Yes, it was. How many orgasms did you have?"

"I can't believe it. I've never had more than one. I must have had—three. Maybe more? I don't even know."

"Mmmmm."

They were silent a few minutes. Scarlett began tracing her fingers through Steve's chest hair.

"I love hearing your heart beat."

"Mmmm. I'm totally exhausted now. Remember, I'm an old man."

"Yeah, right. I'm exhausted, too. What does that make me?" Scarlett said through a yawn.

Before long they both were asleep. They slept soundly for an hour until Steve jumped at the sound of the doorbell. Scarlett remained motionless but when Steve flew out of the bed, he woke her. Grabbing his swim trunks from the floor, he collected Scarlett's swimsuit and tossed it to her before pulling on his own. "Get dressed!"

"What's the matter?" Scarlett asked, still groggy and unaware of the doorbell.

"We fell asleep! It's late and someone's at the door!"

"Could it be Katie?" Scarlett shot up and started putting on her suit.

"I know we're estranged, but I don't think she would ring the bell to her own house." Steve looked in the mirror over the bureau and patted down his bedhead. "I'll be right back."

Racing down the hallway, Steve headed for the front door when he suddenly realized someone was in the kitchen.

"Marty! What the hell are you doing in here?"

"I should ask you the same question," Marty said, holding up Scarlett's sarong he'd picked up off the entryway floor.

"Um, I live here, Marty," he said, ignoring the dangling garment.

"Scarlett's bag was outside."

"Yeah, so? Katie told her she could use the pool until hers is finished. How did you get in here?"

"I went around back. The boys forgot their swim goggles. No one was there, by the way. Didn't look like *anyone* had been there since we left. Yeah. So, anyway, I let myself in," he gestured to the French doors leading out from the kitchen to the backyard. He looked over Steve's shoulder and saw Scarlett approaching from the darkened hallway. She was wearing a Beverly Hilton robe, which she pulled more tightly around her when she spotted Marty.

"Hmmm. I think this is a breach of the game's rules, don't you think? *Counselor?*"

Steve turned to see Scarlett in the kitchen doorway.

"The game's over," they both said.

"I can't believe you two!" Marty bellowed.

"What do you think is going on here?" Steve asked.

"I know *exactly* what is going on. I'm sure Katie would like to know, too. And C. Thomas." He alternately was glaring at both of them.

"Are you threatening us, Marty?"

"What do you two plan to do? Go off over the rainbow and live happily ever after?"

"Whatever, Marty," Scarlett said.

"I'd shut the hell up and get out of here, man. *Now,*" Steve warned.

Marty picked up the boys' goggles he'd placed on the kitchen table and brushed past Steve, intentionally ramming him in the shoulder with his own. Steve and Scarlett could hear the front door slam behind him.

"Oh, my God, Steve. What should we do?"

"Nothing. I know Marty. He'll cool down. This falls into guy code."

"I don't know. He scares me. *Really* scares me."

Steve took Scarlett into his arms and kissed her on top of the head, breathing deeply and taking in the smell of her. He'd never felt so intoxicated by another woman in his life.

"We'll work it out, my love." They embraced for a few moments.

"I'd better get going. I guess we were lucky it was Marty not Katie and the girls."

"I guess so. Oh, don't forget your bag—Marty said you left it out on the front step."

"Jeez. Sorry."

Steve walked Scarlett to the door. They embraced one last time before Scarlett slipped out.

## 21

## REVELATIONS

"We really should do this more often!" Katie cackled, pursing her lips after tossing aside the lemon wedge she sucked on following the shot of tequila. "I forgot how much fun I could have without my husband."

"I'll drink to that," Erin responded, holding up her beer as a mock toast before taking a long swig and emptying it. The pair had been at the local tavern for less than an hour and already were through their second round of shots and beer. "Another round?"

"Absolutely!" Katie signaled the cocktail waitress and ordered two more beers and two more shots.

"This place is packed tonight," Erin commented, looking around. "But I don't recognize anyone here. Then again, my circle of friends lately is down to about a *half-dozen*," she teased.

"Mine, too."

"Anyway, I don't expect too many of the local school parents go out boozing on the weekends."

Katie chuckled. "You know, you really look great, Erin. As you sometimes say, you have that 'well-laid' look about you. Things better with you and Marty? You getting some action on the home front?"

"Not on the *home* front," Erin couldn't contain the smile that overtook her entire face. "But I am getting some *action*." She was seriously buzzed.

Katie was about to take a drink. She paused with the bottle touching her parted lips and raised an eyebrow.

"What?! You're having an *affair?*"

"I'm not exactly sure it qualifies as an affair. It was only one night—so far!"

"Oh, my God, Erin! You didn't tell me?! Who? When?"

"Don't worry, it's not Steve," Erin said with a laugh. Katie snickered, moving closer, waiting for the big reveal.

"Tell me!"

"I'll say first, it has resulted in me going back to teaching this fall."

"Huh?" The beer and tequila had gone to Katie's head, too, and it took her a full ten seconds for it to register what she was hearing. "You mean you slept with the guy from your interview?!"

Erin sat coyly, enjoying the torture she was heaping upon Katie. When it looked as if Katie was going to fall off her bar stool from anticipation, she finally responded.

"Umm, not exactly. Actually, his wife—while he watched."

Katie could do nothing but chug her beer, rendered completely speechless. Afterward, she recovered enough to choke out, "How—how—how in hell did that happen?"

"Well, you know I had my interview yesterday. I actually had gone back to the mall and bought that dress you suggested. It looked great, if I do say so myself—perfect for making an *impression*. Anyway, we were nearly through with the interview, which had been going really well, I might add—"

"Cut to the chase!"

"I am!" Erin scolded. "So he offered me the job almost right away—I am going to be teaching fourth grade at Winnifred Roberts Elementary in Brookfield. God only knows how I'm going to manage being around maniac nine-year-olds there and at home from sunup to sundown, but anyway—"

"Oh, my God, Erin. You're killing me."

"Okay, okay. Let me finish. Soooo, we're walking out of his office, and all of a sudden this beautiful blonde walks up to him and plants a big ole kiss on him, then she looks right at me. Looked me up and down. I guess it was the dress. I was sort of flabbergasted. I started laughing. I don't really know why. The two of them started laughing, too. It turned out it was his wife and she'd just gotten back from a business trip, so she came to see him."

"Yeah, yeah, and?"

"They walked me out to my car. We realized we all had a lot in common. We stood outside in the parking lot talking for like ever. They invited me out for a drink. Then one thing led to another."

"Oh, my God, Erin! So you ended up in their bedroom?" Katie shook her head in utter amazement.

"Yeah, just like that. It was great!"

"I hope you know what you're doing."

"Look, Katie. I feel great. I should have swung years ago!"

"But I don't understand. I mean, I don't care, but do you still like men?"

"Of course I do. But I guess I've just never had the kind of intimacy or passion with a man that I felt with her or even with Scarlett. I've never been sexually fulfilled to be honest. It's hard to explain. I didn't even know I *liked* sex until now!"

"Really?"

"My first relationship before Marty was with my high school boyfriend. I was never even physically attracted to him, but we were together a while, and it seemed like the natural next step. He was a virgin, too, and was so anxious our first time he couldn't get it up and never did after that, either. So, suffice it to say, it was totally unsatisfying."

"Wow."

"Yeah. We spent nearly two years like that."

"Why?"

"Call it stupidity. Lack of self-confidence. I don't know. But there is something about women though. I guess we just naturally know how to please each other. It's not just sex. It's like a connection. Sort of the emotional piece I never had with Marty, either. But don't get me wrong. I want men. I just wish Marty was a *better* man in more ways than one."

"Yeah. I can understand that. I'm happy for you—I think." Katie laughed.

"It sounds funny, but I think it's just a phase. Maybe some kind of self-exploration. You'd know more about that than me, Mrs. Freud." She paused a moment. "Anyway, I don't ever want to play the game again, but I'm glad we did it. I never would have known what I was missing." She picked up her beer to toast. "To the game."

Katie picked up hers to toast and they clinked their bottles.

"To the game—" Katie began, when two men approached their table and cut her off.

"Hello, ladies," the first man said. He was in his late twenties or early thirties and had well-trimmed stubble. His eyes were dark, and his hair perfectly unkempt. He leaned his elbow on the table and continued. "You two look like you're having such a wonderful time. I thought my friend John and I could join you. You know, the more the merrier? What do you say?"

He gestured to John, who had been standing a step or two back, and then pointed to the two open stools at their table. John was blonde and blue-eyed, wearing a golf polo and plaid shorts, looking like he just came off the green. He looked a bit older than his friend and slightly more reserved. He brightened when he approached Katie and Erin.

"Whoa. Wait a minute," Erin said, the alcohol evident in her tone, making her bold. "We have to test you first. If you pass the test, then you can join us. Are you game?"

The first man responded. "Fire away." He sat down on one of the stools. John leaned against the other, one foot on the bottom rung and the other still planted on the floor. They both set down their glasses.

Erin smiled at Katie. "You start."

"Okay, first, there's the physical test." Katie turned to Erin, "I think these two gentleman have passed the physical test, don't you?" She turned back to the men and looked them up and down in a very slow and obvious manner.

"Uh, I don't know, Katie," she said, staring at them and purposely drawing out each word. "Show me your teeth."

The men exchanged puzzled looks, but then shrugged and opened their mouths, exposing their teeth.

"Okay, you pass the physical test." The men looked at one another again, but smiled. "Katie, do you want to ask the rest of the questions, or should I?"

"That's okay, you can," Katie said. The first question was easy, but she wasn't completely sure where Erin was going with this. Nevertheless, she was eager to find out.

"Okay, guys, ready for the lightning round?" The men nodded. "Do you guys like to play cards?" The men exchanged looks, smiled and nodded again. "Do you guys play poker?"

"Sure," Dark Eyes said.

"Yes," John said.

"How about Texas Hold'em?" Erin asked.

"Love the game," Dark Eyes said, leaning in showing more interest.

"My favorite," John said.

"Okay. Last question. And this is the most important one."

The two men beamed, sure that they had nearly passed the test.

"Would you cheat on your wives?"

The men exchanged looks. "Uh," John began.

"We're not married," Dark Eyes said.

"Oh, well, of course you're not. But if you were, would you?"

"No way," Dark Eyes said, satisfied with his answer.

"Absolutely not," John said, sitting back on his stool and folding his arms across his chest.

Erin and Katie looked at each other, then simultaneously said, "Wrong answer," laughing and high-fiving one another.

"What the—" Dark Eyes said, standing up.

"These two are nuts," John said, waving his hand, dismissing them. He abruptly picked up his glass and backed up his stool, almost knocking it over. The two headed into the crowd near the bar, surely intending to find two much more normal women to chat up.

The cocktail waitress came by, cleaning up discarded lemons and dirty napkins. "Another round?"

"Absolutely," Erin said.

As the waitress left for the service bar, John returned to the table. "I think you two may be needing this," he said, sliding a business card across the table to them before turning on his heels and heading back to the bar.

"Wha—" Erin began.

"He's a divorce attorney!" Katie said, breaking into hysterics. Erin did the same.

While the two tried to pull themselves together, wiping tears from their eyes with their cocktail napkins, a woman about Erin's age and with a similar build and hair color approached the table. She looked surprised to see Erin.

"Erin?"

"Oh, my God, Brenda. How are you? Long time, no see!" The two women hugged.

"Katie, this is my cousin, Brenda, who I haven't seen for ages, even though we *always* say we are going to get together." Erin was slurring. "And Brenda, this is Katie, my best, best, bestest friend in the whole world."

"Hi, it's a pleasure!"

"Nice to meet you," Katie responded.

"Brenda's husband is a state trooper," Erin said to Katie.

Katie nodded.

"So how is Eddie?"

"Ah, he's tired of his job. He wants to retire and move to Florida."

"You guys are too young for that, but on the other hand, Florida does sound great! God, what I wouldn't give for a change of scenery."

"Well, he can't retire just yet anyway. I mean, he has another *fifteen* years. So for now, I'll just sit in the kids' plastic turtle pool and pretend I live in a chic condo with an in-ground." The three women laughed.

"So what are you doing out?"

"I'm meeting a bunch of people from work. Eddie's supposed to stop by after his shift. What about you?"

"Girls' night. A *well-deserved* girls' night. We needed a break from our husbands."

"Yeah, I understand. You certainly do deserve one after all that's been going on."

Erin looked at Katie. Could she somehow have heard about the game? How? They both were thinking the same thing.

"You don't have to worry with me. You know I wouldn't say anything."

"Huh?" Erin said, feeling an odd lump in her throat. "Brenda, I really don't know what you are talking about." Could she know the elementary school principal or his wife?

"C'mon, Erin. The whole thing with Marty."

"What whole thing?!"

Brenda leaned in to Erin out of Katie's earshot. Just above a whisper, she said, "Are you being serious, or are you just playing dumb for Katie's benefit?"

"I have no idea what you're talking about," Erin said, loud enough for

Katie to hear. "If there's something that you know that involves my husband, please let *me* know. Katie's my *best* friend, and there are *no* secrets between us."

"Um, okay—"

---

Erin rushed through the front door, tripping over action figures and avoiding a glut of squished marshmallows. She could hear the television blaring with the sounds of machine guns and sirens. As she passed by the living room, Devin and Daniel, who still were clad in the day's clothing despite the late hour, were standing and jumping up and down on the couch playing on the Xbox. Uncharacteristically, Erin didn't stop to say hello or admonish them for their raucous activities. She only wanted to find Marty, who was, of course, in his study.

Erin slammed the door against the wall as she threw it open, waking Marty from his near-comatose state. Next to him was a jug of Jack Daniels, with little more than an inch left in it.

"What? What the fuck, Erin? What's going on?" he slurred.

Erin picked up the bottle and poured the remainder over his open laptop which displayed nude photos of young, buxom women in mostly very vulgar sexual positions. Then grabbing the computer by its screen, she threw it, and the bottle across the room.

"What the fuck are you doing?" Marty screeched.

"I should just cut it off! Just cut off your dick, you lying, cheating bastard! You just couldn't keep it in your pants! Just couldn't do it!" She was in a fury, spitting as she spoke. "Even with the game! Even with all the porn you watch! You had to look for something more! A prostitute?! How could you?!"

Erin reached out and in one sweeping motion, knocked everything she could from the desk onto the floor and into his lap.

"What are you talking about?" Marty said, a look of fear spreading across his face.

"My cousin Brenda—you remember Brenda—and *Eddie—the cop*! She told me *everything*!"

Marty blanched.

"Yeah! The whole family knows what kind of dirty scumbag you are! Oh, my God! I can't believe you were arrested for soliciting a hooker!"

"Erin, calm down! I was drunk! It was just a misunderstanding!"

"Don't you *dare* tell me to calm down! And a misunderstanding? Are you fucking kidding me?! The only misunderstanding is our *marriage*! I want you out! Tonight! Now!"

Marty got up from his chair, knocking pens and papers from his lap to the floor. "Erin, let's talk about this."

"Get the hell away from me, Marty! There's nothing to talk about!"

"Erin, please. Be reasonable," he groveled.

"Be reasonable?! Are you kidding? Are you really kidding me?"

"Erin," Marty said, approaching her.

"Get the fuck out of this house! Now!" Erin was so beside herself that her head was spinning. She had never felt such rage.

"Where am I going to go? It's late. Please, let's talk about it tomorrow. Both of us have had too much to drink. We can figure this out." He reached out to put a hand on her arm. She flipped it off, and slapped him across the face as hard as she could, leaving her entire handprint on his cheek. He stumbled back.

"I deserve that. I know. But Erin."

"Don't 'but Erin' me! I want you out of here! And away from my sons! Right this minute before I call the police!"

"Police? What for? What are you going to tell them?"

"I don't care! I'll tell them you attacked me! I'll tell them you went after the boys! They'll believe me, too! You already have a record! You—you *pig*!"

Suddenly Erin heard voices behind her and turned to see Devin and Daniel standing in the doorway, ashen.

"Is everything okay, Mommy?" Daniel asked.

Erin rushed over to them. "Yes, boys. Mommy and Daddy are just—talking about something."

"But you're yelling," Devin said.

"I know, honey. Sometimes mommies and daddies do that. I'm sorry. Let's go get ready for bed, and you can tell me about your night." She turned to Marty and mouthed the words "Get out! Now!" then headed for the stairs.

From the study, Marty could hear Erin telling the boys that there would be a lot for them to clean up tomorrow. He looked around the floor of his study at the mess before him. The laptop was blinking and the screen was shattered. Several of the keys from the keyboard were sticking up or missing. He kicked it to the other side of the room and fell to his knees.

## 22

## FAST FORWARD

*Autumn is the eternal corrective. It is ripeness and color and a time of maturity; but it is also breadth, and depth, and distance. What man can stand with autumn on a hilltop and fail to see the span of his world and the meaning of the rolling hills that reach to the far horizon?*

— HAL BORLAND

"I JUST DON'T UNDERSTAND why you have to leave *tomorrow*," Katie said, sitting on the edge of the bed watching Steve pack. "Your business trips are *always* planned in advance. The travel department would never tolerate it if they didn't have time to find the cheapest deals on hotels."

"I don't know, Katie," Steve said, getting visibly annoyed. They'd been going around and around for ten minutes now. "Don't ask me. I'm just the worker bee. They say go, so I go."

"Whatever."

Katie began taking his shirts out of the suitcase and refolding them, then replacing them in a neatened stack. "So what is your agenda?" She handed him back a shirt, "This one has a stain."

"Thanks." Steve tossed it on top of the hamper.

"You know, now that the girls are back in school, they're all over the place between work, cheerleading, student council, and their social calendars. And you know the parts for Jamie's car haven't come in yet, so it's all on me—it's hard to do all the running myself."

"What do you want me to do, Katie? Say no? As if I could? I lose my job, and you won't be able to stay home playing Susie Homemaker anymore."

"Screw you, Steve! As if that wasn't a joint decision. How dare you throw that back in my face after all these years. And I do work. Plus, I'll have you know that I *am* planning to go back and finish my licensure. I only needed a few hundred more supervised hours before the licensing exam. I spoke to a few local psychiatrists already about working under them."

Steve didn't say anything. He was thinking about this trip and *only* about this trip. Katie might as well have been Charlie Brown's teacher saying, "Wah wahh woh wahh." He tossed a few more polos and a pair of jeans on top of his khakis and his business clothes.

"Why are you packing so many casual clothes? Aren't you just advising on a trial?"

"Of course, but there will be a lot of down time, and I'm not going to sit around in a suit all day every day."

Katie got up and walked over to the mirror. She ran her fingers through her hair. It had gotten long this summer and she liked it. "I think I'm going to let Ayanna give me those highlights. Maybe when you come back, you won't recognize me. It will be like having another woman in the house."

Steve stopped dead for a moment. He looked down at the bed and thought about his tryst with Scarlett right there in Katie's and his bedroom, on that very bed. His heart skipped just remembering it. Fearful that Katie might somehow read his thoughts as she often did, he resumed packing. He went over to the dresser and took his Ray-Bans from his leather valet. When Katie wasn't looking, he lifted the tray and pulled out a small envelope, stashing it in the suitcase under the refolded clothing stack.

"I'm going to go start dinner," Katie said, abruptly walking out of the bedroom.

"What time will it be ready?" Steve called after her. She didn't respond.

Steve took his cell phone out of his pants pocket. He'd felt it vibrate a short time before, and he saw there was a text from Scarlett. He wasn't too concerned about occasional texts between them, since all of the triptych were *supposedly* still friends. But he was careful to be cryptic in his messages, as was Scarlett, just in case Katie or C. Thomas happened to see. He read her text.

*Need some help with the paralegal stuff. I know you're leaving for the city at 7 a.m. tomorrow right?*

He responded.

*Yes, leaving at 7. Let me know what you need when I get back Sunday. Should be around 8 p.m.*

Steve felt like he was courting again. An old-fashioned term, but it was exhilarating to be with Scarlett and he loved treating her like a queen. It had been barely over a month, but he loved their long talks, their lovemaking. Mostly he loved being himself with her. Plus, they shared so many common interests. This little getaway would make them feel like they were really dating. It was hard to sneak away most days, but having direct access to the cabin helped as long as they could account for their time. He was looking forward to surprising her with so many things in the city—shows, restaurants, even a concert. As luck would have it, Scarlett's favorite band was performing at Madison Square Garden.

He finished packing and went into the kitchen. Even as he watched Katie cooking and dancing along to her iPod, he felt nothing. He suspected she felt a lot less about him these days, too. Maybe he needed to think that to assuage his guilt, but he was going to New York, and maybe for the first time ever, he was going with someone he truly loved.

---

STEVE HAD LEFT EARLY and after Katie drove the girls to school, she came back and made herself a pot of coffee. The September days were still warm, so she brought her mug outside and set in on the patio table. She sat with her feet curled under her looking out at the woods behind the house and wondering when the leaves might start to change. Fall was her favorite time of year. The commencement of each new autumn made her wax poetic. In a way, it made her wish she had become a writer. In college, she spent countless hours reading the works of different authors and exploring new genres, sometimes getting so caught up in a book that she would run late for class. But no matter what, she always read something of substance.

Since Erin was now busy teaching and she wasn't available to chat over morning coffee, Katie figured she'd try calling Scarlett. When the phone went directly to voicemail, she sat staring at the handset for a moment, contemplating what to do with herself. Like a firecracker under her, she leapt to her feet and headed for the basement.

Once downstairs, she ran her fingers over the neatly stacked and labeled boxes until she found her old college books. Actually, there were several boxes, but she knew which one she wanted to get her hands on. The first book she pulled was *Mr. Tompkins in Paperback* and the second, *The Phenomenon of Man*. She headed back upstairs and grabbed a muffin, then took it and her books back out to the patio.

She began thumbing through the dog-eared and highlighted pages. These were books she devoured in college after her professor recommended them to his eager student. Although she often thought of Mr. Leo as a wild man, she had something of a crush on him. It was his passion and his diverse interests which roped her in. She liked the eccentricities. She'd always been so conventional, so predictable. Mr. Leo and his ideas were the complete opposite. Initially she thought of these principles as pure whimsy, but she soon grew excited by them. But like the books, they had been packed away since she and Steve got married, and her only concentrations since then had been of the traditional kind.

Before she knew it, she caught herself daydreaming about Zack Braun, but was rudely snapped out of her reverie by the ringing of the telephone.

"Hello?" She hadn't checked the caller ID display.

"Hey, Kate. It's me. Just wanted to let you know I'm in the city."

"Oh."

"Yeah, I just got out of Grand Central."

"Hm. Funny, you never call when you get anywhere."

"Oh, yeah. Well, I just wanted you to—ah—let me know if the mail came yet."

"Um, no. How could it? It's not even nine o'clock. Are you expecting something? Are you okay?"

"Uh, no. And um, yes."

"Okay, well. I'll let you know if anything interesting comes."

"Okay. Bye, Katie."

"Bye."

---

STEVE AND SCARLETT had just arrived in New York. It wasn't the first time Steve had lied to Katie, nor was it the first time he'd kept something from her, but he wasn't very good at it. His impulsive decision to call her was certainly a faux pas he now regretted. Steve was a bad liar. Thinking fast on his feet was never his strong suit. In a weak effort to try to cover his tracks, he knew he had made worse because as Katie pointed out, he never checked in with her. He was sure Katie *knew* he was up to no good. He tried to brush it off. He reached for Scarlett's hand and waved for a taxi. The next to drive by pulled over and after the driver helped put their bags in the trunk, they climbed in.

"TriBeCa," he told the driver.

"Address?"

"Three-seventy-seven Greenwich Street."

"So, what did she say?" Scarlett asked. She'd been fixing her hair in her reflection in a store window while Steve paced on the phone with Katie a few feet away.

"Not much," Steve said, sounding glum.

"What's wrong?"

"I shouldn't have called. I think I screwed up."

"I'm sure it's fine," Scarlett said, entwining her slender fingers through his strong, masculine ones. She pumped their hands up and down. "I love your hands."

"Mmm."

She beamed up at him and changed the subject. "So where to?"

"Not telling. But what I will say is that you've never had a better frittata or lemon ricotta pancakes in your life."

"Mmm. Good, because I'm starved." She pulled out her cell phone and tried to look up the address when she didn't think Steve was paying attention. He put his hand over the screen.

"Don't be sneaky," he scolded.

"You know I don't like surprises," she said with a chuckle. She instead clicked the phone onto camera mode and attempted to take a selfie of the two of them in the cab.

"No, no. Scarlett, you can't."

"C'mon, Steve. No one else will see it." She leaned back against him and clicked the camera button. The photo captured an unsmiling Steve, however Scarlett looked stunning; their image immediately transformed into a frozen tableau with New York City behind them through the rear window of the cab.

"There can't be any pictures of us, Scarlett. You can't put that out there. Not yet."

Scarlett pouted.

"I mean it. There can't be any trace of us. Please delete it," he pleaded.

"Okay, Steve. If it means that much to you," she said as she pressed delete.

"We're almost here," Steve said, reaching for his briefcase which he'd only taken as a cover.

Locanda Verde was a casually elegant, rustic little place tucked between tall, older buildings in TriBeCa; one of its claims to fame was that it was co-owned by the one and only Robert De Niro. Steve had taken a client there for breakfast not long before and couldn't find a better reason to go back. It was ironic to him that he'd once read a review that referred to their cuisine as "food porn." It was.

"Sooooo, I take it you're not telling me anything about what you have planned for us this week?"

"Nope." Steve smiled slyly. He finally was on the verge of release from his sullen mood. Thinking about Scarlett and porn amused him. He was not a fan of the stuff, never had been. But their lovemaking bordered on the pornographic and he began to feel himself getting hard. He wasn't sure they'd make it through breakfast.

MARTY SCRATCHED at his unshaven face and threw back the cold, bitter dregs of a miserable cup of coffee he'd bought at the Citgo. He now had to take a leak and didn't feel like driving back to the gas station. He knew Erin's mom wouldn't have left the house yet after getting the boys on the school bus, so he couldn't go back there. Instead he adjusted himself and wiggled in his seat. He still had plenty of his belongings to pack up from the house, but Erin wasn't letting him in again until Saturday. She didn't know he let himself in regularly while she was at her new teaching job. Thankfully she hadn't had the locks changed yet.

He continued to drive up and down Scarlett's street passing by her house looking for some signs of life. She and C. Thomas usually parked their cars in the garage, and while he was tempted to peer in through the window to see if her car was there, he was afraid of being spotted. He'd been on patrol since about seven-thirty a.m. It had been shortly after that when he saw C. Thomas pull out on his way to work. Chances were that C. Thomas would be gone most of the day. Now he was hoping to catch a glimpse of Scarlett through a window, or better yet, that she might come out to sit on the porch swing, coffee in hand. He'd been doing this for weeks and he knew her habits well. It was after nine now. Where the hell was she? He headed across the street into the construction site and clicked off the ignition so he wouldn't waste gas.

Marty pulled his cell out of his pocket and scrolled through his photos. Long ago he'd sent himself the naked pictures of Scarlett from Aruba. Thank God, since that bitch Erin had smashed his laptop. He reached down into his elastic-waist athletic shorts and jerked off. After he finished, he fell asleep. It wasn't until the construction workers came and blared their horns at him that he woke up. Damn! It was nearly eleven.

Marty navigated down the muddy, chunked-up driveway to the street, giving the finger to the burly workmen who shouted epithets at him as he passed. He squinted in the late-morning sun to see if Scarlett was outside or if he could see her from the window.

"Shit, damn, fuck!" he grumbled as he passed the house. At this hour, he could have missed her and wouldn't have known it. From the previous weeks of stalking, he knew sometimes she left for work by ten. He hadn't been sleeping well since Erin kicked him out and his drinking became no less than twice-nightly binges. Sometimes more if he awakened from his passed-out states and it still was early enough for another go-round.

He punched the steering wheel. "Now what?" he screeched. He didn't want to go back to the cheap motel where he had been staying. The room was filthy. Management already warned him that housekeeping wouldn't do anything more than change his sheets and bring in fresh towels. It reeked of alcohol and vomit, and he had clothes, take-out packaging, and empty bottles strewn everywhere. They'd already shut off his television because he'd racked up astronomical charges in porn on the Pay-Per-View.

Veering toward his house, he figured he'd go in and score some food and get some more of his stuff, including the box of dirty magazines he kept up in the attic along with some poetry books. He didn't need any more clothing since he'd taken a leave from the University until the whole solicitation charge issue was resolved. He hadn't told them what was going on, but he was unnerved during the meeting with Human Resources. The HR manager looked at him sideways, and Marty had been concerned that maybe Heather had blown the whistle on him.

He parked at the street corner then walked around to the backdoor of the house. He couldn't be certain whether Erin had asked the neighbors to keep watch so he always snuck in the back. He pulled out his keys from his shorts pocket and tried to unlock the door but it wouldn't budge. He looked at the key ring thinking he'd used the wrong key. He hadn't.

"Fuck, fuck, fuck!" he screeched. He headed around the side and tried a few windows, then the basement door, but it was to no avail. Erin had finally changed the locks, likely having grown wise to Marty's uninvited entries.

Marty sat on the stone wall surrounding the patio and pulled out his phone. When he found Steve's contact, he pressed SEND. He needed some legal advice—Erin only had had him served with divorce papers the week before and he didn't recall it saying anything about the use of the house. Then again, he spilled Jack Daniels on the documents before he could read them.

When the phone went to voicemail, Marty left a message. "Hey, Steve. It's me. What the fuck! Erin had me locked out of the house! Can she do that? Why aren't you picking up? Call me!"

# GOING ALL IN

The week had been a whirlwind, and it was already Saturday night. There was one day left before their Cinderella liberty was over. Steve and Scarlett had been to two Broadway shows and a concert, walked the city, strolled some sidewalk festivals, ate every conceivable kind of food, and the rest of the time they'd spent in bed. They'd cut back on their outside activities in order to accommodate more of the latter. Up until this point, Steve had counted forty-one phone calls from Marty, none of which he had answered.

Scarlett was taking a shower when Steve finally decided to listen to the slew of voicemails. He put it on speaker and pressed the play button.

"Hey, Steve. It's me. What the fuck! Erin had me locked out of the house! Can she do that? Why aren't you picking up? Call me!"

"Steve, where the fuck are you?!"

In the third message, Marty sounded totally drunk: "Steve, are you gonna answer the fuckin' phone?!"

"Steve. man, you're my best friend. I am losing my fucking mind. I haven't heard from Paul either. Where the fuck are you?"

"Katie says you're in fucking New York! I should meet ya—"

The next one was garbled and hard to understand as there was what sounded like a television in the background, followed by loud banging. "Get the fuck outta here!" Marty yelled to someone.

About half a dozen were only background noises for a second or two. A few more were hang ups.

"Hey, Steve! It's fucking Thursday already. You don't call? I need to talk to you! I called Scarlett. That bitch is avoiding me. I saw C. Thomas outside the house, and he said he came back from a convention early and doesn't know where the fuck she is! What a cun—" Click.

The next was received only a moment after the previous one. "Steve. Oh, my fucking God! Is Scarlett with you?!"

"Steve, I know she can't be with you. You'd never do that to Katie. You'd never want Katie to *know* if you did, though. Right? *Steve-O?*"

After several more hang-ups and even more drunken calls which were totally unintelligible, the last message really rattled Steve. Just as he was listening to it, Scarlett appeared in the bathroom doorway wearing only a

273

towel. She was ashen, despite her lingering summer tan. He never should have put the phone on speaker. He wondered how much she'd heard. He reached to take it off speaker when Scarlett stopped him.

"Don't," she said, putting speaker back on and replaying the message. "I should hear this, too."

The final message sounded totally lucid. It had been left just a few hours before when he and Scarlett were at the hotel spa. This one was different. It wasn't the words so much as it was the tone that was disturbing, even chilling.

"Steve, I know where you are, and I know what you're doing, *Buddy*. See you when you get back. Oh, and say hi–" He had hung up before finishing the last sentence. Scarlett looked up at Steve. He reached for her, and they held each other a long time before either spoke.

"It's nothing, right?" Scarlett said. "I mean, Marty's just being Marty. It's Marty being a prick. Just being his prick self. Right? Tell me I'm right about this." She was rambling and shaking.

Steve pulled back and looked directly into Scarlett's eyes. "Yes, it's nothing. Marty is a weak wimp who drinks too much. He screwed up his marriage and maybe his job, and he's spiraling out of control. He's just mad because he thinks he didn't do anything wrong, and he's busting my balls because I haven't called him back. That's all."

"But—"

"Shhhh. Don't worry, Scarlett. I really think he's just being a drunk ass and taking it out on me. There's nothing more to it. I think he's still healing from the shock that Erin kicked him out and changed the locks. I think the idiot actually thought she'd forgive him and take him back."

"Okay. But, he really sounds insane."

---

*Dear Diary and Mom,*

*I've found him. I've really found him—the ONE. I've just spent six of the most incredible days of my life with a loving, kind, intelligent, cultured man. A man who can and would take care of me—but the best part is I get to take care of him right back.*

*PLUS*—*the sex is mind-blowing! I can't believe there are men who exist who care about their partner's needs before their own—or instead of!*

*Did I say he's mine? I have to break it off with C. Thomas. I know Steve has more to deal with because of the divorce process, the kids, but I can wait. We have our whole lives ahead of us—together.*

*Maybe I'm just being paranoid about Marty. Steve says don't worry. He's just a blow hard, and he'll get over it. Plus, Steve says we should break it to everyone soon, so it won't matter what Marty says.*

*I AM IN LOVE!!!*

## 23

## CHANGE

"God. I don't want to go, but I think I have to," Steve said, kissing Scarlett on the top of the head. She'd been nuzzled against him, lazily running her fingers through his chest hairs.

"C. Thomas won't be home until tonight," she pouted. "His uncle's funeral isn't until three o'clock, and there will be a family gathering after. Do you have to?"

"I know, but I have to do a couple of things." Steve was being coy. Today was the day he planned to tell Katie. Things had been strange between them since he'd returned from New York the day before. Katie hadn't said anything, but he suspected she knew something was awry.

"Are you going to do it right away?" Scarlett asked, propping her head up on her hand.

"As soon as I get home." Steve started to get up when Scarlett pulled him back and kissed him passionately.

"No regrets?" she asked.

"God, no."

"No second thoughts?"

"None."

"So by this time tomorrow—"

"It will have been done, my love."

This time Steve got up, and Scarlett didn't stop him. She did not want him to go, but she was eager for him to tell Katie. Neither of them could stand to be apart since returning from the city. She watched him as he began to pull on his pants, then leapt out of bed and pressed her naked body against him from behind.

"Mmmm," he said, reaching around behind him and grabbing Scarlett's rear.

"I love you. I have for a long time, you know," Scarlett said, barely above a whisper.

Steve turned around to face her, holding her tightly. He felt himself getting hard. He opened his mouth to speak, when Scarlett put a finger over his lips.

"Don't say anything. Not now."

He bent down to kiss her then picked her up and carried her back to the bed, letting his pants fall back around his feet, kicking them aside. He reached down and felt her wetness, pushing two fingers inside of her. She cried out, grabbing him by the shoulders so she could feel his full weight on top of her. He reached under her thighs to pull her legs over his biceps and entered her deeply, thrusting hard. When he was sure Scarlett had had enough, he let go of her legs, allowing her to rest them back on the bed as he gyrated his hips.

"Oh, my God!" Scarlett cried out.

Lifting his knees one by one, Steve pushed Scarlett's legs together between his thighs. He shifted his weight slightly forward so that the shaft of his erection was exerting firm pressure and friction on her clitoris while he thrust harder and harder. Her body went rigid, and she screamed in ecstasy. He came with her.

---

SCARLETT OPENED the front door just as Steve pulled her back into an embrace. It was still warm outside, but a cool breeze drifted over them accompanied by the sound of the barely yellowed, rustling leaves. In just a week, fall had teasingly begun.

"I'll miss you," Scarlett said.

"Me, too, my love."

"Good luck."

Steve slid out of the front door, still holding on to Scarlett's hand. He didn't want to let go, nor did she. Finally he smiled and tugged his hand from her grip. She beamed back at him with a look of both radiance and melancholy. He knew what she was feeling. This day marked both a beginning and an end.

Steve headed to his car, which he had cavalierly parked on the driveway expecting he'd be gone early, before anyone might spot it. Steve had told Katie he was going to stay in a hotel the previous night after working late, instead of catching the midnight train and taking the risk of falling asleep and missing his stop. He said that he did it for her benefit, so that she wouldn't have to come to retrieve him further down the train line at some ungodly hour. He explained he was still recovering from his business trip and jumping right back to work the next day had been a mistake—so he'd be home early and take the day off. Of course the real reason was that he'd planned to make good use of C. Thomas's unexpected absence—and his bed.

---

MARTY WAS PLANTED in his usual spot across the street, taking in the whole scene. His car was riddled with empty liquor bottles and garbage—and it *stank*. What may have started out smelling like dirty gym socks, now had become the richer, more pungent odor of pure, unadulterated filth. Marty hadn't bathed in a week, nor had he changed his clothes. He stared intently as Steve backed out onto the street and drove toward home.

Marty had been there all night doing his usual stalking and sulking. He knew C. Thomas was gone. The night before he saw C. Thomas tossing a small suitcase in the trunk before heading off in his Jag. Marty must have passed out though, because he became enraged when he awakened somewhere around ten thirty and found Steve's car on the driveway. He was going around and around his head, trying to think of excuses for Steve, even holding out hope that he might just have stopped by to talk to C. Thomas, not knowing he was gone. When the Audi stayed into the wee hours, he knew for certain there was far more than that happening behind the closed doors.

As soon as Steve's car was out of sight, Marty pulled past the bulldozer and straight for Scarlett's house. He scrambled out of the car and sprinted to the door where he rang the bell repeatedly until he heard footsteps from within. Thinking it must be Steve, Scarlett, wearing only a scanty pink robe, swung open the door with a beaming smile and said, "What did you forge—"

Her face quickly turned to a scowl when she saw Marty. Her eyes grew wide with horror as she took in the entirety of his disheveled appearance.

"Well, if truth be told Scar-*lett*, I did forget to give you something—something to remember me by." His tone bordered on sinister and he looked utterly frightening.

Scarlett tried to slam the door shut, but he placed his foot in the way before shoving his shoulder between the door and the jamb, forcing it open. The move knocked Scarlett to the floor. Scrambling to her feet, she ran toward the kitchen with Marty at her heels. She reached for the butcher block and grabbed the largest carving knife, brandishing it at Marty as he burst in.

"Ha! You going to cut me, bitch?" Marty lunged for Scarlett, who swiped at him, driving him back.

"Marty! What are you doing?!" He ignored her, his eyes wild.

She swiped at him again.

"Yeah, baby. I like this game! Maybe even better than poker!"

He lunged at her again. This time, her swipe hit her mark. She cut his left shoulder, but only superficially. Marty laughed loudly. "You think that hurt, bitch?"

Scarlett screamed. She looked around in a panic for some way to escape. He had her trapped behind the center island. Marty climbed up on a stool and threw himself over the island, charging at her. They crashed to the floor, the force of which knocked the knife from Scarlett's hand.

"You're not so tough without your knife, are you?" Marty snickered.

Both scrambled to get to their feet. Marty was first. He punched Scarlett in the face, immediately splitting the skin across her cheekbone and knocking her back to the floor. She screamed out in pain.

"Marty! What the hell is wrong with you?" She tried to get up. Her life was flashing before her eyes.

"What is wrong with *me*?! What is wrong with *you*? You didn't know a good thing when you had it!" He tried to kick her but missed as she wriggled away.

"Oh, Marty, please!" Scarlett pleaded as he lunged at her again, grabbing her by the hair. She kicked out at him and screeched, "Marty!"

"Oh, you want it now, do you, bitch? Oh, Marty! Oh, Marty! Yeah, I'll give you 'Oh, Marty!' " Like punting a football, he let go of her hair just as he kicked her in the ribs with all of his might, sending her sailing across the floor. Her head smashed against the corner of the ornate French stove.

"What else do you got?" Marty taunted as he approached her.

Scarlett was dazed and barely conscious. Her robe had opened, and she was spectacularly naked.

"Yeah, that's a girl," Marty said, leaning down and grabbing a breast. She responded with a faint moan. "Atta girl. I know you want it."

Marty picked Scarlett up, throwing her over his shoulder, then he carried her to the bedroom. She was moaning softly. "Yeah," Marty said, tossing her on the bed like a ragdoll.

"I guess I'll have to make do with sloppy seconds," Marty said, unfastening and removing his pants then climbing on top of her, pinning her arms down with his knees. "Are you ready, Scarlett? I'm about to take what's mine."

---

"ARE THE GIRLS AROUND?" Steve said as he walked into the kitchen where Katie sat with a cup of coffee doing a crossword puzzle.

"Are you kidding?" she said, looking up. She was momentarily taken aback. Steve's clothes were wrinkled, and he had that just-fucked looking kind of hair. "You're home already?" She looked at the clock.

Steve ignored her last question. "So, we're alone?"

"Um, yeah. The girls both stayed over at friends' houses last night after the football game."

"Good," Steve said. He washed his face in his hands. "I need to talk to you."

Katie froze. It was his tone. "Oh, so I take it you've finally decided you know how to open your mouth."

"Please, Katie. We really need to talk."

Katie pushed aside the newspaper and took another sip of her coffee. "Go ahead."

"The game is over." Steve was pacing back and forth. "We're not playing anymore. Any of us."

"Hard to believe lately that we can agree on anything, but of course it's over. You've caught on. It has been for most of us for a while."

Steve stopped pacing and stood facing Katie. He looked right into her eyes. "This is hard, Katie, very hard for me to say." He massaged his forehead. "Katie, I'm attracted to Scarlett."

"Oh, God, Steve. I know. Everyone knows. It's about time you finally owned up to it."

Steve looked at the floor. "I mean. It's more than that. I—I have—feelings for her." He paused to gauge Katie's reaction before continuing. She stared stone-faced at him. He chose his words slowly. "We've been together—outside the game."

Katie put down her coffee cup. An expression spread across her face which Steve could not discern. "What are you saying? You *love* her or something?!"

"Maybe. I don't know. I'm still sorting it all out." Steve sat back on the edge of a kitchen stool, his feet still on the floor.

"*Sorting it out?!* What could you possibly have to sort out? It was only a game. Are you telling me you're willing to walk away from everything? From me? The girls? Our home? This is our life, Steve."

"I—I don't know." He wasn't looking at her.

Katie got up and walked over to the kitchen window searching for strength. She pounded a fist on the counter. "Maybe we shouldn't have played the game. The stupid, goddamn game. We let the devil into our marriage for a couple of cheap thrills. We destroyed what we had."

"You're talking foolishness."

"Am I? How can you say that?"

Steve started to answer when Katie interrupted him. "Everything was fine before the game. I thought the game might—I don't know—spice things up—spice up our lives—and our sex life, too. God knows it needed *something*."

"Katie—"

"I never thought it could ruin our marriage." She began to cry.

"Katie. The game didn't ruin our marriage. We were not fine before."

"Oh? That's a surprise to me."

"C'mon, Katie. We were just going through the motions for a long time." Steve paused. "Are you telling me you really thought we had a *solid* marriage?"

"Yes. Yes, we did, or so *I* thought. Sure, we had our ups and downs—just like any other couple. In my opinion, at least the bedrock was solid."

Steve was shaking his head. "We had problems."

"What *problems* exactly?" She was staring at him.

"I don't want to go over it."

"You don't have a right to say that. You can't throw something like this in my face and expect me not to question it." She walked over, mere inches from his face and was looking right into his eyes. He felt uncomfortable, weak. "We *have* had a solid marriage. *Everyone* has always said that. If you don't think that's true, then you better tell me why. For once in your goddamned life—in this marriage—be honest with me."

Steve stood and walked over to the kitchen table, gesturing for Katie to sit next to him. She complied, and they sat nearly knee-to-knee.

"I have done everything possible for this marriage, Steve. I've done everything to hold us together…" She trailed off, looking away.

After a moment, he began. "First, I don't know what you think went on at the firm Christmas parties, but—nothing—*nothing* ever did."

"Okay, fine. It didn't. So?"

Steve bit his lip. "But something else—something did happen—about six years ago. I was supervising a case in Georgia."

"Georgia, yes, I remember that trip. It was fall."

Steve nodded. "The lawyer I was advising. We spent some time outside of the office. We had dinner. We had a few drinks. One thing led—"

"Led to another? Were you going to say *one thing led to another*? You had an affair? Is that what you are saying?" Tears now were streaming non-stop down Katie's face in a combination of fury and total devastation.

Steve nodded, silent.

"Was it a one-night thing?"

Steve shook his head, averting his eyes.

"How long did it last?" Katie asked, her voice barely audible.

"About a year."

Katie put her head in her hands. Abruptly she looked up. "Six years ago. That was the year I found out about the endometriosis. When I had my surgery, wasn't it? I was trying to get pregnant again. Oh, my God. You stayed longer than you were supposed to."

"Yes."

"You weren't here when I was going through all those tests. Christ, that awful laparoscopy. The biopsy."

"No, I wasn't."

"You never wanted another baby."

Steve hung his head.

"Who broke it off? Did *you* break it off?"

He paused. "No, she did."

Katie was shattered. She'd wanted to hear that he was remorseful. That he had broken it off because he felt guilty about betraying the marriage. That he loved her.

"There wasn't—there weren't. Oh, God. There couldn't be," Katie stammered. "Were there any children?" She held her breath, waiting for Steve to answer.

"Yes. One. A boy. She's raising him—alone. He doesn't know anything about me. She plans to tell him she was artificially inseminated when he's old enough to understand."

Katie doubled over, clutching her stomach.

"I support him," he continued. "I send her money."

"What? Well, how gentlemanly of you. God, Steve. I can't believe this is my life!"

"I never meant—"

"Never meant for what? To knock up some woman? Some stranger? Haven't you ever heard of birth control?!"

"Katie."

"This is unreal! Have you met him? Your *son*?"

"No. But she tells me about him from time to time. I've seen photos."

"How could you? You have Jamie and Anna. They have a brother—a half-brother. They don't even know it. I—I—God, I don't even know what to say." She stood, but he clutched her forearm and pulled her back down.

"Not a day goes by that I don't agonize over what happened."

"Poor you. My heart bleeds for you. Why are you even telling me this —*now*?" Katie bent forward, facing the floor.

"I guess—I wanted to be totally honest with you about everything."

"So after eighteen years of marriage—eighteen years of *lies*—you wake up one morning with an attack of conscience?"

"Katie." Steve reached out to put his hand over hers, but she snatched it away. "It's not like that."

"You know what, Steve?" Katie snapped, facing him again. "You're right. We *didn't* have a solid marriage all these years. Our marriage was built on lies, because *you're* a liar. You hid your true feelings and paid lip service to what you thought a marriage should be."

"Katie—"

She stood. "No, you don't get to talk. Not anymore. You're a liar and a hypocrite. You know why you didn't want to play the game? Because you knew that playing it would expose you for what you really are. A coward. You've betrayed me. You've betrayed your daughters. And you know what? You've betrayed *yourself*."

"Katie," he began again.

"No. I said you don't get to talk," she said, walking out of the kitchen.

---

MARTY HAD Scarlett draped over the bed. He was holding her face down with his right hand and her waist firmly with his left as he plowed into her from behind. She struggled weakly at first, but Marty held her fast until finally she stopped.

"That's it, bitch. Just lie there and enjoy it. Yeah. Yeah. We are going to do *everything*. Did you let Steve take you up the ass? I bet you did. That's next, baby."

> *"Love is a discord and a strange divorce*
> *Betwixt our sense and rest, by whose power,*
> *As mad with reason, we admit that force*
> *Which wit or labour never may divorce (?):*
> *It is a will that brooketh no consent;*
> *It would refuse yet never may repent."*

Scarlett let out an unnerving moan, the sound muffled and trapped within the bed sheets.

"That's Edward de Vere, Scarlett. You wouldn't know, of course, because you're so fucking stupid. But he was a very underrated Elizabethan poet. I bet C. Thomas and Steve didn't quote poetry while they were fucking you."

Marty went rigid as he climaxed. He cried out and collapsed on top of Scarlett. "I bet Steve never fucked you like that!" He rolled over onto his back. She was still lying face down, motionless next to him.

"I hope you enjoyed that as much as I did."

He turned to her. "Answer me, bitch!" He grabbed a fistful of her hair and shook her head. "Did I knock you out? It was that good, huh?" When she didn't answer, he reached out again, this time shaking her by the shoulder. Then again, harder. "Answer me!"

The realization that something might be terribly wrong hit him like the shockwave of an electric current searing down his spine. He sat up, shaking, and finally mustered the courage to turn her over. He gasped; the gash she had sustained on the front of her head when she hit the stove had created a massive pool of blood covering the sheets and much of her beautiful face, now frozen in a grotesque mask of deathly horror. A thousand thoughts raced through his mind as he vainly tried to wake her, to no avail. Suddenly his boyhood, college, career, marriage, fatherhood, and even his future were all but erased in the blink of an eye.

She was dead, but it was also his life that had just terminated. He looked into her eyes wide with death and screamed. The sound wasn't human. It was savage and unearthly. It was the scream of a doomed animal waiting in line to be slaughtered.

"Noooooooo! You can't do this to me!"

---

STEVE FINALLY ROSE from the chair and walked out of the kitchen to look for Katie. He needed to resolve this, if nothing more than for closure. He found her sitting on the bed lost in thought. Her face was red from crying.

"You're right, Katie," he said, startling her. "You're right about everything. You always have been. I am a liar and a hypocrite, and I'm a coward. I was so much more concerned with appearances and how things were supposed to be, that I lost sight of what they were—and what they had become."

"I know you so well, Steve. You wouldn't be telling me all of this unless you were certain you could make a go of it with Scarlett. I know you don't plan to be alone. You're playing me."

"Katie, can you honestly tell me you've always been happy?"

"Who is *always* happy? I said before, all marriages have their ups and downs! Sometimes they even flounder completely! Do you know I looked into a pro se divorce once?"

Steve looked surprised and shook his head.

"You know what? Coincidentally—or not—*ha!* It was when you weren't here for me when I was sick! Funny. I guess that was the universe overlapping. It was when you were having that *affair!*"

Steve washed his face in his hands but said nothing.

"I was devastated. I needed you. But I gave you a pass. I've always given you passes. Tons of them. But when you love each other, you work to get it back. That's what I did. That's what I've always done."

"But we were so young when we met, and your parents, the way they pushed the wedding. Then all of a sudden there was Jamie."

"Don't you dare blame the kids or anyone else for this. This was you. All you."

"We rushed into it all though. We didn't know who we were at that point in our lives."

"I knew what I wanted, Steve. Maybe it's true that girls mature earlier. I knew what I wanted, and I always believed it was you. That is, the man you *professed* to be. But you were a poser. Just a fake and a phony. A cardboard cut-out, pretending to be something you weren't."

"I really don't know what to do," Steve said, leaning against the closet door.

"You're still lying! I can see it in your eyes! Even now, you can't be honest," Katie stood up, wringing her hands. "Go find Scarlett. Our *friend,* Scarlett. Go run off into the sunset. Don't worry, Steve. You'll get your divorce. I won't fight you on that."

"Katie—"

"But you will pay *dearly* for it."

## 24

## HOUSE OF CARDS

*Delicious autumn! My very soul is wedded to it, and if I were a bird I would fly about the earth seeking the successive autumns.*
  *Letter to Miss Lewis*, October 1, 1841

— GEORGE ELIOT

KATIE WAS DRIVING along scenic Route One-thirty-three. The air was crisp, and October's vibrant colors blanketed the landscape. Rich gold, amber, and crimson leaves fluttered to the ground from the now-exposed branches of the abundant New England foliage. It had been three weeks since Steve moved out, and she was surprised to find that she truly was enjoying her new-found freedom.

She could feel her heart racing as she recognized the approaching rolling hillsides and came upon the diminutive apple orchard, frequented by the locals. She pressed the brakes lightly, wanting to take it all in. Half a mile further, and only one more left turn to go.

Life had turned on a dime.

A month ago her world had been completely different. Then everything she had believed in, trusted in, and counted upon was exposed as a lie. Her entire married life was built on a rotten foundation, which unbeknownst to her, continued to disintegrate. Someone had once told her that no matter how strong you might think a structure looked from the outside, if the foundation was weak, it was only a matter of time before it all would collapse—like a house of cards.

She was amazed and even proud by how quickly she was able to adapt to a complete change in life's circumstances. Of course she knew from a psychological perspective that adaptation is evolutionary. It is about survival. Adapting to change is hard-wired in us. We must do so in order to meet the demands of our environment. Change means progress, advancement, and embracing new experiences. It means we simply may continue to exist. Refusal to change only means inertia, apathy, stagnation, and eventually, death.

The butterfly finally had emerged from her chrysalis.

Katie had been wholly unaware of the changes she'd been making over the years. She'd only *felt* as if she was playing the dutiful wife. In truth, she'd actually begun to evolve long before the events of *The Game*.

Like a caterpillar on the brink of such a change, she'd lost all interest in life as it had been. She'd begun to wander around almost aimlessly, finally stopping to spin herself a little silk pad, hiding it away as though it were on the underside of a leaf. She'd later returned to it, hastily grabbing that silk pad with her hind legs, and once her hooks were in, her form started to fully transform, nature taking its course. She had completely digested her former self, emerging the triumphant butterfly, her metamorphosis complete.

Over the course of the previous week, Katie had polished the first half of her book and she'd sent the proposal to nearly twenty agents. She'd already heard back from several, some of whom had expressed interest.

And this very morning, she'd finally mustered the courage to call Alice, her little sister.

The two awkwardly began the conversation—years past due—neither knowing where to start. As the big sister, Katie took her rightful place at the reins. It had been high time they both aired their respective issues: Katie's resentment over Alice's flourishing career, not held in abeyance because of a man; Alice's bitterness about Katie's fertility—Katie who had never had any trouble becoming pregnant, at least not until the endometriosis, but Alice hadn't known about that. Katie also learned that Alice hated her job, despite her excellent income. And that her earning status caused problems with her husband whose job wasn't as lucrative. Amazing what assumptions people will make.

It was rocky at first, even downright explosive, but they soon came around. Before long, both were in tears. Throughout the course of the conversation, Katie learned that Alice and her husband were finally expecting. They'd only just found out. Katie told Alice about her impending divorce, her book, as well as the fact that she'd begun the completion of her psychotherapy licensure hours and expected to be finished in a year, two tops.

Katie felt free for the first time in her adult life. With the exception of her daughters, there was no one to please but herself. No parental authority subtly controlling her, no spouse explicitly controlling her, and no peer pressure. Letting go of everything was invigorating, liberating. Katie embraced change, and it looked good on her.

She took the drive today on a lark. Maybe it wouldn't work out. Maybe it was a pipe dream. She pulled up in front of the house and put the Jeep in park.

But on this particular day she felt lucky. Very lucky, and most importantly, *she expected to win*.

Climbing out of the car, she walked up to the front door and knocked. She could feel the pounding in her chest. She wondered vaguely if it was the sound of her heart that she was hearing or footsteps on the other side of the door. She didn't have long to wait to discover the answer.

The door opened, and it was him. He was standing in front of her. Zack Braun raised an eyebrow, cocking his head slightly.

"You once told me that one of the most important lessons in the game—and in life—is to know when to let go. I've decided it's time."

Zack smiled and stepped back. She crossed the threshold and he closed the door behind them.

# EPILOGUE

## THREE MONTHS LATER

*Everything works out in the end. If it hasn't worked out, it's not the end.*

— UNKNOWN

Connecticut was in the middle of its third bad winter in a row. It had been pounded with one Nor'easter after another while the pundits of doom and gloom reported that there was going be be no relief in sight. More than a foot of snow covered the deadened lawns while heaping piles lined plowed streets and driveways.

The Kelly house appeared deserted. All but two of the front windows were shuttered. The driveway hadn't been plowed, and there was so much snow on the roof that one could barely see the top of the chimney peeking out. A gutter creaked as it swung in the winter wind. There was a for sale sign almost completely buried in the front of the yard with only the top visible, the broker's name and number lost amid the hoary drifts. Next to it was a half-buried tag sale sign, ripped and faded; it had been there since the fall. The word tag was crossed out in red paint and had been replaced by the word divorce.

It was Saturday and despite the recent rash of cold weather, this particular day was unseasonably warm for the region, several degrees above freezing. While the town had dutifully salted and plowed, there had been a resistant layer of black ice which only now was beginning to melt, making the streets even more difficult to navigate.

Doogie and the Mole were walking down the middle of the slush-covered street on their way to a friend's house where the rest of their day was to be filled with marijuana, mature-rated videogames, selfies, various social media, and, if they could do so under the radar, view any number of porn websites.

Doogie was in the lead. He stopped in front of the Kelly house, reached down and grabbed a handful of snow then carefully molded it into a snowball. "Good for packing," he said.

"Yeah. So?" the Mole asked, nonplussed. The blunt in his pocket was calling his name.

"So, I bet you ten bucks I can hit the for sale sign from here."

"You couldn't hit the house from here, dickwad. Let's go. My feet are soaked."

"You're the fuckin' dickwad who wore crap sneakers instead of boots!" Doogie hurled the snowball. It fell short of the sign by a few feet.

"Told ya, shithead," the Mole sneered. "Now let's go."

"One more try," Doogie said, fashioning another snowball.

"Okay, but be quick. I think my feet are gettin' frostbite."

Doogie did a wind up like a pitcher on the mound before letting the snowball fly. This time, it sailed clear over the sign, smashing one of the two unshuttered windows. At first it appeared as if the snowball went clean through the window, leaving an almost perfect circular cut out, but before their eyes, the remaining intact glass spiderwebbed outward. Shards began falling out of the frame, creating a tinkling sound which filled the air like wind chimes.

"Now look what you've done, asshat." The Mole looked around to see if anyone witnessed the incident. A car was just turning onto the block, but it was far enough away not to pose a threat. "Let's go!"

"Relax," Doogie chided. "The house has been empty for months."

At that moment the front door opened and Steve stepped out. "Hey! What's going on?"

"Holy shit!" Doogie screeched. He turned and started running, the Mole close in his wake.

"Wrong again!" the Mole screamed.

Steve clumped down the unplowed driveway to the street, but by the time he got there the kids were long gone. "Damnit," he muttered to himself.

He was about to go back inside when a car pulled onto the end of his driveway. It was a brand-new Jaguar. The driver opened the door and got out; it was C. Thomas. Steve could see the shadow of someone in the passenger seat, but the glare from the sun bouncing off the snow obscured any details.

"Hey, Steve-O," C. Thomas said, approaching him. "I thought you were long gone."

"I came back to turn on the oil burner so the pipes don't freeze."

"The house sell yet?"

Steve shook his head. "Market's bad."

C. Thomas nodded. "That's what I hear. Did you move back to New York?"

"Yeah. I'm living in Westchester."

"I take it you'll be back for the trial. I guess that's the next time we'll all see each other. Well, most of us anyway."

"Guess so," Steve agreed.

C. Thomas kicked at the snow with his expensive leather boots which were far from appropriate cold weather footwear. "I never meant for any of this to happen, you know. It was just a poker game,"

Steve shook his head. "That's just it, C. Thomas. It was never a just a game." He paused a moment. "In some ways, we're all just as guilty as Marty."

C. Thomas kicked more snow. The silence was awkward. "Well," he finally said, "I gotta head. Take care." He turned and returned to his Jag.

As C. Thomas backed out of the driveway, Steve caught a glimpse of the person in the passenger seat. It was a woman with long, blonde hair. She turned to look at Steve and she waved at him. Steve was immediately overcome, feeling that he might double over and vomit.

She was a dead ringer for Scarlett.

"Let's go find us a card game, babe." C. Thomas said as he floored the accelerator and took off down the street.

## THE END

**THANK YOU FOR READING**

Did you enjoy this book?

We invite you to leave a review at the website of your choice, such as Goodreads, Amazon, Barnes & Noble, etc.

**DID YOU KNOW THAT LEAVING A REVIEW…**

- Helps other readers find books they may enjoy.
- Gives you a chance to let your voice be heard.
- Gives authors recognition for their hard work.
- Doesn't have to be long. A sentence or two about why you liked the book will do.

**Don't miss out on your next favorite book!**

**Join the Melange Books mailing list at**
www.melange-books.com/mail.html

**Subscriber Perks Include:**

- First peeks at upcoming releases.
- Exclusive giveaways.
- News of book sales and freebies right in your inbox.
- And more!

# ABOUT THE AUTHORS

**Stephanie** is an award-winning writer, director, and producer as well as a novelist, playwright, screenwriter, journalist, editor, and blogger. With a Master of Arts in counseling psychology, she currently also is a professor of psychology at two Connecticut colleges. Psychology and the human condition underscore all of her creative endeavors.

**Wayne** is a four-time Emmy-nominated, two-time winning writer and producer, as well as a novelist, filmmaker, playwright, screenwriter, blogger, and theatre producer/director who has worked with countless industry greats. He also is author of the legal thriller *Mahogany Row*. He currently works as a media attorney and is a part-time professor of communications at a Connecticut college.

Together the married duo (who are parents to a blended brood of seven children, two dogs, and three ferrets) pen "he-said/she-said" reviews for theatre, film, books, and other entertainment media on their website, Pillow Talking, where they also conduct celebrity and artist interviews.

Moreover, Stephanie and Wayne have combined their talents on myriad projects for film, theatre, and TV which are in various stages of development. In addition to *Going All In*, as a literary writing team, they recently published an eBook on Amazon, the first of a four-part series titled *Deadraiser: Horror on Jordan's Bank*.

***Find them online:***
www.facebook.com/Goingallinbook

www.facebook.com/Pillow-Talking-1619864644937154

twitter.com/someday_talking

goingallinbook@gmail.com

www.somedayprods.com

www.somedayprods.com/talking

www.somedayprods.com/talking/category/going-all- in